Seed of Aldebaran

By James Crawford

To all my friends and family who believed in me, even when I
doubted myself. Many thanks.

Seed of Aldebaran

Observational data for M2-9-
Epoch J2450
Right ascension-   17ʰ 05ᵐ 37.952ˢ
Declination-   -10 Deg 08 Min 34.58 Sec
Distance-   2,100 ly (650 pc)
Constellation-   Ophiuchus
Apparent magnitude-   14.7
Apparent dimensions-115 Sec × 18 Sec
Radius-   0.7 ly (0.2 pc)
Notable features-   Bi-polar outflow nebula
Other designations- Twin Jet Nebula, Butterfly
Nebula, PNG 010.8+18.0, PK 010+18.2

.27 mas shift since last observation at AlCent A2.

Personal observation - Opposing columns of cold fire
formed by the vortices of gravity from a white hell
where even hell is compressed into nothingness.

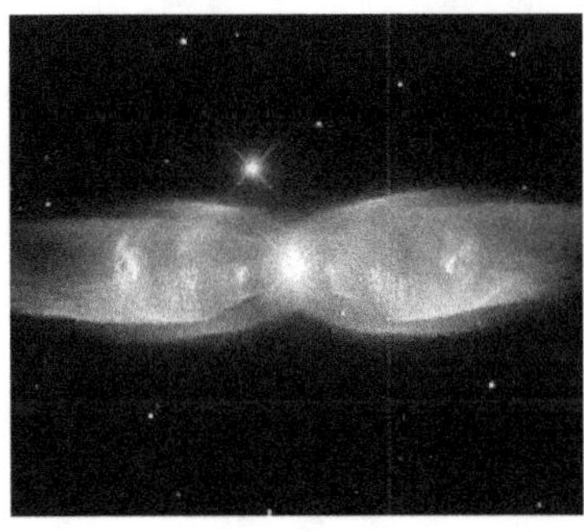

- Entry #64 from Navigator Lawrence "Petey" Peters' personal
star journal.

Chapter 1
"Change of Plans"

The vast emptiness of interplanetary space loomed cold and silent against an uncountable backdrop of stars, galaxies and nebulae. At the center of this emptiness the twin suns of the binary star system Alpha Centauri radiated a yellow and unfelt warmth, illuminating everything within reach of their dual gravitational fields.

By an interstellar scale the realm of the twin stars burgeoned with orbiting planets, comets, and asteroids, but to the crew of the *Black Hawk*-class corvette *USS Kestrel*, inbound for home after a three month patrol, it seemed a colossal void. The vessel, dimly lit now by the cold glow of the remote suns, left an incandescent blue trail of ionized particles in its wake, like a river of micro-stars stretching out to infinity behind it. The ship traveled at great speed yet appeared motionless against the cosmic backdrop, while onboard, the dull routine of watch-standing, meals, and sleep, the staples of underway life on patrol, carried on unbroken.

Operations technician second class Julius Kowalski waited outside the ship's radio room, bracing himself against the dull, familiar thrust of the ship's engines. Before him an electronic chess board lay magnetically adhered to the shelf at the radio room window, his opponent summoned from the game by the receipt of a radio message from the second planet of Alpha Centauri A. Ski studied his next move carefully as another crewman pushed past him in the narrow passageway.

All right, Schroedie, either take the pawn with your bishop and I smash your castle with my rook, or don't take it and I take your pawn and open up the file. Classic forking maneuver. Either way, pal, it's almost over. The check is on the way.

The door surrounding the caged window opened and radioman Schroeder appeared holding a small computer pad in his hand.

1

"We'll finish the game later, Ski. I gotta deliver this message. Maybe after supper."

"Message?" Ski asked. "Who's it for?"

"The old man. Mission assignment."

"Really? Let me see it."

"No, Ski."

"Come on, man. Aren't we friends?"

"I'll have no friends if I end up in the brig."

"You're not going to the brig. Look, we'll find out what's going on soon enough anyway." Ski held out his hand. "Come on, Schroedie. Just a peek."

Schroeder took a furtive glance behind him as he closed the door, then passed the pad to Ski. It read,

```
PRIORTY URGENT SECRET TRANSMISSION

FROM: ADM SELIG, FLEET HEADQUARTERS, ALCENT A2
TO: LTCDR VAN WERT, COMMANDING OFFICER, USS
KESTREL
TIME RECEIVED: 1537 HOURS
SUBJECT: MISSION ASSIGNMENT
THIRTY-SEVEN HOURS AGO, DEEP SPACE
COMMUNICATIONS RELAY STATION CR3 CEASED
TRANSMISSION WITHOUT PRIOR NOTICE. ALL ATTEMPTS
TO RAISE THE CREW HAVE FAILED. YOU ARE
INSTRUCTED TO DIVERT FROM CURRENT TRAJECTORY
AND PROCEED TO CR3 TO INVESTIGATE. BE ADVISED
OF SUSPECTED INSURGENT ACTIVITY IN THAT AREA.
USE CAUTION DURING APPROACH. SECURE AREA AND
LEND ASSISTANCE IF NECESSARY. LIBERTY IS
AUTHORIZED AT YOUR DISCRETION. - SELIG
```

Ski read the message again, then nodded and gave a slight chuckle. "Huh. The guys are going to love this. Can you shoot me a copy?"

"Sorry, Ski," Schroeder said, snatching the pad from Ski's hand. "You're not even supposed to see that."

Ski smiled. "No matter. I'll talk with you later. Thanks."

Schroeder left Ski and headed forward along the passageway, disappearing down the main access tube between decks. Ski rolled up the chess screen and stuck it in his shirt pocket and then walked down the passageway to the smaller access tube that led to the ship's bridge. The pale gleam of the overhead light strips mingled with the light gray paint of the walls and ceiling and cast no shadow on the slate colored deck. As he walked past the ship's damage control central compartment he saw several crewmen gathered around a console doing a watch turnover and realized he was late.

Using his hands against the walls to steady himself in the low gravity environment, Ski approached the ladder well and grabbed the two polished metal poles that ran perpendicular between the decks. He lifted his feet out of the micro gravitational field of the main deck and, now in zero-g, pulled his body upward through the cylindrical tube to the deck above. Once at the level of the ship's bridge he stuck his right foot out into its micro gravitational field and released his hold on the poles. He did this in one smooth motion and without thought. Then he brought his left foot onto the deck and walked to his watch station.

The low ceiling of the compartment, stuffed with various control consoles and computer screens, naturally gave the bridge a cramped feeling, intensified now by the presence of crewmen changing the watch at their appointed stations. Ski edged past the clusters of people to an area just forward and to the right of the captain's conning station. Here heavy curtains served as a partition between the bridge area and the operations and weapons stations, referred to as "shacks" by the crew. Between them a hatch led down and forward to a computer equipment room. Ski pulled aside the ops shack curtain and squeezed into the crowded compartment where the other three operations techs were conducting the watch turnover. His watch partner Sansbury was already seated and Morrell stood beside him.

"Where the hell have you been? It's ten 'till," Cauthen demanded. He was the senior watch stander and sat in Ski's place.

"You'll live."

"Man, I'm going to start relieving you late."

"Dilligaf," Ski replied. He looked at the other two men. "Guess what's up, now?"

"What?" Sansbury said.

As Ski started to speak, navigator Lawrence Peters poked his head through the curtain, his sandy brown hair rumpled from an earlier nap. He reached out to Cauthen with a tiny penlight in his hand. "Here, Cauth. Thanks."

Cauthen took the penlight and tucked it into his shirt pocket. "Anytime."

Sansbury nodded toward it. "Why do you always carry a light?"

"Because you never know when the lights will go out," Cauthen said.

"Like I told you about toilet paper," Morrell offered. "Always keep a roll in your locker. Just in case."

Ski addressed the navigator. "Hey, Petey! I was just going to share the good news!"

"What's that?"

"We've just received a new mission assignment."

"To do what?"

Ski looked around at the faces, savoring their curiosity. Even Cauthen, who had been entering the last log entry, stopped to listen. "We've been assigned to investigate a comm relay station that's shut down. They've stopped transmitting and no one knows why."

"How long will that take?" Morrell asked.

Ski shrugged his shoulders. "Who knows?"

"Oh, that stinks!" Morrell shook his head. "That's freaking typical! A three month cruise chasing phantom radio transmissions, and now this as we're heading home."

Ski tried hard to conceal a smirk. "What are you complaining about? You're the one who was bored and wanted some adventure."

"Yeah, but now the cruise is over! I was supposed to go on leave when we got back. I've got tickets to go see my parents!"

"They'll let you trade in your tickets," Petey offered.

"That's not the point. They do this every time."

"Well, don't worry about it, Morrell," Ski goaded, smiling openly now. "I'm sure they'll make up for it with some awesome liberty at that station."

"Oh, I'm sure."

Cauthen studied Ski's expression. "You're lying! No one's said anything about this."

Ski smirked at Cauthen. "It's hot off the press."

"Peters!" the officer of the deck called.

"Yes, sir!" Petey called back, disappearing through the curtain.

Ski gestured after him with his thumb. "See?"

"Damn," Morrell said.

"Just take the watch," Cauthen said to Ski. He stood up so Ski could take the chair.

Ski sat down and looked up at Morrell. "You shouldn't whine so much. You knew that things like this happened in the fleet. Try to bear up."

"Shut up, Ski," Morrell said.

Cauthen started to leave, but stopped and turned around. "Don't listen to him, Morrell. Ski doesn't have anyone to go home to, so it doesn't matter to him how long we stay out here. Isn't that right, Julius?"

Sansbury grinned and faced Ski. "Julius? Is that your first name?"

"You didn't think it was really Ski, did you?"

"To him," Cauthen continued, "being home or being out is all the same."

Moron. Ski's eyes scanned the computer log quickly and found what he was looking for. The last entry read, "Releive the watch." He sat back in his chair, his voice taking on a nagging tone. "Cauthen, Cauthen, can't you even spell a simple word like 'relieve'? Remember 'I before E, except after C'? I thought you graduated from fourth grade."

Cauthen leaned forward to look at the log. "Just change it."

Ski sighed loudly and corrected the error. "This is an official log, you know. You'd better get it right, or they'll find out that you're an idiot."

Cauthen's face reddened with anger and embarrassment, but he quickly smiled again. "It doesn't take an idiot to misspell a word. However, it does require an idiot to screw up a golden opportunity for an education."

"What do you mean?" Morrell asked, interested in the new attack.

"Back when Julius was still in college, he had a bright idea that the university needed some kind of new science equipment. The Dean tried to explain there wasn't enough money, so Julius here tells him, 'That's why this is a second rate university. No one wants to spend money on important things!' Can you believe that? Second rate, he says! Ha!"

"He said that to the Dean?" Morrell asked.

"Sure enough! They put him on academic probation, not his first, but smart guy here up and quits."

"He quit college over that? What an idiot!"

"You don't know what you're talking about!" Ski snapped.

Cauthen pressed on. "If he had finished school, he could have come out here as an officer. But, instead, he's just a college drop-out! No better than the rest of us."

"You moron," Ski answered. "I'd have more intelligence after a lobotomy than both of you put together!"

"Maybe," Cauthen said. "But, at least I have enough intelligence to know when to keep my mouth shut."

"Course change indicated," Sansbury said, pointing to the console screen.

A voice came over the shipboard address circuit. "Attention all hands. Secure loose gear and standby for a course correction."

The curtain opened and the operations officer, Ensign Clark, stepped into the crowded shack. "Hey, I'm glad you're all still here. I've got some bad news."

Ski turned to face him. "It wouldn't have anything to do with a comms relay station that has mysteriously shut down, would it?"

Clark's expression grew puzzled. "How did you know?"

"Ski already told us a little about it, sir," Cauthen said. "But what's the story?"

"Well, it's just like he said. We're being sent to investigate and help out."

"Do they have any ideas why the station shut down?"

"Possible insurgent activity."

"Insurgents," Morrell said. "Nothing more than stinking pirates."

"How far away is it?" Sansbury asked.

"About forty-two hours at our best speed so stand by for an acceleration." Clark looked directly at Ski. "And how did you know about the mission assignment? That was a secret message."

Ski smiled. "There are no secrets on a little ship, sir. Not even operational ones."

***

In the wardroom, the captain, Lieutenant Commander James Van Wert, sipped a cup of black coffee as he waited for the executive officer to return. He was a tall man, six foot five and built like a linebacker. He rotated his head around, stretching his neck muscles. He felt tired.

Lieutenant Junior Grade Wallsbrook, the systems officer, sat at the table filling out a report. When he finished he looked up at Van Wert. His rural accent was slow but clear, and he removed his glasses as he spoke.

"Any speculation on what we might find on this station, Captain?"

Van Wert took a sip from the cup. "Who knows? If they were attacked, then they should have been able to get some kind of message out. It's strange that they just stopped transmitting."

"Do you think that it could just be some maintenance problem?"

"I sure hope so."

The wardroom door opened and the executive officer, Lieutenant Paul Fischer, stepped in. He shook his head as he walked over to the captain.

"We've got two weeks of food, maybe three at normal rationing. But we could extend that." He pursed his lips. "It's too bad we have no idea how long this is going to take."

The captain nodded. "Yes, I know." *Two weeks would have been enough to get us back,* he thought. "Where's the *Oregon*?" Van Wert referred to the fleet supply ship stationed nearby.

"Five days out, in the opposite direction."

"Damn. I'd like to have gotten fifteen days rations, full water, full air, and an atmosphere scrub. I'm sure they could've provided it. But we'll have to make due."

Fischer nodded. "Do you think our present supply is enough for this side trip?"

Van Wert nodded. "No matter what we find, in a few days we'll either be relieved, dead, or mission accomplished."

Fischer nodded but said nothing.

Van Wert stood up and stretched his back. "I'm going to see if I can grab a couple. Wake me up if there's any comms traffic."

"Aye, sir," Wallsbrook replied.

Van Wert downed the cup and put it in a cleaning receptacle, then left the wardroom and headed forward into officer country. Entering his stateroom, he kicked off his shoes and lay down in his transparent sleeping tube. He had slept only five hours in the last twenty-four, and he hoped that he could catch up before the ship reached the station.

The walls of the stateroom were bare except for some photos and three athletic awards from the fleet academy where he played on the football team. He rolled over onto his side and looked at the photos that were attached to the bulkhead. The woman in the pictures was Jennifer Murray. She was petite with green eyes and light brown hair. She was also a lieutenant commander and commanding officer of the *Blackhawk*, a corvette like the *Kestrel* with an all-female crew. Gender segregation was one of the early experiments of the newly created fleet.

Murray and Van Wert had been seeing each other for almost eight years, whenever their schedules would permit. They had met during training at AlCent A2's fleet academy, and he had fallen in love with her almost immediately. Beyond the veneer of the no-nonsense professional was a complex woman capable of deep intimacy.

They dated for nearly a year before Van Wert proposed marriage. Even at that time he realized that it would be a difficult relationship to maintain with opposing schedules and separate duty stations, but he wanted her. She touched him like no other could and he wanted her more than he had ever wanted any other woman. But when the awkward silence lingered after the question, he knew that it would never be. She explained that she loved him, but she could not give him the total devotion he deserved and still devote herself to her career.

Van Wert had spent a week thinking it out and knew that she was right. Eventually he realized that deep down he felt the same way, so the two continued to see each other whenever they could.

When Van Wert was transferred to his first duty station, Murray suddenly received orders transferring her to the same place. Soon the talk in the fleet was that her orders had been arranged by her father, a senator on the Armed Services Committee. She never affirmed or denied the rumor, but over the years other officers began to suspect that Van Wert's duty assignments were being pre-arranged, also, for his and Murray's on-going affair had been no secret. There was no truth behind the suspicions at all, but every time he received a new assignment, especially a choice one, the talk would begin again. Van Wert could feel the resentment of his peers, and occasionally it would erupt into open accusations. At one time he had even considered breaking off his relationship with Murray. He never felt like his career was suffering, but James Van Wert hated being falsely accused.

Finally he saw an opportunity to quell the rumors once and for all. The position for CO of the *Kestrel* opened for which he requested and received. As a duty station, the *Kestrel* was considered one of the worst. The crew was nearly incorrigible and the ship had been ill-maintained. The assignment was usually given to officers of ill favor, so now no one could accuse Van Wert of anything.

Except stupidity, perhaps, he had mused shortly after taking command. But after eleven months as *Kestrel's* CO he felt that, despite the uphill struggle, he had made some progress. Morale had improved and the ship's efficiency rating slowly climbed up from last place, but something still wasn't right. Despite all that he tried to do, the men still seemed discontented.

Van Wert looked up at the picture of himself and Murray at a ski resort and frowned at the new delay. The two had made plans to return to the resort after this deployment. It had been a long patrol and he was ready for a break.

"Just a little longer, Jenny," he said to the picture. Then he rolled over, closed his eyes, and soon fell asleep.

Chapter 2
"First Contact"

Ski glanced down at the clock at the corner of his computer screen and saw it read 1000 hours. He sighed and rubbed his face. It had been nineteen hours since the receipt of the message and the *Kestrel* still cruised at high speed with all active scanning and passive sensory devices energized and manned. Sansbury sat next to him and yawned deeply, causing Ski to yawn as well. He sipped the last of his coffee, cold now as it came through the pinch straw of the cup's lid.

"I'm kind of bummed out with this extension to our cruise," Sansbury said. "I'm so tired of this one-meter high gravity."

"It takes some getting used to," Ski answered. "Wait until you get home and pick up something heavy for the first time. It stays heavy no matter how high you lift it."

"I know. When I first came on board I lifted up my stow chest and nearly smashed it against the overhead."

Ski smiled. "I remember." He took another dry sip through his straw and frowned. "I've got half a mind to make a dash down to the mess decks for more coffee."

"I haven't touched any of mine. You can have it if you like."

"What's in it?"

"Cream and sugar."

Ski frowned but took the lid from his cup. "All right."

He held the insulated cup down close to the deck and waited as Sansbury did the same. Gingerly, the younger man pried off the lid to his cup and poured the light brown liquid into Ski's cup. Then they both replaced the lids and sat back up in their chairs. Ski tasted the brew and smiled.

"Still warm. I knew you'd be good for something up here."

"You're welcome," Sansbury said.

Peters stepped through the curtain. "Hello, boys! Look what I've got."

"What is it?" Ski asked. He turned around and took the small computer pad from the navigator's hand.

"The in-port watch bill."

"Thank God," Sansbury said. "This underway four on four is killing my sleep."

Ski looked over the schedule. "Then it's official about some shore time?"

"Uh, no. I should say that's the prospective watch bill. If they decide to moor out, then that's the schedule they'll use."

"Am I on it?" Sansbury asked.

"Yeah," Ski replied. "First section, but I'm not on it at all."

"Neither am I," Petey said. "We're usually in first section together."

"I know." Ski studied the watch bill absently. Then he looked up at Petey. "I wonder if I'll still be on it as in-port officer of the deck."

"I'm sure you would be."

"Why wouldn't you?" Sansbury asked.

Ski turned to Sansbury. "Well, if I'm not good enough to be a first class petty officer, how can I be good enough to stand OOD?"

"Oh, that's right. You were passed over for promotion, weren't you?"

Ski nodded. "Damn right, I was. Of course it's perfectly understandable. I've completed all of my advancement requirements. I scored outstanding on the test. I'm even qualified for in-port officer of the deck! How many second classes do you know who are qualified to stand OOD?"

Sansbury shook his head. "So what happened?"

"My evaluations. That's when the officers give you a conduct rating and that's how they hamstring you." He shook his head. "The captain is such a baby. Over one little thing, he'll ruin the devotion of a highly motivated petty officer."

"The captain's not a baby," Petey said. "He just sees things differently than we do. He has different priorities and greater responsibilities."

"I've got the responsibility for the operation, maintenance, and repair of all the sensor and scanner equipment. This stuff is worth a bundle!"

"True, but the captain has responsibility for all of that, too, plus the entire ship, plus the crew."

"Whose side are you on, Petey?"

"It's not a matter of being on one side or another. It's a matter of considering another person's viewpoint."

"So you're saying that what he did was right?"

"No, I'm just saying that it could have been worse."

"Whatever." Ski turned back to the scope. "Any way you slice it, he screwed me over."

Petey took a medicinal inhaler out of his pocket and shook it vigorously. He glanced back toward the OOD and inhaled a quick dose before shaking it again.

Ski looked up at the navigator. "Asthma getting bad, Petey?"

Still holding his breath, Petey nodded and held his thumb and forefinger to mean, "a little."

"It's too bad this cruise has been extended," Ski said. "This ship badly needs an atmosphere scrub. I know that helps."

Petey exhaled. "It does, but I still have plenty of meds left, as well as a lot of puffers." Petey inhaled another dose, drawing in a larger breath this time.

"Man, you can get out of the fleet with an ailment like that," Sansbury said.

Petey nodded.

"He knows that," Ski replied, "but he's saving money to go to school. Since the credit collapse, all of the money for school loans has dried up."

Petey exhaled. "And if they find out, they can kick me out of the fleet. So I would appreciate it if you'd keep it to yourself."

"My lips are sealed," Sansbury said, drawing a finger across his mouth.

"So, Petey," Ski said, "did you get any mail in the transmission today?"

"Yes, a little. I got a letter from my mom. My grandma is staying with her now."

"The one who is terminally ill?"

"That's right."

"Is your mother going to be taking care of her until the end?"

"Yes."

Ski shook his head. "Man, that's a hell of a job. I could never do that."

"You probably could if you had to."

"No, I don't have the patience for it. I mean, I think it's very noble for your mom to do it, but it's not for me."

"I heard someone say that being with a person who's dying can be a privilege," Sansbury said.

Petey nodded. "That's true. Watching a person face death bravely can be a life-changing experience."

I'll bet. Ski nodded once but said nothing.

"Did you get any mail, Ski?" Petey asked.

"Yeah, I got a letter from my mom. She says that some lawyer has started a class-action suit against the tour company. It's for all of the people who got sick on that trip to the Equatorial belt I took."

"That's when you got sick, isn't it?"

Ski nodded.

"What's the name of that virus you contracted?"

"The Schadendorf virus."

Sansbury's face grew alarmed. "You've got a virus *now*?"

"It's in a dormant state." He looked up at Petey. "And, of course, they can't figure out how to get rid of it."

"Are you going to join the suit?" the navigator asked.

"Yes. These people should have known about the water in that area before they took tours through there. They should have checked it out."

Petey nodded. "True."

"How long are we going to be under this communication silence?" Sansbury asked. "I'd like to send a message to my parents."

"Usually until we get close to home," Petey answered.

"And nothing is going out now that we may be getting into a hot area," Ski said.

"You think we'll get into some action?" Sansbury asked.

"You never know," Ski said, with a quick glance up at Petey. The navigator gave no expression.

Sansbury nodded. "Maybe I should do one more manual sweep with all the scan modes before we get relieved."

Behind them someone called out from the conn, "Captain on the bridge."

"Whoop! Gotta go!" Petey said, dashing out through the curtain.

"Uh, yeah. Why don't you run another sweep?" Ski said, turning his attention back to the screen. He looked at the clock on the console. "We'll run through them all one more time."

Sansbury nodded and began touching button images on the computer screen, switching the scanner equipment out of automatic mode and into the highly sensitive manual functions. These were listed as Broadband Omnidirectional Transmission, Narrowband ODT, Short Range Focused Beam, Long Range Focused Beam, and Extreme Long Range Focused Beam. Each one offered a different display on the screen and Sansbury and Ski studied them carefully, adjusting the frequency and sensitivity before switching to the next one.

As Sansbury switched to Extreme Long Range Focused Beam the display screen reset, then they watched as the scanning device swept back and forth across the expanse of open space out ahead of the *Kestrel*. A small dot appeared on the screen and the console chirped twice. Ski and Sansbury saw it at the same time.

"Whoa," Ski said. "Hold it there. Get a course and speed on it."

Sansbury began typing commands on the computer while Ski switched to a different mode and adjusted a joystick on his overview console. He pointed the cursor in the same area as the dot on his partner's scanner but the response was negative. "Man, that's a weak signal." He looked at Sansbury's screen. "Do you still have it?"

"Yeah."

"It's not showing up on mine yet. Have you got the course and speed?"

"I think so."

"You *think* so? Double-check it."

Sansbury ran the program again. Then his voice sounded a bit more confident as he said, "Yeah, that's it."

"All right." Ski called through the curtain, "Officer of the deck?"

Behind him Ski heard the curtain open and the underway officer of the deck, Lieutenant Junior Grade Wallsbrook, stuck his head into the ops shack. "Yes, Petty Officer Kowalski?"

For a split second Ski felt amused seeing Sansbury straighten up in his chair. Then he, too, noticed the captain over his shoulder. The dot on the screen glowed a little brighter now than when they had first seen it. *Good. You don't like to call the captain over unless you're sure.* He pointed to the dot. "We picked up a contact on the E.L.R.F. Range is point zero-six-three astronomical units and closing. They're heading in our general direction, but their course is shearing away from us. Presently, they're predicted to pass within fourteen hundred kilometers of us."

"What's their speed?" Wallsbrook asked.

"Six hundred knots, sir. There has been no deviation in course or speed since we first spotted them."

"Do you think they see us?" Van Wert asked.

"I don't think so, but there's no way to know for sure. I checked and they are emitting no active impulses toward us, but they could be monitoring us passively, sir."

"I see," Van Wert said. He looked at Wallsbrook. "Go to General Quarters."

"Aye-aye, sir." Wallsbrook turned from the Ops shack. A moment later, the Battle Stations alarm, a repetitive gonging tone, sounded throughout the ship, and the lights in the bridge switched to red. From the aft section of the bridge Ski could hear the airtight hatch sliding into place over the ladder well, sealing off the bridge.

"Let me know immediately if it changes course or speed," Van Wert said.

"Aye, Captain." Ski buckled his seat belt as Van Wert backed away, then he turned to Sansbury. "Get the curtain."

Sansbury reached up and pushed the curtain aside and fastened it with a strap. Ski did the same on his side and now the ops shack was a part of the bridge. Next to them, the weapons shack had also opened their curtains, and the bridge seemed much larger now as Ski looked around. One of the weapons techs, whose black hair needed a cut, smiled and winked at Ski. *Gung Ho Gradenko.*

"Ops Shack, Equipment Room," Cauthen's voice came over the intercom.

"Ops Shack," Sansbury replied.

"Equipment Room manned and ready."

"Equipment Room manned and ready, aye." Sansbury turned to the conn. "Officer of the deck, Operations manned and ready."

"Very well," Wallsbrook replied.

Ski could hear the readiness reports being called in from Engineering, Weapons, Systems, and the Damage Control repair parties. As Ski listened, an excitement grew in his heart. This was why he enlisted in Operations. Here on the bridge, in the center of the action, he knew exactly what was going on. He glanced around at the activity and saw the Ops Officer, Clark, standing next to Petey at the hologram plot. He could see that Sansbury had sent the information to Petey already. *Good man.* Clark looked over at him and gave him a thumbs-up sign before calling out to the captain.

"The ship is manned and ready, Captain."

"Very well," Van Wert answered. "Commence maneuver."

Here we go! Ski turned back around and looked at the scope. His stomach lifted as the ship dove and banked toward the unidentified contact.

"Have you ever been in combat before?" Sansbury asked.

Ski looked at him and saw the apprehension on the younger man's face. "Not full-fledged combat, but I was in a standoff once where we shot a little." Ski paused. "The captain was there, too. Don't worry. The *Kestrel* can be a bad-assed bird when you need her to be." He looked at the dot on the screen. "If they know what's good for them, they'll do exactly what we say."

This seemed to put Sansbury at ease. He adjusted the equipment and re-computed the information.

"Hey, Ski! Let's go!" Gradenko called from the Weapons Shack.

"It's still pretty far away."

"Give me what you've got, man. We need a preliminary solution."

Ski activated a command on the screen that transferred the information to the weapons console. Behind him he could hear the captain telling Clark to hail the contact. The ensign's voice sounded overly firm as he spoke into the microphone, as if trying to stifle a twinge of nervous jitters.

"*USS Kestrel* to unidentified vessel. You are ordered to maintain your present course and speed. Any deviation will be to your peril. Stand by for further instructions."

"Weapons!" Van Wert barked.

"Positive return on targeting laser and preliminary solution running, sir."

"Very well. Energize all sand casting units. Ops?"

"They seem to be complying, sir," Ski said. "No deviation."

"Can you identify it?"

"No, sir. It's very small though."

As the *Kestrel* bore down on the object Ski and Sansbury constantly adjusted and switched scanning modes, watching the shrinking distance between the two vessels. At the same time, they monitored the constant feed of updated information to Navigation and Weapons. Ski heard Gradenko announce that he had a firing solution running and both main guns were locked on target. The captain acknowledged and pointed to Clark.

"*USS Kestrel* to unidentified vessel. Identify yourself," Clark said.

Static alone came over the speaker.

He called again but still there came no response. Van Wert ordered that two shots be fired across the bow of the object.

Out of the corner of his eye, Ski could see Gradenko grin as he adjusted his aim and fired. His console twice dimmed briefly as the powerful laser cannons each fired one shot.

As Clark called to the vessel again, a feeling of apprehension began to well up in Ski. *Something isn't right about that ship.* He began to adjust his console, trying to get more information on it. The two vessels were only fifty-five hundred kilometers apart now, practically right on top of one another.

The dimensions came up on screen and showed the object to be cylindrical with tapered, blunt ends, five meters long and two meters wide. It reminded Ski of a fat cigar. As the computer raced through its Identification Memory banks, a sense of dread began to settle over Ski. *My God, what if it's a nuclear mine?* He looked at the closing distance and saw they just passed two thousand kilometers. *Hurry!*

Then the computer flashed its answer on the screen:

```
VESSEL CLASS: Passenger
FUNCTION: Emergency escape pod
CAPACITY: Six persons
```

MANUFACTURER: Olympus Mons Industrial Products, Inc.

Ski read the screen again. *Escape pod? Where the hell would it have come from?* He turned around to where Van Wert was seated at the conn. "Captain, it's a lifeboat!"

"A lifeboat?" Van Wert asked.

"Yes, sir. The computer's verified it."

"Put it on the main screen. Helm, decrease speed and bring us around it."

"Decreasing speed and swinging around, aye!"

Ski felt the blood rush to his face and the press of his seat belt as the reverse engines rumbled slowing the *Kestrel* down. Automatically, he reached up and switched on the optics so the captain could get a visual. He always found it amusing that despite all of the sophisticated scanning and sensing devices on board, the human eye held the final word. That fact always pleased Petey, who frequently said that man's handiwork could never rival God's.

As the *Kestrel* approached the lifeboat, the captain ordered the ship to parallel its course and match its speed. The optical viewer descended from the overhead until level with the captain's face. Unbuckling his seat belt, Van Wert stood up and looked into the device.

"Ski," he said. "Illumination to the port beam, please."

"Aye, sir," Ski said. He selected a command on the console and outside the ship flood lamps bathed the lifeboat in white light. He turned to look at the captain who was adjusting the magnification.

"No sign of life," Van Wert said. "None that I can see in the windows." He stood back from the device and nodded to Ski. "Do you want to take a look?"

Momentarily taken aback, Ski quickly unbuckled his belt and made his way to the device. Peering through the eyepieces, Ski saw that the *Kestrel*'s speed matched perfectly with the boat and it looked as though both ships were stopped in space. He could see no sign of life at all, but the frost on the inside of the windows indicated that there once had been life aboard. Neither interior nor exterior lights showed on the craft, and he could not tell how long it had been out here.

The executive officer, Lieutenant Fischer, stepped up behind Ski. "Where could it have come from? The station?"

"It's quite possible," Van Wert said.

Ski had an idea. "Sansbury," he said, his voice taking on an authoritative tone, "what's one-eighty out from our current course?" It felt good giving a command from the captain's viewer. But he checked himself and turned to Van Wert. "We can assume that it's been traveling in a straight line, sir. We'll plot back to see where it's from." Then he stepped away from the optical device and sat back down in his seat.

"Here you go," Sansbury said. He pointed to a course line diagram on the screen.

Ski looked at it and cross-referenced it to the *Kestrel*'s original course. The two lines met a Communications Relay Station CR3. He spoke to the captain. "It's from the station, sir."

Van Wert looked over Ski's shoulder at the screen. "I see. All right, secure the optics." He turned to Fischer. "Let's get it with the magnet and grapple it to the hull. We'll bring it with us." He turned to Clark. "Helm, come about to original course and increase to full speed when the lifeboat is secured alongside. Secure from GQ."

"Aye, Captain," Clark answered.

The white interior lights came back on as the ship stood down from General Quarters. Ski glanced over at Gradenko who smiled.

"Show's over, Big Shot."

Ski nodded and closed the curtain around the Ops shack again.

Thirty minutes later, with the lifeboat secured to the underside of its hull, the *Kestrel* was underway again, making its top speed toward the station. Cauthen and Morrell relieved the watch at noon, and Sansbury, Ski, and Petey went down to the mess decks together for the midday meal.

Behind the serving line one of the cooks, McElroy, had his earphones on while busily cleaning dirty food containers with a flexible vacuum hose. As he caught sight of the three, Petey waved. Mac nodded and said, "Meanwhile, back in the jungle…"

Ski picked up his tray and gave an uninspired look over the arrangement of colored plastic boxes in the serving line before him.

"Let's see," Sansbury said, "what'll it be today? Menu A, B, or C?"

"What does it matter?" Ski answered. "It's all the same crap we've been eating for the last three months."

"I don't think it's too bad."

"Maybe you've never had real food," Ski said, selecting a blue box and snapping it into place on his metal tray.

"I like to mix and match," Petey said. "It lends variety."

"I need hot sauce to give me variety," Ski said. "I hope there's some left."

"You know what I really miss?" Petey asked. "Soup. You never think you'd miss something like soup until you can't have it for months."

"Oh, soup!" Sansbury said. "I'd love some French onion soup right now."

"Or tomato," Petey said, "with lots of crackers."

"New England clam chowder for me, with oyster crackers," Ski said. His mouth watered at the thought. "Thanks, Petey. Now I hate my dinner even more."

Petey grinned and slapped Ski on the back. "Sorry, buddy."

They filled their trays with assorted boxes and then sat down at an empty table. Ski pressed his tray onto the magnetic table top and opened up his first box. A warm vapor of pasta and tomato sauce rose to his nose. He squeezed in a generous dose of hot sauce from the condiment rack and began eating. As he chewed he noticed that the talk going around the mess decks centered on the lifeboat encounter.

"Ski," Crosly, one of the other crewmen said, "you were there. Did we hit that lifeboat with the gun or not?"

"No. They were only warning shots."

The young man turned to face the others at his table. "See? I told you."

Another man piped in. "Gradenko said he hit it and put it out of action."

"He's bullshit. I saw it myself optically. It was already long dead."

"Is it from that station?"

"Looks like it," Ski answered, lifting another sticky spoonful to his mouth.

Another man stood up as he spoke, large and unshaven. His wrinkled blue uniform looked as though it hadn't been washed in a week. "Why the hell didn't they send someone out to look inside the damn thing?"

The others looked at Ski as if he would know the answer. Ski looked up at the standing man, engineering technician first class William Wilde, who most of the crew called Wild Bill. His accusatory tone silenced the talk on the mess decks.

"There was no sign of life aboard at all," Ski replied.

"But somebody could have been sick or hurt or something. Why didn't they send someone out to check?"

Ski looked up at Wild Bill and knew that Bill didn't care whether anyone had been aboard the lifeboat. He always took a contradictory stance on every subject, but especially subjects concerning ship's policy or actions of the ship's officers. Ski knew he could be very critical too, but he tried to limit his remarks to his friends. *Most of the time anyway.* He contemplated verbally attacking the engineering tech but thought better of it. The larger man was used to settling differences in physically violent ways. He also had no fear of punishment. *God, I hate dealing with these snipes.*

"I think the reason they didn't go out was because we still don't know if there are hostile units in this area. They probably didn't want anyone outside the skin of the ship in case we were ambushed." *There, that's reasonable.*

"Oh, yeah, that's typical," Wild Bill said. He shook his head in disgust and headed aft. "I figured they'd turn yellow when someone needs help." He disappeared through a doorway.

"I'd be surprised if he'd stick his neck out to help his own mother," Sansbury said under his breath.

They resumed their meal as the crowd of men on the mess decks dispersed.

After a few minutes of eating quietly, Ski said, "I hate this ship, Petey. I hate the military and I hate having to deal with these people every stinking day."

Petey nodded but chewed silently.

"You're the only one I can talk to. But the rest of these people, I couldn't care whether they lived or died."

"Me, too?" Sansbury asked.

"No, you haven't been on board long enough to deeply get on my nerves."

"Come on, Ski," Petey said. "It's been a long patrol. Everybody's ready to get off of this ship."

"I know. But for me it goes much deeper than that. I don't belong here."

"Is it that you feel you don't belong, or do you think others feel you don't belong? There is a difference."

"Both! I just feel like I'm destined for greater things, but I'm going nowhere here. I'm forced to operate far below my potential. Do you understand what I mean?"

"Of course, Ski. Why do you think I keep that star journal and save every last penny for school? Because I'm going on to something better. This enlistment is a means to an end for me. So I try to enjoy it while I'm here." Petey paused. "Maybe that's what you should do. Don't wait until you're out of the fleet before you decide where you're going. Start making plans now. I think that when you can see a definite course of action ahead, the day-to-day troubles are easier to manage."

Ski nodded and took another bite. "Yeah, you're probably right. Now all I have to do is figure out what I want to do with my life."

The two men resumed eating quietly.

"I know I'll be glad to get back home," Sansbury said, as if trying to commiserate.

"Yeah, whenever that'll be," Ski said.

"Hey, Ski, what are you doing after chow?" Petey asked.

"I don't know. I had planned to run a maintenance check on one of the transponders, but they're not going to let me shut it down with us cruising on alert."

"I'm going up to the sextant to run a calibration check after we eat. Do you want to come?"

"Yeah, I'd like that."

***

They finished eating and took their trays to the scullery where the containers would be cleansed and sterilized. Then Ski followed Petey up one deck and aft of the bridge tube to a small round hatch called a scuttle located in the overhead. Petey manually opened it and ascended the small tube, disappearing into the chamber above. Ski followed him up and into the low overhead room jammed with equipment cabinets and wiring harnesses, and owing to the zero-g of the compartment he was able to slither easily between them. This was Ski's favorite place on the ship, and a feeling of happy anticipation kept his claustrophobia in check.

The Celestial Navigation Compartment, or 'sextant' as the navigators called it, measured eight feet by ten feet. From deck to ceiling it measured only three feet high except for a four-foot wide hemisphere of glass in the center of the room. Inside the sphere stood the actual sextant, an optical and X-ray sensing device that observed minute shifts in star positions. It also tracked the timing and position of several pulsars and fed the combined readings into the navigation computer. The computer then merged the information with a star chart of all planetary movements and displayed the ship's position on a holographic chart at the navigator's plot table. To ensure complete accuracy, the sextant's alignment had to be periodically checked and adjusted. That was Petey's job, and Ski joined him whenever he had a chance.

Ski pulled himself in the zero-g over to the sextant and waited for Petey's signal. He bided his time by studying the complex system of synchros and servos that positioned the device. Then he turned his gaze upward and saw the stars beyond the glass. The hemispherical shape, clear and free of distortion, gave the impression of an open hole above him.

As Ski waited for Petey to shut down the power, his thoughts drifted to his family. He remembered how mortified his parents had become upon learning that he had dropped out of school. They tried to get him to enroll in another university as soon as possible, even suggesting he go to a school with a similar name so that friends or relatives might not notice. But Ski had refused. He knew that he had yet to decide on what career to follow and was tired of drifting aimlessly. He had also become tired of student life. It seemed to Ski that no matter what one did, a student was always treated as a second-class citizen. *I'm paying for this education*, he remembered thinking, *or my father is anyway. I should be treated like a customer!* He laughed now at the absurdity of that statement. It had only been two weeks after his dropping out of school that he enlisted in the fleet, which had been another blow to his parents. His father, an American Zone congressmen and a partner in a law firm, had tried to get Ski to change his mind.

"Son," his father had said, "I know you're still upset about the school, but joining the fleet is a big mistake. I don't think you realize what you're doing."

"That's the problem, Dad. I don't know what I want to do. Besides, it's only for four years."

"You're willing to throw four years down the toilet?" Ski's father took a deep breath to calm down. "Listen, Son, if you want to be in the military, that's fine. I have no problem with that, but you should finish school and then go out as an officer. Don't you know what kind of people enlist in the fleet? Criminals, bums, and losers. You're better than that."

"How am I so much better than that?"

"Because you're my son!" his father replied. "Listen, it's not just me I'm thinking about, it's your mother. This whim of yours is going to break her heart."

But three years later it was Ski's mother who had kept up a correspondence with him. And he had spoken to his father only once.

"Okay, I've secured the power," Petey said. "You can get up now without getting suddenly crushed."

Ski got up on his knees in the glass dome with his back to the sextant, careful not to touch the device. The glass, only inches from his face, was so clear that only the light mist of Ski's breath betrayed its presence. He gazed out at the stars.

Oh, the stars, the stars! A peaceful lull settled over Ski as if he were in a hypnotic trance. Out here in the void of interplanetary space, with no atmosphere to distort the cold points of light, there seemed to be billions of them. To his right he could see the Milky Way. On AlCent A2 it appeared to be a long cluster of stars, but here in space it became a thick carpet that appeared almost solid and stretched from one end of the sky to the other. The view was interrupted only by the instrument array, a stalk of antennas and sensors just aft of the sextant that stuck out of the hull like a huge spiny fin. The array provided an intricate black silhouette against the celestial backdrop.

He looked to his left and saw in the distance a nebula, an irregularly shaped cloud of blue and green backlit by the stars beyond it. Around him constellations and clusters of stars glowed everywhere, and toward the bow of the ship, right over the bridge, he saw the stars reflected in the highly polished metallic skin of the ship.

All in all, the perfectly unique beauty created a magical sensation. Ski felt it a high privilege to be entranced by the intricate splendor of the universe. As he gazed out, his mind relaxed with celestial suggestions of continuity, permanence, and infinity. Ski knew that indifference was there, too, but the inherent peril that went with space travel only added to the excitement and privilege.

Behind him at the other side of the sextant, he heard Petey scuffling to raise himself up into the glass dome. "Did you finish your work?" he asked.

"Yeah, it all checked out. Kind of chilly up here."

Ski ignored the cold. "What group of stars is that?"

Petey looked to where Ski pointed. "That's Proxima Centauri."

"Proxima Centauri?"

"Yeah. It looks out of position out here because we're seeing it from a different angle."

"Tell me again where Earth is," Ski said.

"Look straight up," Petey said. "That bright star in Cassiopeia is the star of Earth."

"That flat *W*, right?"

"Yes."

Ski stared at the large yellow-white star and wondered at the origin of all human life now present on Alpha Centauri. Like the majority of the inhabitants of AlCent A2, he had not made the great journey from the home planet and felt little connection to it beyond curiosity. His only knowledge of Earth came from lessons in school and books he'd read. Even the old timers who'd made the trip had no direct knowledge of Earth, being the grandchildren of the original voyagers. The only connection they had to the planet was the deep-seated desire to return which had been ingrained in them from their parents. The last radio transmission from Earth had come when Ski was still a boy.

"Do you ever think we'll return to Earth, Pete?"

"I don't see why we would. We have everything we need here, and I doubt that Earth is any better than AlCent A2. Even their view of the stars is no better than this, and most of the people there never saw it like we do from *Kestrel*."

Ski nodded in agreement as his eyes followed the edge of the Milky Way. "You know, Petey, this is why I joined the fleet. I wanted to be out here in this openness and to see the stars from unique viewpoints. Maybe no one's ever seen them from this angle, from this position in space."

"It's quite possible. Most ships don't have windows, so the crew would never see it."

"I wish there were more windows on board. I don't think I could ever become tired of looking out at the stars."

"I know what you mean. As much as I deal with the stars for navigation, I never grow bored with them."

Ski looked around. Beyond the instrument array he could just see the edges of the glowing trail of superheated particles that ran out behind the ship. The exhaust from the *Kestrel*'s two powerful ion engines gave the only evidence that the ship was moving at all.

Ski remembered the first time Petey had brought him up here. Petey, one of the few people that Ski got along well with, seemed to understand profound things and Ski respected him. Because they both worked on the bridge and were in the same watch section, it didn't take long for the good rapport to turn to friendship. One day, when Ski had had a particularly bad day, Petey offered to show him something "special." Ski didn't think he was in the mood for anything, but Petey insisted. The navigator took Ski up to the sextant, explaining that it was a restricted compartment. When Ski saw the stars, he felt renewed. And he felt the same way every time he came to the sextant.

"You know, Petey, when I'm up here all of the troubles and problems seem to vanish. Down below we stand an endless stream of watches, and sometimes I think that I can't stand to be around these people for a minute longer, but when I'm up here it all seems so small, so petty. The bickering seems so pointless."

"I know. It's good therapy." Petey sighed. "When you see all this, does it make you wonder if there's a God?"

"I don't know." Ski disliked it when Petey waxed religious, but he didn't want to be rude about his friend's antiquated beliefs. "I guess if there is an intelligent being behind all of this, he must be magnificent!"

"Oh, he is," Petey said, "and he encompasses the greatest and noblest traits of humanity and much, much more."

Ski thought about those words, and as he looked out across the universe, it didn't seem implausible.

"Well, buddy," Petey said, "I think I'll try to get a quick nap before our next watch."

"Good idea." Ski took one last look around before he crouched down and headed back to the scuttle. "Thanks, Petey."

"Anytime."

Chapter 4
"CR3 Arrival"

After re-energizing the sextant and associated equipment, Petey secured the compartment and headed down the main tube for two decks where it ended. He exited on the second deck and walked down a narrow passageway forward. He glanced into the ballroom and saw Gradenko and a few other men working out with the ship's exercising equipment, and then passed the forward crew's head and through the door to the forward crew's berthing compartment. Here, off-duty crewmen lounged about reading, playing video games, or chatting. He walked over to his locker and opened it to reveal several flat, rectangular mesh bags of various sizes, all held in place by a short strap. Some of the bags held his neatly folded uniforms and civilian clothes, and others contained his toiletries and other personal effects. Beneath the bags and also held in place by a strap lay a collection of astronomical books, navigational manuals, his Bible, and a computer notepad. He grabbed the notepad and shut the locker, then opening his sleeping tube, took a small paper notebook out of his pocket and opened it to a page containing handwritten mathematical figures and astronomical data. Using the tube as a desk, Petey began transferring information from the paper notebook to the computer notepad, typing out his notes in clear and complete astronomical structure.

Observational data for NGC 6543-
Epoch J2450
Right ascension- 17^h 58^m 33.423^s
Declination- +66 Deg 37 Min 59.52 Sec
Distance- 3.3±0.9 kly (1.0±0.3 kpc)
Constellation- Draco
Apparent magnitude- 9.8B
Absolute magnitude- -0.2+0.8-0.6B
Apparent dimensions- Core: 20 Sec
Radius- Core: 0.2 ly
Notable features- complex structure
Other designations- Cat's Eye Nebula, Snail Nebula, Sunflower Nebula, (includes IC 4677), Caldwell 6
Stellar Class- O7 + Wolf-Rayet-type star

28

15 mas shift since last observation at AlCent A2.

Personal observation – Spectacular rose flower of
Joseph's coat colors, petals flung abroad into light
by death's tantrum into diminution.

This was Petey's astronomical log, or star-journal, as he called it. It contained photos, descriptions, and calculations of the many observations that Petey had made in the last two years aboard the *Kestrel*. The present entry, an addendum to a previous observation, described the apparent shift of perspective of the core of the Cat's Eye Nebula. He also entered the apparent separation or merging of several double stars and multiple stars as the *Kestrel* moved through space. Using the numerical setting circles on the bridge's optical viewer he could get accurate figures to calculate actual distance between the stars. The exercise helped him in his mastery of the navigator's trade, but it also provided a deeper enrichment for his love of the stars.

His love of astronomy started when he was fourteen years old. He had traveled with his mother and father to visit his grandparents in the northern temperate region of AlCent A2's American Zone. They lived in an agricultural production area, and in later years he would spend whole summers with them, but on this first trip he was fascinated to learn that his grandfather, whom Petey called 'Pap,' had built an observatory in the field behind his house. In it stood a homemade eighteen-inch reflector telescope, and for Petey it was love at first sight. Petey accompanied his Pap almost every night to the telescope to look at the astronomical wonders. There he learned the names of the constellations and the major stars, as well as the many nebulas, globular clusters, open clusters, and galaxies that could be seen in the summer sky. He even showed Petey the star where Earth resided, the birthplace of all human beings. His grandfather also had a small refractor scope that Petey could use on his own, and with it he would study the moon and planets of Alpha Centauri A's solar system.

As Petey re-copied his data he remembered the night his grandfather showed him how to use the stars to navigate.

"This is how the old sea ships used to find their way across the ocean," Pap had told him. Using an old sextant, the old man showed him how to calculate the latitude and longitude of the observatory. That summer Petey knew what career he wanted. He would be an astronomer.

But there remained a snag. Petey's parents were not wealthy and they couldn't afford to pay his way through college, and his grades, which had suffered because of his astronomical pre-occupation, weren't good enough to land him a scholarship. He had almost given up when some recruiters for the military's deep-space fleet came to give a talk at his high school. They told him that he could earn enough money, both in a college assistance program and by his personal savings, to go to school in only one enlistment. It sounded like his best solution, so he signed up to become a navigator, a job using and studying the stars. It would also teach him a useful trade to fall back on. Later, aboard the *Kestrel*, he began his star-journal. He hoped to one day use it, as proof of practical experience, to help him get into a university.

Petey finished his entries, but before putting the journal away he opened an app that kept track of his financial records. He had already saved enough to pay for four years of school. He only had one more year to go in the fleet, and when the ship got back into port, he would begin sending out applications.

Petey smiled and turned off the computer pad. It was all working out. He replaced the journal in his locker and silently murmured a prayer of thanks.

***

At seven minutes before five the next morning Ski awakened out of his bunk by the obnoxious electronic gonging sound of the General Quarters alarm. He grabbed his uniform and shoes and ran with the flow of men out of the compartment. Some continued aft, but Ski joined the flow of men ascending the tube. Instead of climbing up the pole with one hand, he grabbed the pant leg of the crewman ahead of him and rode with him to the top. Fortunately, the man headed to the bridge also, and Ski thanked him as he got to the top. Still carrying his uniform and shoes, he dodged around other crewmembers scrambling to their own stations. By the time he got to the ops shack his shirt was on but still unbuttoned. He saw the captain smiling and shaking his head at him. He put on his pants as Cauthen explained the situation.

"Here's the contact," Cauthen said, pointing to the screen, "and beyond it, there, is the relay station."

"Nothing else in the area?"

"No, that's it. If you've got it, I'm gone."

"All right. You're relieved," Ski said. Cauthen stood up and went down the forward hatch to the equipment room. Ski, still buttoning his shirt, sat down and began to page through the scanning modes. Morrell sat next to him still.

"Where's your partner?" Morrell said, impatiently.

"He'll be here. Did you guys run an ID on it?"

"No, uh, Cauthen was just starting to when you came up."

Sure he was. Ski began to run the program as Sansbury relieved Morrell, setting a bundle wrapped in a napkin down on the console. On a hunch, Ski entered the lifeboat data into the ID program and the result came on screen immediately. *I'll be damned.*

"Captain," he called. "It's another lifeboat. And it's practically motionless relative to the station."

Van Wert walked over and looked at the screen. "I see. Anything else in the area?"

"We're scanning now, sir. But so far the only other object around is the station."

"Very well. Since we're already at GQ, we'll maneuver to close and grab it with the arm and drag it with us. Get us a good scan of the whole area before we come alongside the station."

"Aye, sir." He and Sansbury did a thorough scan of the surrounding space as the *Kestrel* made a series of course changes to pick up the lifeboat. When Ski felt satisfied that there were no other vessels in the area, he notified the captain.

"Very well," Van Wert said. "The ship is manned and ready. Begin deceleration to close in on CR3. We will adopt a solar orbit fixed relative to the station, but will remain at GQ."

An order was given to the helm. Ski heard a distant rumble and felt his seatbelt tighten against his chest and waist.

As the tension on the bridge relaxed somewhat, Sansbury unwrapped the napkin from around two cinnamon rolls. "I stopped by the mess decks on the way up." Sansbury smiled. "I figured we may be up here a while. Take one."

On an empty stomach and a short night's sleep, the spiral shaped rolls made Ski smile. "Thanks." He took one and it tasted warm and sweet. *They may run out of a lot of things on patrol, but the baked goods are always made fresh.*

Ski studied the image of the station on the screen. The most striking feature was a large dish-shaped antenna that measured eighty meters across. Behind the antenna a metal framework surrounded a large cylindrical pod, and fixed on the end of the pod stood another smaller cylinder with a glass hemispherical cap on its end. Ski knew this to be the Tachyon transmitter, and it pointed toward the second star of the binary system. The dish antenna took in signals from the planet Alpha Centauri A2, amplified them, and sent them on to the vast industrial and scientific complex that orbited Alpha Centauri B.

Below the transmitter pod, also supported by framework, were two other large pods. The first one, the smaller of the two, would be the living quarters for the crew. The larger one would be the nuclear power plant. The whole structure, top to bottom, measured more than two hundred and fifty meters.

"Communication Relay Station Three, Communication Relay Station Three, this is the *USS Kestrel.* Please respond, over," Ensign Clark said into the microphone. After a few moments of silence, he called again and still got no answer.

Ski adjusted some settings on the console, and a large red beam of hazy light appeared that stretched from the right side of the screen to the dish antennae. Although faint, the beam was hitting the antennae squarely in the middle.

"Whoa!" Sansbury exclaimed. "What's that?"

"That's the communications beam. It's sent from AlCent A2 to this station. The station amplifies it and sends it on to the Exploration and Industrial Complex orbiting AlCent B."

"How did you put it on the screen?"

"There's a program that allows you to see if someone is communicating by beam transmission. We don't use it much but it can be helpful. I wanted to see if maybe the station had drifted off its position, but apparently, that's not the case. It's just not transmitting."

"That's pretty neat. I didn't even know it would do that."

Ski looked at Sansbury and smiled. "That's why they put you with me, so you could learn from the best." Ski popped the last bit of roll into his mouth. "Thanks again for the snack."

"Ops," Van Wert called, "bring down the optical."

"Aye, sir." Ski said and activated the optical viewer.

The captain peered into the device. "Nav, bring us around it like an orbit. Do we have a place to park yet?"

"Yes, sir," Petey answered. "Their automated Out-mooring Positioning System has already assigned us a berth. I'm putting it on screen now."

"Very well. Ops, see if you can link into their computer telemetry. I want to know what their atmosphere looks like."

"Aye, Captain," Ski answered. He felt his stomach shift as the ship decelerated and banked and began its orbit around the station. He reached up, and after selecting a new application, he located the station's computer telemetry link and got inside the station's computer system. He passed several display options and chose one for atmospheric gasses.

Behind him the captain studied the station through the optical scope. "What's the atmosphere look like, Ski?"

"Normal ratios of standard gasses, Captain. Nineteen point two percent oxygen, seventy-eight percent nitrogen, and other trace element gasses. We're getting a few unusual ones mixed in, elevated above trace level. The computer is classifying them as possibly taphonomic."

Van Wert looked over at him. "What, like poisonous?"

"No sir, not at these levels. Just traces of basic ammonia, hydrogen sulfide, and the like. Just enough for a smell, possibly, but the air is definitely breathable."

"Very well." The captain returned to the scope and then after a few minutes said, "Okay. Nav, maneuver us to our assigned position and stop the ship. We'll maintain a modified GQ until further notice. OOD, notify boarding party members. I'll be in my cabin."

"Aye, sir."

Ski was about to look up the word 'taphonomic' when he felt a hand on his shoulder. He looked up to see Ensign Clark behind him.

"Grab a quick bite to eat and then go suit up. Also get a side arm from Gradenko."

"I take it I'm one of the boarding party?"

"Yes. Be at the gig in thirty minutes."

"Aye, sir." Clark left and Ski turned to Sansbury. "Well, now I know why I wasn't on the watch bill."

Petey stepped over to them. "Did Mr. Clark talk to you?"

"Yeah. Are you going, too?"

Petey nodded, a slight smile betraying his excitement.

"How many?" Ski asked.

"Nine, I think, including the captain," Petey answered.

"Well, then, I guess we'd better eat now while we still have time." He turned to Sansbury. "Hold the fort."

Sansbury nodded. "Be careful."

"We'll let you know if the liberty is any good," Petey said.

Ski stood up and followed Petey to the mess decks.

Chapter 5
"Station Search"

Twenty-five minutes later Ski and Petey arrived at the hatch to the gig, already in vac-suits and each holding a helmet in his hand. The vac-suit, a sealed, one-piece suit made of a flexible polymer with a helmet, provided an enclosed atmosphere for the wearer that could be used for work outside the skin of the ship as well as in contaminated atmospheres. It could even be used to fight fires. Hot and cold filaments embedded in the material regulated the temperature of the suit's interior. The filaments and atmosphere controls were powered by a battery pack on the belt.

As it was tight fitting over the clothes, Ski found the suit uncomfortable, especially walking around the ship. He adjusted the temperature control to cool to keep from sweating.

"Mind if I jump down there first?" Petey asked. "I'd meant to get here earlier to start up."

Ski stepped aside and took Petey's helmet as the navigator climbed down the hatch into the gig. He thought about when Petey volunteered for boat coxswain's school. *On a small ship, nobody pulls only one job.* Petey reached the deck below and Ski could hear other crewmembers already in the gig greeting him with an encouraging chant.

"Pe-*tey*! Pe-*tey*! Pe-*tey*!" The navigator grinned and looked up, stretching out his hands.

As Ski handed the helmets down to him, he once again felt envious of his congenial friend. Everybody liked Petey and most felt confidence and trust with him. Many even came to him to discuss their deepest and most personal problems. Ski reflected how even though Petey knew many things about the people around him, he had never heard him talk about anyone in a conversation.

Maybe everyone accepts Petey because Petey accepts everyone. Well, I would be more accepting of the others if they made themselves more acceptable to me. And with that thought, feeling vaguely satisfied, Ski descended the ladder into the gig.

As Ski reached the deck of the gig, the excitement of Petey's entrance had died down. Some of the men had looked up at Ski but didn't say anything. Systems technician DeShon Wilson said, "Hi, Fruitcake."

"That's Mr. Fruitcake to you," Ski retorted. He took one of the portside seats and looked around as he fastened his seat belt. Petey sat forward at the helm, warming up the propulsion system. Facing Ski along the starboard side of the gig sat engineering technician Gonzalo Flores, who generally avoided all eye contact. Next to him sat hospital corpsman Bert Foley, a twenty-eight year old who, in addition to being slightly overweight and prematurely balding, seemed to be in a perpetual sweat. Beside Foley sat one of the ship's cooks Jay McElroy, who fiddled with his belt controls, and Wilson, who now leered at Ski. Ski sat portside beside weapons technician Gradenko. Ski looked at the firearm between Gradenko's knees and shook his head. Everyone else had been issued a semi-automatic single-pulse laser handgun, the normal issue for watch standers. But Gradenko had issued himself a fully automatic multiple-pulse laser rifle affectionately known as the 'street sweeper.'

"What did you bring that thing for?" Ski asked.

"Because I'm the gunner."

Wonderful. Ski looked around at the others, listening to the talk as it became animated with nervous excitement.

"I'm telling you, there's nothing here," Flores said. "Some comms glitch."

"What if the station has been infiltrated?" McElroy asked. "We could be walking into a trap."

"That's why I brought this," Gradenko said, patting his rifle.

"I wish I had one."

Petey turned around to join the conversation. "What would you do if some terrorists tried to take the gig?" he asked aloud.

"I'd put down my weapon, sign myself out in the log, and let them have it," Ski said. "Apparently they want it more than I do." A few of the men laughed.

"Not me," Gradenko said, putting his rifle to his shoulder. "I'd cut 'em in half and then toss 'em a bandage."

"Yeah, man. They'd have to get by me," Flores said, drawing his pistol. He pushed the arm button and the weapon began to hum menacingly.

"Hey, don't arm that in here!" Foley said.

Flores turned to reply when Ensign Millus, the second engineer, came down the ladder. The officer saw the drawn weapon.

"Stow that weapon, Flores. It's not a toy."

Flores disarmed the pistol and stuck it back into its holster as Millus sat down next to Ski.

The captain came down the ladder and looked around as if counting heads. Then, satisfied that all were present, he pulled a lever that closed the hatch and stowed the ladder. He sat down and buckled his seat belt. "All right, Peters, let's go."

Petey turned around to face the console screen and took the joystick. On the computer screen he touched an actuator that released the gig from its bay under the *Kestrel*'s belly. Ski leaned forward and looked out of the wide forward view ports as the highly polished underside of the ship seemed to rise up like a curtain, revealing a panorama of stars. Petey turned to the left, and soon the station came into view, silent and cold except for the warm light coming from its windows and the soft glow of starlight on its metallic skin.

"Meanwhile, back in the jungle…"

Ski looked back to see everyone staring wide-eyed through the forward window.

"Nothing seems amiss," Millus said.

No one replied and Ski returned his gaze to the station ahead. The large closed door of the docking bay came into view, and Petey stopped the tiny vessel just a few meters away from the door.

"How are we going to get in?" McElroy asked.

"I'm working on that now," Petey said. "I'm using our out-mooring position as an access code. There… we're in."

Two green lights came on at either side of the door, but nothing else happened.

"What's the delay?" Gradenko asked.

"It's probably closing the interior doors and depressurizing the space," Petey answered.

"Let's knock off the chatter," Van Wert said.

A bar of yellow-white light appeared at the bottom as the door began to slide upward, growing wider until fully open. Then Petey drove the gig inside the brightly lit docking bay, reaching his left hand over to grasp another smaller joystick. Ski could feel a slight surge downward as the gig entered the station's artificial gravity field. Petey steered toward an area near the far corner next to the airlock. The only other vehicles present were a small utility pod in the opposite corner and a smaller cylindrical object next to it. Petey set the gig down securely onto the floor and shut down the engines. Then he turned to face the others.

"Ok, let's get ready to go," Van Wert said. "I want Flores and Gradenko out first to set up a defensive perimeter covering the access doors. Then we'll all head to the airlock."

"What about the bay door?" Petey asked.

"We'll leave it open until the *Kestrel* gets the life boats in."

The boarding party began putting on their helmets and adjusting their suits. Ski put the radio monitor into his ear, adjusting the mic along his cheek before putting on his helmet. Once everyone signaled readiness, Millus equalized the pressure in the gig to match the vacuum in the bay, and Ski felt his suit expand and stiffen. Then the officer opened the side door.

Gradenko and Flores exited the gig, followed by the captain and the second engineer. Ski stepped out onto the floor of the docking bay, pistol in hand, and took up a position near the stern of the gig and waited as the others came out. The lights of the bay contrasted sharply with the star-strewn blackness of the open door, and he felt an apprehensive nausea in the pit of his stomach.

"Clear!" Gradenko called out through the radio.

Ski relaxed his defensive stance but kept his eyes focused on the vista of limitless space beyond him. McElroy stepped up beside him.

"Bizarre sight, huh?"

"Yes it is."

"With this artificial gravity holding us to the deck, it seems like we could just step out of the door and fall through infinity."

Ski nodded and stepped back a little closer to the gig. Beyond the open door he saw the *Kestrel* hanging motionless in space and for some reason he could not explain, he felt a little sad looking out at it.

Mac patted his arm, and he turned around to see the others gathering at the door of the airlock. He trotted toward them and stood next to Petey as they waited for the airlock to depressurize. Once the green light came on, Millus opened the door and they all stepped inside.

As the airlock pressurized again Ski felt the suit clinging to him once more, and he shrugged his shoulders against it. The gravity field on the station, stronger than on the ship, made him feel heavy and sluggish.

"Everyone leave your gear on until we check out the atmosphere," Van Wert said over the radio in Ski's helmet. "Keep your weapons armed but with fingers off the trigger."

Ski held his pistol pointing up and took a deep breath. They watched the pressure indicator and Petey gave him a wink and a smile. Another green light came on and the door slid open. Gradenko stepped out, his weapon at the ready and sweeping back and forth as he looked around, but no one was in sight. The short hall opened into a wide passageway, and Millus pointed toward a flight of stairs at one end.

"Those stairs lead to the central control room."

"Take us there," Van Wert said.

After so many weeks of being aboard the *Kestrel*, Ski found the openness of the relay station strange. It had been built in a time of large budgets and high hopes, and the contrast between it and the warship was striking. The wide passageways, high ceilings, and large rooms seemed plain, unadorned by tracks of conduit and piping. Even the stairs were such as you might find in a planetside office building. The style of architecture would have been ultra-modern twenty years old, but now seemed elegant, almost gothic, as if made to resemble a high-tech cathedral in space.

The group of men ascended the stairs and stepped into the large central control room. They stopped to look around, and Ski saw that most of the men were as impressed as he was. The rectangular room measured sixty feet long and forty feet wide with a high ceiling of acoustic tiles above. The tiles displayed a huge stylized star map painted in the motif of an ancient explorer's chart of the heavens embellished with gods and mythic creatures. A depiction of the station stood out near one corner, and from it a bright red line shot through the constellations to the far corner.

Two semi-circular consoles dominated the center of the room clustered with computer monitors, keyboards, and other operating controls. Each console faced an opposite wall, and judging by the controls, one monitored the communication receiver and transmitter while the other monitored the power plant. Mounted high on the wall at each end of the room were two large computer generated schematic diagrams. The one at far left displayed the various stages of the receiver, amplifier, and transmitter systems. The one at the far right displayed the various stages of the nuclear power plant. Several video monitors were arranged beneath each of the schematic diagram displays. From the chair in the center of the room, an operator could monitor the entire station and see any developing problem by merely glancing up.

The wall opposite from where the group stood consisted of six large plates of glass, each twenty feet tall by ten feet wide and held in place by stout girders. Beyond the glass the *Kestrel's* polished metallic skin, illuminated by the station's lights, stood out in bas-relief against the backdrop of stars. Ski watched as the manipulator arm, so-called despite its tentacle-like appearance, placed the lifeboats inside the docking bay.

"Man, what a palace," Doc said.

Millus and the captain went to the power console, and the ensign sat down before one of the computer terminals. As the men holstered their weapons, Ski studied the nuclear power plant schematic. Everything seemed to be running perfectly, yet the camera monitors showed no one around. He looked at the communications schematic diagram and saw a flashing red light in the amplifier section with every stage beyond it to the transmitter shut down. Ski wondered if the crew was at this moment fixing a problem in those sections but saw no one in the camera monitors there either.

"Meanwhile, back in the jungle…" Mac said over the radio.

At the console, Millus stood up and gave a thumbs-up sign. "The atmosphere in all the compartments is good," he said over the radio.

"Very well," Van Wert said. He reached up and pulled off his helmet, and the rest of the men followed his example, hanging them from hooks on their belts. He walked over to the transmitter console and Wilson joined him. The systems tech sat down at a terminal and began paging through various display screens. Flores joined Millus at the power plant console and also began working at a terminal.

"Man, this is weird," McElroy said. "Where is everybody?"

"I don't know, man, but watch your back," Gradenko replied.

Petey stood next to Ski. "What do you think, Ski?"

"I don't know about the crew, but there's our transmitter problem." Ski pointed to the red indicator on the diagram. "Let's go see what's going on." They both walked over to a communications terminal.

"Power plant checks out fine," Flores said. "Everything is functioning normally."

"I concur, Captain," Millus said. "Automated control system is running everything."

"I see. What have you got, Wilson?"

"There's a coolant pump failure in the amplifier section. An OP/FAIL contingency program in the computer shut down the rest of the system, preventing further damage."

"What about an auxiliary?"

"It's listed as off-line for maintenance, Captain."

"I see," Van Wert said. He rubbed his chin for a moment, then stepped back and turned so as to be heard by all of the men. "Well, aside from the transmitter itself, the equipment checks out. We need to form up into small parties to search for the crew. Ensign Millus and Petty Officer Flores will check out the Engineering Equipment compartments and the Machinery Spaces. Petty Officers Peters, Kowalski, and McElroy will search the Berthing Compartments and the Receiver/Transmitter spaces. The rest of us will go down to the docking bay to check out the lifeboats. Keep your radios on at all times and call if you find anything. And be careful."

Chapter 6
"A Lonely Air for a Lonely Death"

The captain led Gradenko, Doc, and Wilson back to the stairwell and went down. McElroy stepped over to Ski and Petey while Ensign Millus got up from the console chair. Ski touched his arm to get his attention.

"Which way, Mr. Millus?"

"Go up at the stairwell. The next deck above us is the living spaces, and the one above that is the transmitter section."

"Thanks." Ski turned to Petey and McElroy. "Let's go."

The two men followed as Ski left the central control room. At the stairwell Millus and Flores went down as the captain and his group had done. Ski watched them go and then looked up at the silent staircase above them. He drew his pistol once again and armed it.

"Just in case," Ski said and began his ascent. Petey and Mac drew their pistols and followed.

"Naturally we got to be the ones to search upward," Mac said. "Don't they have an elevator?" Mac asked.

"Probably somewhere," Ski said.

"How is it that the gravity is stronger here than on the ship?" Petey asked.

"Probably more varysium filaments in the deck," Ski said. "That's why they have to have the ceilings so high."

"I'm sure not used to it," Petey said.

"Me neither," Mac said. "Hey, how come Mr. Millus knows so much about this station?"

"He used to be in a Mobile Technical Unit that worked on these stations," Petey replied.

"I wish we had Gradenko with us," Mac said.

"Why?" Ski asked. "Because he's got that big gun?"

"Yeah, that. And because he's good in a fight. All the men in his family are military men."

"Huh!" Ski said. "Just because he acts gung-ho doesn't mean he's brave."

"Yeah, but they're hunters, too." Mac turned to Petey. "He killed his first deer at the age of seven. And it didn't bother him at all because he'd already seen lots of 'em killed by his brothers and dad."

"I know," the navigator replied.

"Let's keep quiet in case there's anyone up there," Ski said. They approached the next deck and Ski craned his neck to look above the floor level. Seeing no one, they climbed to the landing and looked around. In the central control room a gentle hum of machinery gave at least a false impression of life, but here in the living spaces a tomblike pall of silence hung over them. Ski felt a tingle go up the back of his neck.

"Hey, is anyone here?" he called out, but heard no reply.

"Eerie," said Petey, standing next to him. "Where do you want to look first?"

Ski looked down the hall and could see partially into the first room where lounge chairs and some tables stood. The oppressive silence outweighed his curiosity, and a desire to be around the noise of machinery grew. He thought about the coolant pump failure in the transmitter section and said, "I have an idea. Let's check out the comm equipment spaces. Maybe the crew is working on something up there."

Petey and Mac quickly agreed and the three continued up the long, narrow stairwell. As there were no other hallways leading from the stairs now, Ski knew they were proceeding up through the connecting tunnel to the communications pod. The stairs topped out at a narrow hallway leading to the right and left. A sign on the wall indicated the transmitter section to the left. The three men stopped to catch their breath.

"They really need an elevator," Mac said.

"Maybe this is how they get their exercise," Petey said.

"Hey, look." Ski pointed to a sliding door next to the stairwell labeled elevator. The other two looked and Mac shook his head.

"Great."

They moved down the passageway past various equipment rooms, and at each one Ski looked in to call but got no reply. When they came to the coolant pump room they stepped inside and saw two large pumps in the center of the floor connected to a maze of piping that hung from the ceiling. One of them had been taken completely apart and a computer terminal by the door flashed the words "Bearing Overheating" in red letters. There were no tools lying around, nor was there any sign of maintenance going on.

"Well, that's the end of that theory," Mac said.

Ski rubbed his chin. *Where the hell is the crew?* He backed out of the room, and they checked every remaining space of the entire communications compartment before returning to the stairs.

"Elevator?" Mac asked.

"No," Ski said. "Let's sneak down the stairs."

They descended and soon came to the level of the living spaces again. With pistol still drawn Ski walked straight to the lounge and looked inside. On a far wall a large video screen displayed only static while a variety of video game consoles and tables for cards or meals stood unattended. An e-book reader on a chair was the only trace of a crew.

"Meanwhile, back in the jungle…" Mac said, looking around.

Ski frowned and led them down the hall to the first cabin where the door stood open. The lights came on as he stepped inside, and he saw that the room was uninhabited. The two bunks were made up and the bunk curtains were open.

"Nice accommodations," Petey said.

They went to the second cabin and found the door shut. Ski passed his hand over the sensor, and as the door opened a chill went up his spine. The lights remained off, and a foul smell of death wafted out from the blackness.

"Uh-uh," Ski said and the three stepped back and put their helmets on. Then, cautiously they returned to the door, and Ski looked around inside. Silence seemed to scream out at him, and a surge of goose flesh passed over his skin. He waved his hand inside the door but the room remained dark.

"What the hell's wrong with the lights?" Mac asked.

"I don't know," Ski said, jerking his hand back.

"Maybe they've got it set for sleep mode," Petey offered. "They have watch standers here, too."

Ski reached around the open door and felt for a light switch but found none. He snatched his hand back and said, "Dammit! There's no switch."

"I bet they have bunk lamps," Petey said, "but voice recognition wouldn't turn them on for us."

"Here, I have a light." Mac held up a tiny pocket flashlight and offered it to Ski, but the ops tech stood back from the doorway.

"After you."

The cook grimaced.

"We'll go in with you," Petey said. "Just flip on the bunk lamps so we can see."

Mac looked from one to the other, then switched on the light and entered the dark room. Ski walked in behind him, and in the darting light beam he could see that the bunk curtains were closed. McElroy bent down and opened the curtain on the lower bunk revealing a made up and unoccupied bed. He switched on the bunk lamp, and a pale white light illuminated the floor. Then Mac stood and opened the curtain on the bunk above it. He shone his light up, but because of the height of the bunk, they could see nothing. The bunk lamp remained out of reach.

Ski watched as McElroy climbed the bunk ladder. With one hand holding the penlight and resting on the edge of the bed, he reached his free hand in toward the lamp. Something seemed to be in his way and he tugged at it. With a flopping motion, the face of a dead crewmember rolled into the flashlight's beam. The man's cheeks were gaunt, and the puffy, half-open eyes stared blankly down at Ski. A black fluid oozed from the open mouth.

Mac yelled and reared back, and his hand slipped off the edge of the bunk. With arms flailing wildly, his feet slipped off of the ladder and he fell against Ski, knocking him backward into a locker. A sharp, gruesome crack rang out just before McElroy hit the floor, and the cook began to scream in pain.

"My leg! My leg!"

"Mac!" Petey yelled. He picked up the flashlight and shined it at McElroy lying on his back on the floor, one of his feet still caught in the ladder rung. His foot was twisted grotesquely, and a broken bone pushed out against the inside of his right pants leg. His screaming merged into a torrent of profanity.

Ski climbed to his feet and shouted, "Let's get him out of here! Grab his shoulders." The two men lifted McElroy as Ski freed the cook's foot from the rung. Then they carried him out to the hall and put him in the middle of the floor.

"What was it?" Petey asked as he removed his helmet.

Ski removed his own helmet and the sickening smell of decay assaulted his nostril's again, more powerfully now. He took a knife from his pocket and began to cut the vac-suit from around the cook's leg.

"A corpse. It startled him. Here." Ski handed Petey the knife and touched the communicator on his ear to switch channels. "Captain, we've got a man down. McElroy has a broken leg. We're on the level just above the central control room."

"We're on our way," Van Wert said.

"We also found a dead crewmember."

"All right. Just stay put."

"Oh, man." Petey said, cutting away the pants from around McElroy's right leg. The broken tibia stuck through the skin covered with blood.

Mac removed his helmet and raised his head to look at his leg, his face writhing in pain. "Oh shit, man! It's broken!"

Ski gently pushed McElroy's head back down. "Take it easy Mac. Foley's coming."

"Oh shit, man. I can't believe it. Damn, it hurts!"

"I know, buddy. It won't be long."

Ski patted Mac's shoulder. "Life in the jungle, huh?"

"Huh!" Mac answered with a nervous chuckle. "Shit, it frickin' hurts!"

Ski heard a commotion behind him as Foley and the captain ran up the stairs and into the hall. Petey stood up to get out of Foley's way as the medic knelt down beside the broken leg.

"Where did this happen?" Foley asked as he took a cylindrical device out of his bag. He inserted a tiny bottle into it.

Ski pointing to the room. "In this cabin. He fell off of the bunk ladder."

"Why did you move him?" Foley held the device to Mac's thigh and pressed a button. With a brief hissing sound the device pneumatically injected a mixture of an antibiotic, regional painkiller, and tranquillizer into Mac's leg. "I tell you guys over and over again never to move the victim."

"No. They had to get me out of there, Doc! That thing was in there! It looked right at me!"

Van Wert squatted down. "Take it easy, Mac. Are you hurt anywhere else?"

"No, sir. That leg is enough!"

Gradenko and Wilson ran up the stairs with a folding stretcher from the gig. Foley stood and faced Van Wert.

"I've got to take him back to the ship, Captain. I can't set the bone here."

"I understand. Can you and Peters handle the stretcher?"

"Yes, sir."

"Good. Then you both take him back to the ship. You'll need Peters to operate the gig."

Gradenko and Wilson opened the stretcher and laid it alongside Mac, then everyone gently lifted the cook onto it. Mac winced with every motion. Then they all stood up and Van Wert nodded to Petey. The navigator helped Foley lift the stretcher.

"I'll get the door," Wilson said. He passed his hand over a nearby sensor and the elevator door slid open. Ski watched as they carried Mac inside.

"Oh, now I get to ride in the damn elevator?" Mac asked aloud, his voice becoming woozy. "Un-frickin' believable!"

Gradenko stood next to Ski, his rifle slung across his back. "You should've seen it down in the bay. We found four bodies in one of the lifeboats."

"Four?"

"Yeah, and they looked really weird. Their armpits and knees were swollen, their eyes were puffed out, and some kind of goo was coming out of their mouths."

"Sounds just like the one in here."

"It's weird. We were about to open the other when you called."

"All right," Van Wert said, "let's continue looking. There still might be someone who needs our help."

The captain stepped over to the door of the next cabin and opened it. Dark like the last one, it had the same foul odor. Ski handed the flashlight to Van Wert who shone it into the room.

On the floor of the room they saw three more corpses laid out evenly side-by-side. All of them had the same swelling around the knees, groin, armpits, and neck, and black fluid encrusted the mouths. Van Wert glanced quickly around the room, then stepped back and closed the door, shutting the terrible smell inside.

"That's three more," the captain said. "Eight total."

They checked the rest of the sleeping quarters and found most of the compartments empty. Two bodies lay in the dark in the officer's staterooms, and as Ski opened the last door soft music floated out into the hall. He recognized it as Bach's Suite No. 3. On the bed inside lay a dead man, his arms cradling two holographic images. The music player, set at continuous repeat, played Suite No. 3 over and over again.

Van Wert stepped up beside Ski. "Damn."

"He must've come here to die," Ski said. He held his breath and walked over to shut the music off. He glanced down at the holographs and saw photos of a young woman and a baby. Van Wert motioned for Ski to step back into the hall.

"Well, that's eleven," Van Wert said. "According to Mr. Millus, this station is assigned fourteen people, so that leaves three others."

"How about the other lifeboat, Captain?" Gradenko said.

"We'll check it out. Ski, have you checked the comm section yet?"

"Yes, sir. We saw no one there."

"Very well. Then we'll check out the other boat." As the group turned to leave, Van Wert spoke into his communicator. "Ray, did you find anyone?"

"No, sir," Millus replied. "The computer's running everything perfectly, but no one's here."

"All right, meet us in the docking bay."

As the four men moved down the hall toward the steps, Ski turned to look at the last cabin once more. He could still hear the music in his mind, sad, gentle, and soft. *A lonely air for a lonely death.*

Chapter 7
"Lifeboat Discovery"

Ten minutes later Ski stood with the others in the airlock waiting
for the docking bay to re-pressurize from the gig's exit. He peered
through a small window into the bay, past where the gig had been, to
where the two lifeboats sat in the corner. He studied the small
cylindrical object that lay next to the utility pod and couldn't decide
what it was. A green light came on over the door and Millus opened the
airlock. They walked out onto the docking bay floor and headed for the
lifeboats.

"Now, this is the second lifeboat we found just a little ways off
from the station and almost motionless, right, Captain?" Millus asked.

"That's right. The other boat is the first one we came across with
the four bodies," Van Wert said. "Gradenko, would you do the
honors?"

Gradenko nodded and stepped over to the door, pushing his
weapon around to his back. He pulled on two red emergency handles
and then, with Wilson's help, he pulled the hatch open. The same foul
odor drifted out, and the two men turned away from the boat.

Van Wert stepped through the hatch and looked around. Light
from the docking bay streamed in through the small windows,
illuminating three bodies. Two were slumped in seats at the rear of the
craft, and the other one sat forward at the control panel.

"Wilson, check the computer," Van Wert said.

Ski watched as Wilson took three large breaths and, holding the
last one, reluctantly stepped through the hatch. He brushed past the
captain and walked to the tiny control panel at the opposite end of the
boat to where the man seated there lay hunched over the controls.
Wilson pushed him aside and read the status board, then pulling his
shirt up over his nose, said "The systems check out normal but the
oxygen is exhausted, sir. Also, the fuel cells are empty."

Van Wert walked over, crouching under the low ceiling, and
looked at the dead man. "All right. Let's go back out."

Wilson nodded and both men stepped back through the hatch into the bay. They pushed the door shut then faced the others. "Well, that's it. There's the last three," Van Wert said.

"Did you say that the fuel cells were empty?" Millus asked. "That's strange."

"What's even stranger is that the man at the controls had no apparent symptoms like the others," Van Wert said.

"He didn't?"

"No, and that might explain what happened to the fuel."

"How's that?"

"Apparently," Ski broke in, "he left with the others, and when he realized that he wasn't going to die like they did, he used up the fuel trying to get back to the station."

"That's plausible," Millus said. "The fuel supply on these boats is mainly for maneuvering. He had enough to stop the boat, but not enough to start moving in the opposite direction."

"And suspended in space, he eventually suffocated when the air ran out," Van Wert concluded. He shook his head.

"But what killed the others?" Gradenko asked.

"That's a damn good question," Van Wert said. "Let's go back and check the log." He started back toward the airlock, and everyone followed him to the central control room.

***

Petey docked the gig and locked it in place on the *Kestrel's* underside. Then he powered down the console before going aft to help Foley with McElroy. Mac drifted in and out of consciousness due to the tranquillizer the medic had given him. He looked up at Petey.

"Hey, Mackie, we're home. How ya doing?"

"Been in… the… all of… yeah." Mac smiled.

"Hey, Petey, let's go. He's still hurt, you know."

Petey nodded and straightened up. He opened the hatch and saw Lieutenant Fischer standing above the hatch, his face etched with concern.

"What happened? Is he okay?" the executive officer asked.

"A broken leg, sir," Foley answered. "We can lift him on the stretcher. Is there someone up there who can give us a hand?"

Fischer nodded and stepped away. Two crewmen stepped up to the hatch and crouched down. Petey and Foley raised the stretcher to the hatch and the crewmen hoisted it up. Then Petey fixed the ladder in place and ascended in turn after the medic. Several crewmen stood nearby, including the two who lifted Mac.

"Carry him to sick bay," Foley said. Then he turned to the XO. "Compound fracture of the right tibia, sir. I've administered standard first-aid compound. I'm going to get a scan and then set it."

"Very well. I'll be by to check on him later. What happened to him?"

"I wasn't there, sir. Petey was."

Fischer nodded and watched as Foley and the two crewmen lifted the stretcher out of the gravity field and guided it to sickbay. He turned to the navigator.

"What happened, Peters?"

"He was up on a bunk ladder and found a body. It scared him and he broke his leg falling from the bunk."

"He found a body of one of the space station crew?"

"Yes, sir. There were lots of them."

Fischer looked around at the other men who had gathered to see what was going on, their attention rapt. "Follow me, Peters."

Petey followed the XO up one deck and forward to his stateroom. They stepped inside and closed the door. "You say there were lots of bodies?"

"Well, I only saw one, sir. But, I overheard Gradenko saying that they had found others."

"What were the conditions of the corpses?"

"They were dead." Petey checked himself. "I mean, they looked bloated and puffy. At least from what I heard."

Fischer nodded. "Listen, don't speak to anyone about this, do you understand?"

"Yes, sir."

Ski and the rest of the boarding party walked into the central control room to the two semi-circular consoles. On the far side of the power console stood a video monitor with a camera built in at the top of the screen. Wilson walked over to it and sat down at the keyboard in front of the monitor. He touched some keys on the menu screen, and some words came up displaying the date and time.

VIDEO LOG INITIALIZING.

The screen went blank for a moment, then read,

SELECT OPTION:
NEW ENTRY,
AUGMENT ENTRY,
LATE ENTRY,
REVIEW.

Wilson touched, REVIEW.

TO? FROM? ENTRY NUMBER (BY DAY)?

Wilson typed, LAST ENTRY.

The screen went blank for a moment, then a man appeared on the screen, sitting in the same chair in front of the console. Ski immediately recognized him as the man in the cabin with the music playing. He watched the man slump his head down and saw his hand reach up to steady himself on the console, as if he'd spent all his energy just switching on the video log. An oxygen tube ran to his nose from a small bottle behind him, and he seemed to fight for every breath. His sweat-soaked sleeveless undershirt revealed swelling under the armpits, and he held his arms away from his body to relieve the discomfort. His labored breathing forced him to speak slowly and in broken sentences.

Heavy mucus made his voice raspy when he lifted his head again to speak.

"I… don't think… there'll be another… log entry… tomorrow… I…" The man began coughing, a little at first, but then the coughs grew more forceful until they wracked his whole body. He held a handkerchief over his mouth but could not contain the spatters of black goo. Eventually the coughing subsided and the man shook his head, weary from the effort. "I really think this is it. I've been…" The man took a deep breath, "…watching movies to occupy myself… I don't want to think about it… I don't want to think… about anything… I'll just sign off… and watch another… movie… Or maybe… some music…" The man looked up toward the glass windows with the panorama of stars behind, and a shadow of defeat seemed to pass over his face. Then his gaze drifted back to the camera. "If anybody ever sees this… please tell my wife… and my daughter… that I love them… that I was… thinking about them… to the last." The man lowered his head and began to cry. After a few moments he switched off.

The screen went blank and the words SELECT OPTION came on again. A pall of silence hung over the group of men clustered around the console. Ski looked at the captain, but Van Wert betrayed no emotion as he stared at the blank screen.

"Start the log from the beginning of their term out here," he said.

Wilson typed the necessary commands, and the screen went black for a few moments before a man appeared. He seemed to be in his mid-thirties and had sandy brown hair with a closely trimmed beard. He wore a jovial expression and appeared to be in good health. Ski recognized him immediately.

"That's Doctor Leonard Fredricks!" he said.

"Who?" Van Wert asked.

"Doctor Fredricks. He did a lot of work on the development of Interplanetary Tachyon Beam Communications. He came to my university and gave a seminar. I met with him afterwards. He's a very smart man."

"He must be a genius if *you* think he's smart," Flores said.

"He is. He pioneered work in light-wave phase shifting on stations just like this. The next generation of Beam Comms will carry twice the information as the present systems." Ski nodded in appreciation. *I wonder what he's doing out here again?*

"Uh," Fredricks said, "are we on here?" He tapped the camera. "Oh yes, Good. Well, here we are, day one of our 'on-crew' stretch. Turnover preventative maintenance went well. Everything is functioning normally. As usual, most of us stood at the windows to watch the transport ship depart, watching it until it was out of sight and then tracking it on the scanner until it passed out of range. It is our last contact with other people for six months." Fredricks rubbed his beard and smiled. "Yep. During turnover, the station seems so crowded and busy with the on-coming crew, the off-going crew, and the transport ship crew all here at the same time. But, now there's peace and quiet. Our crew will settle into a routine, and I can get some unofficial research work done." He smiled and raised is eyebrows.

"But, back to business, we have some new people out here with us this time. Kyu Matsuda is our new Comms engineer. We also have Dana Powalie with us serving as a Power Systems technician. And lastly, Ren Babbitt is now with us in the Station Service/Cook department. Other than that, it's the usual gang.

"One more thing, we brought out two new scenarios for the *Brainstorm* Mind/Sensory Expansion Systems." He held up two flat computer game packages, each one about three inches square with a title and an appropriate graphic. "One is *Nordic Rampage*, which simulates being on a Viking longboat and pillaging Eleventh Century Europe. Sounds interesting. And the other one is *The Sub Continent*, which simulates various adventures in the different regions of India in the latter Nineteenth Century. That one I can't wait to try. These discs are so real, that after spending some time with them, you really could believe that you'd been there. On our last time out I became hooked on *Drone War Battle-Cruiser*. I'd always had a secret longing to be a starship commander.

"But, I bring this up to tell you how much the crew and I appreciate these recreational machines. They turn idle time into harmless diversions. It is money well spent and we thank you.

"I guess that's all for day one. Check in tomorrow."

The screen went blank momentarily.

"Man," Gradenko said, "They sure treat these people right."

"They should," Ski said. "They're out here for six months at a time."

"Have you ever played one of those machines? Every little detail, even mosquito bites and sweat are sensory stimulated."

Before anyone could reply, the words Day Two came on the screen and the image of Fredericks appeared again. He wore light-blue coveralls emblazoned with a communications relay station patch. "Hello, again. Nothing to report today. Everything is running smoothly and the crew is falling into their usual routines. Check in tomorrow."

Day Three: "Nothing to report today, all is well. Now that things are well underway, I've started the next step of my research." Fredericks smiled. "But that will be covered in my personal journal. Until tomorrow."

Day Four: "Everything is running well, nothing to report. We received a news update today. Of course, the data was three days old, but it was refreshing to get some news from home. Tomorrow, our tournament starts. We have competitions in chess, Monopoly, and cribbage. It promises to be a lot of fun for everyone. Check in tomorrow."

Day Five: "Everything is well, nothing to report."

When Day Six came on the screen Ski, was taken aback. Then he started to laugh, encouraging the others to laugh as well. Fredericks was apparently hanging upside down, but the camera was turned upside down as well. The effect made Fredericks look upright and the control room look upside-down. "Nothing to report today. Everything is running well. Matsuda is kicking butt in the chess tournament, and Himmelsbach says her novel is well underway."

Day Seven: "All is well, nothing to report. There is a story making its way around the station and it goes like this." Fredricks told a joke and then laughed aloud. Ski could hear others laughing off screen. Everyone in the control room laughed too, except for the captain. He just watched the screen and waited for the next entry.

Ski realized he was becoming absorbed in the people on the log. Apparently they were a good-natured bunch. *A good trait in such isolation.*

Day Eight: "The Comm techs report that one of the coolant pumps in the signal amplifier system is running a little warm."

Fredericks held his hands up in mock excitement. "At last, an interesting case! They say it's nothing serious, though, and they will monitor it. Other than that, everything is well."

Day Nine: "The coolant pump is running a little warmer, but there is no noise of bearing failure. They're monitoring it, but it is still in the permissible temperature range. Here are the final results of the tournament: Matsuda is the Chess Master Strategist, Tilman is the Cribbage Peg King, and Buis is the Monopoly Chief Acquisitioner. I think everyone had a good time, but there were some complaints about the lack of diversity of the contests. In three weeks we'll go again, but this time we'll add arm-wrestling or things like that."

Day Ten: "The coolant pump is hot. We've switched to a backup. Tomorrow our comm techs, Garlock and Gregory, will disassemble the pump to see what's wrong."

Day Eleven: "Well, everyone got involved with the pump today, much to Garlock and Gregory's displeasure. I don't think they like to be watched while they work, but it was exciting for everyone. They found nothing wrong at all, so they reassembled, relubricated, and realigned the pump and motor. We'll try it tomorrow."

Day Twelve: "We started the pump today and it ran fine. Another mystery of the Comm Relay Station Service. Everything else is running well."

Day Thirteen: "All is well, nothing to report."

Day Fourteen: "All is well. Tonight is pizza night! Yum!"

Day Fifteen: "Matsuda and the comm techs have picked up an object on the scanner. It's still pretty far away, but they calculated that it will pass to just within nine hundred kilometers of us. There's been some talk of going out and getting it, but I don't think I like that idea. It appears to be traveling in a steep elliptical orbit around AlCent A, like a comet.

"According to the International Astronomical Convention rules, Matsuda gets to name it since he was the first one to find it, but he has demurred from giving his name to it. Instead he is preliminarily calling it the 'Aldebaran mystery object' because that is the nearest star from which it seemed to be traveling when he discovered it. I suppose he will modify the name if we find out what it is."

Day Sixteen: "We're still tracking the object, and it's stirred up much excitement around the station. A lot of the crew have asked me if we could send someone out in the utility pod to go get it, and I told them it was too dangerous. We only have one pod and it carries a limited amount of fuel. But most are convinced that it is an artifact of some kind and would be a great boost to science, so after constant persuasion by everyone I agreed that only one volunteer could go, and the trip must be calculated so that only one quarter of the fuel would be used on the initial burn. I stressed a maximum of one quarter of the fuel. That would leave enough fuel for slowing and maneuvering with a reserve to get back. I was hoping that the window of opportunity for interception would have already closed. But they calculated it out and found that at the speed that could be attained using one quarter of the fuel in a burn, it would take four and a half hours to reach the object. I double-checked the figures myself. That means that the pod must be launched by tomorrow evening at 1800. Oh, and by the way, the scanner estimates the object's size as being three meters by one meter. Until tomorrow."

Day Seventeen: "Everything is running well today except for the coolant pump. It's starting to run warm again.

"As to the mystery object, several of the men drew straws today to see who would go out in the pod to get the object. Moody drew the shortest piece of copper wire so he will go." Fredericks looked at his watch. "He'll be launching in about one hour."

D.17 Augment: "Moody has launched and is well underway. The comm team is tracking him and will advise him on course corrections. I must admit that I'm curious and excited, too."

D.17 Augment: "Moody has the object. Our scanner got him close, and the pod's seeker unit guided him the rest of the way. He's on his way home now and I breathe a sigh of relief."

Day Eighteen: "The coolant pump is running hot again, so we have switched to back-up. Gregory and Garlock will disassemble the pump tomorrow.

"As to the excursion, Moody is safely back with us. The object appears to be an escape pod of some kind."

The image on the screen switched over to some handheld video footage that showed members of the station crew gathered around the pod in the docking bay. Some of them had tools and were attempting to open the pod. Others were milling around holding coffee cups and chatting excitedly. Fredericks squatted next to the men with the tools.

The oblong shaped cylinder measured three feet wide by nine feet long and appeared solid gray with no windows. One end was round and smooth but the other end had three small impressions that resembled rocket nozzles. On each side were two small patches of Runic-like inscriptions that bracketed a rectangular shaped seam on the top. As the men tried to pry at the seam to open the object, voices could be heard off-camera talking about the device.

"What if it's some type of torpedo or probe? We might find some kind of new military seeker on board," he said.

"Or get blown up," a woman said.

"I bet it's a religious artifact."

"From who, space people?"

The conversation halted at the sound of a metallic snap as one of the men with the pry bars broke a latching mechanism. The group pressed forward to get a better look as the men with the tools lifted the cover off.

Fredericks continued to narrate from the log as the camera man moved forward to shoot the object's interior. "Ah, here we go. Look at what we found inside."

The camera pointed down into the pod, and inside lay a four-foot-tall humanoid creature lying supine on a bed with straps. A breathing mask and hose covered the face. It wore loose-fitting pantaloons and a broad tunic encrusted with various gems in symmetrical patterns. The being had small hands with long thin fingers and wore bright red slipper-like shoes. The shirt had broad sleeves and tight cuffs. One of the station crew reached in and lifted the mask off of the bald head revealing a tight, thin-lipped mouth and two nostrils set on a hint of a nose. The eyes were slanted and closed tightly. At the being's feet appeared to be a space for another person, but the space was presently vacant.

The hushed conversation around the object resumed slowly.

"What the hell is it?"

"I don't know."

"How long do you think it's been floating around out there?"

"Who knows? Maybe since before human beings got to the AlCent system."

"Maybe centuries before we got here."

"Mr. Fredericks, do you think this is some kind of coffin?"

Fredericks studied the being intently. "I don't think so. The nozzles in the stern, the space for two, and the markings all seem to indicate it's an escape pod. What do you think, Andy?"

"Could be," Anderson answered. "What about his clothes. Do you think he's military?"

"Who could know? Maybe a diplomat or something."

A man who was dressed like a physician said, "I'm sure the cold must have preserved the body, but in this warmth decay will soon set in."

"Yeah, what'll we do with him?"

Fredericks thought for a moment. "Let's drop some cold packs in and button it up. We'll leave it here in the bay and maybe take it back with us."

"Hey, before you close it, let me take some pictures." The woman recorded some images before the others replaced the mask and dropped the door in place. Then the video footage stopped, and Frederick's face appeared on the screen again.

"Well, that's it. Fascinating, isn't it? Much of the initial interest has died down and some of the crew seem disappointed. I guess they were expecting to find some kind of treasure. We'll keep it in the docking bay with some cold packs until we leave. I'll bring it back and find out more about it. Until tomorrow."

Day Nineteen: "Today our comm techs, Gregory and Garlock, disassembled the overheating coolant pump. Mechanically it was in great shape, but the lubricant inside had congealed. It seems that this lubricant had been ordered from a substitution list and two numbers were reversed. This lube is a very high viscosity and is designed for low R.P.M. applications. In our high R.P.M. pumps, the lubricant couldn't dissipate the excess heat. The lube was changed on the last Preventative Maintenance checks and it's the only kind we now have. Power department has some of the right stuff, but they need it for their reserve supply. I inserted a transmission to our home base to have the next crew bring some of the right lubricant. In the meantime, we cannot keep changing out the lube because we will run out before our twenty-six weeks are up. So, we've decided to rotate the pumps on a schedule to get their optimum time. Also, to decrease the load on the pumps, thus extending their service time, we've decided to shut down the scanning unit and the local traffic comm unit. We really don't need either of them. This way the beam comms will still go through, which is the most important function."

Day Twenty: "Nothing to report. Comms people are monitoring the pumps. All is well."

Day Twenty-One: "All is well." Fredericks coughed. "Here is something you should see." He motioned to someone off camera to come to him. A man stepped up holding a detailed scale model of the relay station. He looked a little shy to be in front of the camera. "Babbitt here, in his spare time, has fabricated this model of the station." Fredericks carefully took the model and held it right up to the camera. "Look at that detail. How did you do it, Babbitt?"

"I used mechanical diagrams for most of it and rode around in the pod taking images for the really fine stuff."

"Isn't that incredible?" Fredericks handed the model back to Babbitt. "Thanks." He turned back to the camera. "I know that stuff is irrelevant on an operational journal," Fredericks coughed, "but after a while even the little things excite us. We're bored! How bored? I'll tell you. The five people in Power department are having a contest to see who will have the blackest coffee cup by the end of our term." Fredericks coughed. "They aren't washing them! That's how bored these people are. But, there are better jobs and there are worse ones." He coughed again and Ski could hear the sputtering of phlegm. "God, I must be coming down with something. Anyway, I'm getting a lot of work done."

Day Twenty-Two: "All is well. The pumps are being alternated on schedule." Fredericks coughed several times and seemed to produce a lot of phlegm, spitting it into a handkerchief. He took a deep breath and continued. "Interesting sidetrack today. Tilman, the woman on the video taking pictures, has been digging around in the station library. It appears that she might have uncovered the mystery of our friend we found in the lifeboat." Fredericks looked down at a computer pad. "Judging by the inscriptions found on the sides of the pod he may have come from AlCent B2. The markings are similar to those found on the archeological remains of an ancient civilization discovered in the equatorial region on that planet. If so, then this find really is a coup for science, as it will give us a new look into the people who lived in this star system long before the arrival of the human race."

Fredricks looked up from the pad and smiled. "Of course, Matsuda insists on calling it the *Aldebaran Conundrum* because he thinks it sounds better than the *AlCent B2 Object*. I can't say I disagree.

"Some of the crew seem to be coming down with colds, and there has been some concern over the possibility that the humanoid we found in the pod might have brought a virus with him, but I personally doubt it. The cold of space should have killed any organisms that were present. At any rate, our friend might have some value in a museum. Until tomorrow."

Day Twenty-Three: "The machinery is running well." Fredericks said in a raspy voice. He coughed and coughed, and he looked very sick. After a deep breath he continued. "I am not doing so well, however. I spent most of the day in bed. Many of the crew are sick." He coughed again. "Doctor Shahid says it's some kind of virus. I shudder to think where we might've gotten it from."

Day Twenty-Four: Fredericks was not wearing the usual blue station jumper, but only wore a tank top undershirt. He held his arms outward as if his armpits were sore. He seemed to exert a lot of effort just to sit upright. "Bad news today. Powalie died." Fredericks coughed for a few moments. Then, trying not to trigger another spasm, he slowly took a deep breath and spoke. "He died in his bed of pneumonia. It's a complication of the virus. He was the sickest. I'm sorry that he died. Dr. Shahid has been running tests and suggests that the virus might have a ninety-seven percent kill rate, but I pray to God that this is just something that will run its course and go away." Fredericks coughed and spit into a handkerchief. "Half of the crew is sick. Everyone is keeping to themselves. The station seems deserted. I wanted to insert a message into the beam today, but I just don't have the strength. Maybe tomorrow."

Day Twenty-Five: Fredericks still looked very ill. His eyes, which up to now had seemed clear and alert, seemed tired and distracted. With a voice like gravel he said, "The cooling system failed today and the comms system is down. We lost two lifeboats today. One left at eight in the morning and the other at ten." Fredericks coughed, his whole body wracked by the spasm. Ski noticed that it was taking him longer and longer to recover each time. "Seven of the crew departed, including my power engineer. Oddly, they all seemed to be rather healthy. I guess they wanted to stay that way." Fredericks looked as if he were about to cough, but he held his exhalation until the urge settled. "I don't know where they think they'll go. There's nothing around here. This virus seems to incite panic." Fredericks coughed again. "Now Pruett is my only power tech. He seems well enough, at least not as bad as some. I wanted to send a message home, but Gregory and Garlock left in the boats and Matsuda can't get out of bed. Moody is helping, but we don't know how to put the system back on line."

Day Twenty-Six: Fredericks could barely sit up. He had an oxygen tube running up to his nose. His hair was damp with sweat. "Matsuda died today. So did Randolph. Everyone has symptoms of the virus." Fredericks coughed hard. When it was over, he looked down and shook his head. Then he looked out in the direction of the window. As he stared at the stars, despair and sadness moved over his face. Ski thought he saw a tear in Fredericks' eye as the engineer looked off camera. Then after a long silence, Fredericks said, "I don't know. I…" He closed his eyes and shook his head.

Day Twenty-Seven: Fredericks again had the oxygen hose. He sat hunched over the keyboard and took a breath between almost every word. "Babbitt… died today…. Moody and… Shahid… are bedridden…" He seemed to try to say more, but was too exhausted.

Day Twenty-Eight: This log entry featured a younger man wearing the station overalls. His nametag said "Pruett". He looked tired, sweaty, and sick. In a raspy voice he said, "Moody died. We're using a crew's cabin as a morgue." Pruett coughed and coughed, spitting black phlegm into a handkerchief. "I am becoming afraid as breathing becomes more difficult. God, help us."

Day Twenty-Nine: Pruett was in a t-shirt, swelling evident under his arms. He rested his head on his hands and had his eyes closed. "Shahid and Fredericks died today. That's it." He coughed hard, then raised his head from his hands and looked at the camera. His eyes held the desperate look of a caged animal. "I'm the last one! My God, what am I going to do? It's so hard to breathe!" He coughed hard, seemingly unable to get his breath.

Day Thirty: Pruett was on oxygen. His neck and armpits were visibly swollen. He took a shallow breath between almost every word. His voice was barely audible. "I… don't think… there'll be another… log entry… tomorrow… I…" Pruett began coughing. A little at first, but soon the coughs were wracking his whole body. Eventually they subsided. "I really think that this is it. I've been…" Pruett took a slow deep breath. "…watching movies to occupy myself… I don't want to think about it… I don't want to think… about anything… I'll just… sign off… and watch… another movie… or maybe… some music…" Pruett looked up at the glass windows with the panorama of stars behind and a shadow of defeat seemed to pass over his face. Then his gaze drifted back to the camera. "If anybody ever sees this… please tell my wife… and my daughter… that I was… thinking about them… to the last." The man lowered his head and began to cry. After a few moments he switched off.

The screen went blank and displayed the words SELECT OPTION.

If someone had asked Ski how he felt at that moment, he would not have been able to answer. His mind seemed devoid of thought, his feelings stolen by the numbing shock of the images he had just seen. He only stood there, like the others, staring at the blank screen.

But soon a new feeling began to rise in his heart. *What if the virus is still here?* As the primitive urge of panic welled inside him, he became aware of the others looking at the captain.

Van Wert, with closed eyes and rapid breathing, nervously chewed his thumbnail. His lowered hand would occasionally shake slowly back and forth. Ski could almost visibly see the captain's sense of duty struggling with his sense of self-preservation. Everyone watched him carefully. Each knowing, perhaps unconsciously, that the captain's course of action now would determine the fate of all.

"Skipper?" Ensign Millus said. He waited for a reply, but none came. "Skipper?"

Van Wert opened his eyes and raised his head. He dropped his hand from his mouth and turned to look at the others. His eyes glowed with the self-confidence and authority that Ski had always known.

"We must establish a quarantine," Van Wert said.

"Do you think there's a possibility that we've been infected now, too?" Millus asked.

"I don't know. But we can't take a chance. We must assume that we have contracted the virus until we're certain that we have not."

"What about Petey, Mac, and Foley?" Ski asked. "They've already gone back to the ship."

Van Wert looked over at Ski. "Then the ship will have to be quarantined as well."

Those words and the captain's gaze made Ski uneasy.

"You know sir," Wilson said, his voice tinged with the same uneasiness, "maybe this virus works like the Bubonic plague did. Once that disease killed off so many people, there weren't enough hosts to support it. Then the plague stopped."

"That's crazy," Ski said. "How do you explain the fact that the virus traveled through space for so long?"

"It must go into a dormant state," Flores said. "Don't you think, Captain?"

"How should I know?" Van Wert snapped. "I'm not a damned microbiologist!"

"Skipper, I have an idea," Millus said. "I'll take Flores down to the air filtration system. I think it's possible that in the time this station has been running since the last crewmember died, the filters may have removed the virus from the air. Maybe we can bypass it and isolate the filter."

"I don't think the virus would get caught up in a filter," Van Wert said, but then he seemed to reconsider. "Yeah, go ahead. Be careful and let me know what you find."

Flores said, "Maybe we can vent the atmosphere into space and replenish it. That would get rid of a virus in the air."

"Yeah, that might work," Van Wert said, "providing you had enough air in the banks to replenish the whole station. For now, just go check out the filters."

As Millus and Flores turned to walk out of the control room, Gradenko picked up his auto-rifle and armed it. "Man, I don't believe you people. Can't you see what's going on?"

Millus and Flores stopped. Millus stared at Gradenko. "What are you talking about?"

"All of this."

"Be more specific," Van Wert said.

"It's a ruse, a fake. They've put this on to fool us!"

"Who?"

"The insurgency," the gunner said, his voice nervous, almost jittery. "They've done this before! They kill everyone, take what they want, then cover their tracks with some elaborate scheme."

"What about the log? The bodies?" Ski asked.

"They faked it. I've seen this before. They might even be here still. Or maybe they'll come back."

Ski stared at the gunner. *Surely he can't really believe that.* But, then it dawned on Ski. *He needs to believe that.* It's easier for him to face an enemy he can see than one he can't see, let alone fight.

"Forget it, Gradenko," Van Wert said. Millus and Flores continued out the door.

"If it's all the same to you, Captain, I'd like to stay prepared."

Van Wert started to speak, then stopped short. It seemed to Ski that the captain also understood why Gradenko acted this way. "All right, Gradenko. Carry it if you must, but I want it disarmed."

The gunner nodded and shut the weapon off.

The captain looked at Ski. "Why don't you three go to the mess hall and find something to eat. I want to call the XO."

Ski nodded and the three of them left for the stairwell.

When they got to the dining room, Ski walked over to the meal selector machine. As it was still morning by the *Kestrel's* reckoning, he ordered a Danish and some coffee. The items came out and he took them over to a table where Wilson sat. Gradenko stood at the window.

"Man, this sucks," Wilson said. "This really sucks."

"I know. I hope what you said about the Bubonic Plague applies here."

"I told you people what's wrong," Gradenko said, still facing the window.

"Come on, man," Ski said. "I'd like to believe you, but it just doesn't seem likely."

The gunner turned to face Ski. "Well, I'll tell you one thing, even if it is just a virus, I think it's wrong to sit around here. This is stupid. We should go back to the ship and haul ass out of here. Let the ICA handle this."

Ski didn't reply. He looked at Wilson. "Aren't you going to eat?"

"No way, man. I'm not ingesting anything."

"Me neither," the gunner said.

"Look," Ski said, "if you're going to get this thing, you've got it already. And if you haven't gotten it by now, you never will."

"I'm not taking any chances," Wilson said. "I'll wait until we get back on the ship."

Ski started to argue but decided against it. The precaution seemed pointless, but as he looked down at his danish, he could imagine millions of microorganisms crawling all over it, and he promptly lost his appetite.

***

Lieutenant Fischer, the *Kestrel*'s executive officer, studied Van Wert's face on the comm screen as the captain related what he'd found on the station log and could scarcely believe his ears. "Do you think there's a possibility that you've contracted this virus?"

"I don't know, but given the circumstances it's highly probable." Van Wert frowned. "If it's as contagious as I believe it is, then McElroy, Foley, and Peters probably brought it back with them as well."

Fischer felt a flutter of fear in his stomach but mastered it. "What's our next course of action?"

"Send out a message to Fleet Headquarters. Let them know what has happened. Ask them if there is anything we can do to stop it. Maybe they can research the government medical histories and find something."

Fischer nodded. "It'll take three days for the message to get there, then another three days for the reply."

Van Wert shrugged. "What else can we do?"

"Will you be coming back on board?"

"Not right yet. I want to look at the station doctor's medical journal and records. Maybe they will yield something."

"All right. I'll get that message out right away."

"Good. And Paul," Van Wert said, "let's keep this quiet for now. We'll tell the crew when we find out exactly what we're up against."

"I understand," Fischer said. He watched the screen until the captain switched off.

***

As soon as McElroy arrived in the sickbay, Foley gave the broken leg a thorough internal examination. Then he set the bone and began the electromagnetic speed-healing treatments. Mac would receive one treatment a day for seven days. After that, the bone would be fused and completely healed.

67

Following the first treatment, the cook was brought to the mess decks where he instantly became the center of attention. The tranquillizer had long since worn off, and with the leg well on the way to recovery and a meal under his belt, he felt expansive and communicative. The excitement of his shipmates concerning the discovery of the corpse on the station further propelled his already talkative nature.

"No, man. Its eyes were open but it was already dead."

"And that's when you got scared and jumped off the ladder?" a weapons tech named Crosly said, trying to suppress a smile.

"I didn't jump off. A fastener on the ladder broke."

"At the precise moment this thing reached out and tried to grab you!" Crosly grabbed Mac's shoulder with both hands and leaned over him as the men that had gathered around erupted into laughter.

One of the men, engineering technician Matthew Dresden, listened intently. Being stationed aboard the *Kestrel* for more than two years had given him a keen ear for conversation. Wild Bill had taught him how to listen to find out what was going on around the ship. Bill remained convinced that if information had to proceed down the proper channels to the engineering techs, little, if any would actually make it to them, so he taught Dresden and the other men who worked with him how to listen for bits of information that would be useful.

Dresden, a clean-cut, intelligent technician, had never been prone to trouble. Chief engineer Fukunaga and second engineer Millus had hoped that his arrival would break down Wild Bill's sphere of influence in the engineering department, but circumstances had weighed against him. Dresden first arrived aboard the ship during a holiday period when much of the crew were away on leave. Docked at an orbiting port facility that offered little in the way of entertainment, he felt lonely and had little reason to leave the ship. At that time Wild Bill and another engineering tech named Morris had been restricted to the ship for starting a brawl in a local bar and assaulting a police officer. Bill took Dresden under his wing, and night after night the two restricted men filled his head with all kinds of stories about the supposed harsh command aboard the *Kestrel*. They told him that the officers didn't care about the men in engineering and they had to stick together and fend for themselves to survive.

"Yeah," Wild Bill had told him, "on another ship, just like this one, the bridge crew had run the ship into an asteroid. The engineering crew wasn't told what was going on. The CHENG just told them to keep the power on. So they did it for as long as they could, but no one told them the hull had fractured and the ship was losing air. Finally when it became apparent that the ship was depressurizing, someone went forward for a look and saw that the crew had already been evacuated. They took that man off with the last lifeboat while the snipes, still working in the main spaces to keep the power on, suffocated."

"Snipes?" Dresden had asked.

"That's what we engineering techs call ourselves," Morris had answered.

"And then," Bill had continued, "to top off the criminal neglect with hypocrisy, they made a big ceremony to honor the brave snipes, but they covered up the truth to make the captain and the other zeros look good."

"That's how it is," Morris said. "They stab you in the back and then put on the piety."

"Just like why we're here right now. If it had been some ops tech instead of us with that cop, they'd have just slapped his wrist, but we get maxed out. Forty-five days extra duty, forty-five days restriction, half a month's pay for two months and reduction in rate. Some equality!"

At first, Dresden had scarcely believed the stories, but day after day of the indoctrination took its toll, and Dresden became a committed member of Wild Bill's team.

Now as he listened to Mac's tale of what he saw on the station, he formulated his questions to learn more. "What did the body look like?"

Mac turned to face Dresden. "Well, its face was puffy and it had some swelling around the neck. And it had some black goo around its mouth, but I didn't see it for very long."

A movement caught Dresden's eye, and he looked to see Petey coming up through a hatch onto the mess decks. Someone yelled out to him, "How's your hammer hanging?" Petey blushed and shook his head, smiling. He got his lunch and sat down next to Mac.

"So tell us," Dresden said, "how many corpses were there?"

Petey took a bite of his food. "I don't know. I only saw the one that tried to kiss Mac!" A ripple of laughter made its way around the room.

"But there had to have been others. Didn't Foley say anything to you about what they had found?"

"No, he was busy fixing Mac's leg." Petey grinned. "But even if he did say something, I don't think I'd have heard it over Mac's screaming!" The mess decks erupted into laughter again.

"Come on, man," Mac said. He smiled and nudged Petey in the ribs with his elbow.

Dresden persisted. "But could you tell what had happened to them?"

"You're awfully damned curious," Lyons, another weapons tech, said.

"Maybe we all should be curious!" Dresden snapped. "What about it, Petey?"

Petey chewed his food for a moment and glanced over at Mac. "No, I didn't get a good look at it. It was dark."

Foley stepped into the mess decks and took no notice of the crowd. He took his lunch and sat down at a nearby table and began eating in silence.

"Now here's the man to ask," Dresden said. "Hey, Doc. Petey says the whole station crew has been wiped out. What happened?"

Foley looked up and glared at Petey who shook his head. "I have no idea what happened."

"But surely there were more corpses than the one that Mac saw."

Foley looked at Mac. "We're not supposed to discuss it yet."

"Oh, I see," Dresden said, nodding as he looked around at the other men, "standard operating procedure again. Keep the crew in the dark."

"Look, Dresden, when the boarding party finds out exactly what happened, they'll let everybody know."

"Oh, sure. I believe that."

"Hey, that attitude is the reason why they don't tell you things right away. You take any little thing you hear and collect wild rumors and distorted half truths about it."

"A half-truth is better than no truth at all!" Dresden addressed all of the men on the mess decks. "You guys just remember one thing. This command will tell you anything that's not worth knowing. But if they refuse to let you in on something, it's because you're in danger. And you can bet your ass, you're in danger right now." He didn't wait for a reply, but turned and walked out of the mess decks heading aft.

He traveled through the passageway past several compartments until he reached the main spaces. Plugging his ears with his fingers to keep out the noise, he walked around the compartment until he found Wild Bill. The engineering petty officer stood before an arrangement of equipment monitoring instruments, calibrating the readings. He wore no earmuffs, intent on claiming a hearing disability in future years. He looked up as Dresden approached.

"Hey, what's going on?" he shouted over the noise.

"Foley, Mac and Petey are on the mess decks. Just like you said, big secret."

Bill nodded and recorded the last reading on his computer pad, then he rolled it up and jammed it in his pocket before motioning for Dresden to follow him to the control room. They stepped inside and Dresden removed his fingers from his ears.

"So, what's the deal?" Bill asked, taking a seat.

"From what I can gather, they found more than one body. Foley says they were told not to talk about it."

"Oh, yeah. Of course."

"You know, I think that there's something very wrong happening over there. Even Petey is evasive." Dresden frowned. "We may have to wait for the official version this time."

Bill shook his head and smiled. "I can find out what's going on." He pointed up at a monitor. "I saw a power dip on the mains a few minutes ago. They must've sent out a message." Bill sat back. "And if that's the case, we'll find out this evening."

Dresden nodded, wondering at the statement. Even though some of Bill's methods bothered him, the results were usually impressive.

The power module contained the life support system for the whole station. Flores and Millus, dressed in vac-suits with helmets, entered the separate compartment and sealed it off from the main module. They went to the filtration section, and Millus spoke into his microphone.

"I like that idea that you had about venting the atmosphere to space, but let's try this compartment first. Now that we've isolated it from the rest of the station, I think we could by-pass the filters to the air then vent it to space. What do you think?"

Flores started to answer but the second engineer's tone distracted him. He liked the way that Millus spoke to him now, as if they were partners. He wondered why Millus never spoke to him this way on the ship, but then it dawned on him.

Wild Bill had made himself the self-appointed spokesman for all the engineering techs.

Flores felt a tinge of regret, wondering if he had been missing something in the way of camaraderie or esprit de corps with the officers and other crewmembers on the *Kestrel*. The officers were shipmates, too. He thought again about what Millus had said and nodded.

"Yes, sir. We might even be able to back-flush the filters as we vent to space."

"Even better," Millus said, and stood before the control console.

Flores watched as the officer by-passed the filters and isolated the air ducts from the rest of the station's ventilation system. Then he wedged himself between some piping and placed his hand on the manual emergency exterior vent levers. The automatic vents were designed to be opened only in case of fire. The tech looked back at Millus and gave a nod. "Hold on."

Millus nodded and took a grip on the console. Flores pulled the levers and the compartment began to de-pressurize. As the air rushed out, he reached over and opened another valve that allowed a rush of the station's air through the filter. A burst of dust came out, and when it cleared, Flores closed the valve again. The dust raced to the vents as the last of the air escaped from the compartment. The procedure had taken twenty seconds.

The ensign gave a thumbs-up sign, and Flores nodded and closed the vents. Then the officer re-pressurized the compartment from the reserve banks until it equalized with the rest of the station. Both men removed their helmets.

Millus seemed pleased. "A lot of junk came out of those filters."

"Yes, it did," Flores said. "Do you think there's a chance that the microbes would get caught up in the filter? Enough for us to vent to space?"

"I don't know, but I keep thinking about how a doctor's mask holds germs back." He looked at Flores and shrugged. "We can only try."

"Well, what do we do now?"

Millus pointed to the filters. "Let's leave these out of action for now. We'll tell the captain what we did. Maybe there's something else we can try."

Flores agreed and the two then exited the filtration compartment and headed for the main control room.

***

After speaking to Fischer, Van Wert spent the rest of the morning in Dr. Shahid's office searching through the station crew's medical records. Only the first few cases had been chronicled completely as the doctor's own failing health made it impossible for him to continue.

One of the records documented a crewmember named Powalie and covered all of the symptoms from the first sniffles to the man's death of an acute form of pneumonia, which the doctor referred to as "latuseris distraho." Van Wert compared the Powalie case with the others and saw that from the initial symptoms all subsequent stages were nearly identical. In every case, the disease attacks the mucous membrane first, whether the sinuses or the lungs. Dr. Shahid kept a journal of the disease's progress and had observed that it spread mainly through coughing, sneezing, or merely breathing in an infected atmosphere. In successive stages, the disease attacked the lymph system, causing swelling and in some cases decreased blood circulation and numbness due to the enlarged nodes. This also caused decreased white blood cell production. High fever sets in as the body's defenses are overcome, while the sinus and lung tissues continue to produce large amounts of mucous to resist the virus. This stage culminates in the condition the doctor referred to as "latuseris distraho." Finally, the body succumbs as the lungs fill up with fluid. The whole process took six to eight days from initial contact to death. Once the tissue is exposed, the disease rapidly mutates, always keeping one step ahead of the body's defenses.

Doctor Shahid's records and notes were clear and concise but gave no clue as to how one could combat the virus. Toward the end of his personal journal, as he became increasingly ill, he recorded some work he had done in his lab. He had apparently tried to find a way to retard the virus' growth by creating some type of hybrid bacteria that would act as a parasite to the virus, but his work was never completed. He died two days after the last entry.

And what the hell is latuseris distraho? I wish Foley were here.

Van Wert put the hand-written journal back down on the desk and looked through the door to the adjoining lab. He contemplated going in to examine the doctor's experiments, but Millus and Flores stepped in from the hall.

"Ah, there you are, Skipper," Millus said. "How's it going? Did you find anything significant?"

"No. Just a graphic picture of what the virus did to the station crew. What did you guys come up with?"

"Well, we back-flushed the filters and vented the compartment to space. But, of course, we have no way of knowing if we flushed out the microbes or not."

"A lot of dust came out, though," Flores said.

"Yes, that's right," Millus said.

"Good. Did you check to see if there was enough air in the banks to allow us to vent the station and re-pressurize?"

"Yes. We checked on the way up. They only keep enough on hand to re-pressurize on a room by room basis. There's not enough to do the whole station. We would have to decide which compartment we wanted to do and then just stay there."

"I don't understand that," Flores said. "The *Kestrel* carries enough air to fill the ship twice over. Why doesn't this station?"

"Because *Kestrel* is a warship and the designers expect us to need more," Van Wert answered. "A civilian platform like this would only need to re-pressurize after a fire. And I'm not sure that it would even work for us, especially if we are already infected. But we'll keep it in mind, though."

"Where are the others?" Millus asked.

"I suppose they're still on the mess decks. You two join them. It's about lunchtime."

"Why don't you go on ahead, Flores," the ensign said. "I'll be down in few minutes."

"All right. See you there, sir."

Flores exited the doctor's office, and Millus waited until he could no longer hear the man's footsteps in the hall. Then he turned to face Van Wert. "Well, Jim, it looks like we might be in a hell of a pickle this time."

"Yes, we might be." Van Wert took a deep breath and sighed. "Have you ever heard of a medical condition called latuseris distraho? I'm not sure I'm pronouncing it right."

"No. It'd be Latin, right?"

"I suppose so."

"Hold on." Millus took out a computer pad from his pocket and unfolded it, switching it on as the crinkles flattened out. "I have a translator app right here. How do you spell it?"

Van Wert held up the doctor's journal and pointed to the words on the screen. Millus typed in the words and initialized the translation. His face made a grimace.

"What?" Van Wert asked.

"It says "lungs melted.""

"Lungs melted? Damn." Van Wert shook his head. "The news just keeps getting better."

"And that's from the doctor's notes? Well, I guess it explains the black goo all over their mouths."

"Yep. Their friggin' lungs were melting. Damn."

"Well, we've been in bad scrapes before. Do you remember that time with the smugglers? I thought we were in trouble then."

"Yeah, but at least in that situation I could exercise some control. I had options. I'm afraid there's not much I can do here." Van Wert paused. "Hopefully we'll know something when Fleet Headquarters sends a reply to our message. Until then we need to wait to see if any symptoms appear."

"I hope we can keep the crew occupied while we wait."

"So do I," Van Wert said, nodding slowly. "So do I."

When Flores stepped into the lounge area, he saw Ski, Gradenko, and Wilson standing next to one of the recreational machines, which looked like a cushioned reclining chair inside a low, sound-proofed booth. Across the top at the device a large bold label read *Brainstorm – Mind/Sensory Expansion System*. He stepped over to them. "Hey, what's going on?"

Ski looked up from the operating panel. "We're thinking about cranking up one of these MSES machines. Ever try one?"

"They call it *Mee-sis*," Gradenko corrected.

"No. How does it work?" Flores asked.

"I guess I'm the only one who's ever done it," Gradenko said. "Here, sit down and I'll show you."

Flores sat down and lay back in the reclined chair, his neck supported by a padded cushion. "This is comfortable. Remind me to come back later to take a nap."

"You'll feel like you had a nap when you wake up." Gradenko fixed a helmet to his head with a set of earphones attached. At the front of the helmet a pair of opaque goggles covered his eyes, and inside Flores felt twenty-four tiny, rounded points against his skull. The gunner wiggled the helmet to seat the points directly against the skin.

"Ouch," Flores said. "What are those things?"

"Electrodes. They act as contact points to your brain."

"You going to crank it on and watch him bark?" Ski asked.

"You'll see." Gradenko straightened and powered up the device.

"How does it work?" Wilson asked.

"It's cool," Gradenko replied, now speaking loudly so Flores could hear him. "It works on the principle of brainwave entrainment. First, when you put on the earphones and goggles, you hear a tone and see flashing white lights. This is to synchronize and tune your brainwave frequencies. You see, we mostly operate in Beta range frequencies, which are erratic, and the two brain hemispheres usually operate independently. But the tones and lights synchronize the hemispheres and put the brain in an Alpha wave mode, a slower brain wave pattern."

"It sounds like one of those memory insertion devices," Ski said.

"It works on a similar principle."

Flores listened as Gradenko set up the device on the touch screen as he talked. "Once the Alpha waves are started the earphone frequencies separate slightly, causing extremely low frequency pulsing that the ear cannot hear but that the brain picks up on. This puts the brain into a Theta, then Delta frequency range. This range induces deep relaxation and heightened mental lucidity."

"How long does all of this take?" Wilson asked.

"About three to ten seconds, depending on how stressed you are going into it."

Gradenko finished with the machine and leaned into the booth to talk to Flores. "Hey, man, the program set up now is *World War One Fighter Ace*. Is that all right?"

Flores nodded blindly and gave a thumbs up.

"Okay, I'm starting it up." Gradenko switched on the machine dropped the curtain.

Flores waited and continued hearing Gradenko as he explained the device.

"Once you're in the Theta state different sensory inputs are added depending on which scenario you selected."

"Like virtual reality?" Wilson asked.

"No. Virtual reality compared to this is like a stone axe compared to a street sweeper pulse rifle. These programs are much more complex, and the sensory inputs go directly to the various lobes of the brain via trans-cutaneous electrical impulses. Instead of just seeing and hearing computer generated sights and sounds, you experience real sensory stimulus directly into the brain. You see grass, trees, and mountains. You hear birds, gulls, ocean waves. You smell flowers, perfume, smoke. You feel heat, mosquito bites, snow. Everything is reproduced into a realistic setting."

"But it's still not real," Ski said.

Gradenko looked at him. "Man, when you come out of a program, you'd swear that you were really there."

In the cool quiet of the booth, Flores heard white noise starting in the earphones. An array of tiny lights in the opaque goggles began to flash in time to a pulsing sound, now barely audible in the earphones. As the rhythm altered slightly, Flores began to feel very relaxed. His heart rate and breathing slowed down, and soon he felt as if his body were asleep. Yet his mind remained awake and extremely alert, as if in a lucid dream.

Flores became aware that he stood in a large grassy field surrounded by trees. He wore dark brown pants and a khaki buttoned-up shirt under a brown leather jacket. It must have been summer because the sun shone brightly and a gentle breeze blew across the large field, carrying to his nostrils the smell of a pasture nearby.

Behind him, among several Army tents, stood a small house that had been converted to a military headquarters. In front of him, a low, wide hanger dominated his view, where three British SE5 biplanes parked facing the field, engines running at idle. Several ground crew attended each plane, and Flores saw pilots already climbing into two of the planes. One of them waved him over, and Flores walked briskly through the grass to join them.

As he climbed into the cockpit he could feel the vibration of the engine through the fuselage and smell the gasoline exhaust blowing in the wash of the propeller. He sat down and strapped himself in. Looking over the controls and instruments, it occurred to him that he already knew how to operate the airplane. *Must be a part of the program.* He took the controls and operated them in all directions watching the ailerons, rudder, and elevators move.

A young mechanic in greasy coveralls gave him a thumbs up and Flores returned it. The mechanic pulled the wheel chocks away from the plane, and Flores pushed the throttle forward, excitement surging as the biplane began to move across the grassy field.

To his right he saw the other two planes already airborne. He pushed the throttle all the way forward, and the plane gained speed, bouncing and bumping over the field. His airspeed increased with his heartbeat until the tail finally came off the ground. Flores pulled the stick back and the plane leapt to the sky. As the field fell away he turned toward the other planes now flying in formation heading east. A bump of turbulence made his stomach surge.

Once he had joined the formation, Flores throttled back and looked below him. He saw scattered farms and houses and a river that bordered a large forest to the south. He smiled at the breathtaking view. He seemed to remember being told that they were to intercept a squadron of German fighters heading toward them. He looked ahead and searched the sky to the east.

The propeller produced a steady wind of fresh, cool, invigorating air, and Flores reached up to cock his Vickers machine gun.

The pilot next to him began waving and pointing to the southeast. Flores looked and saw a small line of fighters in the sky. The first SE5 banked to the right, followed by the second. Flores, too, banked over and felt a rush of adrenaline as the plane raced to the enemy fighters.

The Germans had apparently spotted the SE5s as well, for they turned and sped toward Flores' squadron.

As the distance between the two groups of planes narrowed, Flores could count six enemy planes. They would be outnumbered two to one. The planes raced toward each other, and Flores aligned his sights at the nearest one. It seemed to grow bigger than life as he squeezed the trigger. The gun bucked violently and the smell of gun powder smoke blew past his face. The bullets tore through the fabric of the German's wing as the plane flashed past him. Flores banked to the left to pursue.

As he came around he could see that the German squadron had dispersed. Two planes were climbing up and away, out of his reach, but a third plane, the one he'd hit, seemed to be having trouble. He closed in on the German, bringing it into range. He had almost lined up to squeeze the trigger when he heard loud machine gun fire behind him. Bullets ripped through his engine cowling, and oil splattered onto his goggles. He turned to his left and saw a second German plane dive past while a third came weaving in behind him. Flores banked hard to the right but could not get power from the engine.

The German fired and Flores felt burning pain tear through his back. He realized he couldn't move his feet.

He pushed the stick forward and the plane began to dive. The German fired again, and the image in Flores' mind went black.

Flores could hear Gradenko's voice through the earphones. "Hey, man! What happened?"

"What did you see?" Ski asked.

He tore off the helmet and opened the curtain. "What did I see? You mean, what did I hear, feel, smell! It was great! I was a World War One fighter pilot. I took off and got in a dog fight with some Germans, but I got shot down."

"No kidding?"

"Yeah, man!"

Gradenko beamed. "I told you."

"Hey, I want to have some lunch and try it again!" The group became quiet and Flores looked around. "What?"

"We were kind of leery about eating the food here," Wilson said.

"Why?"

"Because of the virus and all," Ski said.

"That food has never been in this atmosphere," Flores replied.

"Are you sure?" Gradenko asked.

"Yeah. It was packaged and sealed probably months ago, and the heating process kills anything in it. Even if there is a virus going around, it can't be in the food."

"That's a relief," Wilson said, "I'm starved."

"Well let's go eat then," Flores said. "Unless the captain says otherwise, I intend to play in these machines for the rest of the afternoon."

After lunch, Petey went on watch on the bridge. His job entailed monitoring the equipment that maintained the ship's position relative to the station, but as there was little to interfere with the *Kestrel,* he engaged in the usual small talk with anyone who happened to be on the bridge.

Weapons tech Brad Crosly finished his maintenance functions on the ship's weapons systems and swung his chair around to face the navigator. "Well, Petey, have we drifted away yet?"

"Not one millimeter."

"I don't see why they have to have one of you guys on this watch. The computer is doing all the work anyway."

"There are only two reasons I can think of," Petey said, counting on his fingers. "One, they want fallible human oversight on an unerring computer, and two, as warships are labor heavy, they need to keep us occupied."

Crosly laughed. "I know that's right."

"Life in the fleet. But at least I'm not scrubbing toilets anymore."

"True enough." Crosly took a glance over toward the aft bridge access tube. "So tell me Pete, what gives about the station?"

"I haven't heard anything since I came back, so I'm in the dark as much as anyone."

The gunner nodded. "I guess you can't talk about it. I just wish I knew when we were getting out of here. We were heading home, remember?"

"I know."

"And if we've got to stay here a little longer, I wish they'd grant some liberty. Mac says that station is huge on the inside."

"It is, and the full gravity is nice, but there seemed to be little in the way of entertainment. Some video games in a crews lounge is about it."

"No lady crewmembers?"

Petey hesitated. "I didn't see any."

"But, at least the video games would be different. Could you tell what they had?"

"No. We really didn't spend much time there."

Crosly nodded and glanced up at the bridge clock. "Well, I suppose I've got time for one more round of checks before knock off. I'll talk to you again after a while."

"Ok."

Crosly disappeared down the hatch between the weps and ops shacks, and Petey stood up and went to the captain's chair. He lowered the optical viewing device and turned it toward the station, studying the great dish antenna for a moment before moving on to the transmitter module. Atop this structure stood a glass dome with a sextant device inside similar to the one on *Kestrel*. Next he turned his gaze to the large windows of the main control room, trying to see if he could locate any of the boarding party, but the room was deserted.

As Petey looked through the device, he thought about Ski's observation of the lifeboat during GQ. It had been a high moment for Ski, and it seemed obvious to Petey that the captain was reaching out to him. But the conversation the two had had on watch just before the second lifeboat was discovered still disturbed Petey. Ski still didn't understand why the captain had passed him over for promotion. Had Ski forgotten his sarcastic song, or the offence it had caused? The ops tech had been way out of line, and Petey remembered the day the captain had heard it.

Some of the off-watch bridge crew had gathered in the forward equipment room after knock off to read, play cards, or just talk. For days Ski had been working on the computer there, putting together some kind of song with a music composer app. He had programmed the computer to play the music and display the words with a bouncing ball so that anyone could sing along. The music was jazzy and upbeat and sounded like an old ragtime song. Petey remembered the words clearly.

"That is the way, that is the Fleet life,
Just how screwed up are we today?
Open your eyes, the regs are all bullshit.
See all the RID's they just can't deal with it.
Scrub out those heads, have some adventure,

Smile or you'll go the Mast today,
Just one more year, and then I'll be gone,
And then you all can carry on!"

RID was an acronym that referred to enlisted men who were getting out of the fleet when their time was up. Mast referred to Captain's Mast, non-judicial punishment administered by the captain in a trial-like setting on the bridge. Ski had been singing the song loudly, joined by a few others, when the captain had come down from the bridge unexpectedly. Not seeing the old man, Ski continued, singing the entire song.

But the other men had noticed the captain standing there, so Ski concluded the song into a silence. Instead of jolly laughter, an oppressive pall of equipment room noise and the distant rumble of the ship's engines filled the compartment. Ski turned around and saw Van Wert, but Ski displayed no embarrassment at all. In fact, Petey remembered that Ski seemed almost proud, as if glad that the captain had heard.

Everyone waited for a reaction from the captain, but, after staring at Ski for a few moments, the old man just shook his head and headed aft through the door.

The incident had occurred just two weeks before Ski's recommendation for promotion to first class petty officer went up before the captain. But Van Wert had refused to sign it, thus passing Ski over for promotion.

Petey understood the profound disappointment that Ski felt, but it had been an amateurish prank and the captain needed to know that the men in the leadership chain of command stood with him. And given the sense of undermining the song carried, the outcome could have been worse. It might've been viewed as seditious.

Petey stowed the optical viewer away and went back to the holographic chart table as Cauthen came up to the ops shack.

"What's happening, Pee-tro?"

"Same old, same old. What are you doing?"

"Just switching off from some checks on the scanners." He powered down the console and then stepped over to the navigation station. "Well, Petey, when are we going to get out of here?"

"I don't know, buddy. I have no idea what they want to do."

"A lot of stories are flying around the ship."

"I know."

"Some are saying that if the crew is all dead, they'll probably want us to hang around until they can get another crew out here."

"Probably. Although if we got the beam running I don't see why they wouldn't let us go. The station practically runs itself."

"Do you think they know by now what happened?"

"I would guess so," Petey said. "I'm just glad I don't have to go back over there."

"Why won't you?"

"Because it's Brown's turn. I've got watch again tonight, and I need to get to bed early."

"You ought to try to catch a nap while you're up here." Cauthen smiled. "Just don't get caught. I'll see you later for chow."

"All right."

Cauthen left the bridge, and Petey took out his computer pad from his back pocket and unrolled it. He opened up a Bible app and went to Psalm Ninety-one. The navigator read it as a veritable list of promises of God's protection, and he found solace reading it whenever the ship was in danger. The corpse on the station, the missing station crew, and the total lack of forthcoming information had filled him with a sense of uneasiness. *If all was well, then why hadn't the boarding party returned, and why the continued secrecy?* But in the quiet of the bridge, he read the words aloud and as he did so his heart warmed. Once again his faith had pushed out his fears and he smiled to himself.

Petey heard voices coming up the tube behind him and turned around to see Crosly and a few other men ascending into the bridge compartment. He rolled up the pad and put it back in his pocket as they stepped over to talk. A glance at the bridge clock told him knock-off time approached.

"You said you have another watch to stand tonight, right?" Crosly asked.

"Yeah, the mid ride."

"We're trying to get up a cribbage game after chow. Want to join?"

"No. I'm going to eat then hit the sack. But thanks, anyway."

"What about Cauthen? Have you seen him?"

"He was here a little while ago. Maybe heading for the mess decks."

"What's for chow anyway?" systems tech Frasier asked.

"I'm not sure. I didn't check."

"So, Petey, when are we getting out of here?" radioman Mullins asked.

"Everybody asks me that." Petey laughed. "I don't know, buddy. I'm just as much in the dark as you."

"I hope we get underway soon. If we can get home within ten days, I'll make my daughter's birthday. She'll be three."

"How many kids have you got?" Frasier asked.

"Just two. Do you want to see photos?" Mullins reached for his wallet.

"We've seen 'em, man. We've seen 'em," Crosly said.

The others chuckled.

"Hey, Petey," Frasier said. "Crosly was telling me that as Alpha Centauri A and B come closer together they'll be the same size in the sky, and that AlCent A2 will have no nighttime. Is that right?"

"Well, they won't be exactly the same size in the sky, but almost. AlCent B is actually smaller than AlCent A, and we'll still be closer to A. But as far as sunshine all day and night, that is true. At certain times of the year the two suns will be in opposition, so as one sets the other will be rising."

"I told you," Crosly said.

"It will be pretty cool," Petey continued. "And since this will be the first periastron since the Alpha Centauri was settled, and since nothing like this could ever have happened on Earth, we will be the first humans ever to have witnessed such an event."

"When will it happen?" Mullins asked.

"In about eighteen years. Then it won't happen again for another eighty years. It will be a strange and colossal time. I hope to be director of an orbiting observatory by then."

"Professor Petey," Crosly said, slapping the navigator on the back. "I like the sound of that."

Petey smiled. "Me, too." He heard a noise and looked over to see Brown coming up the tube. He made his way over to the navigation console.

"You're early," Petey said.

"I know," Brown said. "And if you can return the favor, I'd appreciate it."

"Will do." Petey pointed to the position readouts on the computer screen. "Nothing's changed, as you can see. I stand relieved."

"I got it."

"Let's go get in line for chow," Crosly said.

***

In the wardroom, the officers milled around and talked as the steward finished setting dishes onto the micro gravitational field of the table. Ensign Clark paged through movie choices on the wardroom computer but nothing look appealing. Systems officer Wallsbrook stepped over to him.

"Hey, you thinking about watching a movie tonight?" Wallsbrook asked.

"Yeah, maybe."

"What's in there that you haven't seen five times?"

"I don't know." Clark backed out of the movie app and shut the computer down. Then he reached into a drawer and pulled out a deck of cards. "Do you want to get up a game, instead?"

"Yeah, that'd be good. Hey, Oki, care to join us in a game of cards later?"

Chief engineer Oki Fukunaga sat in a chair in a corner engrossed in technical readouts for the *Kestrel's* auxiliary equipment on his pad. He turned his handsome, Asian face up to where Wallsbrook stood. "I would like to, but I'm afraid I have some work to catch up in main control first. But, I'll probably be through by about nine or nine thirty. How would that be?"

"That'd be fine. We'll play until you get here."

Lieutenant Fischer stepped into the wardroom, and Clark stuffed the cards back into the drawer. The executive officer went to his place at the table and waited for the others to join him, then they all sat down in unison. As the steward came around to serve, arranging the restaurant quality food carefully on the plates, Wallsbrook spoke.

"Well, sir, is the captain returning this evening?"

"No. I just spoke to him from the bridge. He says that they'll remain on the station this evening and probably come back over in the morning."

"Have any of them shown symptoms of the virus, yet?" Fukunaga asked.

Fischer glanced around at the officers, but he waited for the steward to step back into the galley for another tray. "No, not yet. But remember, it could take a few days for the signs to show up."

"What should we be looking for?" Clark asked.

"Basically, flu-like symptoms, except greatly exaggerated. High fever, sinus and respiratory problems, and swollen lymph nodes."

Fischer paused as the steward returned and set another tray on the table. When he had left again the XO continued. "Watch for signs in the crew. Let me or Foley know immediately if you discover anything."

The steward returned and continued serving in a pall of awkward silence. Fischer cleared his throat and said, "So, anything come over the news today?"

"There was another bombing at the AlCent B Port Facility," Wallsbrook said. "Looks like insurgents, again."

This started a lively discussion around the table, but Clark noticed that Fischer remained quiet, seemingly lost in his own thoughts.

Chapter 13
"Threats and Revelations"

Dresden followed Wild Bill, Morris, and Jackson forward from the engineering berthing compartment, past the boat decks and storage compartments and into the forward crews head. At twenty minutes before taps, most of the crew were either finishing up a movie on the mess decks or were already in bed. They entered to find only one crewman brushing his teeth at a vacuum tube who looked over at them, curious to see engineers so far forward in the ship. One of the mist showers was running as well. Bill stared at the crewman who hurriedly finished brushing. He then gathered his things and quickly moved past them out of the door. Morris walked over to the shower tent and held out the towel for Bill to see. The stencil on the towel read "SCHROEDER." Bill nodded and the four men gathered around the shower. Bill reached up and abruptly pulled down the tubular shower tent, and instantly Dresden realized the logic of meeting Schroder this way. The radioman was at his most vulnerable, naked in the shower facing four angry, rough looking men.

Schroeder jumped at the intrusion. With the water running on his face, he peered up at Bill with an expression of bewilderment mixed with fear. He turned his body away from the four men, and Dresden couldn't tell if the move came from modesty or a feeble attempt to protect himself.

"Hi, Schroeder! How's the water?" Bill's jovial tone mocked the radioman.

"All right."

"Don't want to waste it, though." Bill reached in and shut the water off. Then, with his arms folded across his broad chest, he asked, "So, how's it going?"

Schroeder looked confused. "All right."

"I'd like to know what you can tell me about what's happening on the station."

"How… how should I know, Bill?" Schroeder replied.

Bill's face grew cross as he leaned forward into Schroeder's face. "Cause you sent the message that went out this afternoon. That's how."

"It was just position report."

"You're a liar. Why do you want to bullshit me? That message was too long to be just a position report. Don't you think I know the difference? The captain was reporting what he'd found on the station. Now what did the message say?"

"Bill, you know I can't violate operational security."

Jackson leaned forward and gave a leer. "I think you'd better start worrying about personal security."

Schroeder looked at the other engineering techs, and Dresden could see his fear, like a rabbit cornered by wolves. He felt sorry for the radioman, but he tried to maintain a stern expression. The intimidation was necessary. They must know.

"Don't you think the men have a right to know what's going on?" Bill continued. "Don't you think they have a right to know if they're in danger?"

The door opened and another crew member stepped into the head carrying a wash kit and towel. Morris turned toward him and said, "This is not a good time to take a shower, pal. You might slip and break something."

The man backed out into the passageway and closed the door behind him.

Bill pressed on. "The zeros don't care about you or me. They think we're a bunch of idiots, but we've got to stick together." Bill reached out and ran a knuckle lovingly against Schroeder's upper arm, letting his eyes wander over the lithe wet body. "Now what did that message say?"

"Bill, the XO will tell everyone when it's time."

"Don't you see how arrogant that is? They treat us like cattle. We have a right to know what's going on. Especially if we're in some kind of danger." Bill fixed his gaze at the radioman's eyes. "Can't you feel the danger?"

Schroeder looked down at the floor of the shower stall, his face etched with hopeless resignation, but still he said nothing. Dresden could see that he feared the worst. *What could be so confidential that even Schroeder won't talk?*

"I don't know," Bill said, shaking his head. "I was hoping that I wouldn't have to make an issue of this, but you force my hand." Bill paused and Schroeder looked up at him cautiously. "I wonder if the XO would be very interested to know about the sexual orientation of one his radiomen."

Jackson raised his eyebrows. "You mean little Schroeder here is a queer boy?"

"Sure is," Morris said. "He's done a few favors for some of his lonely shipmates on these long patrols."

"No kidding." Jackson smiled and rubbed at his own crotch. "I always thought he had a nice ass." Jackson leaned his face into the stall. "I'd treat you real nice, you know. You'd be my favorite."

Schroeder backed up against the far wall of the shower tent, stumbling at the base of the stall. Morris moved to cut off any possibility of escape. To Dresden, the rabbit-like fear on his face bordered on blind panic. It was one thing to be beaten up, but being gang raped was another matter entirely. The whole situation began to nauseate Dresden. Bill was going too far.

Before Schroeder could reply, Bill spoke again. "And I'd be very interested to know what the XO, or the captain for that matter, would say if they found out that said radioman had, because of his hidden sexual orientation, been blackmailed into compromising some secret information about fleet movements to an insurgent terrorist."

"No kidding?" Morris said. He looked at Schroeder with mock admiration. "I didn't even know about that."

"Yep. He didn't know that I was privy to that one, but I have evidence. Intelligence had been snooping around for weeks trying to discover that leak."

"Man, oh man," Jackson said. "They'll execute you for that."

Schroeder hung his head down and began to cry, and Dresden felt ashamed and angry. But nothing could be done now. Bill had found the right pressure points. Maybe he'd known them all along.

"Now, Schroeder," Bill said. "What did the message say?"

Without raising his head, Schroeder told them everything.

***

Weapons tech Greg Lyons lifted himself out of the feeble gravity zone and swung up into his bunk. The sleeping tube was attached at both ends to frames projected from the wall and floated freely above the bunk below it. The lower bunk, well within the gravitational field of the deck, contained a more traditional mattress and curtain, but Lyons preferred the free floating method of sleep. He wriggled inside, zipped the bunk shut, and then touched a button at his head causing a soft glow of white light to suffuse the upper portion of the tube. He emptied his pockets and placed all of the items into a pouch sewn into the inside of the bunk, except for his computer pad, which he unfolded and held before his face. He touched the smooth screen and activated an email app. With his feet bracing his body still, he pressed the start button and spoke into the device, smiling warmly.

"Hi, Sugar. I just wanted to say a quick hello before I turned in. I shudder to think how many messages you'll receive once we're out of this radio silence. I know they're stacking up, but at least once you get them you'll know we are almost home.

"Nothing new going on, except that we've been briefly delayed, but it doesn't look like it'll be for long. I look forward to our road trip to your parents and then out to the cabin, but first you must promise me at least three days of non-stop kineutling. I *need* my love muffin! Ha! I know you're blushing now.

"I do love you so much. Thank you for staying with me through all of my junk. This fleet idea was the best thing for us. The regimentation has been good for me, and I can't wait to get back out into the world without the addiction. I know I can stay clean and hold a good job this time. I don't care what I have to do for a living as long as I have you with me. I want to spend my life making you happy. Hold on. We're almost there.

"So, goodnight, my love. Give our little Nicole a hug for me. Tell her Daddy will be home soon. I love you both."

He made a kissing sound and shut off the recorder. Then he labeled the message and sent it into the ship's mail system. He yawned, put the pad into the pouch, shut off the light, and drifted off to sleep.

Chapter 14
"Seize the Chokepoints of Power"

"Goddammit!" Bill shouted. "Do you see what I mean? *Now* do you see what I mean? Those bastards!"

Bill paced back and forth inside the aft damage control locker where they'd concealed themselves to discuss what they had heard from Schroeder. Crammed in with various firefighting and depressurization repair equipment, Morris, Jackson, and Dresden sat in the small room listening to Bill while trying to digest the information.

Dresden only half-listened to Bill's rant as he mulled the implications. *So they did know. The entire station crew wiped out by a virus that may have infected us all. A virus that could kill us all! Why would the captain and XO keep that from the crew?*

"Those sons of bitches," Bill growled. "I guess they'll just wait until we're all infected. I'd like to kill every one of them!"

"Well," Jackson said, "even if the boarding party had contracted this thing, wouldn't that leave us in the clear?"

"No! Not when they sent Mac back here with his busted leg!" Bill fumed. "Son of a bitch. They should have fixed his leg on the damn station."

"What are we going to do?"

Bill stopped and looked directly at Jackson. "I'll tell you what we *need* to do. We *need* to get the hell out of here. That's what we *need* to do."

"Do you mean take the ship?" Dresden asked.

"You're damn right, that's what I mean! Even if Mac and the others didn't bring that virus back, you can bet that it won't be long before the rest of them are back aboard." Bill stopped and made eye contact with each man. "We need to get the hell out of here."

"How could we take the ship?" Jackson asked. "It would be four against forty-five."

"I'll tell you how, we cut into the small arms locker and anyone who resists us is dead."

"That's easier said than done," Morris said. He had been quiet since they'd left Schroeder sobbing in the shower, but Dresden knew he was calculating. Morris was the thinker of the group. "We would be stopped before we got the first gun."

"Then we could get the ship underway from main control," Bill said.

"And go where? You can't navigate from main, and we're a long way from anywhere."

"Well, what do you suggest?" Bill said, clearly irritated.

Morris stood up and began to pace thoughtfully as Bill seated himself on an equipment box. "I read once that to pull off a coup properly, you need to seize the *choke points* of power. In this way, a small force can take a large force captive."

"What makes something a choke point?" Jackson asked.

"In a political coup, it would be something that those in power use to control others, such as the media outlets, transportation hubs, traffic intersections, and the like. On a ship it would be places such as main control or the bridge."

"What about the small arms locker?" Bill asked, his expression now shifted from irritation to strong interest.

"That's another one."

"What about the main passageways?" Dresden asked. "When the action starts, we wouldn't want any opposition to be able to move around freely."

Morris smiled at Dresden and nodded. "Precisely. A choke point of power."

"Well, how do we take these choke points?" Bill asked. "Do we just go there with guns and take it?"

"No, we'd still have the same problem." Morris absently kicked at a piece of equipment on the deck while he thought. "We need to buy some time while we get the weapons and get everyone in place."

"Seems to me that the passageways would be the hard part," Jackson said. "How do you keep people out of the passageways while you set up?"

"What if…" Morris started. He stopped pacing and turned around to face them. "What if there was a way we could do both? We need a way to close off the main deck passageway while we get into the small arms locker. Then after the action starts we could keep the passageway secured."

"Deuterium gas leak," Dresden said.

"What?"

"A deuterium gas leak. Remember when we started this patrol? We had a lasing chemical leak and we had to secure the main deck and the second deck while we fixed it and cleaned it up."

Morris smiled at Bill and Bill nodded. "Yes, that's a potent idea. And believable, too, because it's already happened once before."

"Hell, yeah," Jackson said. "You tell the crew we have a deuterium gas leak and you won't be able to drag them through there."

"That's true. But this isn't something that we would announce," Morris said. "We could post someone at each end of the passageway while we went about our business. We should wait until later tonight when most of the crew had turned in. Also, we need more people. Who can we count on?"

"Fontaine and Harper," Bill said. "And everyone in the engineering department."

"What about Walsh?" Jackson asked.

"Forget about Walsh," Morris said. "The chief engineer's got him in his hip pocket."

"He's on sounding and security watch right now," Dresden added.

"We'll have somebody trade with him," Bill said.

"We could," Morris said, "but leaving him on watch might be useful. It would keep him out of the way."

"So let me get this straight," Bill said, counting on his fingers as he spoke. "We secure the main deck passageway from the mess decks to aux machinery."

"Yes. We'd need to cordon off that much."

"Then we'd have two people posted while we cut into the small arms locker. Once we got the guns, we would take main control and then the bridge."

"Right," Morris said. "At that time, we would also arm the guards at the passageways. We should also block off the oh-one level and the second deck. If anyone puts up a fuss, we'll just have to shoot them to keep order."

"What about the forward arms locker?" Jackson asked. "That's in officer country."

"Once we have main and the bridge, we'll go forward and round up the zeros. Then we'll have the forward arms locker, too." Morris smiled at Bill. "After that the ship is ours."

"You know," Bill said, "I'm not worried about the engineers or ships servicemen. But all those spark chasers in forward berthing might be trouble."

Morris nodded at Bill. "Yes, that's true. I think we should post somebody in forward berthing. We'll be spread thin, but we'll be armed and they won't."

Dresden listened to the planning with mixed feelings of excitement and foreboding. He wasn't looking forward to killing anyone in the crew. *They are my shipmates. Maybe the killing could be avoided.* "You know, the rest of the crew doesn't know about this virus thing. I'd be willing to bet that if they knew, they would side with us."

No one spoke for a few moments, and Dresden began to think that he'd spoken out of turn, but then Morris said, "That's true. Once we begin our move, if anyone asks what's going on, we should tell them. After we take the ship we'll announce it on the intercom."

"It sounds like that's everything," Jackson said. "I guess we'll start right after taps."

"Yes, but we need to get set up first. And we need to round up the others and let them know. Taps is about an hour away."

"Then let's get started," Bill said.

Chapter 15
"Virus Confirmation"

In Doctor Shahid's lab on the station, Van Wert finished his careful arrangement of flat computer pads on one of the tables, each one displaying an image and chemical readout of the viral organism during its various stages of mutation. After playing a few games on the MSES machines with the crewmen following lunch, he found that he couldn't concentrate and longed to get back to the station doctor's records. Too many unanswered questions plagued his thoughts. Ensign Millus had expressed an interest to join him, so they spent the afternoon and evening in the lab, even skipping supper to work.

Millus became fascinated with the doctor's lab microscope and had spent most of his time perfecting its use. The microscope utilized an electron beam in a chamber to magnify images. A specimen placed into the chamber yielded an image on an adjoining computer screen, and the image could be magnified to a molecular level, complete with a chemical analysis of the specimen.

"Okay," Van Wert said, "I believe I've got all of the major stages of mutation for this thing in chronological order. Now I want to put it to the test. Let me see one of those slides."

The second engineer handed him a small glass laboratory slide and stood beside him. "You know, it might be too early to tell one way or another."

"Yeah, but I still want to try. If this thing is as fast as the doctor says, then we should see something by now."

Van Wert forced himself to cough repeatedly and then spit a small glob of mucus onto the glass slide. Then the two men stepped over to the microscope chamber where the captain fixed the slide in place and closed the door.

"Do you think you've fiddled around with this thing enough for us to find an organism on that slide?" Van Wert asked.

"Definitely. A little while ago I had magnified a hair of mine as large as a highway." Millus powered up the machine and made adjustments on the control screen until the sputum came into focus. Then he increased the magnification by stages, refocusing each time until the microscope reached seventy percent of its total magnification power.

"Hold it there," Van Wert said, pointing to a cluster of microorganisms on the microscope screen. "See? Right there. Bring that up."

Millus brought the cluster to the center of the screen and magnified it until it became a writhing mass of tiny one-celled creatures.

"See?" Van Wert asked. "The mucus is dead tissue, but those are living organisms. Can you bring it closer and freeze the image?"

"Yes, I can." Millus did so and the captain studied the organism carefully. Then he went to his arrangement of computer pads and immediately picked one up, bringing back to the microscope.

"Here is an observation from a slightly advanced case," he said and held the pad up next to the microscope screen. "They are almost identical. And the chemical compositions match up, too." He lowered the pad and looked at Millus and frowned. "I've got it."

"And if you've got it, then we all probably have it," Millus said, then seemed to catch himself. "No. We all definitely have it. We all were around the corpses as much as you were." He looked at the captain. "And Peters, Foley, and Mac took it back to the ship."

Van Wert nodded and frowned again.

"What should we do now?" Millus asked.

"When I spoke to the XO earlier, I told him we would spend the night here. We can start testing people, but the only thing we can really hope for is that fleet headquarters will be able to find some way to help us out. In any case, it's going to be hard road from here."

"I want to be tested," Millus said. "I want to know."

"All right. Grab a slide."

As Van Wert waited for Millus to cough up some phlegm, he looked up at the screen. *Well, at least now I know for sure.*

***

The girl led Ski by the hand up the grand staircase, the strains of the Strauss waltz fading behind them. With her other hand she held up the hem of her silken ball gown as she trotted up the steps. Her raven hair, pulled up on the back of her head, cascaded down between her shoulders in dancing ringlets. All around, the Czarist Russian décor dazzled him with aristocratic opulence. As they reached the top of the stairs, the girl, who appeared to be about twenty, looked back and smiled at Ski. She had a beautiful captivating smile and even her dark blue eyes seemed to be smiling. She gave a mischievous raising of the eyebrows before tugging him along again.

Ski could still hear the quartet downstairs playing. None of the young dancers or older gentry milling about the ballroom had noticed their retreat from her old man's birthday celebration, and most of the servants were attending the guests.

The girl led Ski down the wide, balconied hall to her room, but stopped short of going in. She looked at Ski and brought her face close to his. "I have a better idea," she whispered. She turned and led him further down the hall.

The stiff woolen collar of the ornate nineteenth century Army dress uniform abraded his throat, but he scarcely noticed as he followed the beautiful young woman down the hall to the master bedroom. The girl waved away a servant posted in the room, and they waited as the matronly person curtseyed and retired, shutting the bedroom door behind her. The raven-haired girl giggled and led Ski by the hand over to the side of the large four-poster bed before turning to face Ski. She stood close to him, her firm breasts lightly pressing against his coat, her sweet, warm breath on his face as she spoke.

"I was conceived on this bed," she whispered, gazing into his eyes. "Take me here."

Ski pressed his mouth to hers in a long searching kiss. With her arms around his neck, she pressed her body to him, and he put his arms around her waist, drawing her closer. Leaning back toward the bed she pulled him down on top of her, legs wide to receive him.

He did take her there, on the luxurious bed in the opulent room with the sounds of the aristocratic party in the background. But the picture-perfect encounter with the picture-perfect girl in the euphoric and passionate coital embrace ended all too quickly, and immediately Ski felt embarrassed.

The girl, however, wasn't disappointed. She hugged him tightly and kissed him all over his face, giggling gleefully. She was beautiful, and as she smiled at him, Ski felt as if he were falling in love with her.

"That's it, Hot Shot. Game over."

The sound of Wilson's voice broke the scene and Ski's concentration. He removed the headgear.

"I found that one earlier," Wilson said. "There must be a thousand different scenarios. Now I know how they could stand being out here for six months at a time."

Ski's embarrassment returned. He would rather have discovered this program with no one else around. Now Wilson stood next to the booth as if expecting a critique.

"Who did you get? The redhead on the sailboat? I was going to take that one, but I went with an Egyptian instead."

Ski didn't want to answer him. Even though intellectually he knew it was silly, he felt as though he would be violating the girl's trust to talk about his experience.

"I found some raincoats in that cabinet over there. Should have told you earlier, huh?"

"Thanks for the public service announcement. Now why don't you shut up?" Ski left the room, wondering ruefully when they would be returning to the ship.

Chapter 16
"Mutiny"

        Engineering Technician Third Class Eric Walsh dutifully entered all of the volume readings in the forward water and sanitary tanks into his computer pad. The roving sounding and security watch he stood took him throughout the ship, checking various tank levels and battery power indicators, and the information manually gathered would be entered into the computer log in main control to calibrate the automated functions. He knew that the other men who stood this watch falsified or 'gun-decked' the log out of sheer laziness, preferring to carry over the old figures and goof off in main control with the watchstander there instead of taking proper readings, but Walsh believed strongly in the importance of accuracy in the log, so he carefully checked every station every hour. He took pride in knowing that at least one watch in three would be accurate.

        The forward equipment room being his final stop on this round, he entered the last reading and headed through the door aft along the main deck toward the engineering spaces where the cycle would begin again. Following the nightly call of taps, all of the passageway lights glowed a soft red and add to the sense of quiet slumber. Walsh came to the door to officer's country and, as is customary for enlisted men, removed his hat and entered. He walked past the stateroom doors and the forward arms locker to the wardroom. By force of habit he looked through the small window, then seeing no one, knocked and stepped through the officer's dining area to the galley.

        As Walsh replaced his hat and entered the food preparation room, he saw Dresden sitting in a chair next to the door to the mess decks. The engineering tech wore a personal respirator and a personal air quality tester and dosimeter on his belt. He stood up as Walsh approached.

        "Hey, Big D. What are you doing up this late?"

        "Passageway is secured, Walsh."

        "What's going on?"

        "There's a small deuterium gas leak. I've been posted here to stop people from coming through while they clean it up."

Walsh looked down at his log readings and saw nothing to indicate a leak. He'd been through that area only ten minutes before. "How long ago did this happen?"

"About fifteen minutes ago."

"Where's the chief engineer?"

"He's been sent for. The fellows wanted to get started right away."

Walsh eyed Dresden for a few moments. *What are you up to?* "Well, I've got to get through to main."

As Walsh stepped forward, Dresden held up his head. "No one is to go through here."

"I'm on watch."

"You'll have to wait. They should be done in a few minutes."

"Dresden, I'm going to go through to main."

Dresden turned around and touched the control pad, shutting and locking the door. "I'm not letting anyone through," he said. Then as an afterthought, added. "It's too dangerous."

Walsh thought about forcing the issue but decided against it. "All right. I'll recheck the readings up forward, and maybe they'll be done by then."

Dresden didn't reply, so Walsh turned and headed back through the galley and wardroom and into officer's country. Here, out of sight of Dresden, he reached up and manually opened a small round escape scuttle, then pulled himself up the tube into the forward equipment room on the deck above. Closing the scuttle behind him, he headed aft through the banks of computer servers and related equipment and into the passageway beyond.

"I guess I had to go over your head, shipmate," he said aloud as he walked one deck above where Dresden sat.

He saw no one as he passed damage control central, the ship's office, the radio shack, and the navigation equipment room. At the far end of the passageway, he inserted his earplugs then opened and stepped through the heavy door into the main spaces. With his pad between his teeth, he stepped off of the platform and pulled himself head-down along a utility pole to the main control room. Righting himself, he entered and saw chief engineer Lieutenant Fukunaga switching off his computer at his desk. Next to his tiny office area stood the control cabinets and consoles where the ship's main propulsion engines, attitude control engines, and all of the auxiliary equipment were operated. Walsh set his computer pad down onto a link-up site and started the data download.

"Did you finally get all your work caught up, sir?" he asked the Chief Engineer, or CHENG.

"Yes. I really wanted to finish it before I turned in for the night."

"Sir, did anyone tell you about a deuterium gas leak?"

Fukunaga turned to look at Walsh, his face concerned. "Did you find a leak?"

"No, sir. That's just it. I didn't find anything like that at all. But Dresden is blocking the passageway to the mess decks telling people that there's a deuterium leak. They said you knew about it."

A look of puzzlement spread across Fukunaga face as he shook his head. "Nothing was said to me, but I'll find out." He stepped through the door into the main deck passageway, and Walsh followed close behind.

They walked past the after damage control locker and opened the door to the auxiliary and life support equipment room. Just inside stood engineering tech Snyder with a respirator and dosimeter hanging from his belt.

"Hold on, sir. We have a deuterium gas leak. The men have stopped it and are cleaning it up."

"Why wasn't I told about this?"

"Someone was supposed to have notified you. The men wanted to get to this right away."

Without another word, Fukunaga stepped toward the far door, but Snyder held up his hand. "Sorry, sir. I was told to let no one through without at least a respirator."

Fukunaga quickly grabbed the respirator off of Snyder's belt and said, "Very well, then." He walked through the auxiliary equipment room, and Walsh followed close behind. As he opened the door at the forward end of the compartment, he saw Jackson standing up smoking a cigarette. Two others knelt by the bulkhead to the small arms locker, the bright flickering light of a plasma arc cutter flashing in front of them. Two others also stood beyond Jackson and one of them pointed. Jackson turned toward Fukunaga, and a look of surprise spread across his face. He threw the cigarette to the deck and called out, "CHENG's here!"

Walsh could see the other two men beyond and identified weapons tech Fontaine and ship's serviceman Harper. *The whole lot of trouble makers.*

The flashes of light stopped and there followed a metallic clang and rattle. Kneeling next to the bulkhead, Morris lifted up his welding mask and shouted to Jackson and the others. "We're through! Come on, this is it!"

Fukunaga started to speak, but when he saw Morris passing the first pistol to Jackson, he and Walsh turned and ran back through the compartment, using their arms to pull themselves forward. Walsh ran ahead of the chief engineer, and when they reached the after door of aux machinery, Snyder raised his foot and kicked Walsh in the chest, sending him sprawling into a bulkhead.

The chief engineer ran headlong into Snyder, shoving his shoulder into the engineering tech's chest and driving him breathless into a heavy pipe. Snyder staggered and fell back, and Fukunaga dashed aft toward main control.

As Walsh tried to stand up, his back sore and his head bleeding, Bill and the others, now armed, ran up to him. Wild Bill stood over him and leveled the humming pistol at his head. Walsh braced himself, lowering his head and shutting his eyes tightly.

"You chickenshit." Bill squeezed the trigger and a pulse of coherent light energy flashed out of the muzzle and into Walsh's head. The laser pulse shattered a thumbnail sized section of his skull and dissipated throughout his cerebral cortex, smoldering a full third of his brain. Walsh's consciousness went black, and he fell to the floor, instantly dead.

***

Fukunaga ran into main control and pushed the button to the XO's stateroom on the visicom. "Fischer! Fischer! Wake up!"

The screen came on and Lieutenant Fischer, groggy from sleep, stood in front of the camera. "Yes, what is it?"

"Petty Officer Wilde and his gang are taking the ship! They've broken into the small arms locker!"

"What? Where are you?"

"Main control! They're armed and they've-" He looked toward the door. "Here they are!"

Morris, Bill, Dresden, Harper, Jackson, Fontaine, and Snyder burst into main control, crowding the small room. Morris reached over and switched off the visicom. Bill raised his pistol and pointed it at Fukunaga's face.

"You're next, Chink!"

Fukunaga stood up straight and faced Bill, unblinking, proud, and devoid of fear. "I am Japanese."

"Sayonara." Bill sneered and began to squeeze the trigger.

"Wait! Hold on!" Dresden shouted. He pushed his way forward though the group of men until he stood between Morris and Bill.

"What?" Bill growled.

"Don't kill him! He might be valuable as a hostage!"

Bill looked at Morris who nodded approvingly, then snapped to the others, "Bind him up."

Chapter 17

"Regaining Control"

Fischer sat momentarily stunned by the image he'd seen on the visicom, but then a sense of urgency galvanized him into action. He had been lying on the bed in his trousers reading when he had dozed off a half an hour before. He leapt for the door, grabbing his shirt and stuffing on his shoes as he half stumbled, half ran into the passageway. He turned toward the forward small arms locker, banging his hand on the junior officers' stateroom door as he ran past.

"Emergency! Get up, now!" he yelled. He stopped in front of the forward small arms locker and pressed his right hand up against the sensor grid. The grid scanned the palm and fingerprints, and in an instant the locks released. He opened the door just as Clark and Wallsbrook stepped into the passageway from their stateroom, still groggy from sleep.

"What's going on, sir?" Wallsbrook asked.

"Mutiny! Wilde and his gang are trying to take the ship! Get over here!" Fischer grabbed a pistol from the small locker and stuck it into his belt, then he handed another to Clark as the ensign ran up. "Clark, you're posted at this locker. They may try to come here. Shoot if they're armed. If they're not, put them on the deck. Shoot to wound if they're unarmed. Do you understand?"

Clark's face was nervous, but he seemed to digest everything. "Aye, aye, sir!"

Fischer handed Wallsbrook a gun, and together they ran to the access tube at the end of the passageway. As they ascended, Fischer instructed Wallsbrook. "Go to damage control central and get on the phones. Your instructions are the same as Clark's, shoot if they're armed. I'm going to the bridge."

"What are you going to do?"

"I'm going to call away G.Q."

As Wallsbrook headed aft, Fischer continued up the tube to the bridge. Navigator Brown, on watch at the holographic chart table, seemed to be playing a game on his computer pad but shoved it behind a panel when the XO came into the bridge. He stood up almost at attention.

"Brown, take this!" Fischer handed the navigator the pistol. "Guard that after hatch! Don't let anyone through."

"What's happening, sir?"

"Wild Bill and his gang have broken into the small arms locker. They're trying to take the ship."

Brown's face looked surprised, but he quickly stepped over to the hatch and closed it. Fischer grabbed the microphone for the ships PA system and shouted. "General quarters, general quarters! All hands, man your battle stations!" He switched on the alarm, and the electronic gonging tone echoed throughout the sleeping ship as red passageway lights switched back to white. He repeated the call, "General quarters, general quarters! All hands, man your battle stations!"

Fischer checked a monitor of the entire ship's airtight integrity and watched as battle doors began closing. The doors could be opened and closed manually as the crew went to their stations.

"Why are they doing this, sir?" Brown asked.

"I don't know." For the first time, Fischer thought about the question, but then dismissed it. *It doesn't matter now. All that matters is regaining control. Calling away GQ is a calculated risk. I hope no one gets hurt, but it's the fastest way to get the crew on station where lines of communication are already set up. Maybe the flurry of activity will help as well.*

Come on, Kestrels! Be quick!

***

"Shit!" Bill yelled at the PA speaker in main control. "Damn it!"

Morris remained calm and calculating. "Hey, Bill, we expected some kind of resistance. We need to hold the choke points. Fontaine, go to forward berthing and keep the men in there. Tell them there's a leak and that's why GQ was called. Go now! Quickly!" He looked at Jackson. "You go cover engineering berthing. Tell them the same thing. Hurry!"

Jackson and Fontaine ran forward to their assigned posts.

"What about the boat deck? Dresden asked.

"What about it?" Bill asked.

"Somebody could take a boat and go get the captain. He's got five armed men with him."

"Good idea. Go cover it," Bill said.

"No, wait. Let Snyder go, I want Dresden with us."

"Why do you always go against what I say?" Bill snapped.

"I'm not. I just want him here because he's got good ideas. "Snyder, go." Snyder turned and ran forward.

"Well, now what?"

"First," Morris pointed to Harper, "go secure the mess decks and hold it until we relieve you." Harper turned and ran forward. "Now there's just three of us. We need to go to the berthing compartments and recruit more men."

"Let's go, then," Bill said, and the three headed forward toward engineering berthing.

***

The sound of the general quarters alarm woke Cauthen up with a start. He sat bolt upright, grazing his head on the sleeping tube above his bunk, and grabbed his pants. He pushed his feet into them and rolled out of his rack, pulling them as he stood to his feet. Then he grabbed his shirt and shoes and looked around at the other men stirring from sleep. Someone switched on the lights.

"What's going on?" Sansbury asked from the bunk above Cauthen's.

"GQ! Grab your clothes and take them with you! Let's go!"

The electronic gonging sound continued as the men in the compartment jumped out of their bunks and hurriedly began dressing. Cauthen moved aft through the men but soon saw a tight knot of people forming at the door. He turned around and headed forward, still holding his shirt and shoes in his hand.

"Sansbury, Morrell, follow me!"

"Where are you going?" Crosly asked.

"To the bridge through the forward escape scuttle. They're jammed up at the door."

108

"Good idea." Lyons said, slipping on his shoes as he fell gently from his bunk into the deck's gravitational field. He landed on his feet and stood upright. "Let's go."

Cauthen, together with Sansbury, Morrell, Crosly, Lyons and a systems tech named DeZurik, pushed forward to the base of the escape scuttle. He opened the small hatch and lifted himself through, emerging into the forward end of the officer country passageway. He looked around and saw Ensign Clark standing at the small arms locker. The officer raised his gun and pointed it at Cauthen.

"Freeze! Get on the deck, now!"

Cauthen fell prostrate on the cold floor still clutching his shirt in his mouth and his shoes in his left hand. Coming out of the hatch behind him, Lyons was also commanded to lie down on the deck. Cauthen looked up at the frightened officer.

What in the hell is going on?

Chapter 18
"Deceptive Recruitment"

Petey had been in a deep sleep when the alarm sounded and took a little longer than normal to wake up. He put his clothes on in his bunk and climbed out into the flow of men moving through the door. As he emerged, he saw Fontaine running up the passageway toward them. He waved for them to stop, and in one hand Petey saw a pistol.

"Hold on, hold on! Get back into the compartment!"

"What for? We've got to go to GQ," one of the men said.

"Not yet," Fontaine said, his voice authoritarian. "There's been a deuterium gas leak. That's why they called GQ. As soon as they know the extent of the contamination, they'll let people through."

The men grew puzzled but they moved back. Petey climbed back into his bunk and waited.

Something's not right.

***

Fischer shut the general quarters alarm off and walked back to the forward stairwell. Brown still guarded the aft hatch. Fischer quickly descended the access tube to the next level and entered damage control central from its forward door.

"Anything from main?" he asked Wallsbrook.

"No, sir, nothing." Wallsbrook turned around and looked at the XO. "Sir, how do you know that someone's trying to take the ship? The phones are dead quiet."

"Oki was back in main when it started. He told me what was going on. He's still back there." He compulsively looked up at the clock. "I'm going to check on Clark."

Fischer left damage control central and descended the tube to the galley on the main deck. Moving forward, he stepped into officers' country and saw Clark pointing his gun at several men lying on the deck. He walked over and saw who they were.

Cauthen looked up at him. "What's going on, XO?"

"Where are you fellows coming from?"

"The berthing compartment. We heard GQ go down and this is the fastest way."

"Get up." Fischer stepped to the locker and grabbed a few pistols. "Listen. Wild Bill and his gang are trying to take the ship. Pass these back." He handed the pistols to the men and grabbed some more, keeping one for himself.

Ensign Clark watched the flow of weapons with increasing alarm. "Sir?"

"These men couldn't be part of the mutiny," Fischer said. "I can tell by the looks on their faces. Besides, these are all good men."

"Mutiny? But, why, sir?" Cauthen asked.

"I don't know. But we need to secure the ship and then ask questions."

"That'll suit me fine, sir," Lyons said, holding up his pistol. "I've always wanted a crack at that son of a bitch."

Fischer nodded. *I hope you get the chance.* "All right, listen. You men, as well as Brown on the bridge, Mr. Clark and Mr. Wallsbrook, are the only ones who should be armed. We need to secure the ship compartment by compartment. I'm splitting us up into three groups, one for each deck. We'll move from forward to aft."

"This'll be weird, sir. How will we know who is on our side and who isn't?" Cauthen asked.

"You won't have to. Anyone you see armed who is not in this group right now is to be shot. Don't ask anything or they'll shoot you. Anyone who isn't armed should be put on the deck. If you get too many to cover by yourselves, call Mr. Wallsbrook in D.C. central." He paused a moment. "Most of the crew doesn't know what's going on so they shouldn't be much trouble. But keep in contact. If there's light resistance, take it out. If resistance is heavy, then fall back and call D.C. central. If you can close and guard a door, that's good. Any questions?"

No one said anything. They appeared nervous but ready.

"All right. Cauthen and Sansbury, go back down to forward berthing and secure it. Then proceed aft. Clark, Lyons and Crosly, go aft from here along the main deck as far as you can go. DeZurik, guard the main hatch. Don't let anyone through unless you hear from me. Morrell, you come with me. Now everyone go, and be careful!"

The men split up into their groups and moved out. Morrell followed Fischer up the main access tube to D.C. central.

***

Wild Bill, Morris, and Dresden walked forward along the second deck to the aft door to engineering berthing. There they saw Jackson standing, brandishing his pistol. Other men were standing at the door. They were mostly the ship's servicemen, a rate combining cooks and laundry cleaners. They were waiting to go to their G.Q. stations, and they looked surprised to see the three engineering techs with sidearms.

"Listen up!" Bill said, his voice loud and direct. "The deuterium leak is a lie. We checked it out." He paused to let the words sink in. "There's something much bigger going on here."

"Why can't we go to our G.Q. stations?" asked Rodgers, one of the men in the compartment.

"Because we're all in danger. The space station crew has been wiped out by a virus."

"A virus that had already killed the population of an entire planet," Morris interjected.

"And there's a good chance that the captain and the boarding party have got it now, too," Bill continued. "That's why the captain and the others are still on the station. He's quarantined us to see if we're going to get it. But I tell you, if he comes back on board, we'll all get it for sure."

"Well, what do you expect us to do about it?"

"We're going to get the crew together and tell the XO that we want to get out of here before we catch this thing, too."

"We're not equipped to deal with this kind of situation," Morris added. "We need to go get help. We need to get someone who knows what to do."

"How did you find out about this virus?" Ryan, a ships serviceman, asked.

"Schroeder told us. He sent out a message on it."

"Well, hell, Foley was there. What did you see, Doc?"

The men at the door turned around to look at Foley. Dresden couldn't see him behind the crowd, but he could hear his voice. "We

112

found a bunch of dead crew members in the lifeboats and another in the station, but I don't know how they died."

"The message says the virus killed them," Morris said.

Dresden looked at the faces of the men. They clearly believed what Bill said about the virus, but remained unsure about what Bill intended to do. The thought of a mutiny frightened them, even Dresden found it frightening, but the thought of catching a deadly virus scared them also. Now, it was a question of loyalty.

"If you're just going to talk to the XO, then why do you need guns?" Rogers asked.

"To show him we're serious," Bill said.

"Well, actually," Morris added, "it's to help keep order. If the rest of the crew finds out about this killer virus, he will need us to keep order."

"Who all is with you?" Ryan asked, looking at each of the four armed men.

"Mainly engineering and a few from up forward," Morris replied.

"And the chief engineer," Bill lied. "He's in main right now."

The men looked around at each other. Believing that there was an officer in charge made them feel more at ease.

"What do we have to do?" Ryan asked.

"Are you with us?" Bill asked.

"Yeah, of course."

Bill and Morris exchanged glances. "Who else is with us?" Four other men raised their hands. "All right. Go up to the small arms locker and grab a pistol. Then two of you go to the mess decks and wait with Harper. He's already there. The others will come with us to forward berthing."

"Hold on a minute!" Foley shouted. "This is mutiny!"

"How's that?" Ryan said. "Mr. Fukunaga is organizing it."

"I don't care who is doing it. It's still mutiny. If you go get a gun, they'll execute you for sedition. You can bank on that."

"Look," Bill shouted, "if you don't want to help, then just stay here and shut up. The rest of you, move out now."

One of the men hesitated and stepped back in. Ryan and the other three went to the access tube that led to the small arms locker on the main deck.

"Jackson," Bill said, "stay here. Don't let anyone out. Shoot to kill if you have to." Then he motioned for Morris and Dresden to follow him forward.

As they walked, Dresden considered the lie about the chief engineer. It bothered him that these men were being deceived into going with Bill. *How will they react when it's all over? When they know the truth?*

Chapter 19
"Hold the Line"

Cauthen and Sansbury stepped over to the open scuttle and looked down inside the compartment below. Seeing no one, Sansbury started to climb down.

"Hold on," Cauthen said. He squatted down and placed his pistol on the deck next to the small hatch. Then, with his hands holding onto the rim, he leaned over and stuck his head through the scuttle. He could see several men milling about just inside the compartment's aft door. He raised himself back up and grabbed his pistol.

"Everyone's standing around next to the door. They didn't notice me. Let's go down quietly and quickly."

Cauthen stuck the pistol in his belt and eased through the scuttle. Once on the deck below, he drew the gun and waited for Sansbury. The other operations tech came down and the two men moved silently between the bunks and lockers to where the men stood clustered inside the door. As they rounded a laundry locker, radioman Mullins turned around and saw them.

"Hey!" he exclaimed. "What the hell is going on now?"

Several men turned around to look and seemed more amused than surprised.

"Security breach," Cauthen answered. "Everyone get down on the deck, please. Now."

A few of the men sitting on their bunks climbed to the deck and sat down. Two men at the door looked at Cauthen, then looked out the door, then looked back at Cauthen again.

"Get on the deck, now!" Cauthen said.

The two men at the door sat down, and beyond them Cauthen could see Fontaine holding a pistol at his side. For a moment the two men stared at each other. Then Cauthen raised his pistol and shouted, "Drop it!"

Fontaine raised his pistol and fired wildly. The shot struck the upper edge of the door opening and sent a shower of sparks over the two men in the deck. Cauthen crouched down and fired, but Fontaine was already diving behind a storage locker. Sansbury stood behind the

115

laundry locker and fired two shots over Cauthen's head, hitting the far wall in the passageway. Fontaine fired several shots rapidly into the door, and the men on the deck began shouting and screaming and scrambling to get out of the way.

Cauthen took careful aim at the edge of the storage locker and fired, but most of the shot's energy deflected away from the weapons tech. Fontaine was well covered and Cauthen was not. He realized that they wouldn't be able to proceed any further aft on this deck. *We must seal the compartment and hold the line here. At least for now.*

"Hey, shipmate," he called to a man crouched at the doorway. "Close the door!" The man gave no response, as if too scared to move. "Hey! Close the door!"

Another young crewman stuck his head out from a bunk next the door, his face ashen. He looked at the man crouching by the door and then looked over at Cauthen. With a frightened expression, he slowly shook his head.

Damn!

Fontaine began yelling to someone down the passageway. "Hey! Come on! Hurry up! There's someone in the compartment!"

Cauthen could hear running on the deck and raised his pistol just as Morris, Dresden, and Wild Bill ran into view. He fired and grazed Bill's left shoulder, and the engineer shouted in pain as all three darted out of sight. Dresden dove behind the locker, and Morris and Bill went into the crew's head.

"Who the hell is up there?" Bill shouted.

"It's Cauthen!" Fontaine answered.

There was a pause, and then Bill shouted, "Let's rush him! Go, go, go!"

The four men charged for the door firing a barrage of shots into the compartment. Cauthen and Sansbury fired back, striking Fontaine twice. He fell screaming to the deck.

The men hiding in the bunks began shouting curses and exclamations as shots hit all around the room, exploding against the bunks and lockers and sending fragments of hot metal flying through the air.

A shot hit the side of a bunk frame next to Cauthen, and fragments of hot metal sprayed onto his face. He winced and staggered backward from his crouching position onto the deck. From behind the laundry locker, Sansbury fired rapidly at the three men, hitting Dresden in the hip as he and the other two took cover just outside the door.

"Hey, man! Are you okay?" Sansbury called.

Cauthen crawled to cover behind the locker. "Yeah, yeah. We've got to get the hell out of here." He wiped blood from his eyes and raised his voice so the other crew members could hear. "You fellows just keep down, no matter what happens!" He got to his feet and gestured to the scuttle. "Let's go!"

As the men sprinted back to the scuttle, Cauthen saw Petey out of the corner of his eye crouched behind a bunk and felt guilty for deserting him. "We'll be back," he said aloud, but he had a nagging feeling that he would never see the navigator again.

***

Dresden sat against the wall on one side of the door. His belt and a section of his uniform had been burnt, and through the opening he could see seared skin.

"You okay?" Morris asked.

Dresden nodded and spoke through clenched teeth. "Yeah, it just hurts."

"There must be two of them in there." Bill said. He looked down at a crewman inside and pointed his gun at him. "Where are they? Tell me or I'll blow your head off."

The crewman pointed forward and to the right. Bill waved his hand in front of the door and got no response. He looked inside past the scared crewmen crouching on the deck and then snapped his fingers. "The scuttle!"

Ryan and Hughes came jogging up the passageway and Bill waved them over.

"We're going in now. Go, go, go!"

The two men ran into the compartment with Bill and Morris close behind. Dresden struggled to get up.

***

Sansbury passed through the scuttle, and Cauthen was just starting up when a shot hit the handle above him and someone behind him yelled, "Shoot him!" He pushed himself back down and pressed against a locker as a volley of shots erupted against the access tube. He pointed his pistol around the locker and fired a few shots blindly, then looked up to see Sansbury looking down at him.

"Drop me your pistol," Cauthen said, "and go get the others!" Sansbury threw it down and Cauthen caught it with one hand. He looked up at Sansbury. "Hurry!"

Sansbury ran down the passageway at top speed to where DeZurik guarded the main access tube hatch.

"What's wrong?"

"Cauthen's pinned down in forward berthing!" Sansbury leaped and pulled himself up the tube before heading aft to D.C. central. The XO, Lieutenant j.g. Wallsbrook, and Morrell looked at him as he ran through the door.

"Sir! Cauthen's pinned down in forward Berthing! He's under the scuttle."

"How many are there?" Fischer demanded.

"At least three."

"Wallsbrook, stay here. Morrell, come with me."

Sansbury led them back out of D.C. central and down the access tube. At the main deck next to the hatch stood Ensign Clark, Lyons, and Crosly, summoned by DeZurik's call. Fischer pointed to each man as he spoke. "Clark, you and Crosly continue aft and hold the line. And be careful, it's started. Lyons come with us."

Clark and Crosly moved aft and the rest ran forward to the scuttle, leaving DeZurik at the hatch. They reached the scuttle and crowded around to see Cauthen below shooting both pistols while shots exploded around him. Blood streamed from small wounds in his neck.

In the compartment they heard Bill's voice shouting. "I said move in!"

Lyons stood up and pointed to Morrell. "Go to the D.C. locker and get an emergency respirator hose. Hurry!" Then he turned to Fischer. "If you please, sir."

Fischer nodded and Morrell ran up the passageway. Lyons quickly walked over to the locker and put his pistol back. Then he grabbed a "street sweeper," a full auto pulse rifle. Arming the weapon, he stepped back to the scuttle and knelt down beside it. He looked up at Sansbury and said, "Grab my belt and hold on. And when I say 'pull,' you pull me back up in a hurry."

Sansbury nodded and grabbed Lyons' belt. The gunner pointed the rifle down and leaned over and into the compartment. Hanging upside down, he pointed the rifle to where the shots were coming from and squeezed the trigger. The rifle shuddered as high intensity bolts of light exploded rapidly from the weapon's muzzle, tearing through the metal bunk frames and lockers and scorching the mattresses. Over the jackhammer din of the street sweeper, Sansbury could hear the screams of the men on the other side of the compartment.

"I've got something for your asses now, you bastards!" Lyons yelled as the weapon tore the compartment to shreds.

In the light muzzle flashes, Sansbury saw Cauthen huddled on the deck, his arms covering his head. Fischer leaned over and grabbed the gunner's belt also.

The weapon's overheat warning alarm sounded, and Lyons yelled, "Pull!"

Sansbury and the XO snatched him back up into the passageway. Morrell ran up with a coil of black hose, panting to catch his breath.

"Tie a bowline!" Lyons said.

Morrell paused for a moment, then dropped the coil and tied a bowline knot with a large loop.

"Throw it over that pipe, there."

Morrell tossed the loop over a pipe in the overhead and sent it down into the compartment. The knot fell on Cauthen's lap, and Lyons made a gesture for him to put the loop under his arms. Cauthen did so and Morrell pulled out the slack.

"Now, I'm going to fire again to keep them down," Lyons said. "When I say 'pull,' hoist me up, then hoist him up right after, okay?" Everyone nodded. "All right, let's go!"

Lyons leaned back over into the compartment and began firing again. In the flashing light Sansbury could see no movement save for the fragments of glowing metal spraying across the room.

"Pull!" Lyons yelled and was hauled swiftly up. Then Sansbury and the XO grabbed the hose with Morrell and furiously pulled Cauthen through the scuttle. As he hung suspended, Lyons closed the scuttle hatch and locked it shut. Then the three men lowered Cauthen down and released the hose. Everyone visibly relaxed.

"Are you all right?" Fischer asked Cauthen.

"Yes, sir. Just minor scratches."

Fischer nodded. "Okay, Sansbury, stay here and guard this hatch." He's stepped over to the small arms locker and grabbed a few communicators. "I should have thought of these before." He handed two to Lyons. "Here, go forward and get back with Ensign Clark. Give the second one to DeZurik. Try to take the small arms locker if you can. We need to keep him from arming anyone else."

Lyons stood up and headed aft.

"The rest of you come with me to D.C. Central."

***

With the sound of the scuttle slamming shut, the forward berthing compartment grew very quiet. Petey slowly raised his head and looked around to see the berthing compartment in shambles. Several of the other crewmembers had begun to stir, but others remained still. Petey looked down the aisle between the bunks and saw Fontaine lying dead outside the door.

So much death. Why? Why?

Across the compartment Wild Bill stood up. He had not been seriously hurt during the melee, and Petey watched him as he walked over to Hughes who lay motionless and face down on the deck. Bill pushed him over with his foot and took the ship serviceman's pistol. Behind him, Morris stood up. His face and neck oozed blood from dozens of small cuts from the flying debris. Ryan leaned against a locker holding one hand over a wounded shoulder.

As the three men came toward Petey, a feeling of dread washed over him. He averted his eyes and contemplated pretending he was dead, but the men walked past without incident. They stepped through the door and stood before Fontaine while Bill took the gunner's pistol.

"He won't be needing this anymore." Bill looked at another person in the passageway. "Where the hell were you?"

"I tried to help Fontaine," Dresden answered. "When I realized he was dead, I came forward but it was already over."

Morris looked back into the compartment. "We need to post Ryan here and get back with the other group. We've got to move fast now." He turned to Ryan. "Stand here at the doorway so you can listen

121

for the scuttle and the main hatch. We'll send someone back to check on you after everything else is secure."

"You want me to guard both hatches by myself?"

"Yes. We'll send someone back as soon as we can." Morris faced the compartment and spoke loudly. "If anyone here tries anything, Ryan, you shoot them dead." He turned to Bill. "We should head aft now and check on Harper's gang."

The three moved quickly down the passageway. Petey wiped blood from the back of his neck and realized that he was shaking.

God help us. God please help us.

Chapter 21
"Impasse"

Crosly dashed into the wardroom and crouched behind a dining chair, his pistol aimed across the table at the galley door at the far side of the room. All quiet. He nodded and heard Ensign Clark come into the wardroom behind him and watched him take up a position adjacent to the galley door. Crosly started to rise but froze when he noticed Clark looking at someone behind him. He turned back to see Lyons entering the wardroom, the muzzle of his street sweeper pointing up and humming menacingly.

Crosly smiled to see the gun. "You traded up!"

"Have you guys seen anything yet?" Lyons asked.

"Not yet," Ensign Clark whispered. He gestured with his thumb. "But I'm sure there will be resistance up ahead."

"Because of the small arms locker?"

Clark nodded. "Crosly will open the door. If it's clear, I'll go in. Then he will come in, then you. But I want you to provide covering fire if it's not clear."

"I understand." Lyons lowered the weapon toward the door.

Clark looked at Crosly. "Go ahead."

Holding his pistol in his right hand, Crosly reached his left hand up and unlatched the door, giving it a gentle push.

As the door swung wide open, Clark peered inside and, seeing no one, scrambled through. Crosly soon ran in, taking up a position behind a freezer. Lyons followed.

Clark made a circular motion with his hand, and the three men quickly searched around the galley's various cooking and food container heaters. Satisfied that the galley was clear, Crosly went to the wardroom side to a covered rack filled with sweet rolls. He reached inside and took one.

"What are you doing?" Clark asked.

"Just a little hungry, sir." Crosly took a bite of the roll and said, "If I'd have known there was going to be an insurrection tonight, I'd have eaten more at dinner."

Lyons began to laugh aloud but stifled it.

Clark shook his head. "Well, hurry and finish it. We've got to secure this deck."

"Don't mind me, sir. I'm ready." He jammed the last of the roll in his mouth as he stepped over to the door to the mess decks. He turned around and, with cheeks full of food, said, "We going to do the same thing?"

"Yes," Clark said. The two men took up their positions by the door. Lyons stood behind them with his weapon ready at the hip.

Crouched down, Crosly looked to see if the others were ready, then he unlatched the door and pushed it open.

Against the far wall of the mess decks stood Harper, Rodgers, and Falk. They appeared to have been talking when the door opened. Lyons pointed his gun and began firing. The three men dove to cover behind some tables.

Lyons fired short bursts at the men, but there was no return volley. He stopped firing and crouched down. Clark spoke at the men through the door.

"Throw down your weapons and lie down on the deck. If you cooperate, you will not be hurt."

A long pause followed by quiet murmuring from across the room. Then came the reply, "Screw you!" Several shots erupted from behind the tables causing Clark and the others to shrink back into the galley.

Clark shook his head. "We've got to get to the small arms locker."

Crosly crouched low and tried to see under the tables. "I can see them moving," he carefully aimed and fired. The shot ricocheted between the legs of the tables and chair supports. "But I can't hit them from here."

"We should close this off," Clark said. He bit his thumbnail as he spoke, his eyes darting between the two weapons techs. "We should secure this door and fall back."

"Hold on, sir," Lyons said. He pointed along the starboard wall. "If I can get behind the ice cream machine, I'll make my way down the serving line, and from there I'll be able to get a bead on them."

"But... but what if..."

"Go ahead, buddy. I've got you," Crosly said. He started firing as Lyons ran behind the ice cream machine.

***

Bill, Morris, and Dresden ascended the aft hatch to aux machinery, along with Snyder who had joined them from the boat decks. Morris had insisted that they needed an extra man now more than they needed the boats secured. As they approached the forward door of aux machinery, they could hear gunfire coming from the mess decks. Bill tore the door open, and they broke into a run forward.

As they passed the small arms locker, Bill stopped in front of the door. "Hold on."

Ahead, shots could be seen flashing back and forth across the room. Bill leveled his pistol at the door lock and fired several shots, scattering metal fragments around the passageway. Then he grabbed the handle and jerked the door open. Stepping quickly over to a shelf, he opened a box and took out a couple of plum-sized fragmentary hand grenades. Hooking them onto his belt, he turned and led the others forward through the passageway once again.

***

Crosly watched from the galley as Lyons slowly made his way along the mess decks serving line, firing short sweeping bursts as he went. Crosly waited for Lyons to get in position to get a clear shot at the men from the left before he would dash through the door and attack from the right. He hoped they would be able to overpower them without having to kill anyone.

A flicker of light caught his eye from the darkened passageway beyond the opposite door of the mess decks. Someone was shooting at a wall. There was a pause. Then he could see four figures running to the mess decks.

"Oh, man." *Lyons will be caught in the open.*

"What's wrong?" Clark asked.

Crosly didn't answer. "Lyons! Fall back! Fall back!"

125

The weapon's tech couldn't hear or didn't want to hear. He kept firing, moving closer to the men behind the tables.

Crosly fired through the opposite door at the new group of men, and they split up, taking cover next to the open door.

"Lyons! The door! They're coming up behind the door!" Crosly screamed. A wave of fear swept over him. *Why doesn't he come back?*

Crosly's fear turned to dread as he watched a hand come around the door and throw a small object toward Lyons. Time seemed to slow down as the small hand grenade, flying above the low powered gravitational field of the deck, made a straight line across the room, spinning slowly and leaving a faint curling trail of smoke behind it. Lyons saw it but did not move. There was no time to move.

Crosly felt the stinging slap of the concussion on his face as the grenade exploded in mid-air. Only two feet away from Lyons, it sent out shards of metal propelled by the high explosive charge, striking the weapons tech and causing him to stagger backward and collapse to the deck.

"No!" Crosly yelled in horror. Without thought he ran out onto the mess decks, and for a few moments the room remained quiet, the acrid smell of smoke hanging heavy in the air. But then shots began to burst around him, and he ducked down below the level of the tables to the serving line.

The sight of his friend writhing on the deck shocked him. Lyons lay covered in blood that ran from as many as twenty small wounds across his face, neck, and chest. His eyes squinched in pain, and he groaned through clenched teeth and shook his head from side to side as blood spurted from a wound in his neck.

"Oh, shit, man!" Crosly said, stuffing his pistol into his belt. "Take it easy, shipmate. I'm gonna get you out of here." He knelt down and grabbed Lyons under his arms, lifting him onto his shoulder, then grabbed the strap of the rifle and turned for the galley door. As he started into an awkward run, he glanced back over his shoulder to where the mutineers were clustered near the aft door.

***

Harper, Rogers, and Falk lay sprawled on the deck, still stunned by the grenade's concussion. Dresden and Morris stepped inside the door, and Dresden had a clear shot at the two weapons techs, but seeing a shipmate carrying a friend to safety, with no thought of danger to himself, overwhelmed him and he lowered his pistol. Morris, too, seemed affected by the act of mercy and also refused to fire. But Bill shoved past them both and aimed for Crosly's back, firing once.

***

Hearing the commotion at the aft door, Crosly crouched lower and nearly fell through the galley entrance. Clark stood up and reached over to help, but the gunner nodded toward the door.

"Seal the door or they'll throw a frag in here, too!"

As Crosly laid Lyons down on the deck, Clark snatched the door shut and pushed a red button. A large steel fire door slid in place. Then he stood over Lyons and Crosly and said, "Oh my God."

Lyons' eyes stared blankly at the ceiling. While he had been tense and writhing on the mess decks, now he lay limp and still. Crosly prodded him for a moment and began to frantically check for vital signs. There were none.

"What the hell happened?" Crosly cried out loud. "He was alive just a few seconds ago!"

With his arms covered in blood, Crosly began to attempt CPR. He pumped down on Lyon's chest several times then listened for breathing.

"Come on, man! Dammit! Come on!" Crosly reached his hand behind Lyons head to reposition it and felt the charred hole. He rolled the head to one side, and a smell of burned hair and flesh rose as he saw the wound.

"Oh shit!" Crosly released the head and slumped back against a stainless steel cabinet. "Oh shit, man." The image of his friend's face began to swim as tears welled up in his eyes. He clenched his teeth as his face contorted with grief and anger. "Sons of bitches. Damn them all to hell."

Clark knelt down and took the communicator from Lyons' belt. He pushed the button and spoke. "XO, this is Clark."

127

"Fischer, here. What've you got?"

"We've been stopped in the galley. We've shut the fire door, and I don't think they can come through here, but we can't go any farther, either." Clark took a breath and looked at the fallen weapons tech. "Also, we've lost Petty Officer Lyons."

There was a long pause. "Do you think that you and Crosly can defend that door?"

Crosly picked up the rifle and wiped his face on his shirt sleeve. He nodded to the officer.

"Yes, sir," Clark said.

"Very well, stay right there for now. If you need help, call."

"Aye, sir."

"I'm really sorry about Lyons," the XO said.

"Me, too. Clark out."

Chapter 22
"Assessment"

Bill walked over to the door to the galley. In disgust he fired several shots at the fire door and kicked it with the bottom of his foot. Morris walked over and stood next to him. "We'll never get though there now. To open it, we'll have to access the computer to get an explosive gas check and reflash…"

"I know what has to be done!" Bill growled. "This whole plan is screwing up." He kicked the door again.

"Hold on now. This isn't so bad. We've got main, aux machinery, the small arms locker, the entire second deck and half of the main deck. We're doing good."

"Yeah, but it ain't gonna make a damn bit of difference if we can't go any further."

"Look, I don't know how many they have, but they've got to be spread as thin as we are, and as long as we hold the men in the berthing compartments, they can't get any stronger."

"Well, Einstein, then what do you suggest now?"

"Let's go for the bridge. If we can get that and keep the men penned up, we can start getting the ship out of here."

"Should we leave someone here?" Dresden asked. Thoroughly tired of the fire fights, he hoped they would post him at the door.

Morris thumped the smooth steel with his fist. "Nah, they can't get through either. But we ought to send someone back to stay with Ryan." He turned to Falk. "You go help Ryan defend forward berthing and the main hatch. Everyone else, to the bridge."

***

"Please, Ryan," Petey said, "just a little water so we can clean up some of these wounds."

"No, Petey. I'm not letting anyone out."

"Well, if I gave you a basin would you get some for me? You're right next to the head."

"No, Petey."

129

"I'll clean up your wounds, too."

"No. Now forget it."

Petey nodded in futility and turned back into the forward compartment. He had been working with radioman Mullins to treat the wounded as best they could. The casualties consisted of either lacerations and minor burns from the shrapnel or deaths from direct hits. Oddly, there were no major injuries. The dead, three in all, lay neatly in the three bunks farthest from the door and covered with sheets. Petey had struggled to choke back his anguish as he carried his friends to the bunks. Nineteen, twenty, and twenty-two years old, and now their lives were irreversibly snuffed out.

"What did he say?" Mullins asked, applying a piece of torn sheet to a crewman's bleeding neck as the man winced in pain.

"Nothing doing."

"Asshole," Mullins said. "Well, we're going to need something. This is the last of my aftershave."

"I've got another bottle. Hold on." Petey turned back to his locker. Most of the men in the compartment were either sitting and talking quietly or trying to sleep. Schroeder sat in his open sleeping tube next to Petey's locker, silently staring at the deck. He hadn't moved since the fighting had ended, only looking up as a dead crewmen was being carried by, then closing his eyes tightly. He didn't look up now as Petey approached.

"You all right, buddy?" the navigator asked.

Slowly Schroeder raised his head and looked at Petey, his expression a mixture of apprehension and dread. He looked around as if to see if anyone else would hear him, then whispered, "I caused this."

Petey opened the locker and took out an unopened bottle of aftershave. *He must still be in a state of shock.* "No, pal, you didn't cause this."

"Yes, this is my fault." The radioman gestured toward the dead crewmen. "They're dead because of me, just as if I'd shot them myself."

"I don't follow you."

Schroeder sighed. "Those crewmen you found on the station were killed by some disease. The captain thinks that maybe the boarding party got it, too. We sent out a message on it."

A tingling went over Petey's scalp. *That makes sense, but wouldn't that mean that I have it, too? I was there.* He glanced at the bunks where the dead crewmen lay.

"All right. But how does that make you guilty of this?"

Schroeder looked as if he were about to cry. "I told them. I told them everything."

"Told who?"

"Wild Bill and the others. They made me tell them."

Petey paused, unable to believe his ears. "Is that what this is all about?"

Schroeder nodded and blinked, and a tear flew away from his eye and up toward the ceiling in the zero G.

So that's it. They intend to take the ship and leave. They think that they'll prevent being exposed to the virus by stranding the boarding party on the station and leaving. But once they commit mutiny, where will they go?

Petey opened his mouth to ask another question, but before he could speak, Mullins walked over to Schroeder's bunk, his face angry and his voice filled with loathing having overheard the conversation.

"You rotten son of a bitch. You always did like to share classified information. I always knew that one day we'd all pay for it."

"Hey, Buddy," Petey intervened, "he said they made him tell."

"Yeah? Well, they knew right where to go, didn't they?" Mullins clenched his fists as he stood over Schroeder's bunk. "I gave you a chance to stop it, didn't I? I should've had your ass busted then."

"I'm sorry."

"You will be."

Mullins grabbed Schroeder's feet and yanked him down out of the tube causing him to strike the deck hard with his buttocks and bang his head on the edge of the lower bunk. Mullins dropped his feet and kicked Schroder hard in the groin before repeatedly kicking him in the ribs.

"You son of a bitch!"

Petey grabbed Mullins and tried to hold him back and away from Schroeder who writhed on the deck. "Come on man. It's over," he said as he struggled with the radioman. They awkwardly fell back against a locker. "Just let him go. Please."

Mullins stopped struggling and calmed down, still breathing hard from the exertion. He pointed at Schroeder. "You'll be the next one to die, you son of a bitch. If someone else dies because of you, you're going with 'em. Do you hear me? I'll do it myself."

Schroeder didn't acknowledge him, but instead crawled into the lower bunk.

"Get out of my friggin rack!" Mullins screamed, shaking Petey loose and kicking Schroeder hard on the buttocks before the navigator could restrain him again.

Schroeder crawled back onto the deck and made his way back to where the dead crewmen lay. He reminded Petey of a dog who had been scolded. Mullins shook loose again and walked back to where the other men waited to be treated. They had watched the confrontation but said nothing.

***

In D.C. central, Fischer went to the aft door and sealed the heavy fireproof door over it, then stepped back over to the table where Wallsbrook had brought up a holographic three-dimensional schematic diagram of the interior of the *Kestrel*. Wallsbrook had outlined in green the sections of the ship that were still under the XO's control. The other sections glowed red. He pointed to the different areas of the diagram as he spoke.

"Well, sir, the entire second deck is in Petty Officer Wilde's control. But I believe that we are effectively holding them at the forward scuttle here, the main deck access tube here, and the galley fire door over here."

"And this door is now secured," Fischer said, pointing to the aft door. "Along with the aft bridge hatch." He studied the chart for a moment. "Where do you think they'll try next?"

"It's hard to say, but I reckon that, even though the hatches are more difficult to overcome, they'll try for those because the doors are definitely shut tight. But the real question is, will they attack in one place together, or will they attack these three hatches simultaneously?"

"Excuse me, sir, but they'll probably attack together," Cauthen said. "Bill's not the type to do his own dirty work. He'll go with a group."

Fischer nodded. "But we need to be ready for either situation. Let's do a radio check with everyone. Then we'll stay here and be ready to respond to whatever happens."

As Cauthen asked for a radio check from each man, Wallsbrook leaned back and spoke quietly to Fischer. "It might be beneficial to speak to Wilde directly. Perhaps he can be reasoned with, or at least we might learn something about his plans."

"I agree. But first I want to talk to the captain. He needs to know what's going on. I'll be on the bridge."

Chapter 23
"Counsel of War"

Ski took off the wide-brimmed pith hat and mopped the sweat off of his forehead with a small towel. The broiling midday sun beat down on the dry grass and scrub vegetation of the Rajasthan Province of India that now stretched out before him. He rode an elephant in a howdah, a type of basket strapped to the animal's back, and next to him sat a local guide. On the back of the animal's neck rode the mahout, or driver, who, like the howdah, swayed from side to side as the elephant lumbered through the four-foot tall grass of the broad plain. Several miles ahead the grass merged into a tree line of dense forest, and beyond it rose a range of mountains.

Three other elephants traveled line abreast in the hunting party, each occupied in the same fashion with a guide, a driver, and a European hunter. A few days earlier a tiger had been spotted in the area, and the expedition quickly assembled. To the left and right of the elephants stretched a V-shaped line of nearly a hundred men who beat the bush with sticks to drive the tiger into the path of the hunting party.

On Ski's lap rested a large four-gauge Greener Big Game gun, a heavy, smooth-bore single-shot weapon, accurate only at close ranges but with terrific shocking power. In his belt he wore a .722 caliber Westley Richards "howdah pistol," another single-shot, smooth-bore weapon that would be used as a backup at close ranges. The two guns had awesome killing power, even compared to modern pulse rifles. Ski found himself constantly shifting the long gun's weight from one thigh to the other.

The guide stood up and shouted an order to the men in the grass, then sat back down and spoke in English to Ski. "I have ordered the men to begin closing the loop. We do not want the animal to escape into the forest."

Ski nodded and removed his hat to mop the sweat from his brow again. He looked out over the expanse of grass and wished that he had a pair of binoculars to study the beautiful landscape. The cloudless sky seemed to glow a rich blue, and the slight breeze that cooled his damp hair carried the sound of the men beating the tall grass. The smell of wicker and unwashed elephant filled his nostrils.

He replaced his hat just as a scream broke out from the line to his left. Some of the men rushed to where a man had been startled by the big cat, and Ski felt a twinge of apprehension. He lifted the gun and placed the barrel on the edge of the howdah. Voices began shouting back and forth between the lines of men and the hunting party. Ski's guide shouted to the drivers, and the four elephants turned and headed for the commotion.

"Be ready now, Sahib. We are very close."

Ski cocked his gun and watched the grass. The thrill of adventure surged through his being and his heartbeat quickened, partly in expectation of seeing the tiger and partly out of fear. He studied the grass ahead but saw no movement.

A deep roaring sound to his left caught his attention, and he turned to see the tiger, a full ten feet from nose to tail, spring up from the grass and sink its claws into the elephant's side. The elephant trumpeted and shook himself violently, trying to loosen the tiger's hold. The guide and the driver had been holding on when the tiger attacked, but the hunter had been holding his gun with both hands, and now, thrown from the howdah, he fell hard into the grass. The tiger released the elephant and leapt on the hunter.

Ski watched in shocked disbelief as both the man and the tiger had disappeared into the grass. The men on the ground began running to the scene, and everybody started yelling. Then, out in front of his own elephant, Ski saw the tiger dragging the hunter through the grass. The cat held the hunter's left thigh in his teeth while the hunter struggled to grab his own pistol. Ski raised his gun to shoot, but the hunter's head and torso blocked a clean shot at the cat. A shot now could just as easily kill the hunter as the tiger. In a few moments they would be out of range.

"Now, Sahib! Now!"

Ski tried to aim the big gun carefully. The hunter finally drew his pistol and fired at the tiger. The shot missed, but the big cat, startled by the report of the gun, stopped and turned around. Now Ski had a clear shot at the tiger's broad side. He held his breath and squeezed the trigger...

"Hey, Ski, come on!" Gradenko's voice crashed into his consciousness.

Ski's concentration was broken, and the images went blank. He removed the headgear and leaned out of the MSES machine. "What's wrong?"

"Something happening on the ship!"

Ski climbed out and followed Gradenko and Flores out into the hallway and down the stairs. As they reached the main control room, he saw the rest of the boarding party gathered around the communications console. On the screen Ski could see the bridge of the *Kestrel* but saw no one monitoring. Off screen he heard sounds of straining and scuffling with an occasional pistol shot.

"What's happening?" Ski asked Wilson.

"I'm not sure. The XO came on and started talking about some kind of mutiny happening, but then suddenly ran to the aft hatch. It sounds like someone is trying to come through."

"Who?"

"A bunch of guys led by Wild Bill."

Ski's mouth dropped open with incredulity, but as he watched the screen he saw Cauthen and Morrell running past, each armed with a pistol. Then he heard several loud pistol shots followed by a loud metallic clank. The XO stepped back in front of the screen, breathing heavily.

"Are you okay?" Van Wert asked.

Fischer nodded. "We've held them at the hatch."

"How much of the ship do they have?"

"The entire second deck, aft of the galley on the main deck, and aft of DC Central on the 01 level."

Van Wert shook his head. "How did they get weapons?"

"Oki said they broke into the small arms locker."

"Where is he?"

"They have him back aft."

Van Wert took a deep breath and looked down at the floor. "Who do you have with you?"

"Clark, Wallsbrook, Cauthen, Morrell, Brown, Crosly, uh, Sansbury, and DeZurik. Lyons was with us, too. He was killed in action."

Van Wert shook his head. "What about the rest of the crew?"

"These are the only ones who reported to their stations. The rest are being held below. Some have apparently joined Bill."

Van Wert lifted his head to look at the *Kestrel* floating beyond the large windows, and Ski could see the concern and frustration on his face. "Is there no way to get me back aboard?"

"No, there isn't. Not until we retake the boat deck." Fischer paused. "Maybe it's possible to-"

A sudden and constant barrage of gunfire against the aft hatch interrupted the XO's words. He turned and looked aft, staring at the hatch. "Oh, hell."

"What's wrong?" Van Wert asked.

"The constant fire at the bottom of the hatch is causing a hot spot. The metal is getting red."

"Paul," Van Wert said, his voice grave. "Get him on the visicom. Find out why they're doing this. Get more information. See if you can get Fukunaga back. I'll stay on the line.

Chapter 24
"Madness"

Bill and the others fired continuously at the large disc of glowing metal at the underside of the hatch. The hardened alloy became softer as it approached its melting point, causing an increasingly dense shower of sparks to cascade to the deck. This continued until a three inch piece at the center of the disc fluttered and then fell away, striking the side of the tube in a burst of sparks.

"Shoot at the edges!" Bill shouted.

The men did so, and the hole grew until large enough to freely admit a man's arm.

"Cease fire!"

"Get back!" Morris shouted. "Watch out for shots coming out!"

Bill handed Rodgers a fragmentary grenade. "Throw it through the hole!"

"Be careful! Those edges are still hot!" Dresden said.

Rodgers cautiously stepped up to the underside of the sealed tube hatch, but a volley of pistol shots drove him back. He faced Bill with a worried expression.

"Here." Bill said, holding out his hand. Rodgers handed him the grenade, and Bill took it and pulled the pin. Then he put the grenade back into Rodger's hand and drew his pistol, pointing it at Rodgers' chest. "Now, throw it through the hole."

Rodgers stared at the grenade for a moment in astonishment, then ran to the hatch, jumped up, and tossed the frag through the glowing hole in the metal.

***

Cauthen stood over the hatch trying to get a bead on one of the mutineers. When the grenade flew up, it struck him in the chest and ricocheted back down next to the hole. Cauthen yelled and pushed it back into the hole and Sansbury covered it with a seat back.

***

Rodgers had not had time to get away from the hatch before the grenade fell back down. Bill and the others pressed themselves hard against the wall and behind storage cabinets as the grenade exploded, killing Rodgers instantly.

The concussion of the explosion in the narrow passageway deafened Dresden. Pressed against the door to the radio shack, he felt as if his head would cave in. He reached up to rub his aching ears and felt blood trickling out of his right ear. His face still stung from the concussion.

He leaned forward and looked down the passageway toward the hatch. Rodgers lay under it, the front of his uniform covered in blood. Dresden felt sick.

Bill went berserk, screaming and shouting and repeatedly shooting two pistols at the hole now covered up. "Come on, you bastards!"

The XO's voice sounded over the PA system, cutting through the engineer's frenzy. "Petty Officer Wilde, pick up on the nearest visicom. Petty Officer Wilde, pick up on the nearest visicom."

Bill stopped shooting. "Hey, screw you!"

"There's one in radio," Dresden offered, hoping now that the situation might still be resolved peacefully.

"I don't give a shit! Screw him!"

"Hold on, Bill," Morris said. "If we talk to him, maybe we can find out how strong they are. They might be ready to fall."

Bill gave no response. He walked over to the door to radio and tried to open it, but it was locked. He raised his leg and kicked the door hard with the bottom of his foot. With a loud snapping sound, the door flew open. He walked inside and went to the visicom, switching it on as the others followed him in.

Dresden could see the XO on the screen. Behind him stood a few enlisted men and an officer, but he could only see the uniforms not their faces. The XO looked confident and relaxed.

"Petty Officer Wilde. I order you and those with you to lay down your arms and surrender. You have committed mutiny, but if you surrender now, we will plead for leniency at the court-martial. This will be the last chance any of you will have to surrender."

Bill hesitated and Dresden began to hope that he would all just end it here, but it was not to be.

"You must be out of your friggin' mind! We have the ship and we have the crew. I order you to surrender."

The XO shook his head. "You know that's not going to happen." Fischer stared at Bill and shook his head. "Why are you doing this? What could you possibly hope to gain?"

"Our lives!" Bill spoke louder to address the others on the bridge. "Hey, did the XO tell you people about the virus on the station? It killed the entire crew! The boarding party surely has it now, and I think that they would just as soon wait to see if we all get it!"

"We don't know that anybody has it yet," Fischer insisted.

"So you'll just keep it a secret from the crew?"

"Listen, this is madness!" shouted the XO. "Where the hell do you think you'll go? Even if you did take the ship, the entire fleet would hunt you down. You'd have nowhere to hide!"

"We've got the whole friggin' star system!" Bill shouted.

Morris stepped up behind Wilde to be in sight of the visicom. "Listen, shipmates, we know what that message said that went out this afternoon. They want to quarantine us, but I'm telling you if we wait here, we're as good as dead. Join us now and give yourselves a chance to live."

"No one is joining you, Petty Officer Morris. And let me make this clear, you men are not taking this bridge, and you are not taking this ship." Fischer made eye contact with every man in the radio shack. "And I guarantee, I'll see to it personally that those of you left alive will see a court-marshal and execution."

The XO's words gave Dresden a chill. *These stakes are too high for someone only twenty years old. Bill is only seven years older and doesn't seem to care a bit. He just stands there glaring in arrogance at the XO. How could he escape from the fleet? The XO is right. This is madness.*

For the first time since the insurrection started Dresden began to see a way out. *It's so easy. I'm armed. All I have to do is kill Bill and maybe Morris. How many others standing here right now are wishing this was over? Maybe if I did it in front of the XO, they would be merciful on us. They'd understand.* Dresden armed his pistol and began to raise it.

"There are other ways to break you," Bill said. "I'm going back to main. You have until the time I get there to surrender, or the CHENG is dead." Bill switched off and abruptly walked out of radio. Everyone followed except for Dresden. *I could talk to the XO alone now.* He started to reach for the visicom but noticed Morris staring at him from the door. He hesitated, then left radio to join the others.

Chapter 25
"Checkmated"

Fischer sat down at the comms panel where Van Wert waited. "He says that-"

"I heard the conversation. Listen, you've got to make an offensive. Is there any way you can get to forward berthing? With more help you can probably retake the ship."

"We could try. What about Oki?"

Van Wert nervously rubbed his chin, then he shook his head. "We can't negotiate with them. We can't start bartering for people's lives. If Wilde knows we won't negotiate, he won't be able to use that against us."

Fischer looked away and shook his head slightly.

"I know," Van Wert said, "but we have no choice."

Bill's voice boomed from the visicom. "Fischer!"

The XO went to the visicom and saw Bill and the others in main control. In front of the camera, Fukunaga sat tied to a chair. Bill held a pistol to his head. Fischer tried to say something but words wouldn't come. Fukunaga looked at him, his eyes stoic.

"Well?" Bill asked.

Fischer could hear the pistol faintly humming and tried to conceal the quaking in his voice. "Bill, committing murder will solve nothing. Please let him go." *Oh, God, please don't let him do this!*

"I guess that means no," Bill said. He squeezed the trigger and a flash of light entered the chief engineer's head. It rocked violently to the left and then righted itself. Fukunaga closed his eyes tightly and then opened them, and for the first time in the thirteen months that he had known the chief engineer, Fischer saw profound fear in his eyes. Then the light that seemed to glow from behind the eyes diminished, and the head slumped forward. Oki Fukunaga, the chief engineer of the USS *Kestrel,* was dead.

A wave of nausea, hot with rage, swept over Fischer. He screamed, "You son of a bitch! You stupid son of a bitch! Do you realize-?"

"Let that show you how serious I am!" Bill shouted. "And I have two compartments full of men who will go next, one by one, until you surrender!" Bill switched off.

***

The first class engineering tech turned around from the visicom to face the others in main control. He looked at the dead man in the chair, revealing no emotion on his face whatsoever.

Dresden had always been afraid of Wild Bill, but now he felt mortal terror, nearly overcome with the desire to run away somewhere and hide.

"Well, that's that," Bill said. His tone carried a sense of satisfaction, as if he had just completed a minor task. "Let's get this carcass out of here and bring up another."

"Hold on, Bill," Morris said. "We can't just start killing off the crew."

"Why not?"

"Because we'll need them later to run the ship. Besides, if the XO didn't give up to save the CHENG, he's not going to give up to save some lousy crewmen. They're probably going to try something."

Bill shrugged. "Then we'll just go after them."

"I have an idea. With main, we control enough of the ship to leave. Let's disengage the mooring position sensor and get underway. Then we'll go to the ventilation transfer section in aux machinery and just cut off the life support to the bridge and DC Central. After they die off, we can get the crew to the bridge and navigate out of here. We'll be home free."

"Where will we go?" Snyder asked.

"Hell, where wouldn't we go? We have a warship! We'll head to the AlCent B frontier and just drop people off a few at a time. Then we'll ditch the ship and live happily ever after. They'll not find us in a million years!"

Bill started to speak, but Harper interrupted him. "What about the virus? Mac and Foley were on that station. What if they brought it back with them?"

143

No one spoke for a few moments, then Bill said, "Then we'll just put 'em off now. Get 'em in a boat and put 'em off."

"Let's do it before we get underway," Morris said. "Snyder and I will switch the ventilation. Why don't you guys round up Mac and Foley?"

"And Petey," Snyder said. "He was with them, too."

Bill nodded. He seemed to be getting excited again as the mutiny was nearing completion. "Pull air from the other sections that they have while you're at it. When they start choking, they'll start joining."

"Will do," Morris answered.

The group split up. Dresden wanted to go with Morris, but Bill motioned for him to descend the tube to the second deck. Reluctantly he went.

***

"He just killed him!" On the screen Fischer's face was a mixture of desperation, confusion, and rage. "Just like that! He just killed him!"

Ski had never seen the XO this way and it troubled him.

"Mind your bearing," Van Wert said, staring impassively at the screen.

Since the beginning of the crisis, the captain had been as tense as a steel trap, constantly shifting his weight from foot to foot and biting his thumbnail, but he never took his eyes off of the monitor. To Ski, he seemed like a caged lion, and the operations tech realized the enormous pressure and frustration that the captain must be under. His ship was being taken over, and he was powerless to stop it.

On the screen, Fischer took a couple of deep breaths and tried to calm down. He was being checkmated and he knew it. Ski began to regret the way that he had acted toward the officers. They were not fools. They were men of enormous responsibility, and they relied on the support of the crew assigned to them. They'd had little of that support.

"Listen to me, Paul," Van Wert said. "Millus and I have been reviewing the station doctor's data. He had isolated the virus. We tested ourselves and we definitely have it. All of us here probably have it. And most likely Foley and the others brought it back with them."

Van Wert paused, and in the silence, the news fell on Ski like an enormous weight. The faint hum of machinery in the station's central control room seemed to roar at him. *So I have it, too.*

Van Wert continued. "We cannot allow them to leave with the ship. If they contact even one civilized outpost, this disease will spread rapidly across both solar systems. Once it reaches the trade routes there'll be no stopping it. There is no way to know the extent of annihilation it will cause. We cannot let them leave."

Fischer stared at the screen and said nothing, his mind obviously lost in thought. Van Wert also said nothing, letting his words sink in until the XO understood the enormity of the situation.

Finally Fischer spoke. "The EDS?"

Van Wert nodded slowly. "If we have to, as a last resort. But tell them about it. Warn them. Let them know that they won't leave here alive."

Fischer nodded slightly. As Ski watched the conversation between the captain and his first officer, a heavy, sick feeling began to well up in his stomach. Most of the crew didn't know about the EDS, but because his job kept him in close proximity to the bridge, Ski knew only too well. The Emergency Destruct System was a series of explosive charges rigged at various locations around the ship that, when detonated, would rend the *Kestrel* into pieces. Designed to keep the ship from falling into enemy hands, the system was equipped with a timer that allowed the crew to abandon ship. *Would the XO really blow up the ship, killing the crew and stranding the boarding party? Maybe if Bill and the others realize that they can't escape, they'll give themselves up. Maybe they'll realize they can't win. Maybe...*

"Ventilation's cut off!" Cauthen said from behind the XO. The others on the bridge reached their hands up to feel the air at the vent. The XO dropped his hand and looked at Van Wert.

"Call them, Paul," Van Wert said slowly. "Tell them."

Fischer nodded and slowly stepped over to the visicom, out of sight to those watching on the monitor. Ski looked at Cauthen, holding his pistol barrel up, his face tense. He, too, deserved credit for his service on the ship. He was a good man. Cauthen turned his head and looked at Ski.

"Good luck, shipmate," Ski said.

Cauthen grunted, then smiled weakly. "Thanks," he mouthed silently.

"Man, this is bullshit!" Gradenko growled.

"What is?" Flores asked.

"This! Here we sit when all hell's breakin' loose over there. *That's* where we should be."

"Yes?" Millus said, clearly irritated. "Your partner over there is dead."

"Better to die honorably in action, sir, than to sit around and let some disease rot you."

No one answered him. His logic sounded reasonable, but Ski doubted that Cauthen would agree.

Chapter 26
"Banishment"

Bill, Harper, and Dresden walked up to the door to aft berthing. Jackson sat on a tool box with his pistol on his lap and didn't get up as the group approached.

"Get Foley and McElroy out here," Bill said.

Jackson stood up and looked into the compartment. Beyond the door, Dresden could see the men in the compartment sitting on the floor or in their bunks. They looked up as Jackson stuck his head through the door. "Foley! McElroy! Get out here!"

The men on the floor looked around behind them. A sound of movement came, but no one appeared. Bill became irritated and walked over to the door.

"Foley! McElroy! Get the hell out here, now!"

"Hold your damn horses!" Foley shouted.

"What did you-?" Bill stopped short, then stepped back from the door. Dresden walked over and looked inside. The men on the floor stood up to make way for Mac and Foley. The medic had his arm around the ship's serviceman and was helping him to walk through the narrow aisle between the bunks. Mac held his broken leg in its cast up off of the deck and hopped along on his good leg.

Dresden had forgotten about Mac's leg and apparently Bill had, too. As the two men made their way to the door, Dresden stuck his pistol into his belt and helped Mac across the door's high threshold. When they were through the door, they stood facing Bill.

"You two pick him up and carry him to the boat deck. We've got to move, now."

"Where are we going?" Foley asked.

"Back to the station."

"Uh-uh! No way, man!" Mac said, shaking his head. "I'm not going back there! Forget it!"

"You'll do whatever I damn well say!"

"Why are we going back there?" Foley asked.

Harper spoke. "Because we're leaving, and we don't want to take your virus with us."

"Shut up, Harper," Bill snapped.

Foley's face became incredulous. "Oh, my God. What happened to the XO and the other officers?"

"Don't worry about it."

"What's gonna happen to us?" Mac asked.

"Who cares?" Bill answered. "Now, pick him up and let's go!"

Foley grabbed Mac under the arms while Dresden picked up his feet into the zero-g, and the two started forward through the passageway.

Jackson leaned toward Bill and gave a happy, childlike smile. "Are we really going now?"

"In a few minutes."

"So the XO and them are taken care of?"

"In a little while. We're gonna suffocate them." Bill turned and followed the other four men forward.

When they reached the boat decks, Dresden put Mac's feet back on the deck, taking care not to jar his broken leg. Harper opened the hatch to the portside gig, the same boat that had been used the previous morning.

"Foley," Bill said. "Get down inside and we'll pass him to you."

"Bill, I need some things for him. If we don't have the EMPH it's going to take a lot longer for him to heal. I don't even have my medic's bag."

"There's stuff on the station you can use."

"Just let me take five minutes to go to sick bay and grab some pain killers and bandages and my bag. I'll come right back."

"No. Get in the friggin boat."

"Bill, I-"

Wild Bill quickly reached up and struck Foley in the temple with his pistol. The medic's head spun around to the right, and he stumbled trying to maintain his balance. A trickle of blood floated off toward the opposite wall.

"I'm not telling you again," Bill said. He pointed the pistol at Foley's chest.

Foley said no more. He wiped the oozing blood off his temple and wiped his hand on his pants. Then, without looking up at anyone, he walked over to the hatch and climbed down the ladder. To Dresden, he looked as if he had resigned himself to the situation. No matter what would happen, he still had his job to do.

Bill pointed to McElroy and said to Dresden, "Help lower him in. I'm going to get Petey."

Bill turned and walked forward. Dresden helped Mac to the edge of the hatch where Harper took his other arm. Below, Foley stood in the hatch, blood still oozing from his head. The two men lifted Mac up over the edge of the hatch, then lowered him down. Foley guided his feet, and when he was down far enough Mac grabbed the handles for himself. As Dresden let go, Mac looked up at him, his face scared, like an animal caught in a trap, and his eyes seemed to implore, "Why?" Waves of guilt began to sweep over Dresden, and he wondered again how he had gotten himself mixed up in this terrible situation.

"Go on," Harper snapped.

Mac looked down toward his feet and, with Foley's help, climbed down into the gig.

***

Petey sat on the edge of one of the bunks and looked over at Schroeder, still sitting on the floor between the bunks that held the dead crewmen. His forehead rested against his arms, which were folded against his knees. He seemed to be sleeping, for he hadn't looked up once.

In the passageway outside of the berthing compartment Petey heard Bill walk up. The big engineer stopped and talked to Ryan for a few minutes and Petey heard the voices but couldn't make out the words. He looked over and saw the men near the door straining to listen.

Bill stopped speaking and walked up to the door. He searched the room with his eyes until he saw Petey. He pointed to the navigator and said, "Come with me."

A fresh wave of dread washed over Petey, and he hesitated for a moment, not sure of what to do. He looked at the other men in the room, but they just stared silently back at him.

"Now!" Bill growled.

Petey stood up from the edge of the bunk and, as a man going to the gallows, began to walk slowly down the aisle to where the engineering technician stood, his great bulk eclipsing the light from the passageway. As Petey approached, Bill backed away from the door.

"Where am I going?" the navigator asked.

"He's sending you back to the station," whispered one of the men at the door. "I heard him tell Ryan."

"The station?" Petey hesitated.

"Yeah," another answered. "They're gonna leave anyone who was in the boarding party on the station."

"Run for it, Petey. Go out the forward scuttle."

"Don't try it," Bill said. He pressed the arm button on the pistol and it began to hum.

"What about my stuff?"

"Leave it, and come on."

Petey took a step forward and then remembered something. "My journal." He turned around and ran back to his locker. He opened the lock, grabbed the notebook, and locked it shut behind him before he ran back to the door where Bill stood glaring at him.

"I had to bring my journal," he said.

Bill said nothing, and the two men started down the passageway aft.

"Good luck. Pete!" yelled one of the men in the compartment.

Petey turned around to see his shipmates gathered at the door. He waved and tried to say something, but couldn't through his clenched throat, so he waved again and continued aft.

When they reached the boat deck, they saw Morris and Snyder standing over the portside hatch looking down. Dresden and Harper stood beside the wall. Morris looked up as Bill and Petey approached.

"Well, we cut the ventilation off," Morris said. "Is that the last of the boarding party?"

"Should be," Bill answered. He poked Petey in the ribs with a pistol. "Was there anyone else who came back with you?"

"Just Mac and Foley."

"Good. Get in the hatch."

Petey stepped over to the hatch and tossed his journal down inside. He looked around at the faces of the mutineers and saw no anger or compassion in any of them, except Dresden. He looked sad. Petey bent down and began climbing into the hatch.

At that moment Dresden sneezed. He took a deep breath and sneezed again, sniffing hard so that mucus could be heard.

Angrily, Harper pushed against Dresden's shoulder and stepped backward. A look of disgust on his face. "Shit, man! He's got it too!"

Dresden's face registered surprise. "No way! How the hell would I have gotten it?"

"You were with them earlier today on the mess decks," Snyder said.

"But… so was everybody!" Dresden looked around at the angry faces. "I've always had sinus trouble!"

"I've never seen it," Morris growled.

"And you were following us around all night." Bill said through clenched teeth. He raised his pistol and pointed it at Dresden's chest.

"Wait a minute! Please!" Dresden held up his arms in a futile effort to protect himself from the shot.

"Bill, hold on!" Petey shouted. "If he's sick, then send him with us! Please don't kill him!"

Wild Bill paused a moment. He was still pointing the pistol at Dresden.

"Please, Bill," Petey begged. "Just let him come with us."

Bill looked at Morris, who gave a slight nod. Then he said, "Hurry up before I change my mind."

Petey dropped down to the boat's deck, and Dresden quickly scrambled to the hatch. As he started to climb down, Bill kicked him in the side of the head. The force of the blow sent him bouncing against the hatch combing to the boat's deck where Petey helped to steady him.

"Are you all right?"

Dresden nodded. Then Petey stowed the ladder and shut the hatch while Dresden strapped himself onto a bench. Petey walked forward to the control console.

"You murdering slob," Mac said to Dresden. "This is all your fault!"

Dresden looked up at McElroy but said nothing.

"It's not going to make any difference, anyhow," Foley said. "If we've got it, then they're all dead, too."

Everyone sat quietly as Petey powered up the gig, but before he could disengage, a surge was felt from the *Kestrel*.

"What the hell was that?" Mac asked.

"They're getting underway," Petey answered. "Here we go."

He released the gig from the *Kestrel,* and the small craft fell away into space.

Chapter 27
"Trump Card"

Gradenko pointed past the huge window at the *Kestrel*. "Look! Look at the ship!"

"It's getting underway!" Wilson said.

Ski, Wilson, Flores, and Gradenko ran over to the window. Flores squinted as if to see more clearly. "What's that?"

"It's the gig," Ski answered. He walked back to the main console. "Captain, the gig is falling away from the ship."

Van Wert looked out of the window and then back at the screen. "Paul, what's going on there?"

Fischer stepped back in front of the monitor, his face desperate. "Main control has powered up the plant. We've tried to stop it, but they've overridden our systems. DeZurik and Wallsbrook went to the foreword equipment room to see if they can reroute the circuitry." Fischer took a deep breath. "I don't know what Wilde thinks he's doing. He won't be able to navigate."

Van Wert frowned. "Who was in the gig?"

A puzzled look came over Fischer face. He looked over at an indicator. "I have no idea."

"Have you spoken to them about the EDS?"

"I haven't been able to raise them."

"Call main. Tell them about it. And if they still don't back down, then…" The captain's words trailed off, as if searching for the right phrase. "Then you know what you have to do."

Fischer nodded, his face grim. "I understand."

"I'm sorry, Paul."

Fischer took a deep breath and exhaled slowly, trying to regain his composure. He rubbed his face with his hands and then said, "Don't be."

***

In main control, Bill sat in the chief engineer's seat in front of the large control and display panels, smiling in his self-satisfaction.

Jackson stood next to him while the rest of the men were scattered throughout the machinery spaces manually controlling the equipment. Bill spoke into his headset.

"Bring the Coulomb grids up to fifty percent."

"Aye, aye, Chief Engineer," came Morris' reply over the speaker.

Bill grinned, and Jackson patted him on the back.

"I know you're loving this."

"Hell, yeah. This is power, but it's only a taste. Soon I'll be captain."

"Total power over the entire ship." Jackson nodded. "Sweet."

"Hell of a way to get a promotion, eh?"

Jackson smiled. "I'll say. You sure know how to move up the ranks." He looked up at an atmospheric indicator for the bridge. "I wonder how long those bastards have got."

"I don't know, but it can't be too much longer."

A light flashed on the visicom indicating a call from the bridge. "Well, speak of the devil," Bill said. He switched on the visicom.

The XO's face appeared on the screen, stern and still very much in command. "Petty Officer Wilde, I order you to stop this ship immediately."

Jackson and Bill looked of each other and chuckled. *What an ass.* "How's it going up there Paul? Things getting a little stuffy?"

"Wilde, listen to me." Fischer held up a small, flat, rectangular electronic part, no bigger than the XO's palm. "This is a coded card that initiates the ship's Emergency Destruct System. Only the captain and I have these. The system is designed to keep the ship from falling into enemy hands." Fischer lowered the device. "It's confirmed that the captain and the boarding party have contracted the virus. That means that it's already on board, and we have been exposed to it. You probably have it now." Fischer lifted the card again and held it close to the screen. "I'm not going to let you spread this virus across the solar system. I'll blow the ship to pieces first."

Bill and Jackson looked at each other, then Bill folded his arms and said, "You gotta be friggin' kidding me. Is this the best you could come up with?" Bill leaned forward and put his face right up to the screen. "You don't scare me with all of this bullshit. I've never even heard of an Emergency Destruct System. To hell with you and your card."

"It looks like a music player to me." Jackson sneered.

Fischer clenched his teeth. "I mean it. You're not taking this ship away from here!" Fischer looked past Bill. "Let me speak to the others."

"My men are busy carrying out *my* orders. Go speak to your own men, while you still can." Bill reached up and shut off the visicom.

"Hey, what if he really does have a way to blow up the ship?" Jackson asked. "Do you think he would?"

"No way. He's just bluffing. But even if he isn't…" Bill called the power distribution room on the visicom and saw Snyder monitoring the equipment. "Hey, cut off all power to the bridge. Everything."

Snyder nodded and Bill sat back in the chair. "He ain't gonna blow up nothing now."

***

On the bridge the power to the all of the lighting and equipment panels went out. In the tomb-like blackness and stale air, Fischer felt a chill of dread pass over him. Death seemed to be standing behind him, breathing fear down his neck, paralyzing him. Then a small lamp came on at the other end of the navigation table. Cauthen's penlight pushed back the sense of fear and doom as it pushed back the dark.

In the dim light the XO could see the faces of all of the men staring at him, waiting to see what he would do next. He wanted to say something encouraging and heroic, but nothing came to mind. He sighed and said, "Well, it looks like-"

"Just do it, sir," Cauthen said.

Fischer, taken aback, looked around at everyone, but no one had even moved. Apparently weary from the prolonged fighting, they just wanted to get it over with.

"We're all dead anyway," Brown said. "We'll be suffocated within the hour."

"And the whole crew is doomed with that virus," Morrell said.

Fischer hesitated, then nodded slowly. He held his hand out toward Cauthen. "Let me have that light."

Cauthen handed the XO the penlight, and Fischer directed the beam to a small door in the overhead. He opened the panel and pressed the power button. The indicator glowed red and a small screen displayed. "Ready."

Fischer inserted the card and pressed his thumb against the small sensor pad. The screen displayed, "E.D.S. Initiated."

There was no alarm, no flashing lights, and no sound. The designers had reasoned that no one would be aboard when the system was activated. Besides, anyone left aboard would not realize what the alarms would mean anyway. Fischer looked around at the men. He wanted to say he was sorry, but somehow it just didn't seem proper.

Chapter 28
"Stranded"

As the men on the station waited for the XO to return, the screen went blank momentarily and then turned to static.

"Hey, hey," Wilson said, tapping the side of the set. He worked the controls for a few moments and then said, "We've lost the signal."

"They've stopped transmitting," Millus said.

"Why?" Flores asked.

"Main must have cut the power," Van Wert said.

"Does that mean that the EDS is disabled?" Ski asked.

Van Wert shook his head "It's on its own circuit that's powered by a battery."

"Then it's all over," Ski said.

No one answered him. All eyes turned to the window where the ship could be seen moving away. Being driven manually instead of with the computer operated bridge controls, the ship jerked and oscillated as it veered away from the station. The lack of grace and fluidity of motion made the *Kestrel* appear injured, broken. The gig powered down out of view toward the docking bay.

The *Kestrel* continued turning until only its stern faced the station. Ski saw a faint glow coming from deep inside the main engine nozzles and thought about the mutineers. *Where could they go? None of them knew how to navigate, and they were millions of miles from anywhere. Maybe if we can quickly get aboard the gig with our weapons, we could catch up to them. Surely another six armed men could tip the balance in the command's favor. Without the bridge's scanning instruments, they would be taken completely by surprise. If only-*

A blinding flash of light interrupted Ski's train of thought. The *Kestrel* instantly became a fireball, shooting burning fragments out in all directions. The large window shook as the expanding ball of hot vaporized metal hit the station. Several small burning pieces struck the window and melted into place. After a few moments, the fireball extinguished with nothing left in its place except several burning pieces streaking away into the background of stars.

Ski had stepped back when the explosion occurred, but now, in shock, he just stood before the window watching a single fragment burn a path away from the station. It continued for several moments until the flame of the burning metal went out, and the object disappeared into the blackness of space.

No one said anything. Although they had realized the possibility of the ship being destroyed, no one had believed that it would really happen. And now, even though it had already happened, it was still unbelievable. The ship and the entire crew were gone as if they'd never existed.

Petey's voice over the communicator broke the pall of silence. "Hey, can somebody open the barn door, please?"

Ski snapped back into reality. Almost as a delayed reaction he became consumed by a fear bordering on panic. He hadn't even thought about Petey, but he was alive! "He's on the gig!"

Everyone in the room ran down the stairs to the docking bay. At the docking bay control panel, Ensign Millus depressurized the room and opened the large door. Through a small window, Ski watched the gig floating gently inside. Petey piloted the craft toward the access door and set it down lightly on the floor. Millus closed the outer door and pressurized the bay again. When the green light came on above the door, Ski opened it and ran out to the ship's boat with the others following closely behind. The gig's side door opened, and Petey stepped out onto the floor. His uncombed hair and lack of socks told Ski that he had been awakened abruptly, but he had remembered his journal, now stuck into his belt.

"Hey, guys. I wish I could say I was glad to be back." He smiled warmly. "What happened out there?"

"The ship is gone, Petey," Wilson said.

"Yeah? Well, I heard them say they were leaving, but I didn't think they would blast off so close to the station."

Everyone looked at each other. Ski spoke. "No, buddy. The ship was destroyed. The XO used the EDS to keep Bill from leaving with it. He had no choice."

Petey looked down and his face contorted into a bitter frown as if he'd just chewed on an aspirin. "Why? Why would he kill the whole crew?"

"He had to, Peters," Van Wert answered. "The crew on this station was killed by a virus. We all have it, and you and Foley and Mac brought it back to the *Kestrel*. By this time the whole crew would have been infected."

Petey rubbed his face with both hands, then sighed. "I had prepared myself for being stranded here, but I had no idea."

"Hey, Petey. Give me a hand, will ya?"

Petey stepped back and turned around to face the door, and Ski saw Foley helping Mac approach the hatch. Dresden, who had been sitting on the bench, stood up and took Mac's elbow to offer support, but Mac violently snatched his arm away from his grasp.

"Hey! Keep your filthy hands off of me, you traitor!"

"I was just trying to help."

"I don't want your stinking help." Mac stepped through the door with Petey's help, quickly followed by Foley and then Dresden. Mac and Petey stepped forward to join the circle of men that had formed around the side of the gig. Foley backed away and left Dresden standing alone while the others stared at him.

"What do you think of our little passenger, Captain?" McElroy sneered.

Van Wert said nothing. He looked at Mac and then back at Dresden.

Mac continued. "He was one of them. He was one of the ones with Wild Bill who were taking the ship."

The captain's eyes seemed to bulge, and a look of subdued fury spread across his face. Ski had never seen Van Wert like this and it disturbed him. "Is this true?"

Dresden looked like a cornered animal, his face pale and frightened. "I… I didn't know…"

In a flash Van Wert's right fist darted forward and struck the engineering tech squarely in the mouth. Blood sprayed down over his shirt as he reeled backward, falling onto the ramp of the gig. He looked up, but didn't stand.

Van Wert stood still for a moment, staring at Dresden and quivering like a volcano about to blow, but then moved away toward the inner door of the docking bay. The others silently shuffled after him. Dresden went back inside the gig and sat down out of sight on one of the benches.

Petey sat down on the edge of the gig's ramp and put his head down, his hands covering his face. Ski walked over and placed a hand on his friend's shoulder.

"It'll be all right, Petey."

Petey looked up at Ski, his eyes wet with tears. "I was just there. I was with them all. And now you guys tell me that they're gone. They're blown up. Everyone we've known, and worked with, and lived with for the last year is gone. There were still injuries that needed our help. And they're gone. They're just gone."

Ski sat down on the ramp next to the navigator and stared down at the deck. In the shock of the vessel's destruction, and in his fear of the virus, he hadn't even considered the loss of so many young men who had deserved better than an untimely death. In his mind he saw Cauthen's face on the visicom screen, brave and determined and worried, and he felt his chest tighten.

"And now," Petey continued, "with this virus, we get to end up like the people on this station? I don't think I'm afraid to die, but I don't want to go out like that. Not like that."

Ski thought about the station crewman they'd found in the stateroom, and the images of Dr. Fredricks on the video log and shivered. *Maybe the Kestrel crew were the lucky ones after all.*

They sat quietly for a few moments, then Ski spoke. "The captain sent out a message to fleet headquarters. Maybe help can come from them."

"They better hurry," Petey replied. He took his inhaler out of his pocket and took a puff, holding the medicine in his lungs for several seconds before exhaling.

Ski looked at the inhaler and shivered again.

Chapter 29
"Midnight Parley"

Ski stood in the main control room of the space station at one of
the large windows, his face only inches away from the thick glass. He
watched the *Kestrel* as it completed its raggedy turn and began to move
away from the station. The outline of the ship stood out in stark relief
against the backdrop of limitless stars.

His mind raced as he watched the ship, torn with anguish
because he knew what would happen. He'd seen it three times before
and although he knew the precise moment, it always took him by
surprise.

The blinding flash of light startled him as the *Kestrel*
transformed into a fireball. Burning fragments scattered in all
directions, and the large window shook as the expanding ball of hot
vaporized metal struck the station. Then the fireball extinguished, and
all that remained were several large pieces of burning wreckage
streaking away.

Ski saw crewmembers flying away through space. Many of them
were still alive, kicking and flailing their arms wildly. Ski heard the
muffled bumps of men striking the glass of the station and bouncing off
and away into space.

A man in khakis, an officer, struck the window right in front of
Ski, and he recognized Lieutenant Fischer, the XO. The officer
remained on the window, lying prone across the glass looking in. His
face wore the same desperation that Ski had seen earlier during the
mutiny. The XO reached over to the edge of the glass where the seam
met the frame and began trying to dig through the seal with his fingers,
suffocating now in agony as he frantically tried to get inside.

Ski watched in despair. He knew he couldn't help him, and he
just wished that the XO would go away. But then his despair turned to
horror as the XO transformed into a hideous monster with huge teeth
and ears and still wearing khakis. Terrible claws began to virtually tear
out handfuls of glass and metal. Ski looked around the control room
and saw that he was alone. The monster was almost inside. He
screamed...

Ski woke up with a start, his heart pounding and the vivid image of the dream still fresh in his mind. He sat up and looked around the lounge. In the dim red glow of the nighttime circadian lighting, he saw the other crewmembers of the station boarding party still sleeping. Some were sitting in chairs or curled up on the sofas. Wilson lay on his back on a table snoring. In the corner of the room the control panel of one the Mind Sensory Expansion System machines glowed, and he could see the legs of the person inside.

He stood up from the recliner and walked out of the lounge into the hall. Here the quiet openness and silence brought a feeling of loneliness, and the entire station seemed to be asleep except for the distant rumble of the power plant. He paused to look at the closed doors of the staterooms where the station crewmembers lay dead and he shuddered inwardly. Then he walked over to the stairs and descended to the next level.

The lights here glowed red also, and Ski followed the short hall to the main control room. He stepped through the door and saw Van Wert standing at the large window, silhouetted against the stars and gaseous nebulae beyond. The captain leaned motionless against the rail staring out into infinity. Ski walked over to the window, his gentle footsteps echoing through the still room, and stood next to the CO.

Van Wert didn't acknowledge Ski's presence at all, but stood impassive, momentarily fogging the glass with each breath, his eyes wandering over the panorama of the universe beyond the glass. Ski stood next to him and also looked at the cold and uncaring stars.

"Couldn't sleep, Captain?" Ski asked.

Van Wert made no reply.

"It's hard to believe, isn't it, sir? That we're stranded here, I mean."

Van Wert grunted. "Yeah. I'll bet the RID's will have a hard time dealing with this, eh?"

Ski felt embarrassed by the captain's sarcastic tone, quoting a line from his own derisive song. *Maybe he wants to be alone.* He considered walking back to the lounge, but stayed. *I guess I deserved that.*

For the first time Ski began to contemplate the role, however minor, that he had played in fomenting the mutiny. *Could it be said that I contributed to the discontent that led to it? Is that what the captain is thinking?* A feeling of shame began to well up inside him, but before he could turn away, Van Wert took a deep breath.

"Belay that," he said, rubbing his face with his hands. "Yeah, I couldn't sleep." The captain brought his hands back to the railing and stared out of the window again.

Ski stood quietly for a moment. "Captain, I'm really sorry for what happened. I can only imagine how this feels for you."

Van Wert nodded. "Do you know what I feel the most?"

Ski shook his head.

"Betrayal. Raw betrayal. They abandoned me when I needed them the most."

"Not all of them, sir. Many were trapped, and others fought with the XO."

Van Wert nodded. "True. And I'll make sure Admiral Selig knows the name of everyone who did stay loyal." He chuckled bitterly. "That is, if we get back." He looked at Ski. "I guess I'd better leave a list."

Ski looked down at his hands on the rail. His stomach seemed to turn over at the captain's words.

Van Wert sighed. "But, you know, I've thought about it over and over, and I just can't figure out why they did it."

"I think Bill and the others were just looking for an excuse, and this virus gave them one."

"But, why? I bent over backwards for this crew. From the beginning I tried to build morale with everyone. I tried to make every man feel like a valued team member. I even pulled strings to get the best liberty ports. But whatever I did, I felt like I was banging my head against the wall."

Ski didn't know how to answer. He remembered when Van Wert had taken over as CO of the *Kestrel*. The ship, ranked twelve out of twelve, stood as the worst ship in the squadron. To take over command of a ship like that had been a daunting task.

But Van Wert had done well with the crew. In training, exercises, and the various fleet inspections, he'd pushed them hard, and they performed. And afterwards, or on patrol, he always had a ship's party or landed some good liberty for them. "Work hard, play hard" was his motto, and it had worked. The ship's ranking jumped to sixth place, and the crew came through a difficult combat situation with flying colors. But no one in the crew seemed to take account of that, not even Ski himself. If was as if the ship's ranking and rewards were expected, and murmuring and complaining came easier than pride and professionalism. The phrase "A bitching sailor is a happy sailor" didn't seem so cute now.

"It wasn't your fault, sir. The men got a bad attitude with Captain Donaldson. He was a pompous ass. He talked to the crew like they were a bunch of idiots, and his officers could do no wrong. No one respected him. That's why his service record got hacked. It was a gag, just to anger him. One for the road, sort of. But you're right about our attitude, captain. We had no excuse for how we acted. And Wild Bill and the others had no excuse to do what they did. I think most of the men would complain, but they would never dream of having a...a mutiny."

Van Wert nodded, his eyes still fixed on the stars beyond the window. Ski noticed his hands on the railing, alternately gripping tightly and relaxing, as he fought some inner turmoil. The CO sighed, then spoke in a voice barely above a whisper.

"I shouldn't have told Paul to blow the ship. I thought that if..." He shook his head slightly. "I thought that if he threatened it, they would back down." Van Wert looked down at his hands on the railing. "Maybe I should have just let them go."

Ski's heart grew heavy in his chest. It wasn't like the captain to confide in someone, especially an enlisted man. He tried to measure his words carefully. "You did the right thing, sir. They would have spread the virus to all parts of the Alpha Centauri system. Thousands, maybe tens of thousands, would have died. Bill and the others would have killed the officers anyway. It would have been a real mess. And then Fleet Headquarters and God-only-knows-who-else would have wanted to know why YOU didn't stop it." Ski paused. "You did the only thing you could have done."

Van Wert looked back out at the stars. "I hope so." Then he took a deep breath and looked at Ski. "Well, I guess you'd better try to get some more sleep. Tomorrow will be a busy day."

"Busy?"

"Yes. I've decided to break the group up into teams. We'll try to get the comms up and PM the equipment."

"Didn't you say there was a message sent out?"

"Yes. We won't get the reply because it will be encrypted, but maybe we'll hear something."

"Do you think they'll send someone?"

"Maybe."

"Do you think there's a vaccine?"

"I don't know. I don't think anyone has ever heard of this disease, but we can hope. They can do wonderful things with diseases these days."

Ski yawned. "Excuse me."

"You ought to lay back down."

"I think I will. Goodnight, Captain."

"Goodnight."

Ski turned and started walking toward the door.

"Ski?" the captain called to him.

"Yes, sir?"

"Thanks."

"Any time."

When Ski returned to the lounge, it appeared as if no one had even stirred. The MSES machine was still on, so he walked over to it and peered inside the booth. Behind the visor Gradenko's face twisted into a cruel grimace, and Ski wondered if the Gunner was having nightmares, also. He considered turning on one of the other machines for himself, but decided against it. He would go back to sleep on the sofa, and he didn't think he would have the dream again.

Chapter 30
"Die Like a Man"

The Viking longship plowed steadily through the three to four foot swells of the North Sea under a dark and overcast sky. Every fourth wave would crash against the hull showering cold spray over the oarsmen. The racing clouds overhead glowed from the light of an unseen moon. Gradenko stood at the bow with the ship's master looking over the dark English coastline, faintly visible between the black water and pale sky. The wind coming off the land carried the smell of smoke from the fireplaces of the village beyond the starboard bow. They were close now, and soon he would see the faint glow of the fires themselves before the ship would turn to shore. Gradenko licked his salt-sprayed lips in anticipation.

The rhythm of the oars splashing into the water and the steady throb of the drumbeat sounded like the immense heart of a mighty sea dragon. Above Gradenko, the dragon's wooden face craned back defiantly toward the sky. He looked astern and could hear the heart beats of the other dragons behind his ship, but he could not see them in the darkness.

The gunner felt a nudge at his shoulder and turned to where the ship's master pointed to the coastline. Faint points of orange light glowed through the trees, and the smell of wood fires intensified. The man chuckled and patted Gradenko on the back, his teeth grinning beneath the full red beard. He shouted to the man at the steer board to turn for the coast, and another man relayed the order to the other ships. The time had come to strike.

The ship began its turn toward the shore. Ahead in the darkness an estuary opened up just north of the village. The wind and waves calmed as the land seemed to draw around them, and Gradenko felt a rush of adrenaline. The element of surprise remained intact.

As the longship came to a rest in the soft mud of the bank, the oarsman lashed their oars and dressed for battle. Gradenko jumped over the bow of the ship to the bank, shield and sword in hand. Others followed, tramping up the firm mud to the gravel of the bank. Behind him the gunner heard the heavy press of the prows of the other ships as they came to rest against the mud. The muffled clank of steel and leather spread along the bank as the Vikings came ashore.

From the dark woods ahead came the sound of hoof beats. A rider galloping to warn the village! The element of surprise would be lost, but the resistance would heighten the excitement. The men began to pour from the longships and into the woods, yelling as they went. Gradenko gave a war cry and ran with them.

As they came upon the path the horseman had used, the hordes of Viking soldiers ran south along it until they came to the village. A group of hastily prepared Englishmen formed a line to meet the charge. Swords were drawn, and the melee began.

Gradenko met with a man who appeared to be in his forties. He carried an axe and swung at the gunner, but Gradenko ducked under the blow and brought his sword up into the man's abdomen. The man shrieked and dropped the axe before falling backward onto the ground. Gradenko roared his elation. This was real warfare, fighting at its most basic level. This battle at its essence was unlike shooting a blip on a scanner scope. He felt powerful and invincible. Now possessed with a lust for blood, he ran further into the village. All around him the shouts of the Vikings punctuated the screams of the terrified villagers and the cacophony of steel and wood and leather.

A man holding a pitchfork ran out from behind a small cottage. He stabbed Gradenko in the right arm and pain shot through him. The man kept pushing on the handle, trying to force the gunner off his balance. He grabbed his sword with his left hand and swung at the man, cutting into his neck. The man let go of the pitch fork handle and tried to staunch the flow of blood. Gradenko pulled the pitchfork out of his arm and dropped it, then buried the blade into the man's chest.

By now several of the thatched huts were ablaze, and the smoke filled his nostrils and stung his eyes. He let the man fall from his blade and onto the ground, and to his right he heard a young woman screaming. *Ah, yes! So that's part of the adventure, too!* He moved toward one of the huts but heard heavy hoof beats coming toward him. Gradenko looked to see an armor-clad rider bearing down on him, sword poised to swing. The flickering orange light of the fires danced across the knight's chain mail as the gunner turned to meet him.

The horse galloped closer, and the sword began to fall. Gradenko swung upwards to meet the blow, and the weapons clanged harshly. Gradenko's hand shuddered, but he had deflected the attack.

The horse ran on before turning around to make another pass. Gradenko charged forward and hacked at the knight's leg, severing it to the bone just above the knee. The knight screamed and chopped down at Gradenko, striking his helmet and driving the headband hard down on his head. Blinded momentarily by his helmet, he pointed his sword up at the knight and thrust forward. The point of the sword entered the knight's abdomen just under the ribs. The frightened horse bucked forward, and the knight fell off, hitting the ground hard. Gradenko stumbled back and loosened his helmet, then aimed his sword and ran the knight through again.

Gradenko stood upright and looked around. The sounds of the fighting had subsided, and an eruption of sparks rose into the air as one of the burning roofs caved in. He turned to look behind him and saw a young woman standing in the doorway of a hut, her face twisted with grief as she looked at the fallen knight. But then she noticed Gradenko, and with a gasp of fear, backed inside the door and slammed it shut.

Gradenko walked over to the door and kicked it down. Holding his sword in front of him he stepped inside. Against the far wall of the dimly lit room stood a family huddled together in fear. An older woman, apparently the mother, stood in front of several small children in a feeble attempt to protect them. The woman that Gradenko had seen now stood to the right of the mother. She was the oldest daughter, and her dark hair fell in front of her shoulders, framing a beautiful face. Gradenko stepped forward and thrust the sword between her and her mother, and drew the girl away from her family.

In fear, the mother shouted something to Gradenko. She was begging him to leave the girl alone. Gradenko lowered the sword and wrapped his left arm around the young woman's slender waist, drawing her to him. She writhed and squirmed, trying to break away from his grasp, but this only excited him further. His other arm wrapped around her back and pulled her to him. He could feel her breasts pressed against him as he kissed her neck.

Then he released her. As she stepped back in confusion, Gradenko took her by the hand and led her out of the hut. He led her back outside and into the smoke of the burning village. Coughing once, he turned and started back for the ship.

Before he could lead the girl ten steps, a sharp pain exploded in his back. He released her hand and turned around. Next to the hut stood an older man holding a bow. The girl ran over to the man and stood behind him as he fitted another arrow. Gradenko raised his sword and ran toward the man. He shot again, and the arrow penetrated the gunner's breastplate. The wind was knocked out of him and Gradenko staggered back. His consciousness went black as he fell to the ground.

"Yes!" Gradenko shouted. He tore off the goggles and earphones and jumped out of the booth. "Ha! Fantastic!"

"Shut up, man!" Wilson said. He rolled over onto his side facing away from the gunner.

Gradenko stood next to the MSES machine smiling broadly. Around him the other crewmembers were sleeping in the dark lounge. Only Ski remained awake on the sofa.

"Hey, man! Have you ever played the Nordic Rampage scenario?"

Ski smiled at the gunner's excitement. He held his finger to his lips. "Shh. Hold it down," Ski whispered. "No, I haven't. Is it good?"

"Oh, man! It's incredible!" Gradenko walked over and sat down on the sofa with Ski. "In this one, you're a Viking. I fought with these dudes and I rolled a knight! I had this gorgeous babe, and I was taking her back to the ship when her old man shot me in the back with an arrow!"

Ski laughed "No kidding!" Is that when you died?"

"Yeah. But I'm gonna go back," Gradenko said, sitting back. "Have you played any of the scenarios, yet?"

"Yes, I did. I went on an Indian safari, and I hunted for tiger from the back of an elephant."

"Yeah? That sounds like a good one, too."

"Oh, it was. I had this old smooth-bore monster gun. It was really great."

"What happened?"

"One of the other hunters was grabbed by a tiger and I had to shoot the tiger to save him."

"Did you do it?"

"Well, I was just about to squeeze the trigger when they came and got me for the, uh," Ski hesitated. "For what was going on the ship."

"Oh," Gradenko said. He and Ski sat quietly for a few minutes, each lost in his own thoughts. Then the gunner said, "This really sucks, doesn't it?"

Ski nodded. "Yes, it does."

"We're out here in the middle of nowhere, we don't even have the ship to go to. And we're all infected with this bug." Gradenko shook his head. "This really sucks. We're gonna buy it, just like the station crew."

"Well, the XO did send a message out."

"So? Didn't you see that log? These people died in about a week. No one's going to be able to get to us in time." Gradenko sighed. *Ski's being really cool. Maybe he'd understand.* "I'll tell you something. I'm not gonna die by some bug. You can bet on that."

Ski looked puzzled. "But you just said that we all are going to die here."

"That's right. But I'm not going to die by some stinking bug." He pointed to the MSES machine. "It's just like that scenario. If you have to die, then that's the way. Die in your boots, standing up, like a man. Not sick in bed."

"You don't mean suicide, do you?"

"No," said the gunner. "I mean dying like a man."

Ski woke up the next morning to a nudge and a smile from Petey. He could smell breakfast and heard conversation and an occasional laugh coming from the dining area.

"Come on, buddy. We've got to go to quarters in fifteen minutes."

"What time is it?" Ski asked as he sat up and stretched.

"Almost nine."

"We're going to have quarters at nine o'clock?"

"Yeah. The captain let everyone sleep in a little."

That was nice. Ski stood up and stretched his legs and back, sore from sleeping upright on the sofa. He looked around and saw Gradenko sleeping on the opposite end of the same couch. "What about him?"

"He asked me to wake him up when it was time for quarters. I woke you up early because I thought you might want breakfast."

"Thanks."

They walked to the dining area where the rest of the boarding party, except for the captain and Mr. Millus, sat at the table finishing breakfast. Dresden sat quietly by himself while everyone else sat together as if they were on the ship. The mood seemed somber, except for Flores and Wilson, who talked excitedly and laughed. Their jovial attitude irritated Ski.

"What's got them so happy?" he asked Petey.

"I don't know. I still can't get over last night."

"Me, neither. How soon they forget."

As Ski and Petey stepped up to the table, Ski saw Flores with a plate of pancakes and sausage. It looked and smelled good so he went to the server console and ordered the same as Petey sat down at the table. When he got his food, he sat down next to the navigator.

"Up all late bunks," Wilson said. "Hey, sleepy head, you and Gradenko sure looked cute lying together on that couch. I wish I would've had my camera."

Ski nodded and gave a weak smile. He thought for some witty reply, but nothing came to mind, so the conversation continued on without him. Lost in his own thoughts, he wondered what lay ahead for them all. He finished eating just as Mr. Millus' voice came over the P.A. speaker.

"Quarters, Quarters. All hands to quarters for muster, instruction and inspection. Quarters will be held in the Main Control Room."

"Oh give me break," Mac said, as everyone stood up.

"You've already got one on your leg," Flores replied.

"Maybe he should pass the word, 'All remaining hands to quarters,'" Wilson said.

Ski got up and put his plate in the wash chute, "Hey, guys," Mac said. "As soon as I'm on my feet again, I'll make us up some real food on the conventional galley equipment."

Ski nodded but said nothing. As he walked out of the lounge he said to Petey. "I wish I had a tooth brush."

"I wish you had one, too," Wilson said, smiling and slapping Ski on the back.

When they reached the Main Control room, the men formed two ranks under the large communications panel. Foley pulled up a chair for Mac to sit on, and Gradenko came in last, rubbing his eyes. Mr. Millus, who had been sitting at the main control panel, stood up and walked over to face them. The captain stood at the windows looking at the stars, and Ski wondered if he had been there all night.

"Meanwhile back in the jungle…" Mac said.

As Ensign Millus stepped up to the group the men quieted down. Then the captain walked over to join them, and the "Old Man" looked tired. He didn't usually join the men at quarters, but today's muster would be a combination of officer's call and quarters.

"Attention on deck," Millus said, and the men came to attention.

"At ease," Van Wert said. He made eye contact with each man as he spoke, his tone slow and reserved. "It would be redundant for me to explain what happened last night since we all saw what happened. But no matter how we may feel about the loss of our shipmates and the *Kestrel*, it is important for us right now to prepare for what may be ahead. We are facing what is in essence a combat situation. But we must fight it with weapons that are contained within ourselves."

"Our immune systems," Foley said.

"Exactly. First, I want to get the station in ship shape. It's our home for now and we'll have to take care of it. We'll work to get the comms up and do all of the scheduled maintenance. I know that we're not familiar with the equipment, but we'll do what we can. Then we'll take it easy. Like any virus, the only thing we can do is ride it out. We'll try to conserve our energy so our bodies will have the best chance of fighting it off. Are there any questions?"

"We really don't have a chance, do we, sir?" McElroy asked.

Van Wert frowned. "This is a deadly virus, to be sure, but I believe it can be fought off. Remember the man we found in the lifeboat? He had no symptoms whatsoever. We will each be given vitamin boosters, and we'll get lots of rest. That's the best thing we can do."

"What about fleet headquarters?" Flores asked. "Somebody said that a message was sent out."

"There was a comm sent out yesterday evening, but it may take a little while to respond. The message explained our situation, and I'm sure the admiral will send help, but we must take care of ourselves until help arrives. Any other questions?" Van Wert waited a moment, then said, "All right, then, here are the assignments." He nodded to Millus who read off of a pocket pad.

"Flores and Dresden will go with me to check out the power plant. Kowalski, Peters and Gradenko will go to the comm unit and do what needs to be done to get it operational again. Wilson, you are to check out the computer system. See if there's anything that needs to be done on the computer to get the comms ready." He turned to Van Wert. "And what about Foley sir?"

Van Wert looked at the medic. "Foley, I want you to join me in sick bay." Foley nodded.

"Hey, what about me?" Mac asked, waving his hand.

Ski saw a slight smile appear on the captain's face. *Good old Mac.*

"You can keep Wilson company," Van Wert said. "Okay, if anyone needs help just pick up on the intercom and call. Work safely. Dismissed."

The group broke up and headed to their various stations.

Chapter 32
"Work Details"

Five minutes later, Ski, Petey and Gradenko exited the elevator at the communications unit level. Everything seemed eerily quiet, as on the day before.

"Didn't we just do this yesterday?" Petey said as they stepped into the hallway.

"Yep. Déjà-vu, all over again," Ski said, pointing down the hallway. "If I'm not mistaken, it was the transmitter that was down, not the receiver. So let's look at that first."

"I don't know what they expect we'll accomplish," Gradenko said. "None of us are comms techs."

"No, but we are technicians and there's a lot commonality between this stuff and our own equipment."

"At least in the electronics," Petey added.

The three walked down the hall to the coolant pump room where one of the pumps still lay in pieces on the floor, tools scattered around it. The other remained intact, though not running. Ski walked over to the control panel, and the other two stood next to the pump.

"Let's give it a try." He pushed the "reset" button on the touch screen, and the failure light went out. Then he pressed the "start" button. With a sudden whirring sound the motor started and the meter showed a flow. He joined Petey and Gradenko.

***

Wilson sat in the chair at the console in the main control room, and Mac sat in a chair at the end of the panel with his leg propped up. Wilson rapidly paged through various screens of the station's computer system, occasionally typing on the keyboard.

"Man, oh man. This is one complex system," he said.

"How's that?"

"Well," Wilson said, typing at the keyboard, "the whole station is interfaced into this access terminal. I can control every system from here, unless overridden at the local control stations. But mainly I can just monitor everything from here."

"I thought they said this station was old."

"The station is, but they've apparently upgraded the control systems recently."

"Fascinating," Mac said, glancing up at the high ceiling. Technology never his forte, he had dropped out of electronics school early in his enlistment and had given up on technical rates altogether. He liked cooking, but he wasn't cooking now. *I'm gonna be bored outta my skull. I can see it now.* "Meanwhile, back in the jungle…" he said.

"Hmm?" Wilson said, without looking up from the screen.

"Hey, man. Isn't there anything I can do to help you?"

"Umm," Wilson grunted, still typing vigorously. He stopped for a minute but kept his eyes on the screen. "Uh. What?"

"I said, is there anything I can do to help you? Can I punch some buttons?"

"No. You're here for moral support."

"Well, how can I boost your morale?"

"I don't know." Wilson chuckled and grinned. "Why don't you sing a song?"

"I don't think I can sing a song, but I'll tell a joke. Did I tell you the one about the mining prospector?"

"I don't think so."

"Well, here it goes. This mining prospector walks into a saloon on AlCent B1 and he orders a whiskey-"

"Is this the one with the baboon?" Wilson asked.

"Yeah. Have you heard it?"

"Yes."

"Okay. There once was a salesman traveling through the rural districts. He stepped out of a diner and saw this three-legged chicken-"

"I heard that one, too," Wilson said, eyes still focused on the screen.

Mac sighed. "All right. Let's see. Here's one. A guy walks into a bar and sees a robot for a bartender. The robot welcomes him, then asks him what his I.Q. is. The guy says-"

"I heard that one, too," Wilson said. "Sorry, Mac."

"How have you heard all these jokes?"

"We've been on the same cruise for three months. Do you want to just tell them, and I'll laugh at the right part?"

"No."

"Why don't you try and make one up?"

"Why don't I just try and take a nap?"

Wilson grinned and shook his head as Mac leaned his chair back against a console and closed his eyes.

***

Millus, Flores, and Dresden stood in front of the large monitoring panel in the control booth of the power plant. Mr. Millus held one of the station's flat, transparent computer pads, and read from a screen titled "Preventative Maintenance Schedule." The control panel shared many features of the one on the *Kestrel,* but, like everything else on the station, spread out over a larger area. Dresden studied the features of an auxiliary panel.

"Visually verify gauge pressure on header. If panel reading does not correspond to actual gauge pressure, then go to calibration section 9-C, now," Millus read aloud. He traced his finger across the schematic diagram located above the window. "Here's the header. So…" He pointed out of the window." It's probably over-"

"There," Flores said. He pointed along the left wall of the power plant." I see it against the wall there, sir."

"Very well. Now one of us has to go read the gauge."

Flores grabbed a pair of hearing protection earphones and shoved them at Dresden. "Here you go, dirt bag. Turn-to."

Dresden hadn't been listening. Confused, he took the earphones and looked at Mr. Millus. Then he looked up at the schematic diagram. Header?

"Out there," Flores snapped. "Against the wall, the big pipe that says fifteen hundred pounds, one-five-oh-oh-pound sign."

"Tell us what the gauge pressure is," Millus said.

Dresden nodded. He put on the earphones and reached for the door handle.

"You aren't back yet?" Flores said. "Go on now, dammit! Get hot!"

Dresden quickly stepped out of the door and onto the floor of the power plant. The heat seemed to choke him as he started his way over to the left wall. The earphones couldn't keep out all of the whining, rumbling noises as he skirted his way around machinery and piping, and his shirt became wet with sweat by the time he reached the header.

Dresden looked up. The header ran along the ceiling some fifteen feet above the floor with the gauge attached directly to the pipe. For a moment he contemplated giving them a made-up number but decided against it. He would have to climb up the other pipes, and he had no gloves. Reaching toward a bracket for support, he began his climb.

The heavily insulated pipes still felt hot to the touch, and as he climbed, he found it necessary to brace himself against a pipe hanger periodically to cool his hands. He continued until he came to the bottom of a small platform where he could see the dial face of the gauge. The gravity here felt noticeably weaker than it did at floor level. The gauge read fourteen ninety-five, and he started back down.

As he neared the floor again, Dresden mistakenly put his right hand on an exposed hot pipe flange. Jerking back, he saw two red marks on the heel of his hand, which began to hurt badly.

Dresden jumped down and walked quickly back to the control booth, grateful to be back in the cool once again.

"Fourteen ninety-five."

"What took you so long?" Flores snapped.

"It was up near the ceiling."

"Why didn't you use the rolling scaffold out there?" asked Mr. Millus, frowning.

Dresden looked out the window. "I didn't see it."

"We've got a lot to do. Don't waste any more time. I don't want this to take all day."

Dresden felt his heart sink. "Yes, sir." He rubbed his throbbing hand.

Millus looked at his hand, "What happened?"

"I accidentally touched a flange."

"Oh, poor baby. Do you want me to kiss it?" Flores jeered.

Despair and guilt kept Dresden's anger in check. He dropped his hand to his side.

"Do you need Foley to look at that?" Millus asked.

"No, sir. It'll be all right."

"Are you sure?"

Dresden nodded. He looked down at the floor and wished they would send him out again.

"Very well. Go to Stirling number one and read the gauge there," Millus said. "And use the scaffold if you need it."

Dresden nodded and walked out of the door into the heat again.

***

"Oh, my God," said Foley, looking at the opened files, scattered papers, and microscope slides strewn about the station doctor's desk. "Where do we begin?"

"Over here." Van Wert walked over to the desk and started straightening the files. "I did some of this yesterday."

"What exactly are we looking for, Captain?"

Van Wert stood up from the desk. As he spoke he counted on his fingers. "Well, first, I want to know exactly what the symptoms are and how long before they begin. This way we can know what to expect. Second, I want to know the order in which the crewmen died and their jobs. Also their medical histories. This may give as a clue as to what might make us more resistant to the virus. Thirdly, I want to see if the station's doctor had come up with anything that would slow the virus' progress, such as vitamins, or some medication, anything. And lastly, I want to see if there was anything that the doctor might have missed that we can do. He might not have been at his best being inundated by sick crewmen as well as being sick himself."

Foley nodded slowly as he looked around the room. He tried to appear compliant, but his face failed to conceal a feeling of futility. The medic had never been the complaining type, but Van Wert wondered if he would protest now. "Sir, between you and I alone, don't you think that all of this effort could only be valiant at best? In the end it's going to be a toss-up as to who makes it and who doesn't."

178

Van Wert had thought about that same question since they first realized the presence of the virus. He rethought it again, now, and still came to the same conclusion. "I can't deny that this situation looks hopeless. But I just can't stop thinking that there might be a slight hope. And no matter how slim the chance of our survival might be, if there is a hope, then we've got to do everything in our power to preserve it."

Foley conceded with a nod. "You're right, sir." He looked around the cluttered sick bay. "So, do you want to work together, or shall we work in two different areas?"

"Well, since you have the medical background, why don't you go over the doctor's journal and all of the information about the virus? I'll draw up a chart of the crewmen in the order they died. I'll also show where they worked and anything else that might have affected how fast the virus overtook them. We might glean something from that."

"All right."

The two men began to sift through and separate the pile of papers. After a few moments, Van Wert looked at the medic and said, "By the way, Doc, thanks for trying."

Foley shrugged. "It's my butt, too."

Chapter 33
"Station Doctor's Log"

In the coolant pump room of the transmitter unit, the three men knelt down and held their hands on the pump.

"No, see, it's vibrating too much," Gradenko said.

"Maybe that's the way it always runs," Petey offered.

"No. These bearings are fried."

"It feels like it's getting hotter," Ski said. He removed his hand and walked over to the control panel. The indicator showed the pump running at the top end of the heat range, and it had only been running for ten minutes. Soon it would go into the red and automatically shut down. Gradenko and Petey also stood up from the pump.

"Go ahead and shut it off," Gradenko said. "It's not gonna run."

Ski did so, and the pump made a slight rattling sound as it slowed to a stop. He walked away from the panel and joined Petey and Gradenko, who stood looking at the puzzle of pump parts that lay scattered across the floor.

"We'll have to rebuild this one and get it on line," Gradenko said.

"Do you know how?" Ski asked.

"Nope."

"You knew that the bearings in the other one were fried," Petey said.

"Yeah, but that doesn't mean I can rebuild a pump. I know enough about them to know that I don't know enough."

"Who would know?" Ski asked.

"Probably Flores."

"Well, we better call the captain and have him send Flores. I think he wanted this system up today if we could manage it."

***

Dresden extended the scaffold platform all the way to the ceiling. As he rose, the oven-like heat forced him to breathe in short, shallow breaths, and his face began to tingle. He read the gauge and pressed the down button, then crouched as low as possible while the scaffold inched its way back to the floor. This was the sixth time he'd checked a gauge reading, and the almost constant exposure to the heat had drained all of his strength. He felt his legs quivering as the scaffold touched the bottom. He would tell Flores to do the next one.

As he walked to the door he bolstered himself for the inevitable confrontation. He had hoped that Flores would volunteer at some point, but he never would. Now it didn't matter. Dresden knew himself, and he knew he needed to cool off.

He stepped inside the cool control booth and saw Millus talking to the captain on the intercom.

"Does it matter who?" the ensign asked.

"No," Van Wert replied. "Just so long as he can fix a pump."

"Aye, aye. He's on his way." The screen went blank and Millus turned to the two men.

"Do you want me to go, sir?" Flores asked.

"No. I think Dresden needs a break from the heat." He pointed to the young engineering tech. "Go to the comms unit and see Petty Officer Kowalski. They need you to help fix a pump."

Excellent. Dresden nodded and left the booth quickly, afraid the officer might change his mind.

He exited the elevator on the main floor and headed for the lounge. His sweat-soaked shirt in the cool air of the hallway gave him a chill. He got a cold drink from the machine and sat down on a sofa to rest.

Fifteen minutes later he stepped into the coolant pump room, still holding the drink in his right hand. His shirt was almost dry. Gradenko looked up from a toolbox as Dresden came in, and a look of disgust spread across his face. He was alone.

"Did they send you to fix this pump?"

Dresden nodded.

"Well, what the hell took you so long to come up here?"

"They just told me," he lied.

"Can you rebuild this pump?"

Dresden looked at the pile of parts. "Rebuild?"

"Yeah."

"What's wrong with this other one?"

"It's fried."

Dresden walked over to the pile of parts, and a feeling of uneasiness rose up in him. He had never been allowed to do a pump, or anything, by himself before. He was about to say no when he remembered the PM checks in the Power Plant.

"Can you do it?"

"Uh, yeah. Let me see what parts they have around here," he said as he went to the parts cabinet.

***

"Captain," Foley said, reading from a computer pad, "the journal says that the first symptoms appeared on the second day of exposure to the virus."

Van Wert stepped over while Foley paraphrased the entry. "Day nineteen. Power technician Powalie reported to sick bay with a persistent cough. Symptomatic of a bronchial infection he had one month previous. The doctor prescribed antibiotics in the usual dosage and scheduled a follow up for him five days later."

"I'm glad you can read all of these abbreviations," Van Wert said.

"They teach us that in corpsman school."

"So it was on the second day. But the doctor said it was something Powalie already had and gave him antibiotics."

"That's true. But three days later…" Foley scrolled down to the next page. "Powalie came back saying that he was much worse, and the doctor said he put him on bed rest and fluids. That's when he realized that he had a virus. He said it seemed that he was coughing up actual lung tissue."

"That's the melting lungs symptom he wrote about."

"Yes, sir."

"When did he die?"

Foley scrolled forward. "In the early morning of the seventh day."

"Do you think there's a connection to his earlier infection?"

182

"Absolutely. I think that the previous infection made him more susceptible to the virus. It seems to attack the respiratory system primarily."

Van Wert nodded. "Who were the next two to report sick?"

"Um." Foley scanned the journal. "Matsuda and Randolph. They reported on the twenty-first day, the fourth day of exposure. And the next day Fredricks reported. On that day, the doctor went around to everyone to see how they were. He says that there were some who still had no symptoms. He also said that some of the men were alarmed because they found out the correlation between the markings on the alien capsule and the ruined civilization on AlCent B2. Someone had read the speculation that the ancient people on that planet were wiped out by an epidemic, and they were scared. He wrote, 'I tried to tell them that there was no proof of this, but they seemed convinced. I, too, am concerned about the possibility. The station manager has already retired for the night, so I will speak to him about this tomorrow. Incidentally I am also showing symptoms of the virus.'"

"Does he say anything about fighting it?" Van Wert asked.

"Not yet. It seems that it took a few days to dawn on them that they might have an epidemic looming. But the next entry says, 'The station manager agrees that this must be the same virus as the one that destroyed the ancient civilization on AlCent B2. I will begin isolating the virus immediately. My problem is that this takes time, and I am needed to care for the sick crewmen. Powalie is in critical condition. I have put him on oxygen. He doesn't respond to the standard treatments. I, too, am feeling weak with fever, but there is no time to lose.'"

"And that's on the sixth day?" Van Wert asked.

"Yes. Uh, let me see. He says that Powalie died and that half of the crew is sick. The last entry in the medical journal was written on the twenty-sixth day, the ninth day of exposure. I guess he was too ill to keep it up. And the last entry in the station log was on the thirtieth day, so the thirteenth day of exposure."

Van Wert nodded. *Not very encouraging. Maybe there is no chance.* "Okay, let's go over the symptoms again. Fever, sometimes high fever, persistent cough with lots of phlegm, body aches, and swollen lymph nodes causing painful joints. Did all of them die of the lungs melting?"

"No. Matsuda died with a runaway fever."

Van Wert shook his head. "All right. I'll start on my chart. You keep looking for something that the doctor tried or wanted to try."

***

As Dresden unwrapped the new bearings, he noticed Ski and Petey step into the room from the hall. Gradenko stood at a locker fooling around with some tools.

"Well, receiver unit area checks out," Ski said. "Now all we need is this equipment." He stepped over to Dresden. "Did they send you to fix the pump?"

Dresden nodded as he arranged the parts on the bench.

"How long do you think it will take?"

"About an hour or so."

"Well, then, I'm going to go down to get some coffee."

"That's a good idea," Gradenko said. He put down the tools and walked over to where Ski stood. Petey walked over to the bench.

"Are you coming, Pete?" Ski asked.

"No, go ahead. I'll stay up here to lend a hand."

"Suit yourself." Ski and Gradenko left the room.

Dresden worked in silence. Petey helped the Engineering tech put the pump shaft into the padded vice and then set up the induction bearing heater. Dresden inserted the first bearing and set the temperature at two hundred and seventy degrees. Then, as they stood waiting for the bearing to heat up, Petey spoke.

"How are you doing, buddy?"

Dresden shrugged. He leaned up against the bench and looked at the floor.

"Remember, this is your friend Petey. If you feel like you want to talk to someone, you know I'm here."

Dresden nodded. "Thanks."

"How did everything go down in the power plant?"

Dresden sighed and raised his head, looking off in the distance.

"You know," he said, "I can take everyone being mad at me. I understand it, and I guess I deserve it. But of all people, I can't believe Flores is acting that way now. He's running his mouth more than

184

anyone else." Dresden looked right Petey. "And if he was on the *Kestrel* last night, he would have been knocking people down to join with Bill."

"I know. He was in thick with that group."

"You're damn right he was. And now he's kissing up to Mr. Millus as if they were long lost pals."

They listened to the buzzing of the bearing heater, then Petey spoke, his voice gentle and inoffensive.

"How did you get tangled up in that crowd, Big D? They're not your type."

Dresden looked away at the floor again and sighed.

"I don't know. I never did feel like I belonged with them, but I wanted to. Even though Bill was always a jerk to me, the Snipes always had gallows camaraderie. They always said everyone was out to get us. We were on our own and had to take care of ourselves. They made it seem true at the time, but now I see it was just bullshit."

"Bill used that mentality to get the loyalty of the E.T.'s back aft, and most of the guys went for it."

Dresden nodded.

"Given the circumstances, it probably could have happened to anyone."

"I doubt it. Just anyone who was dumb enough to get suckered into that way of thinking."

"Not really. Looking back I see how he did it. He used the same method that the fleet uses in boot camp. They break you down and then raise you in their own way."

"I guess." Dresden thought about all of the men who were killed and shuddered. *I should have known better.* "Petey, I am really sorry for what happened on the ship. When we heard about the virus, I was afraid, and everything that Bill had said about the captain seemed true. I was afraid of catching it, and it seemed like a good idea to just leave. I had no idea that it would have gone this far. And when I did realize it, I wanted to stop it. I really did. But by then it was too late. The whole mess was out of control." Dresden gestured around the room. "And now here I am. The ship is gone, the crew is dead, and I'm probably going to die of the virus anyway."

Petey patted Dresden on the shoulder. "Come on, buddy. You can't do anything about the past. But one thing is for sure, you are alive right now. And no matter what happens, you have a chance to do something good." Petey pointed to the pump. Then he looked right into Dresden's eyes. "You have another chance to show them who you really are, to show them the real you."

Dresden nodded. He was about to speak when the tone on the bearing heater sounded. He put his gloves on and went back to work.

Chapter 34
"Evening Assessment"

By late that afternoon, most of the assigned work on the station had been completed, so the crew gathered in the dining area of the lounge at five o'clock, the same time dinner had been served on the *Kestrel*. McElroy insisted that they all sit down and he would take their orders.

"Everyone has worked so hard," he told them, in a poorly-done French accent. "So now I will work for you."

He hobbled from man to man carrying a hand-held computer pad. "I punch the order in here, and then le garçon Petey brings the food from the server console to the table. Voila!"

"Hey," Millus said, grinning, "now this is more like it. What do you think, Flores?"

"Feels like I'm in the wardroom, sir," Flores said.

Van Wert laughed.

"Hey, Mac," Wilson called. "How do you say, 'Meanwhile, back in the jungle…' in French?"

Mac looked to Ski for the answer.

"Uh, Je ne sais pas," Ski replied.

Mac turned back to Wilson. "Je ne sais pas."

Everyone laughed.

"And now, monsieur Ski, what would you like to order?"

"I think I would like to try the chicken. How is it prepared?"

"Ah, good choice, sir. It is finger sized portions of breast meat, lightly breaded and quick fried to a golden perfection. May I suggest a dash of basil to be added in the preparation?"

"Can you do that?"

"Oui, oui! I have been playing with the machine all afternoon!"

"Ah, very good, then. But not too heavy."

"As you wish. Garçon!" Mac tapped the computer screen and nodded to Petey. "Tout suite! And go light on the basil." He leaned over to Ski again. "And to drink, monsieur?"

"Est-ce que ce possible pour moi avoir le vin blanc avec mon poulet?"

"Come again?"

"Could I have some white wine?"

"I must ask le capitaine." He turned to Van Wert who was seated at the head of the table. "Captain, may we serve wine?"

"By all means."

A cheer rose from the table.

"White wine, it is! Magnifique!"

The scene continued until all were served. Then the captain addressed them while they ate.

"I've been hearing good things about the work that went on today. Wilson, how did you and Mac do?"

"Well, sir," Wilson said, "most of the time I was learning the system. But I did check out the comms system, and I'll be ready to start up tomorrow."

"Good."

"Oh, by the way, Captain," Mac said, "please don't put me with Wilson tomorrow. If I'm to sit and do nothing, then at least I should go to sleep somewhere."

"You slept today!" Wilson said.

"Where would you like to be?" Van Wert asked.

"Here in the galley. Maybe I could throw something homemade together for the guys."

"Cinnamon rolls!" Gradenko said.

"That sounds like a good idea," Van Wert said. "And speaking of the comm system, I saw you guys got the cooling pump running again."

"Yes," Ski said, "although we were dead in space until Dresden came up. He became our lead man for rebuilding the pump, then installing it and aligning it to the motor."

"What do you think of engineering tech work?"

"As a bystander, it seemed very slow and tedious, but I suppose it's just the meticulous nature of the work."

"The more meticulous you are, the longer the equipment will run," Flores said.

Ski nodded.

"It gives you a greater appreciation for the ETs' work, doesn't it?" Millus asked.

"Yes, it does," Ski agreed.

"When I got up there," Van Wert said, "you said it had been running for about an hour, right?"

The comms team nodded, and Petey slapped Dresden on the back.

"D looked a little nervous when we hit the switch."

"Good," the captain said. "Then we'll be ready for a full load test tomorrow." He nodded his head toward Millus. "What about our engineering team below? How did you make out?"

"We completed all of the backlogged preventative maintenance checks, then went on to complete the ones that were currently due. The plant's in excellent shape."

"Good. A casualty in the power plant is the last thing we need right now." He took a bite and smiled. It pleased him that Flores worked well with the officer. *Probably the lack of Wilde Bill's influence, as well as the sobering effect of recent events. Still, I'm glad for it.*

"What about you, Captain?" Gradenko asked. "Were you and Doc able to make any headway in the medical office?"

Van Wert exchanged a glance with Doc. *So much to say, but none of it encouraging.*

"You can tell us straight, sir," Wilson said.

Van Wert could feel all eyes on him. "Well, there's not much to tell at this time. I was making a chart of the station crewmembers, when they first showed symptoms, and how long it took them to succumb. I was hoping to see a pattern connected to their workstations. For instance, if it took the engineering people longer to…longer for the virus to take effect, then that might give us a clue as how we may stave off…the more severe symptoms."

"Was there a pattern?" Gradenko asked.

"It's still inconclusive. I've got to keep looking at it."

"What about the people in the lifeboats?" Ski asked. "One of them had no symptoms at all."

"That's true. The only thing that we know about them is that none of them had ever seen the doctor about having symptoms of the virus, and that they had left on the eighth day of exposure. But I'm still looking. I know there's a connection with that one person in particular. There's got to be."

"What were you doing, Doc?" Gradenko asked.

"I was going over the station doctor's journal, trying to see if he'd come up with any ideas on how to fight it. Before he got too sick, I mean."

"And?" Wilson asked.

"And he'd mentioned gene therapy and vector transduction, but said he had neither the skills nor the equipment on the station to do it."

"So we're screwed," Gradenko said.

"Not necessarily," Van Wert said. "We sent out a message to Fleet Headquarters last night. If the station doctor knew of a cure but didn't have access to it here, then maybe the admiral can bring something. Meanwhile we take care of ourselves and minimize the symptoms. That is our duty, now. We'll be doing a lot more resting from here out."

"What about the water?" Petey asked.

"What about it?" Flores asked.

"This station's got to have a water reclamation system like on the *Kestrel*. If this virus is being collected out of the air with the moisture from our breath, then aren't we taking in higher concentrations of virus microbes when we drink?"

"No," Millus said. "After passing through two layers of filters, the water is fed into a catalytic oxidation reactor which incinerates any bacteria or viruses. The water we drink from the reclamation is purer than anything you'd drink at home."

"Well," Gradenko said, "what if the reclamation cleaned all of the virus microbes out of the air before we got here? We'd be free of it right now."

Van Wert shook his head. "Yesterday, Mr. Millus and I tested samples from our blood, and we both have it already. Every one of us was exposed to the virus whenever we were near the bodies of the station crew, or was around someone who had been. Rest is what we need now to fight it."

Van Wert looked around at each of the men. Some were lost in thought as they stared down at the table. Others studied their water glass carefully.

"And speaking of rest, I need help to remove the bodies from the cabins and staterooms after dinner. This way we wouldn't have to sleep in here. If we're going to be on this station for a few days, we may as well be comfortable."

The men looked around the table at each other, as if waiting for someone else to speak. The cook finally broke the silence.

"I'm sorry, Captain," Mac said, "but I'm not going to sleep in those rooms, even if we removed the bodies. Those cabins give me the creeps."

"Yeah, man. They were even using one of them as a morgue."

Van Wert looked around the table. "Does everyone feel that way?"

Everyone agreed, nodding their heads or saying so out loud

"Come on, men," Mr. Millus said. "It won't be so bad. And it would be nice to have a bed to sleep on."

Van Wert tapped Millus' arm and shook his head slightly. Then he said to the crew. "All right. But let's see if we can find some blankets or some pads to lay on. That'll be better than nothing."

The crew agreed. Then Wilson suggested watching a movie. "They came out here only a month ago. Let's see what they have."

Chapter 35
"Station Sextant"

Ski sat through the first fifteen minutes of the movie, a police action story that took place on colonial Mars, but could not get interested in it. He had noticed the captain leaving shortly after it started and contemplated following but decided against it. He didn't feel like company, and the captain probably didn't want any either.

He wandered downstairs and ended up in the Main Control Room. As he walked over to the large windows, he unconsciously looked out for the *Kestrel*, but the vast field of unblinking stars remained conspicuously void of any ship, and a pang of loneliness gripped him. So he wandered back to the main console and looked at the blank screen where the station log had played the day before. He still remembered the last entry, the hopeless words from a man gasping like a fish out of water, and he tried to resist the urge to watch it again, but the log seemed like some kind of bizarre oracle of his own future. Almost against his will, he switched on the computer and touched the keys that Wilson had used the day before.

VIDEO LOG INITIALIZING.

The screen went blank for a moment, then read,

SELECT OPTION:
NEW ENTRY,
AUGMENT ENTRY,
LATE ENTRY,
REVIEW.

Ski touched, REVIEW.

TO? FROM? ENTRY NUMBER (BY DAY)?

Ski typed, First Entry to End.

192

The screen went blank, and then Doctor Fredricks, the station manager, appeared. He looked so happy and easy-going, just as Ski had remembered him from the university. He had been so easy to talk with and so willing to share his knowledge with Ski.

"Uh," Fredricks said, a smile showing through the close trimmed beard, "are we on here?" He tapped the camera. "Oh, yes, good. Well, here we are, day one of our 'on crew' stretch. Turnover Preventative Maintenance went well. Everything is functioning normally. As usual, most of us...."

As Ski watched the image, he felt sorry for the station manager. He seemed happy and confident and totally unaware of the disaster that loomed before him. At one time, Ski had been the same way, but unlike Fredricks, he now knew what lay ahead. As he continued to watch each log entry, a profound feeling of loneliness pressed down on him, as if a large stone rested heavily on his chest.

Ski knew that he should switch the log off, but he couldn't stop himself. He watched the train of events from business as usual on the station, to the retrieval of the object, to the start of the illness and the abandonment by the ones who left in the lifeboats, and then the procession of names of those who died. As the last entry played he heard an inhaler discharge and a deep breath. Ski turned around to see Petey standing behind him.

The navigator exhaled. "Hey, buddy, why are you watching this stuff?"

Ski sighed. "I don't know."

Petey patted Ski's shoulder. "Come on with me. I've found something that I think will interest you."

"What is it?"

"Just come on."

Ski stood up and followed Petey out of the door and into the elevator.

"I found this a little while ago. You know how I love to explore."

Ski nodded. "I thought you were watching the movie."

Petey shrugged. "I couldn't get into it."

They rode past the lounge deck up to the communications pod, and Petey led Ski down the hall to a small ladder that hung from an open hatch in the ceiling. Motioning for Ski to follow, he climbed the ladder and disappeared through the hatch. Ski followed him up into a low tunnel that led to a room similar to the navigational equipment room on the *Kestrel*. A large sextant stood at the end of the room surrounded by a seven-foot diameter glass sphere enclosing the wall and roof on the transmitter side of the station.

"What do you think?" Petey asked. "It's the station's optical positioning equipment."

"Pretty cool. It's a lot bigger that the *Kestrel's*."

"Yeah, it is. Come here and look at this."

Ski walked over to the device and turned to look where Petey pointed. Through the glass, Ski could see the huge dish antennae receiver behind the sextant. It blanked out most of the sky. Above it he could see the carpet of stars that made up the Milky Way. He also noticed small clouds of bluish colored gas backlit by the stars beyond them. Once again a feeling of tranquility began to settle over him. The stars, serene in their heavenly places, calmed him and filled him with peace.

"This equipment does a lot more than the one we had on the ship," Petey said. "Here, step aside and watch this."

Ski stepped back and watched as Petey worked the keyboard on the hand held control box. The sextant's telescope slewed down until it rested parallel with the deck. "This thing is essentially a large telescope on a computer directed, precision aligned mount. Right now I've got it synced to the AlCent B's Central Port Facility that this station transmits to. This is how you direct the beam to its exact destination."

"You say it's a large telescope?"

"Yes, it is." Petey turned a video monitor around toward Ski and touched the screen. An electronic image came on of a long cylindrical object with many odd shaped modules sticking out of it. At the far end, a huge cone extended out from the hull designed for the collection of interstellar hydrogen. At the near end stood a large rocket nozzle surrounded by enormous tanks, each one studded with solar panels and various sized dish antennae. Although it had undergone extensive modification, it's origin as an interstellar space ark remained obvious.

"The old *Fu Sang*," Ski said. "Have you been there?"

"Not since the conversion," Petey said. "I was hoping we'd get to go there on this trip."

"Me, too. We were out here long enough to get there and back." Ski studied the interstellar vessel turned space station and remembered the stories of how those who'd left earth had vowed never to talk about the home planet as a way to ward off melancholy and homesickness. Then, as they approached the Alpha Centauri system, broke their vow as a way to encourage their space-born children and/or grandchildren to leave the only home they'd ever known to explore the new found planets. Ski marveled at the telescope's ability to make out any details at this distance.

"What did your grandparents do aboard the *Fu Sang?*" he asked the navigator.

"Hydroponics," Petey said. "Later on AlCent A2 they always kept a garden at their house. Natural born farmers. How about yours?"

"Waste reclamation," Ski said with a grimace of embarrassment. "Not very glamorous."

"No, but critical on a multigenerational journey. What did they do on AlCent A2?"

"They retired right after they got there. My grandfather pushed my dad to go to school, and he got into the real estate and development business." Ski studied the Central Port Facility carefully. "Imagine. There are kids being born right now who've never been in space, much less lived in space. All they know is planetary living."

"Like our great-grandparents."

Ski nodded. "Is it possible to view it optically?"

"Yeah. Right here." Petey opened a small cover on the end of the telescope opposite the objective lens and pointed to it. "Have a look. It should be pointed right at it."

Ski leaned over to peer into the eyepiece. Most of the background stars were lost in the glare of Alpha Centauri B, but he could make out one tiny speck of light at the center of the field of view. "Wow. Sure is small."

"No image processing."

"What is that tiny star to the left of the Port Facility?"

He backed away from the eyepiece to give Petey room to look. "I believe that's AlCent B3."

"That's the one I hear is the gem of the system, right?"

"Yep. And I'll bet you there'll be a fight over it before settlement starts."

Ski nodded. "Can we see Earth with this?"

"Absolutely," Petey said. He backed away from the eyepiece and touched the screen on the hand held control box. The telescope slewed up and came to rest in a nearly vertical position. The navigator knelt down and peered into the eyepiece. "Ahh. Here, look at this."

Ski bent down to the eyepiece and fine-tuned the focus until a bright, yellowish star became clearly visible. There was no twinkle, as there is in a planetary atmosphere, but still it seemed to burn like a steady fire. "The cradle of the human race. I wonder if they're still proud of us and what we've been doing out here."

"I would think so," Petey said. "Do you want to see Sirius? It's a radiant blue, although not as bright as it is from on Earth."

"No," Ski said, "let me see a galaxy."

"Okay. I'll find one for you."

Ski stood up and watched as Petey moved the telescope around. *What a pro.* "You really know your astronomy, don't you?"

"Yeah, I love it."

"Can I ask you something?"

"Sure."

"How do you reconcile your knowledge of the universe with your belief in God? Most cosmologists deny the existence of Him."

"That doesn't mean He can't exist."

"I know. But they deny Him because of what they know about the universe."

Petey made some fine adjustments to the telescope, then turned to Ski, his expression thoughtful. "Their knowledge of the universe rules out His existence because they wish it to be that way. If one has an open mind to all things, even the things of God, then one finds that everything declares His existence. Knowledge of the universe and knowledge of the Almighty go hand in hand, each one enhances the other."

"But might it be said that your belief in God is just wishful thinking, too. How is your belief in God different from their lack of belief?"

"Because when you open your heart to Him, He makes Himself known to you. He touches you in the inner most parts of your soul and then you cannot deny Him. His is the small, still voice that comforts you and guides you. That's why, despite all of the attempts over the centuries to banish him from the hearts and minds of people, each new generation that comes along seeks Him out. A least part of the new generation does."

"Can He save us from this mess here?"

"Yes, He can."

"But, will He?"

"I can't know. He has set everything into motion and many things that happen proceed as we influence them. He intervenes here and there, but I think that mostly it's a matter of time and chance. To me, it doesn't matter if I die here, or somewhere else, wherever it happens, I'll go to Him, to be with Him, and to be a part of Him."

Ski nodded. "Do you think we'll die here?"

"I don't know. The Book of Ecclesiastes, written by Solomon, says, 'For man also knows not his time: as the fishes that are taken in an evil net, and as the birds that are caught in the snare; so are the sons of men snared in an evil time, when it falls suddenly upon them.'"

"How did you memorize all of that?"

"It just kind of stuck with me."

"So do you think that there is nothing we can do?"

"Oh, no! That passage refers to how bad things happen to us, like this virus. But we should do what we can to overcome it."

Ski nodded and sat quietly for a moment, then said, "I always thought that, as a general rule, people are taken in death when they finally reach a level of understanding. Sometimes they are taken too soon, or they lag behind for a long time, like you said, time and chance. But for most of us, I think we stay around until we reach certain knowledge, like a lesson to be learned, and then we're off to a higher existence. Does that make sense?"

Petey nodded. "Yeah, it does. I sometimes think about that when I see good people die young, and seemingly bad people live on for a long time."

"Let every man in mankind's frailty consider his last day; and let none presume on his good fortune until he finds life, at his death, a memory without pain," Ski said and smiled. "Sophocles."

Petey nodded and smiled, too. "Good words."

Chapter 36
"First Symptoms"

Van Wert pushed back from the breakfast table and wiped his mouth. Then he spoke to the rest of the crew as they finished eating.

"This morning, as soon as we're all done here, I'd like to bring the comms online. Millus and Flores, I want you both in the power plant to adjust the power output to meet the new load. Gradenko and Dresden, I want you two in the coolant pump room to monitor the equipment there. Ski, you will switch on the amplifier and transmitter from the comms control panel. And Petey, I want you at the optical positioner to finalize the beam's alignment. Everyone else can watch from main control. Any questions?"

There were none.

"Very well. Let's get to our stations."

Ten minutes later, the captain stood behind the communications console in the Main Control Room with Wilson, Foley, and Mac seated nearby. He picked up the intercom mic and spoke into it.

"Millus?"

"Ready and standing by, Captain."

"Peters?"

"It's right on the money, sir."

"Ski?"

"Everything's ready to energize, Captain."

"Very well. Throw it."

Van Wert watched the big board as Ski energized the equipment. The various points of the diagram lit up in succession until it reached the transmitter. Then an image of a beam appeared, signifying that the amplified tachyon transmission wave was being sent onto its destination. Wilson and Mac gave each other a high five.

"Yes!" the systems tech said.

Van Wert studied the power plant status board. The plant took the load smoothly, and everything was running as normal. He spoke into the intercom again. "All right. Everything looks good. Now commence holiday routine."

"Thank you, sir!" Mac said.

"Not that you earned it," Wilson said with a grin.

"Help me up, will you? And get me to one of those MSES machines before they're all occupied."

Wilson helped the cook up, and they headed for the elevator with Foley and the captain trailing behind.

"So, what now, sir?" Foley asked.

"I'm going to the doctor's office to continue my diggings."

"Need some help?"

"No. Take the day off. I'll join up later." He looked up at the indicator and saw that the elevator seemed stuck at the top floor. *Probably the guys are trying to all cram in at once. Come on fellas. Someone can take the steps.*

Finally the elevator began to descend, but instead of the expected stop at the lounge level, it continued straight to the Main Control level. The elevator door opened, and Petey stepped out, patting his chest and trying to speak. His eyes seemed to bulge, and his mouth gaped as he tried to gulp air. Ski and Gradenko supported him by the arms.

"Doc!" Ski said. "Petey's having an asthma attack!"

Foley pushed Gradenko out of the way and pulled Petey back inside. "Let's get him to sickbay."

"I'll meet you there," Van Wert said, and ran for the steps, ascending two at a time. He reached the top as the elevator door opened again and followed the three into the doctor's exam room. He helped get Petey onto the table as Doc prepared a nebulizer treatment. "What happened?"

Ski gestured toward his own chest. "He has asthma."

"All right, but-"

"Excuse me." Foley stepped forward holding the nebulizer and held it out to the navigator. Petey grabbed the bubbling, vaporous pipe and put the end in his mouth. "Inhale normally."

"What is that?" the captain asked.

"It's a bronchodilator to open his airways," Foley answered. He faced Petey. "You've been on the peace pipe before, haven't you?"

Still inhaling the vapors, Petey nodded sheepishly.

"How long have you had this?" Van Wert asked.

"He's always had it," Ski answered, "but I've never seen it get like this."

Foley put a stethoscope to his ears and placed the diaphragm to Petey's back. "Deep breaths now."

Petey took a deep breath and coughed hard. Foley listened to his lungs in several places, then removed to stethoscope and said simply, "Hmmm."

"What does that mean?" Ski asked.

"What do you mean, 'he's always had it?'"

Ensign Millus stepped into the exam room. "What's going on? I heard Peters was sick."

"Asthma attack," Van Wert said.

Petey removed the nebulizer from his mouth. "It's starting to clear up now, sir."

"Asthma?" Millus said.

"Yes, sir. Apparently he's had it for a while," Foley said.

Van Wert looked at Peters. "How long?"

"Since I was a little kid. But I can usually keep it under control with my inhaler."

"Why would you keep something like that a secret?"

"Yeah," Millus said. "They'd let you out of the service for a condition like that."

"That's why he kept it to himself," Ski said.

"Usually it doesn't bother me until we've been out on patrol for a while and the air gets stale. But I've been fine on the station. I woke up a little tight and it rapidly got worse."

"Where's your inhaler?" Foley asked.

"It ran out and I left my spare one on the ship."

"You boogerhead!" Ski said, smiling. "You remembered to bring your star journal but forgot to an extra puffer!"

Petey grinned and shrugged as he continued breathing in the vapor.

Van Wert sighed and turned to Foley. "Can we get another inhaler for him?"

"Probably, sir. I'll have to check the station's medical supplies. I can probably give him steroids, too." He turned to Petey. "Have you taken steroids for this?"

Petey nodded yes.

Foley spoke to Van Wert. "They take about twenty-four hours to kick in, but they usually work well."

"They do," Petey said.

Foley held an electronic thermometer against his forehead until it beeped. Foley read the indicator. "He's got a fever."

"All right," the captain said, "I want you to rest, do you hear me? You can go lie down in the first cabin."

Petey raised his eyebrows, and Ski seemed to read his mind.

"But what about the…?"

"The first cabin is empty," Van Wert said. "We'll have to remove the crewmen from the other rooms to have more bed space. Millus and I will do it. Can I get you two to help? I'd rather not bother the others with it right now."

Ski and Foley nodded.

"Good. Thanks."

"But where can we put them?" Millus asked.

"How about in the lifeboats?" Foley suggested. "We can open the docking bay to space and the cold will preserve them."

"Good idea." Van Wert nodded. "Ski, help him get settled and then come back here, all right?"

Ski nodded.

Van Wert pointed his finger at Peters and his voice stern but not cross. "And no more scares, please. I'd like to know about these things beforehand."

Petey smiled. "Yes, sir." He handed the peace pipe to Foley and hopped off the table. Then he followed Ski out of the exam room.

Foley waited until they were out of earshot, then said, "I believe that's the start of it, Captain."

"But that was an asthma attack."

"Yes, but he's got a fever, and I heard fluid in his lungs. The fluid caused the asthma attack. Patients with asthma are more susceptible to respiratory ailments than most people are."

"Why wasn't this in his medical record?"

Foley shrugged. "He probably went to a civilian doctor for treatment."

"What can we do?"

"Well, the steroids will keep the asthma attacks away, but I can't do anything about the virus. The only thing I can do is to try to keep the fluid from building up."

Van Wert nodded. "Do what you can. As soon as Ski returns, we'll start clearing out the cabins."

"Yes, sir," Foley said. "And the sooner the better. I'm sure the symptoms will start showing up soon."

"When will the *Kestrel's* radio message reach home?" Millus asked.

"Already has," Van Wert replied. He sighed deeply and looked at the other two men. "And so it begins."

Chapter 37
"Message in a Bottle"

An hour and a quarter later, Ski and Millus carried the last corpse across the docking bay floor, taking care to skirt around the splash of vomit Ski had deposited there on the first trip. They had all been wearing dust masks in an attempt to keep out the horrific smell, and Ski also wore a towel around his face, but it wasn't enough.

The captain, Doc, and Dresden stepped out of the way of the lifeboat door as Millus and Ski approached, ducking low under the entrance. Millus backed carefully past the stack of bodies, but as Ski came aboard he stumbled and lost his grip on the bed sheet. The corpse fell against the deck with a thud, and a stab of anguish went through Ski's heart. He took it up again, and the two laid it carefully on the pile before retreating from the makeshift morgue. As they stepped out, Dresden and Van Wert lifted the door into place and latched it shut.

Without a word the five men walked to the interior entrance of the docking bay and waited as Millus closed the door and depressurized the space. Only then did they uncover their faces, but Ski could still smell traces of the decay lingering in the air.

Millus turned to the captain. "What's next?"

"Well, first, we need to turn the mattresses over and put new sheets on the beds."

"We've also got to get rid of the smell in those rooms, sir," Ski said. "No one's going to sleep in them like that."

"That's true." Van Wert rubbed his chin. "Can we increase the ventilation to the rooms?"

"I believe so," Millus answered.

"I can get some disinfectant for the floors," Foley said.

Van Wert nodded. "Good. We'll swab the floors with disinfectant and air out the rooms. Once that's done I think they'll be better received."

***

Ski listened to the sounds of clinking silverware at the table as he halfheartedly picked at his lunch. No one spoke a word. News of Petey's attack had gotten around, a fresh reminder of their fate, and as the men arrived for the meal a somber mood descended over the lunch table like a fog.

The captain finished his meal first, putting down his fork with a clang against the plate. He cleared his throat, breaking the thoughtful silence. "I think by now everyone knows about what happened to Petey. His asthmatic condition makes him more susceptible to respiratory illnesses that you or I would be, but Doc tells me that they have medications on board that can keep it under control. Right, Doc?"

Foley nodded in agreement.

"How are you doing now, Petey?" Van Wert asked.

"I'm still a little tight, but otherwise okay."

"Good," Van Wert. His voice tried to be lighted-hearted. "So we're not all going to die tomorrow."

"Just the day after tomorrow," Wilson said. Everyone at the table remained quiet.

"That's not true," Foley said. "Petey's condition just accelerated the symptoms. That's all."

"Well, so what? The end result will be the same," Wilson said. "With all due respect, Captain, no pep talk will change what's ahead for us." He dropped his fork and stared down at his plate.

Van Wert drew a breath as if to say something, but he thought better of it.

"Did you and Doc find anything significant in the medical notes, Captain?" Petey asked. "I understand you were making a chart."

Van Wert hesitated a moment before speaking. "Uh, yes. I made a chart of all the station's crew and when they died, but there was no real pattern to it. I was hoping that there would be some correlation between how long they survived and their occupation, but there was none that I could see." He glanced over to Foley. "Doc?"

Foley took a deep breath. "This corona virus is a lot like the influenza virus on Earth. It is basically a strand of RNA covered by a lipid envelope which is studded with two kinds of spikes. It periodically will change the configuration of its spikes to elude the antibodies. But unlike influenza, which must merge with another virus to produce a new strain, this virus is able to radically alter the surface spikes without the advent of the different virus. It does it by itself, and therefore always keeps one step ahead of the immune system."

"What the hell does that mean?" Flores asked.

"It means we're screwed," Wilson said.

Foley slammed his fist down on the table. "Dammit! What the hell do you want from us? We're doing everything we can! It takes a long time just to learn about this thing!"

No one replied. Ski could almost feel the tension tingling on his skin. "Is there any way to know how long it takes?"

"It's different for everybody," Foley replied.

"Well, what makes it different?"

"That's what the captain was trying to find out. So far the only factor seems to be how strong one's immune system is."

Ski looked around the table and realized that, like himself, no one had eaten much. From deep inside came a surge of panic, and he felt trapped here with nowhere to run.

"I'm going to send out another message right after lunch, to make sure headquarters knows our situation," the captain said. "Our only chance is to try to ride it out as long as we can until help arrives. We got to keep rested so our bodies can concentrate on fighting the virus."

"What will headquarters do? No one's ever heard of this virus," Wilson asked, his tone gentle now.

Van Wert glanced at Foley. "Doc?"

Folly stared at the table as he spoke. "I don't know," Doc said, "maybe gene therapy or some kind of vaccine."

"But anything they might bring won't help us if we're dead," Van Wert said. "So let's stay healthy for as long as we can, and that means rest."

With that the conversation seemed to be over, and everyone drifted silently back to their own thoughts.

***

After lunch Ski watched as Gradenko went right back to MSES machines and sat down in one. Flores walked over to him.

"Hey, man, come on. You've been hogging that one all morning."

"So what? There're two others," Gradenko said.

"Yeah, but we've got to keep sharing those to give everyone a chance. You've been playing this one over and over again."

Gradenko nodded. "Let me play just one game, and I'll get off."

Flores looked at the control screen. "All right, but I'll be watching you."

Gradenko nodded and gave thumbs up.

Flores looked at Wilson who was setting up another booth. "Are you still doing those girlie programs?"

"Yeah. I'm up to nineteen women. I might as well go out with a bang."

"Damn, man. We're supposed to be resting."

Wilson smiled and donned the equipment.

Ski stood up and took his and Petey's trays to the recycle disposal chute, then said, "Well, Petey, what do you want to do this afternoon?"

"I don't know. I'm feeling kind of tired. I think I'll just go lay down."

Ski nodded. "All right. Maybe I'll go sit with you for a while."

"You don't have to do that."

Ski gestured to the station around him. "What the hell else am I going to do?"

Petey nodded and the two headed for the door, but as they got to the cabin Petey looked at Ski.

"Hey, buddy, if you don't mind, I think I'll probably just take a nap. I really feel tired."

"All right," Ski said. "I'll come back later."

"Could you give me one favor?"

"Sure."

"Would you go to the optical positioning room and get my star journal for me? I don't feel like climbing that ladder."

Ski patted the navigator on the shoulder.

"Sure, Pete. I'll bring it down for you when I'll drop by later."

"Thanks, buddy." Then the navigator turned and went straight to bed.

***

In the Main Control Room, Van Wert stood next to the comms panel as Millus set up the radio transceiver. Then he stood up from the panel and looked at the captain.

"All right, it's ready. All you've got to do is press the screen here and speak. Your words will be printed on this screen so you can edit them. When you're finished, we'll transmit the message. I've got it going out on all the main frequencies."

"Good. I'd also like to insert it into the beam comms. You can do that, right?"

"Sure."

"Then that's what we'll do. If the Central Port Facility relays it back to AlCent A2 right away, it might even get there before the radio transmission."

"Very likely."

Van Wert leaned forward and gathered his thoughts, then he pushed the button on the screen and spoke. "Any station, any station. This is Lieutenant Commander James Van Wert of the USS *Kestrel*, transmitting from communications relay station CR3. This is an urgent request for assistance. The crew of this relay station has been killed by a deadly virus. The USS *Kestrel* has been destroyed. A small number of her crew are aboard the station and have also been infected with the virus. Anyone receiving this message is urged to contact Admiral Selig at Fleet Headquarters on AlCent A2 as soon as possible. At this transmission, we are in our third day of exposure to the virus."

Van Wert watched the screen as the last words appeared. He read the message over, and then added, "Please help us. End of transmission." He released the switch and stood upright. "Okay let's send it."

Millus stood over the keyboard and typed in some commands. "Okay it's going out on all the frequencies…now. I'll have it repeat at regular intervals. Next…"

He changed screens and accessed the beam comms where a graphic showed the communications traffic as it flowed through the comms systems. He selected some commands and said, "Information flow will stop here and…" He selected another command, "message insertion scheduled."

They watched as Van Wert's message rode the flow like a bottle in a river. It flowed to the transmitter end and disappeared.

"That's that."

Van Wert nodded. "Now, I want to make an entry into the station log. We need to let whoever finds it know what happened here."

Millus nodded and stepped over to the video log console.

"Just in case," Van Wert said, and gave a lop-sided smile.

Millus nodded again.

***

Ski wandered into the lounge where Ensign Millus, McElroy, and Foley were setting up a card game. Dresden sat on one of the sofas with a computer pad in his hand, and all three MSES machines were occupied.

"Care to join us, Ski?" Millus asked. "Easy stakes."

"Did you bring any money with you?" Mac said with a grin.

"No I didn't. And no thank you," Ski said. "What about Dresden, here?"

No one answered or even looked up.

All right, then. Ski walked over to the sofa and nodded toward the computer pad. "What are you up to?"

"Reading up on the station's power plant."

"Is it much different than on board the ship?"

"Somewhat. But it's also very similar in some ways, just more spread out," Dresden answered. "What are you doing?"

"I'm trying not to be bored." Ski looked over at the MSES machines. "Who're in those right now?"

"Same people as always."

Ski walked over to the first one and looked in at the monitor screen. Gradenko was in southern Africa defending a small British outpost against a horde of Zulu warriors, their Assegais spears flashing as they came over a wall. In the next booth Flores was flying a biplane over London at night, pursuing a German Zeppelin as anti-aircraft shells burst all around. He walked by the last machine and saw Wilson in another sexual encounter, but he didn't stay to watch. He started for the door, wishing Petey were awake.

"Let us deal you in, Ski," Millus called.

"No, thanks. I've got an errand to run." He went out into the hall and entered the elevator.

Chapter 38
"Star Journal"

Ski climbed through the hatch and walked down the short access way to the Optical Positioning Room. He studied the universe beyond the glass for a short while, then picked up Petey's star journal from the control panel and looked over the protective cover. *This is what Petey had taken from the ship, instead of a second lifesaving inhaler.*

Although Petey had offered to show it to him, Ski had never had an interest in reading the navigator's log, but now it piqued his curiosity. He released the strap that held the cover shut and opened the pad. Selecting the table of contents, he randomly opened an entry.

The page opened to a detailed holographic image, colorized and intricate, and labeled NGC 6543. A white glowing center seemed to be living inside an undulating blue and purple envelope. Surrounding the envelope coiled a red double helix edged with green and gold. Listed below the image were several lines of astronomical notations which Ski did not understand, and at the bottom Petey had written his own personal observations. These were descriptive and poetic and seemed to tell the story of the object observed. They also lent a heartfelt beauty to the otherwise sterile astronomical jargon and numbers.

```
Observational data for NGC 6543-
Epoch J2450
Right ascension-      17ʰ 58ᵐ 33.423ˢ
Declination-          +66 Deg 37 Min 59.52 Sec
Distance-             3.3±0.9 kly (1.0±0.3 kpc)
Constellation-        Draco
Apparent magnitude- 9.8
Apparent dimensions-Core: 20 Sec
Radius-               Core: 0.2 ly (0.2 pc)
Notable features-     Complex structure
Other designations- Cat's Eye Nebula, Snail Nebula,
(Includes IC 4677), Caldwell 6

Stellar classification is O7 + [WR]-type star

.02 mas shift since last observation at AlCent A2.
```

Ski studied the image and realized that the star at the center had exploded, sending colorful waves of stellar gasses and material out into space. The image processing had captured all of the colors and ripples of the backlit matter, but it was Petey's words that clarified what had happened and the poetic beauty of the result. Ski went back to the start of the log and began studying the images and reading the observations.

The very first image was a wide angle shot of a star field that seemed to reach into infinity itself. Petey's words read, "I ponder the night sky from a place of perpetual night where wonders abound in deafening silence. I see uncountable glowing gemstones set in orderly chaos against an onyx void, an emperor's ransom of wealth to the beholder, always close at hand and yet out of reach, of limitless value, bartered for nothing, sole utility in knowing their relative position and distance, and in making one humble."

Another entry was of the star Sirius, and the observation read, "The eye of the dog, electric with blue fire, crackling soundlessly in everlasting night." The next one was a gorgeous image of a nebula. "Blue fog lit from within, the indiscernible perimeter lost near the threshold of vision, its secrets awaiting greater efforts and costlier devices." Another was of an emission nebula. "Exploding nursery fixed in time as in a portrait, yet burning with new life, flaming clouds of mist and fire where the aged perish and the young are born."

Ski read passage after passage and became touched with emotion. In each entry Petey had captured the beauty as well as the science of the astronomical subject, and after lingering on each object Ski felt compelled to see the next one. One image caused him to gasp. It showed two spiral galaxies that had collided and were now separating, with individual stars flung out in all directions. The observation read, "Stellar hurricanes collide sending showers of home world suns into the intergalactic void, condemned forever to travel in lonely darkness, viewing a splendid panorama of light from afar."

Ski stared at the image and tried to imagine the view from a planet around one of the displaced suns. A portion of the night sky would be intergalactic blackness, and opposite would be a spectacular view of two colliding galaxies filling the sky. A breathtaking goodbye as the world moved into a stygian exile. *Incredible.*

The next entry showed the Trifid Nebula, an explosion of light and color roughly divided into three lobes by long, irregular shadows. A close up inset showed protostars forming into young stars as they sped off into the cosmos. Petey's observation read, "Billows of living smoke rising like contemplation from God's own peace pipe, new life for embryonic suns coming into being from a solidity of thought."

Ski remembered Petey telling him that he hoped to publish the log one day and wondered at the intended readers he had in mind. Surely most astronomers and cosmologists would scoff at the references to God. But that was the beauty as Petey saw it. The navigator was reflecting the rapture of the visible universe in terms familiar to him. Could there truly be a penalty for such honest expressions?

Ski remembered when Petey made that observation. Before Van Wert became captain of the *Kestrel,* the navigator had to conduct his observations in secret. Captain Donaldson didn't like for the enlisted men to use the optical viewer for any reason, citing a privilege reserved for bridge officers. But Lieutenant, j.g. Mackey, the operations officer at the time, respected Petey's work and thought that the rule was ridiculous. Whenever they were on watch together, Mackey freely let the navigator use the device. It had worked out well, until one day on a long patrol the captain came up to the bridge unexpectedly.

"Peters!" Donaldson said. "What are you doing? Who gave you permission to use the viewer?"

Petey hesitated, and Ski wondered if Mackey would back him up or not.

"I did, Captain," Mackey said.

"You? You know what I've said about this."

"Sir, that man is doing valuable scientific research that may directly benefit the fleet. Besides, he plans to have his work published, and this sort of thing gives the fleet a good image."

Donaldson looked over at Petey. "Well, why does he have to use the viewer?"

"Because," Mackey said, "the setting circles and indicators give him better figures for his calculations."

Donaldson frowned. "Very well, carry on," he said, and left the bridge.

Ski never knew for sure whether Donaldson had given in because of Mackey's reasoning or because he was due to leave in a few weeks. But he did know that Mackey was the most admirable officer he had ever known.

Ski flipped through the journal again. Scanning over the pages he stopped at an entry that showed a binary system of two red dwarf stars. They were very small and very dim and had not appeared on Petey's primary chart. In close orbit around the stars was a dense asteroid field and further out were three barren small rocky planets. Petey spoke excitedly about the discovery.

"You see," he said, "the inner debris wouldn't condense into planets because of the gravity flux caused by the two stars."

"You still haven't found the name of this system?" Ski asked.

"No, but I've got to check the old astrographical charts." Petey beamed. "Maybe it's never been discovered. Maybe I'll get to name it!"

As it turned out, the system was on the astrographical survey charts. Apparently the stars, being so dim and hard to see from the shipping lanes, didn't make the primary navigational chart. But the discovery whetted the navigator's desire to continue his observations.

Ski flipped through the pages and came upon an entry that made him laugh. It was to be Petey's crowning achievement in his log. The hologram showed a large moon, apparently knocked out of orbit long ago and set adrift. Its course was taking it nearer and nearer to some shipping lanes. The entire first page was taken up with information about the moon, and the next page was covered with images of the moon taken at various angles and distances.

This time Petey searched all of the records and charts and found nothing. Van Wert had taken over as commanding officer and was very excited for Petey about the find. He had the radio shack send out a Navigational Hazard Warning to all ships and stations in the vicinity. He also reported the discovery to the Celestial Cartography Commission who in turn named the moon Peters 115, the entry number of the moon in Petey's log. Future navigational charts would feature the moon with that designation.

After the messages were sent out, the captain flew all around Petey's moon, taking the ship wherever the navigator suggested. This gave Petey the opportunity to collect as much information and take as many pictures as possible. He kept only the best ones for his journal.

After the lunar flybys, the *Kestrel* returned to its original course, and the captain assembled all of the officers into the wardroom for a briefing of the discovery. To everyone's surprise the briefing was to be given by Peters himself.

Intimidated at first, Petey soon fell into a stride talking about his favorite subject. He spoke to them about the moon and how to best use the ship's equipment to spot other navigational hazards. He also gave them a brief overview on navigation and a quick run-down on the basic points of astronomy. The officers were impressed.

Only now did Ski realize how wise the captain had been in the matter. Most of the officers had served under Donaldson and still clung to the prejudices of the former CO. Van Wert knew that a briefing given by an enlisted man, a very talented and knowledgeable enlisted man, would help them to cast aside their old ways and conform to the thinking of the new CO. For the most part it had worked, and it had become the first step in smoothing out relations between the ranks, and therefore adding to the efficiency of the ship. The captain proved an expert at team building, which Ski knew that was the most important skill of all in a fleet ship.

Ski flipped forward in the log to the last few entries. They had been taken on the station's optical positioning equipment.

"This scope," the entry read, "has a much narrower field of view then the one on the *Kestrel*, but the optics are very good. The image is completely free of chromatic aberrations and coma. Color resolution is also superb." The entry went on to describe the nearby stars. Then it read, "Once again, Lord, I thank you for my eyes to see these wonders and I thank you for my mind that I may gain understanding of them."

Interesting foot note, Ski mused. *This log is getting more personal.*

The next entry read, "I observed Sirius again. It is so beautiful. Its fiery blue light dazzles like a brilliant sapphire. I believe it is my favorite, Lord, and I hope that when it is my turn to join you, you will show me these wonders of your creation first hand. I can think of nothing finer than to tour the universe with you. Father, I long to see the infinite beauty and power and to know the secrets of the cosmos as I travel by your side. You are truly the Wondrous Father of lights."

Ski skipped to last entry, written earlier this morning. It read, "Lord, I'm beginning to feel the onset of this disease and it scares me. I'm trying not to be afraid of dying. I reassure myself that I'll be with you, but still I'm afraid of the process of death. If this disease attacks the lungs, then I know that I will probably suffocate. That is what frightens me the most. To be unable to breathe is a completely helpless feeling. Dear God, please stay near to me when the hour comes. Please hold my hand when I am to go. Only with you can I face this bravely. And please, Father, keep me strong for the others, to help out when I can and to provide an example of what it means to live in commitment to you. I wish I had my Scriptures with me."

Ski turned off the journal and sat back in the chair, feeling embarrassed at his intrusion of Petey's personal notes. It also saddened him to know that his friend felt fear about the onset of the virus. They all did, but hearing Petey express it filled him with pathos, and the loneliness of being here at the extreme end of the station gripped him sharply. He closed the protective cover and headed back to the elevator.

Chapter 39
"More Symptoms"

Ski woke up with a severe sinus headache. He had been sleeping in the bunk above Petey in the first cabin, and as he sat up, he also noticed soreness in his armpits and groin and muscles. For a moment this puzzled him, but as the grogginess of sleep passed, a familiar sense of dread welled up in its place. He lay back down and stared up at the ceiling. *So it's got me. I knew it was coming, but I didn't expect it so soon.* In his mind he could see the station manager Fredricks gasping on the video screen.

He heard a cough from the bunk below him and the sound of a medical inhaler. He sat up and looked over the edge of the bunk at Petey.

"Hey, how're you doing?" Ski asked.

Petey shook the inhaler to mix the contents, still holding his breath. Then he exhaled. "Not real good. This puffer isn't working very well. I really hope the steroid kicks in soon." He shook the inhaler some more and then puffed again.

"Are you going to breakfast?" Ski asked.

Petey exhaled. "No, I just want to lie here. I'll get up later. How do you feel?"

"Not too good. I'm pretty sure I have a fever."

Petey shook his head.

Ski climbed down from the bunk and sat down on a chair as he put on his shoes. "Do you want me to bring you something to eat? I don't mind."

"No, thanks, buddy. I'm hungry but I just don't feel like eating. You know how it is."

Ski nodded. "Yes, I do." He finished tying his shoes and stood up.

"If you feel sick, you'd better go see Doc."

"I will." Ski opened the door and walked out into the deserted hall. He heard no sound from the lounge as he walked to the station's clinic. As he stepped inside he saw Foley taking McElroy's temperature.

Mac nodded to Ski. "Meanwhile, back in the jungle..."

Foley turned to Ski. "Are you having symptoms, too?"

Ski nodded.

"All right, sit down there." The medic pointed to a chair. The thermometer beeped and he read the indicator. "One hundred one point two."

"Is it the virus?" Mac asked.

"What else?"

"Damn." Mac looked over at Ski. "If you're sick too, then I'll bet we all got it from that room."

Ski nodded.

"Mac, how's your leg doing?" Foley asked.

Mac looked down at his cast and rotated it gently from side to side. "It doesn't hurt as much now as it did at first."

"How many pain pills are you taking a day?"

"Four."

Foley nodded. "Cut it back to one or two and only take them as needed."

"All right."

Foley took the thermometer to Ski and placed it against his forehead and began to feel around his armpits and joints until the thermometer beeped.

"One hundred two point five," Doc said. "Where do you feel sick the most?"

"In my sinuses."

"Okay." He took a stethoscope and listened to Ski's chest and heart, then dispensed some pills to both of them to ease the symptoms, as well as some vitamins. "Now, I want you to rest and drink plenty of fluids. All I can do is treat the symptoms. You must rest to fight off the virus."

"Is that it, then?" Ski asked.

"No, there's one more thing." Foley took a pneumatic hypodermic needle and injected a compound into both men.

"What's that for?" Mac asked, rubbing his arm.

"It's a hemoglobin enhancer to allow your blood to carry more oxygen. The captain thought it might help."

"Doctor Van Wert," Mac said.

Foley didn't answer him.

Ski helped McElroy up, and together they walked to the lounge. A few of the others were getting their breakfasts, and Ski saw Gradenko coming out of one of the MSES machines. His clumsy gait and bleary eyes told Ski that he had been up all night again. He passed them as he headed for the dinner table.

"Hey, man," Ski said. "Were you up all night again on that thing?"

Gradenko didn't answer but kept walking.

"What's it this time?" he asked. "Roman Gladiators?"

Mac coughed and Ski heard loose mucus.

The gunner stopped and looked at McElroy, then at Ski. "Are you both sick now, too?"

"Yes, I think so."

"Damn," Gradenko growled.

Flores, sitting on a couch, said, "Well, keep the hell away from me!" He stood up and walked quickly to the other side of the room, an angry scowl on his face.

Gradenko backed away, too. "Damn." He walked quickly out the lounge door knocking over one of the chairs on the way.

"Well," Mac said. "Spank you very much!"

***

Gradenko stormed down the hall, pausing at the top of the stairs. "Man, screw this place!" He kicked the wall with the bottom of his shoe, and a small placard came loose and hit the floor. On the verge of rage Gradenko picked it up and threw it down the hallway where it hit the floor and bounced against the far wall. He turned and walked down the stairs.

At main control room he stopped to look around but saw no one. He wanted to be alone. *I'm so sick of running into people. There's nowhere to go without having someone gawking at me.* He reached into his pocket and pulled out his stiletto switch blade knife. Its weight felt good in his hand.

He pressed the button, and the long, high-carbon steel blade snapped straight out from the handle. He always carried the knife, a perfect last ditch weapon.

As he looked at the knife he realized the numbness of his mind due to lack of sleep. The guys on the ship always joked that life in the fleet was a study in sleep deprivation, but now he wondered if perhaps he had overdone it, especially concerning how he acted toward the other guys. *No, I'm sick of this place and these people. And now Ski and Mac are sick.*

He stared at the knife and smiled as he pushed the button repeatedly, the blade snapping in and out of the handle. There was a sense of security in holding a weapon in one's hand. He nodded and thought about another weapon that gave a much greater sense of security.

Gradenko stuck the knife in his pocket and walked down the stairs to the docking bay. Next to the docking bay door stood a large gear locker where the boarding party had stowed the vac-suits and weapons. He opened the door and took out the "street sweeper" automatic rifle. The weight felt good in his hands as he held it at attention. He turned around to the hall behind him and lowered the weapon as if he were firing a hip shot, then he pushed the arm button and the weapon vibrated subtly in his hands.

"Purr, baby," he said to the weapon. "You've been lonely, haven't you?"

He moved the weapon back and forth across the width of the hall in a sweeping motion as he made shooting sounds with his mouth, his finger hovering just over the trigger. Then he disarmed the gun and stood at attention, holding the weapon at present arms. A thought formed in his foggy consciousness. *I could end this now, for all of us.* He lowered the weapon and relaxed. *Maybe it's time.*

Chapter 40
"Cognizance"

Ski lay back on the couch in the lounge and tried to rest as some of the other crewmen came in for lunch. Despite a cloth laid over his eyes he couldn't get to sleep. He ignored the shuffling of feet but opened his eyes when the cloth lifted from his face. Doc pressed his hand against Ski's forehead.

"Damn, Ski. You're burning up. You should be in bed."

"I feel like crap and I can't get comfortable."

"I want you to try to eat something, and then go to bed for the rest of the day."

"Try some chicken soup," Flores said. "Mom's remedy was right, scientifically proven."

"I can't eat anything."

"Go back to bed and lie down. I'll bring you something to help you sleep. We need to get that fever under control."

Ski nodded and tried to stand up.

"Come on," Doc said. "I'll help you to your rack." He helped Ski to his feet and led him to his room.

***

Van Wert sat at the station doctor's desk engrossed in a medical book when Ensign Millus opened the door and stepped in.

Millus smiled. "So, there you are."

"Good morning."

"Have you been here all night?"

"Not all night." Van Wert gave a wry smile. "I've been reading about viruses in these books. Listen to this. There are some kinds of viruses that contain only RNA, but when they infect a cell's nucleus they cause the cell to change its own DNA."

"Really?"

"Yes. For a long time researchers thought it impossible, but they found out these viruses carry a reverse transcriptase code that causes the cell to create new viruses instead of new cells."

"Is that how our virus works?"

"As far as forcing the cells to create new viruses, yes, but I don't know about the reverse transcriptase."

"Pretty amazing," Millus said. "Seems strange to be talking about something that's killing you with such admiration."

"I know," Van Wert said.

"Do you want to hold quarters this morning?"

"Is the work all caught up?"

"Yes. The PM's are up to date or ahead of schedule."

"Then let's not bother with it. There's no work to assign, and there's nothing to tell them."

Millus opened his mouth to reply, then stopped himself.

"I don't want to make up some pep talk just to have something to say."

Millus nodded. "Did you hear about Ski and Mac?"

"Yes." Van Wert sighed. "Well, I guess it makes sense. Those two and Petey were the first ones to find the bodies. Did Foley try the hemoglobin enhancer?"

"He says he did."

"Good. How are you feeling?"

"All right. I'm a little tired, but I don't feel like I'm getting sick. How about you?"

"I feel okay," Van Wert said. "By the way, have you been checking on the plant?"

"Yes, I have. Everything is running well. Dresden's been down there a lot."

"He has? What's he doing?"

"Every time I go down there he's reading the tech manuals or scanning the equipment readings on the computer."

Van Wert shook his head. "I'm not sure I want him down there."

"I think he'll be all right. It seems like he is trying to learn the system."

"Do you feel comfortable with that?"

Millus nodded. "Yes. I don't think he means any harm. He's been working hard and laying low. I think he feels bad about what happened."

"Well, he should." Van Wert looked back down at his tablet.

"I wish the rest of the men would take an interest in something productive instead of those high tech fantasy machines," Millus said.

"How do you think they're holding up?" the captain asked.

"It's hard to say. They seem to be all right, but we don't know what they're thinking."

"No one's spoken to you about how they feel?"

Millus shook his head. "I doubt that they would talk to an officer anyway. But everyone seemed to crash emotionally when Peters became ill."

"I noticed that, too." Van Wert said. "I wonder how they're going to hold up under this kind of pressure, fearing for their lives."

"They've all been under pressure before."

"But not for this long. It's this sort of situation that can cause a person to crack."

***

Gradenko plugged his ears with his fingers as he walked through the station's power plant module to the control booth. He stepped into the dim coolness and closed the door, shutting out the noise behind him. Dresden sat at one of the consoles munching on a sandwich. He regarded the gunner as if he expected to be in trouble.

"Hello, D," Gradenko said. "What are you doing in here?"

"Just monitoring the systems and learning the equipment." He took another bite.

"Keeps your mind off everything, doesn't it?"

Dresden nodded. "It's interesting to me, and besides, the MSES machines are never available."

"Well, one's available now. I'm getting tired of them." The gunner sat down in one of the chairs. "It's just like the movies. They're great, but after so many of them I just want to get out and do something."

Dresden nodded, eyeing the gunner curiously. He took another bite.

Gradenko looked out at the power plant beyond the glass. "This system is different from the one we had on the ship, isn't it?"

"The power generation on the *Kestrel* is similar, but much more compact. The *Kestrel* class is fairly new, and these stations were placed in orbit back when they sent the *Fu Sang* over to AlCent B. The station has no propulsion, except for attitude control."

"No propulsion?"

"None. All this is for power generation. That transmitter takes a lot of power."

"What are those big humps on the deck?" Gradenko pointed out beyond the glass to where eight hemispherical objects lay arranged in a circular symmetrical pattern on the floor. Each one had large insulated pipes that ran from the floor to the top of the structure. In addition to the large pipes stood maintenance platforms, small tanks, power lines, and pipes with valves. Some of these pipes extended like spokes toward the outer hull of the station.

"Those are the Stirling Converters, covered with insulation, of course. They convert the heat energy from the reactor core below us to mechanical energy to drive the generators. That's those cylindrical objects sticking out from the side of each converter."

"The Stirlings are the same double-piston, heat-differential generators like we used on the ship?"

"Exactly, but the *Kestrel* only had two little ones. This station has eight large ones. Heat pipes bring heat up from the reactor core, which powers the converters."

Gradenko looked over the control screen on the main console. "Are all of them running now?"

Dresden glanced at the computer screen. "Yes, but only five of them are under a load. The other three are kept running to help dissipate the heat from the core."

"They run all the time?"

"More or less, but you can take them down one at a time for maintenance or repairs. You just can't have any more than two down at any one time."

"What would happen if you shut them all down at once?"

"You can't. There are failsafe features in the control program to prevent anyone from doing that."

"But what if someone bypassed the failsafe features? Would the core go super critical?"

"In theory, yes, but each Stirling unit has variable conductance heat pipes that are connected to a non-condensable gas reservoir system. When the heat at the Stirling gets too high, the gas shifts and ports the excess heat to radiators outside the skin of the station."

"Could those be isolated?"

Dresden eyed the gunner curiously. "Why do you want to know all of this?"

"I'm just curious. Bored, I guess." Gradenko pointed out beyond the glass. "All of this is very new and interesting to me."

"This technology is actually quite old."

"Yeah, but it's new to me." He looked at Dresden, and the tech didn't seem satisfied. "It just seems rather big and dangerous, and vulnerable. I mean, what if an insurgent came in here and shut these units down after having isolated the NCG system? They could blow this station up, right?"

"In theory, but those valves that isolate the radiators are locked open and can only be closed for maintenance or repair when the reactor core is removed."

Gradenko could feel Dresden's suspicion rising. *Time to change the subject.* "The station's heating and air conditioning is controlled from down here, too, right?"

"That's right." The engineering tech pointed up toward some large boxes mounted along the wall above the Stirling units. "You can see the ventilation ducting above them running up to the rest of the station."

Gradenko nodded. "Would you mind showing me around? I would really like to see how they did things back when they built these stations."

"I guess so." Dresden finished his sandwich and stood up. "Grab a pack of earplugs from that box behind you."

Gradenko stood up and inserted the plugs in his ears. Dresden did the same and led the way out of the control booth.

Chapter 41
"Indications"

Ski spent the afternoon in bed, his body alternating between sweats and chills. He dozed fitfully, awaiting Doc's sleeping remedy to take effect, and listened to the rasps and gurgles of Petey's labored breathing. At some point around supper time, he drifted off into a deep sleep. That was when the nightmares began.

The dreams had a common theme, frightening and intensely vivid. In one recurring dream Ski found himself in a colossal room in darkness so complete he couldn't tell if his eyes were open or shut. The air felt cool and still, and a heavy mist settled on his naked body. Around him he could hear shuffling of heavy feet and the slow labored breathing of unseen creatures moving through the blackness. One moved close behind him, and a tingle went up his spine that caused his hair to stand on end. He turned quickly around, afraid of being grabbed, but the creature moved off. This encounter repeated constantly and nearly drove him to panicked flight, but fear of running into a creature kept him fixed in one spot. In despair he knelt down on the cold, wet floor and curled himself into a ball. The shuffling came closer, from all sides now. He curled himself down tighter. They were on him…

Ski awoke with a gasp, sitting bolt upright. It took a few moments to realize that he was in one of the staterooms on the station. Below him, Petey coughed and turned over. A digital clock on the desk read 3:37 a.m. He lay back down and waited until his breathing returned to normal. His skin felt sticky against the damp sheets, and he wanted a shower, but slowly his mind drifted back into sleep. His last thought was a feeling that his fever had passed.

***

Ski awoke to the sound of someone entering the room, and he looked to see Doc with his medical bag. He switched on the lamp above the bed as the medic approached the bunk.

"How are you doing, Ski?"

"I feel weird but not bad."

226

Foley reached up and placed a thermometer against Ski's forehead as he took Ski's wrist and counted his pulse. When the thermometer beeped he read it.

"That's strange."

"What?" Ski asked.

"Your fever's gone. How do you feel?"

"Really weak, but hungry."

Doc shook his head and knelt down by the lower bunk. Petey's slow breathing made a fluttering sound.

"Petey sounds terrible," Ski said.

"I know. The rails are getting worse. Petey, I've got to take a blood gas test." The navigator nodded, and Foley took out an instrument from his bag and slipped it over Petey's finger.

The navigator slowly rolled his head toward Doc and opened his eyes. Then he erupted into a violent spasm of coughing that wracked his whole body. When it was over he spit into a tissue that Foley held for him, then he settled down again and looked up at the medic. Ski saw that the mucus was tinged with blood. Petey closed his eyes and went back to sleep.

Foley checked the instrument and shook his head. "I'm going to have to put him on oxygen." He made an impression on Petey's forearm with his thumb and the impression remained. "I'm also going to run an IV. He's dehydrating."

"What about food? He hasn't eaten in two days."

"His body doesn't need food now."

"Can you do anything about his lungs?"

"Not here." Foley covered Petey with the bed sheet, then stood up and looked at Ski. "You'd better hope we get some help fast."

A feeling of cold dread filled Ski's heart.

"You want me to bring you something to eat?" Doc asked.

"No. I'll go get something. I've got to get out of this bed."

"All right. I'll help you there."

He helped Ski down onto the floor and supported him as they walked to the lounge.

"How are you feeling?" Ski asked the medic as they entered the hall.

"Not worth a damn."

They entered the lounge to find Mac leaning against one of the MSES machines looking inside. He turned around when Ski and Doc entered the room.

"These two are pathetic."

"What's wrong?" Ski asked as Doc helped him to a chair at the table.

"They're on these machines day and night! Flores is in that one having another war scene, and Wilson is in this one buying women at some desert bazaar. I haven't even been able to try one out yet."

"Who's in the third one?"

"No one. It's doing some system reset."

"I'm sure one of them will be done in a few minutes."

"One of them's going to be done right now." Mac clicked a command on the control panel, and the monitor screen inside went blank. Wilson removed the headgear and climbed out.

"What the hell happened?" he asked.

"Time's up. Game over." Mac held his hand out for the headgear, a smug look on his face.

"What the hell are you doing?" Wilson asked.

"You've been hogging that machine ever since we got on this station!"

"Well, so what?"

"I'm gonna try it out!"

"Wait until I'm finished!"

"That's the frigging problem! You're never finished!"

Wilson stepped forward until the two men's faces were only inches apart, his hands clenched into fists. "Don't mess with me, Mac."

"Man, get out of my face." Mac said, shoving Wilson backward. The systems tech quickly regained his balance and stood upright with teeth clenched, then he balled up his first and moved toward Mac. Foley ran over to the two men.

"Hey! Knock it off!" he said.

Wilson threw a fist at Mac's face, but the cook deflected it just as Foley wedged himself between the two men.

"Dammit! I said knock it off," he shouted.

Wilson and Mac struggled around the medic for a few moments and then ceased.

"You guys are acting like a couple of kids fighting over a toy."

"What's wrong with that one?" Wilson asked.

"It's down," Mac said.

Foley turned his head toward Mac. "Let him finish his game..." he looked at Wilson, "then you get out and let him have a turn."

"The hell with it," Wilson snapped. "He can take it." Wilson let go and walked past the two men toward the door, knocking Mac in the shoulder on the way out.

***

Ensign Millus walked quickly across the floor of the power plant to the main control module, a bead of sweat making its way down his right temple. He stepped in and saw Dresden sitting in front of the computer terminal.

"Good morning, Mr. Millus."

"How're you doing?" Millus patted the sweat off of his forehead with a handkerchief.

"Okay. I was just scanning through the system checking readings."

Millus nodded. "Yesterday I saw a pressure increase on the chill water pump. We might want to check out the filter. It could be clogged."

"It was. I switched over and cleaned both filters out last night. The amp draw is back to normal."

"Oh, good." Millus watched as Dresden continued to scan through the computer. "You've been pretty busy down here. Is everything else running smoothly?"

"Yes." Dresden looked up at Millus. "As important as this system is to us, I figured that it'd be good to keep watching for any problems while they're still small."

"I agree." Millus saw a reading tablet on the console and recognized the text. "You're reading Sun Tzu's *The Art of War*?"

"Yes. It's one of my favorites. At one time I had it practically memorized. It's a great book."

229

"Yes, it is. When I was in officer candidate school I wrote a paper on the qualities of a good general based on Master Sun's writings. It went over real well."

"I bet it did. It's amazing that something written more than twenty-three hundred years ago would still be applicable in the military today."

"And in industry. Wherever leadership and management skills are needed."

"Some truths never go out of style." Dresden turned back to the computer.

Millus watched the technician at the keyboard and marveled that this was the same person who, only four days before, had taken part in a treacherous act of mutiny. *How could that have happened? How could someone like Dresden get caught up in a crowd like Wild Bill's gang? He had never been in any trouble before.* Millus considered asking him, but decided against it. "How long do you think you'll be down here?"

Dresden shrugged. "I don't know."

"I think they're going to put on a movie again today."

Dresden nodded but didn't say anything.

Millus turned to leave. "Don't work too hard."

"Sir?" called Dresden. He stopped typing at the keyboard and looked up at the ensign. "Is it true that Doc is sick now, too?"

Millus nodded.

"Do you think that someone will come, like the captain said?"

"Someone should. We sent a radio message out and inserted another message in the beam."

Dresden sighed, then spoke while averting his eyes from the officer's face. "If someone does come, and we make it, what will happen to me?"

Millus frowned. "The proper course of action would be arrest and court martial. A lot of people died because of what happened."

Dresden slowly nodded, shifting his eyes to the floor.

"But," Millus said, "we'll cross that bridge if we come to it. Given your conduct the last four days, I'm sure that the captain would put in a good word for you. I know I will."

Dresden looked up and nodded. "Thank you."

Chapter 42
"Petey"

After a morning of reading and dozing in the lounge, Ski had a light lunch and decided to sleep the rest of the afternoon. He entered his room and, leaving the light off, headed for the bunk. He heard the steady whisper of the oxygen unit, but no lung noise came from Petey. *The oxygen must be helping after all.* Ski leaned over Petey and listened but heard nothing. A tingle of dread grew in his stomach. He felt for the navigator's wrist, and the arm was cold. He switched on the bunk light and saw the navigator lying on his back, motionless, his eyes closed and mouth open.

"Petey? Hey, Petey!" Ski put his ear next to his friend's mouth and heard nothing, so he felt for a pulse. Again, no sign of life.

"Oh, God." Ski stood and walked quickly to the lounge. A few of the guys were having lunch. "Hey! Has anyone seen Doc?"

They shook their heads. "Check the sick bay," Mac offered.

"What's wrong?" Dresden asked.

"Petey's in trouble." Ski jogged to the doctor's office where he found Foley asleep at the desk. "Doc, wake up!"

"What's wrong?"

"Petey's in trouble. Please come quick!"

Foley grabbed his medical bag and followed Ski to the room. When they got there, Wilson, Dresden, and Mac had come from the lounge and stood inside the door.

"Make a hole!" Foley shouted as he pushed his way through. Ski followed him.

As soon as the medic saw Petey he stopped short. Calmly, he walked over to the bedside and felt for a pulse. With his stethoscope he listened for a heartbeat and breathing, then took the stethoscope out of his ears and shut off the oxygen unit. He gently removed the tube from Petey's face and turned toward Ski.

"How long has he been like this?" Foley asked.

"I don't know. I just found him and then went to get you."

Captain Van Wert and Ensign Millus came through the knot of men inside the door. The captain looked run down, aged by the virus.

"What's going on?" he asked, then he saw Petey. "Oh, damn." He sighed. "When did it happen?"

"I don't know. Ski found him like this a few minutes ago." The medic covered Petey's face with the bed sheet.

"Hey," Ski said, incredulous, "aren't you going to even try something?"

Foley looked up at the captain and then at Ski. "Ski, he's uh... he's at room temperature." Foley tried to sound gentle. "He didn't just now pass away. He's been gone for at least an hour."

"Great." Ski shook his head. "Modern medical technology.

"We're in a remote location, Ski."

Ski nodded. "Yes, I know."

"I'm sorry, Ski." Van Wert said. "I know he was your friend."

"He was everybody's friend," Wilson said.

Ski nodded. "Excuse me." He made his way through them and walked out of the room.

***

Ski stood at the window of the main control room looking out at the stars. His eyes settled on a nebula, its tenuous wisps of gaseous clouds glowing with the light of condensing star matter at its heart. As he stared at it, he thought about Petey and marveled at the depth of numbness that filled him. Petey's death was too surreal for any emotion, even sadness.

In his mind he could still see his friend's face in death, could still feel the coldness of his skin, and with those reflections came the realization that Petey had spent his last hours totally alone. *I should have been with you, buddy. You would've stayed with me, but I left you in that cold dark room to die all alone. I'm sorry, my friend.*

Ski could feel a new emotion inside the numbness of his heart, rising and swelling like a magma chamber, and he struggled to hold it down.

"I'm sorry, Petey," he whispered to the nebula, and considered letting the emotion vent but heard footsteps approaching. He looked and saw the captain step up beside him.

"Are you all right?" Van Wert asked.

Ski nodded.

Van Wert stood quietly for a few minutes as if to give Ski a chance to talk, but Ski remained silent.

"I came down here to ask you something. Doc is wrapping Petey in a makeshift shroud, and Wilson found a stretcher. Did you want to help carry him downstairs? It would be like being a pall bearer."

"Where are we going to take him?"

"To one of the lifeboats with the others."

"Captain, I have a better idea. Why don't we bury him in space? Given his love of astronomy it would only be fitting to commit his body to the stars." Ski pointed out past the window. "See that nebula out there? Petey told me that that's where stars are born. I thought that maybe we could put on our vac-suits and send him off from the docking bay toward that nebula."

Van Wert shook his head. "No, Ski."

"I think it would be nice to know that one day he would reach it and would become part of a new star system."

"I can't do that, Ski."

Ski looked at the captain directly. "You have the authority. It's at your discretion."

"That's right. It's at my discretion, but because of the virus, I can't. That's how we got into this whole mess."

"They've buried people who have died of viruses in space before."

"But only if there is a planet with a suitable atmosphere to consume the body during reentry. We can't do it here."

Ski nodded, still looking out at the stars. "Well, if you can't, then you can't."

"I'm sorry, Ski," Van Wert said, "but at least this way he'll eventually get the full honors he deserves."

"I suppose," Ski said.

A half an hour later the entire party loaded Petey's body into one of the lifeboats. Keeping the docking bay vented to space had kept the bodies frozen, but it didn't eliminate the smell of decay, and Ski felt miserable about putting his friend into the makeshift sarcophagus. No one had spoken and once it ended everyone gathered in the lounge, standing awkwardly as if wondering what to do next.

Mac stepped up to the captain, came to attention, and saluted. "I respectfully request permission to get drunk, sir."

"Granted," Van Wert replied. "Don't break anything."

Wine was passed around, and Ski stayed for a few minutes to have a toast for Petey but soon left. He had been on his way to bed when he found Petey, and he still felt weary now. He didn't want to be in the room, so he grabbed his blanket and pillow and rode the elevator up to the communications level. He climbed the ladder and lay down under the station's sextant, then looked out at the stars until he fell asleep.

Chapter 43
"Search for Clues"

Later that afternoon, Wilson shambled into the lounge, now deserted except for Gradenko seated at one of the tables. Spread before him was a sumptuous supper of steak, mashed potatoes and gravy, salad, pie and ice cream, and a large glass of wine. The sight of so much food made the systems tech feel nauseous.

"Have you seen, Doc?"

"Not in a while." Gradenko coughed violently before taking another fork full of food. "Come and join me."

"No, thanks. How can you eat so much food? Don't you feel sick?"

"I feel like crap."

"Then why are you stuffing your face?"

"A last supper should be a feast."

"Don't write yourself off so quickly. There's still hope of a rescue."

Gradenko took another bite and shook his head. "We're all going to be like Petey real soon."

Wilson opened his mouth to reply but thought better of it. *No use arguing with dramatics.* He left the lounge and walked to the station clinic. He found Foley in the adjoining doctor's office asleep at the desk. A computer tablet lay across his lap and another one lay on the table beside him.

"Hey, Doc?"

Foley startled awake and looked up at Wilson. "Yeah. What's going on?"

"I don't feel worth a damn. I'm sore all over and my head hurts. I think it's my sinuses."

Foley nodded and gestured to a chair. "Sit down."

Wilson sat down while Foley took his blood pressure, his temperature, and felt around his face, neck, and armpits. "You've got a fever. I'm going to give you something to relieve the symptoms."

"Doc, is it true that Ski got better?"

"It appears that way."

"Does this mean that my chances are better?"

"I wish I knew. Just take care of yourself. Here." He handed Wilson some pills. "Are you getting any sleep?"

Wilson nodded.

"Where are you sleeping?"

"On a couch in the lounge."

"Get a real bed in one of the rooms. Sleep is your best weapon against this virus."

"Have you found anything promising with those medical records?"

Foley shook his head. "I'm not a virologist. Hell, I'm not even a doctor. I'm just a hospital corpsman with battle surgery training. I don't know what the hell people expect me to find in all this," he said, gesturing toward the computer pads. "The captain wants me to identify it, but even if I could, it wouldn't do us any good. It's all pointless."

Wilson felt taken aback. "I'm sorry, Doc."

"No, I'm sorry." Foley rubbed his face with his hands. "I've just been thinking about my wife and little boy. I was supposed to go on leave when we got back. We were going to take a trip to the equatorial area. My boy wanted to see the animals there."

"Maybe you'll still be able to."

Foley nodded and looked at the computer pad on the desk. "Yeah, maybe."

"Do you think-"

Wilson stopped mid-sentence as the captain stepped into the office, looking haggard and bleary. He coughed, and Wilson could hear the rattling of mucus in the captain's lungs.

"Hello, Doc," Van Wert said. He looked at Wilson. "Don't tell me you're sick, also."

"Yes, sir."

Foley held up a hypodermic needle. "I was just going to give Wilson his hemoglobin enhancer. Are you ready for yours now?"

"I suppose so." The captain gestured toward the computer tablets on the desk. "Did you make any headway?"

"Not really." Foley gave Wilson his shot and then administered one to the captain. "As I said before, it's a corona virus a lot like the flu, but its genetic structure is different, more complex."

Van Wert rubbed his arm where Foley had stuck him. "It's not a strain of flu?"

"It's not a close enough match to be considered a strain."

"I see," the captain said. "Have you given any more thought to viral attenuation?"

Foley sighed. "I really don't think that's an option for us, Captain." He started putting away the hypo and medications.

"What are you talking about? Isn't that how they defeat viruses? That's how Pasteur cured rabies, and Jenner cured small pox, and Salk cured polio. That book said-"

"Yes, that's how they did it back then, but it doesn't work for all viruses. Nowadays, they use genetic engineering to kill viruses."

"So you're not even willing to try?"

Foley sighed and shook his head. "Captain, when you start tinkering around with viruses and go injecting them back into people, you could just as easily kill someone as you could cure them. You have to know exactly what you're doing." Foley coughed hard and spit into a tissue. "It's a lot more that just reading in a book."

"Well, if I had your medical background-"

"You'd realize, as I do, that this is pointless."

Van Wert stood quietly for a moment and frowned. Wilson wondered if Foley had said too much. The captain bit on his thumbnail, then said, "Have you tested Ski to find out why he got over the virus?"

"He's supposed to come in tomorrow morning for that."

"Good. I also want you to compare the blood work of the station crewman in the lifeboat who did not have any symptoms. I want to know why he and Ski didn't die from this thing. It may give us a clue."

Foley nodded, and the captain turned and left the room.

Foley shook his head. "He just doesn't get it."

"Maybe he doesn't want to," Wilson said. "You know the old man. He never gives up."

Chapter 44
"Search for a Friend"

Ski awoke from a deep sleep and stared stupidly at the base of the station sextant, trying to remember where he was. His left shoulder and left hip ached from sleeping on his side on the floor, and his left hand felt numb and tingly. He sat up and looked out at the stars, still fixed in space, their lack of movement revealing no passage of time. But his extreme hunger told him he must've been sleeping for a few hours. The clock on the computer showed the station time to be 10:34 p.m.

He got to his feet and recollected the events of the day. They seemed years in the past and unreal, especially Petey's death. That part seemed far too strange to be real.

And yet it is real. Petey is gone.

The dying expression on Petey's face came to mind, and he blinked his eyes tightly and shook his head to dispel the image. He stared out at the glow of the distant Alpha Centauri B, then his growling stomach prompted him to turn away from the dome of glass and climb down the hatch, leaving his pillow and blanket behind.

Ski found the lounge deserted except for Wilson, who had nodded off on a couch. On his lap lay a computer pad opened to the Gospel of Mark. Ski went to the food selector panel and chose a ham biscuit. Wilson stirred awake at the noise of the machine. He glanced up at Ski and shut the pad off.

"I'm sorry," Ski said. "I didn't mean to wake you up."

"That's all right. I guess I should go find a bed. What are you doing up?"

"I woke up hungry."

"That's probably a good sign," Wilson said. "You must be feeling better."

"Yeah. It's pretty weird." Ski took his food out of the warmer and blew on it before taking a tentative bite. He felt glad that Wilson was still up, but as he turned to face him, he saw the systems tech stand and head for the door.

"You turning in?"

Wilson yawned and nodded. "Doc says I need all the sleep I can get to fight this thing."

"Ok. Well, goodnight."

"You need anything?"

Ski would've liked to say, *Yes, I'd like some conversation to keep my mind off of things.* Instead, he took another bite and shook his head.

Wilson pointed to one of the MSES machines. "If you can't sleep, those things are great diversions."

"Thanks. Good night."

Wilson left the lounge, and Ski finished his biscuit. Then he sat down in the nearest booth and read the menu of scenarios. Nothing appealed to him until he came to the one with no label, the adult one.

He thought about the raven-haired girl, her lovely eyes and warm smile and her loving willingness. *Man, she is so beautiful.* He felt a tingle in his chest at the thought of being with her again and wondered if it was possible to have a conversation with her. *Is it possible to interact with the characters in the programs outside of the scenario limits? Has anyone tried? It would be nice to be candid with a total stranger, especially one who couldn't blab to the other guys on the station. Was it possible to tell her about Petey, and how much it hurt to know he was dead?* He decided to find out.

Ski selected the file and the specific scenario and donned the headgear. Soon he heard the steady frequency of the sound in the earphones and saw the flashing white lights in the goggles. The sound altered almost imperceptibly as his brain waves synchronized with the infrasonic rhythmic pulse. Then an image began to suffuse his mind of a grand ballroom with chandeliers and colorful draperies and formally dressed nineteenth century aristocrats whirling around the floor. The music came next, and Ski recognized Strauss' "Wine, Women, and Song." Then he became aware of *her,* and his heart seemed to stop beating in his chest. The girl's face was jubilant, and her curls tossed from side to side as they danced. Ski held her right hand with his left and his right hand against the small of her back. They danced, with the flow of the other couples on the crowded floor and passed a quartet of musicians playing in the corner.

She was indeed beautiful. Her delicate features accentuated her black hair tied up on the back of her head. Several long curls cascaded down her neck. As they danced he lowered his right hand until it rested just at the top of her buttocks. She stared into his eyes with an alluring desire, and her intention was understood.

When the music ended, the girl led him by the hand through the other people toward the stairs. At the bottom of the staircase Ski tugged her hand.

"Wait a moment. What's your name?"

"Anne," she replied. Giggling, she led him up the grand staircase as the quartet began a new piece.

Ski had planned to stop at the top of the stairs and ask the girl some questions. He wanted to learn more about her, or to see if there was any more to learn, but by now he was far too aroused. He followed her, first to her room briefly, then into her parent's room where the two made love on the bed as before.

When it was over, Ski felt overwhelmed with emotion for the girl named Anne. He held her tightly and kissed her. It was long enduring kiss, and he felt deeply fulfilled to hold another human being so closely with such affection. The isolation of a long patrol eroded a man's soul, and Ski hadn't realized how empty he had become.

After several moments he broke the kiss and looked at her angelic face, now smiling at him happily.

"I love you," he told her. She reached up and ran her fingers through his hair as his consciousness went black.

Ski came out of the program physically satisfied but disappointed to have not spoken to her more. But now he had an idea. If he could delay the conclusion of the program, he might be able to keep her with him longer.

After a trip to the restroom, Ski reset the machine and restarted the program. The situation proceeded as before until they reached the top of the stairs. Then Ski, still holding her hand, stopped and turned her toward him.

"Hold on a minute. I want to talk to you."

Anne tugged on his arm smiling. "Come with me."

"No, please. We'll get to that in a minute. I want to know more about you. Stay and talk with me a moment."

The girl craned her head back, pulling on his arm harder. She gave an expression like a child about to whine. "Uh-uh. Come on."

"Anne."

The girl snatched her hand away from Ski's and stood before him, a disappointed, almost angry look on her face. She hesitated a moment as if expecting him to change his mind, then she stomped past him and went back down the stairs.

"Anne!" Ski called, but the girl gave no response. He watched her until his consciousness went black. He quickly reset the machine and went back in. He had one more avenue to try. It seemed that the sex act alone would hold her attention, and that gave him an idea.

Soon he was with her again going up the staircase. The program continued as before until they were both on the bed. Ski had planned to stop here, but her insistent begging almost overwhelmed him. He forced himself to concentrate and spoke to her.

"Anne, listen. I want to talk to you."

"Please…please don't stop."

"Anne, I love you. I want to know more about you. Please talk to me."

"Oh…" The girl seemed determined to continue the encounter even if it meant going on without him. His self-control crumbled, and it was soon finished. Anne reached up and took his face in her hands and kissed him hard. Then she broke the kiss and looked up at him, smiling gleefully.

At that moment the whole scene took on a synthetic quality. The girl would not sit with him, she would not stop and talk to him, and she could never fall in love with him. She was only there to provide a scenario for his sexual gratification and that was all. Anne was nothing more than an electronically induced fantasy for the male point of view.

Ski felt disappointed, but kissed her anyway and held her tightly, savoring the falsity for the last few moments, but he felt hollow inside. He knew he wouldn't be going into the program again.

Soon his consciousness faded out. He removed the headgear and stepped out of the booth. His heart felt more empty and lonely that it had before he started the machine. He ordered a glass of wine from the vending machine and drank it down, then headed for his bed.

His quiet footfalls in the empty hall accentuated his smothering loneliness. Everyone else was surely asleep by now, and he doubted if there was even one of them to whom he could unburden himself. Petey was the only one he could ever talk to, the only one who seemed to understand him, and Petey was irreplaceably gone. He hoped the wine's intoxication would kick in soon and allow him to drift off into sleep quickly.

As he stood outside his room in the red glow of the nighttime lighting, he remembered his pillow and blanket still under the station sextant. He contemplated going up for them when he was startled by an alarm that began to blare throughout the station. The tone started at a low pitch and rose swiftly in a repeating pattern. The daytime lights came on and emergency lamps began flashing at each end of the hall, and Ski looked around in confusion. Wilson opened one of the doors and shouted to Ski.

"What the hell is going on?"

Ski shrugged. "I don't know."

Wilson came out of the room. "Come on. We can see everything from Main Control."

Chapter 45
"Gradenko's Gambit"

Ski followed the systems tech down the stairs, much faster than the elevator, and ran into the main control room of the station. On the big wall screens, the communications side showed falling power level readings in all areas, but the power side was afire with red alarms and warnings. One stood out in particular to Ski. It read, "REACTOR CORE TEMPERATURE ELEVATED AND RISING."

Wilson saw it, too. "Whoa!" he shouted, taking a seat at the console. "Six of the eight Stirlings are offline!"

"Can you restart them?"

Wilson battered the keyboard with commands as Ski watched the temperature increase steadily. The various equipment representations flashed red in unison. Wilson continued typing and using the touch screen and hand interface.

"Can you restart them?" Ski repeated.

"No! This access point is locked out." He faced Ski. "It's being run locally from the plant itself."

"What the hell are you two doing?" Van Wert shouted as he entered the control room. Millus ran beside him.

"It's not us, sir," Wilson said. "Someone's doing this from the control booth in the plant. They've locked out this panel."

"Where the hell is Dresden?"

"I'm right here, Captain," the engineering tech answered. He coughed hard, and Ski could see he was pale and shivering.

Van Wert squared off to the tech and jerked his thumb up toward the screen behind him. "What the hell do you know about this?"

Dresden took a step back. "Nothing, sir! I swear! All was well when I went to bed at eight."

"We'll see." Van Wert faced Millus. "Muster all hands right here, A.S.A.P."

"Aye, sir." Millus picked up an intercom mic and pushed the button. "Now muster all hands in the main control room, on the double!"

The remains of the *Kestrel* crew exited the elevator or ran down the stairway, some having already been on their way before the announcement went out. Ski saw that they were in various stages of the sickness. They assembled around the captain, bleary but visibly anxious of the alarms and the power plant display.

"Who's missing?" Van Wert asked.

The men looked around at each other until Millus blurted out, "Gradenko."

"Oh, no," Dresden said.

"What?" Van Wert demanded.

"He's been down in the power plant the last couple of days learning the system. He said he was tired of movies and the MSES machines and wanted to get his mind off of things."

"What did you show him?" Van Wert took a step closer to the engineering tech.

"Nothing! Just general stuff, like you might show on a dependent's cruise."

"Captain," Wilson said, "earlier he was talking about having his last meal."

Dresden went pale. "He did say something about blowing up the station."

"Damn!" Van Wert went to the intercom and pressed a button. "Gradenko! Gradenko, answer me!" He turned to Millus, but he and Flores were already heading for the stairs. He turned back to Wilson. "Try breaking through to the control panel. Do anything to restart those motors!"

Wilson turned back to his keyboard, and Ski watched the temperature still rising on the overhead screen.

"Hello?" Gradenko said over the intercom. His voice sounded as calm as if he were answering a front door.

"Gradenko, this is the captain. Restart the Stirling generators immediately."

"I can't do that, sir."

"What the hell do you mean you can't do it? Start them up right now! You're cooking off the reactor!"

"I guess I can do it, sir, but I'm not going to."

"What are you talking about? You're going to blow up the whole station if you don't restart right now!"

"Yes, sir. But isn't that better than going out like Petey? Wouldn't you rather die like a fighting man instead of like some sick old wretch in bed? I know I would."

"Gradenko, that's not your call. Petey had a preexisting condition that the virus made worse. The rest of us have a fighting chance."

"There is no chance. I'm sorry, Captain."

"Gradenko! Start those generators now!"

"I'm signing off now. See you on the other side."

"Gradenko! Gradenko! Dammit!" Van Wert threw the intercom mic down against the console and ran toward the stairwell. Dresden was already descending the steps to the lower level. Ski followed them.

At the bottom of the stairwell Millus and Flores were struggling to get the door open. They looked up as the others approached.

"He's locked the door from the inside," Millus said.

"Can't you override it?"

"No, sir," Dresden answered. "As soon as the reactor incident system kicks in, the doors are sealed shut."

Van Wert turned to Millus. "Go get our weapons." The ensign ran back up the stairs.

"You can't blast through, Captain," Dresden said. "The doors are too thick. But I think there's another way in."

"Where?"

"I'll show you." The engineering tech ran back up the stairs, and Ski and the others followed.

Millus joined them at the top of the stairs holding a few pistols. "These are all that's left. The street sweeper is gone. He must have it."

Dresden staggered against a wall and Flores caught him. Van Wert faced him.

"I'm sorry, sir. I just got a little dizzy running up the stairs. Follow me."

He led them into a short corridor where a small hatch was set into a wall. Steel dogging levers held the door shut. Here, Dresden had to shout over the blaring alarm.

"This is the main service conduit that runs externally along the entire length of the station. Inside are the ventilation ducts, piping, and electrical lines. There's another hatch on the power plant deck near the control booth."

Van Wert pointed to Flores and gestured toward his ear. "Get us some comms." Then he took one of the pistols and handed it to Ski. "You're going in with us."

"Me?"

"Yes. You're the healthiest among us. The rest of you wait by the door below."

Flores brought the communications headsets, and Van Wert passed one each to Millus and Ski before donning one himself. He passed the other one to Dresden. "As soon as we're inside and have secured the area, you need to give us instructions on how to shut it down."

"Why can't I go with you?"

"You're more valuable out of harm's way." He faced Millus and Ski. "All right, let's get this open. The rest of you wait by the door below. We'll open it as soon as we can."

Ski kicked at the locking dogs to loosen them, then swung them out of the way and opened the hatch. Van Wert shoved past him and entered the conduit, followed by Millus. Ski bent down and scrambled in after them.

The conduit had no gravitational field, and Ski immediately "fell" against a pipe running along the far wall. After so long on the station Ski found the microgravity very disorienting. He tumbled for a moment, then looked around in the dim light for the captain and Mr. Millus. They seemed to be above him and moving higher, but one look back at the hatch confirmed that they were actually moving down. Sticking the pistol in his belt, Ski grabbed at the electrical cables and began to pull himself along after them.

The alarm here was not so loud, and after what seemed like a few minutes he caught up with them as they had stopped to talk.

"Is it possible we already passed it?" Millus asked.

"I suppose so," Van Wert answered. "Hey, Ski. Look around and see if you can find that hatch. I'll look ahead."

"Aye, aye." He began to search nearby and found the hatch above him. "Here it is!"

Unable to kick at the dogs in the narrow space, he braced himself between a pipe and the wall and strained at the dogs until they were all loose. The door opened to a cacophony of wailing alarms piercing the whine and rumble of the machinery. A blast of hot air flowed past Ski's face as he looked out. He was at the operations level of the power plant control room with the floor above him. As he pulled himself through, he struck the back of his head on the deck as he tumbled out. He came to rest against the nearest generator casing and was pulling his pistol free when a shower of sparks erupted against a nearby wall. Even in here, where the alarms blared the loudest, Ski could make out the distinctive sound of the street sweeper.

"Behind you, to your left!" Millus shouted from the hatch. A hail of laser fire drove the ensign back inside.

Ski crawled cat-like around the left side of the casing, then cautiously peered around the edge. From this vantage he saw the control booth, the door held open by a piece of wire around the handle. The air felt super heated, and his shirt was already sticky with sweat.

Another burst of laser fire erupted, and Ski looked to see the hatch blasted by sparks and metal fragments. Gradenko was keeping the hatch covered. He was alone with a madman.

A heavily armed madman! I must get to the control booth and start those generators. The booth was no more than ten yards away, and the alarms here were deafening. He caught a movement out of the corner of his eye and recoiled as a burst of laser fire exploded the insulation from the generator casing, causing a snowstorm of white particles around him.

A few single shots erupted behind him from the hatch, quickly answered by the street sweeper. Van Wert seemed to be shouting in his ear through the headset.

"See if you can get a shot at him while we draw his fire!"

"The booth door is wide open! I'm sure I can sprint to it while you get his attention."

"That's no good if he follows you inside. You've got to take him out first!"

"Can you see the panel from there?" Dresden called.

"Yes," Ski answered. "There's a big touch screen with six red squares flashing."

"You have to touch each block one at a time and hit 'RUN' in the pop up."

"Ski," Millus called. "We're running out of time. If we don't start cooling the reactor soon, we won't be able to stop it from cooking off."

"You've got to kill him now," Van Wert shouted. "We'll draw his fire while you shoot. Keep shooting until he goes down."

"Is that you, Ski?" Gradenko called out over the alarms.

"Yes!" Ski yelled. "Don't shoot!"

"I don't want to shoot you, so you'd better stay where you are."

More sporadic fire came from the hatch, answered by a volley from the weapons tech.

"Ski!" the captain shouted in his ear. "Shoot him while we draw his fire!"

"Gradenko!" Ski called out. "Stop this madness! Let us get those motors running!"

"I'm not going to die like those people on the station. I'm not going to die like poor Petey, choking on his own melting lungs. I'm not doing it!"

"Okay, I get that. But why kill everyone? We might be saved yet. Hell, I'm over it! You're going to kill me?"

"I don't want to kill you, Ski. But you'd better keep away from that booth."

If you don't want me in the control booth, then why did you prop the door open? Then Ski realized the situation. The gunner was determined to die in his boots. He'd said so earlier.

"Nick, you've always been brave, probably the bravest man on the ship. And even though this virus is a very frightening thing, you've got to be brave against it, too."

"We're out of time, Ski!" Millus shouted.

"This isn't like you, man. You never give up for anything," Ski reasoned. Above him, still high above the gravity layer, insulation began to crack and break off, spinning lazily in the shimmering air. "I'm coming out, Nick."

"Don't move toward that control booth!"

"I won't. I just want to talk."

Ski slowly rose to his feet, holding the pistol down at his side. Standing, he could see the gunner crouched behind a generator casing, completely immune from fire from the hatch. He smiled at Ski, serene despite the noise and heat.

"Don't do this, Nick."

"I'm sorry, buddy, but you see, I've already decided."

"Ski!" Van Wert shouted into his ear. "What the hell are you doing?"

Another piece of insulation broke loose above him, and Ski detected a subtle vibration through the soles of his feet.

"Ski, there's no time!" Millus shouted.

"They must be screaming at you to shoot, Ski." Gradenko smiled. "Don't keep them waiting."

"Come on, Nick. Stand with us. We need you."

Gradenko shook his head. "Here's how it is. You go for that booth, I kill you. You stand there, we all die. There's only one way out."

"Nick…"

"Would it help if I pointed the gun at you? Would that help you to do this one last favor for me?"

"Ski!" Van Wert yelled.

There came a thump through the deck and a piece of insulation fell at his feet. Without waiting for an answer, Gradenko pointed the gun at Ski. Ski raised the pistol and shot his shipmate three times in the chest. The gunner jolted backward and let the gun settle to his lap.

Van Wert and Millus tumbled out of the hatch and ran past him into the booth. Ski stepped over and squatted next to Gradenko, who lay clutching his chest. The weapons tech smiled through his grimace and took Ski's hand.

"Thanks, Ski." Gradenko chuckled then clenched his teeth. "Damn. This really hurts." Then a look of deep concern came over his face. "Tell the captain I'm sorry."

Choking back tears, Ski nodded and forced a smile. He held the smile as Gradenko faded away and wondered if he could ever be forgiven for such an act. He knew he would never forgive himself.

"Ski!" Millus called out, coming out of the booth behind him. "The generators are all back on, but it's not enough to wick off all this heat! We've got to open the NGG radiator valves!"

Ski released the gunner's hand and stood, looking up to where the ensign pointed.

"On each of these elevated platforms is a large red valve. Get up there and open that one, then open the next one, and so on. I'll start over here." He ran toward a ladder next to the far wall.

Van Wert came up and patted Ski's shoulder, smiling as a father trying to be brave for a suffering child. "Come on, Ski. We can still save the others."

Ski nodded and looked up at the platforms, then, dropping the pistol, he reached over and began to climb the nearest one. As he ascended, the ladder rungs became painfully hot and the air seemed to sear his lungs. He reached the platform and nearly fell over backward, and grabbing a hold of the burning handrail, realized that he was above the gravity field. He tugged himself over to the valve and removed the broken locking mechanism, then turned the valve handle. He heard a muffled whoosh inside the pipe and continued turning until the valve fully opened.

The next platform was only forty feet away, too far a jump in gravity, but not so here. He aimed himself and pushed off against the handrail, knocking a floating piece of insulation out of his face on the way. At the next platform he quickly opened the red valve, and moved onto the next.

Van Wert and Millus had been opening valves as well, so after Ski's third one opened, the job was complete. By now Ski's hands were shaking, his face tingled, and he felt like vomiting from the heat. Before descending, he looked around and saw that the captain wasn't moving. He shook the sweat from his face, the drops flying out like fragments of a bomb burst, and pushed off toward the captain.

Once at the handrail he grabbed the captain's collar and looked around for the ensign. "Mr. Millus!"

The officer appeared on the floor below and held out his arms. Ski pushed the captain down toward the deck and watched the frightful acceleration as the captain fell back into the gravity field, knocking Millus off his feet. He soon recovered and dragged the captain into the control booth. Ski hurriedly climbed down the nearest ladder and raced across the floor to join them, closing the door behind him.

Here much of the outside sound was muffled by the thick walls and glass, but the repeater alarm on the console continued to buzz. Ski held his hand up to the air conditioner vent and felt the rush of cold air, but it would take some time to cool the booth completely. He looked down to where Millus was removing the captain's clothing, directly under one of the vents. He looked up at Ski.

"We've got to cool him down. He's going into heat stroke."

"What can I do?"

"Go prop open the main door, but tell the others to stay out of this booth, except Dresden."

Ski took a glance at the control panel, which showed the core temperature still climbing, but much slower now. He pushed through the door and back into the noise and heat.

"Ski," Dresden called through the headset. "What's happening?"

"How do I get this main door open?"

"Break the glass on the panel next to the door and pull down on the emergency release handle. We'll help you pry it open."

Ski did so, and willing hands helped him slide the heavy doors apart.

"Man! It's hot in there!" Flores said.

"Everyone stay out here," Ski said, "except Dresden."

The tech nodded and ran in toward the booth. Ski moved along the wall until he was out of the rush of hot air coming through the door. He sat down against the wall and breathed in the comparatively cool air. His limbs were shaking, and his face seemed to radiate heat. He slid down the wall to a sitting position and listened to Millus and Dresden talking through the comms gear.

"Call Wilson and send Doc down here," Millus said. "Tell him the captain is down, possible heat exhaustion."

"Aye, aye," Dresden said. "It looks like the core temperature has stopped rising. No wait, it's starting to creep back down."

"Thank God. Get Doc down here."

Ski sighed in his relief. Then he thought about Gradenko and put his head down against his knees.

Chapter 47
"Know Your Enemy"

Ski awoke the next morning feeling sticky from an uncomfortable night's sleep. Despite taking a cool shower before he went to bed, the excessive heat of the power plant had elevated the temperature throughout the station, and though the air was noticeably cooler now, he'd slept in a sweat for most of the night.

After wetting his face and neck in the restroom, he went to the dining area where he saw Wilson eating breakfast alone at one of the tables. Ensign Millus stood at the food dispenser and looked over as Ski came in.

"Hi, Ski. How are you doing this morning?"

"Tired."

"Me, too. I couldn't sleep worth a damn. Couldn't get cool."

Ski nodded and looked over the food selection. Behind him Flores came through the door.

"Hey, where is Doc?" he asked.

"I don't know," Ski said. "Why?"

"I've had this headache all night, and it's getting worse."

"It's the virus," Wilson said not looking up from his plate.

Flores shook his head. "It might be the heat from last night. I'll check his room after I eat."

"Doc's in bed," Millus said. "And I don't think he'll be holding sick call today."

"Is he pretty bad now, too, Mr. Millus?" Ski asked.

Millus nodded.

"Another one getting ready to bite the dust," Wilson said.

"That's a screwed up thing to say," Flores said.

"It's true, isn't it?" Wilson pointed out beyond the door. "It's getting us one by one, like it did those guys on the station log."

"It might not be as bad for us as it was for them," Ski offered. "After all-"

"Oh, great! Words of encouragement from the picture of health." Wilson glared at Ski, a decisive smirk on his face. "Might not be as bad, huh? That's easy for you to say. It doesn't look like it'll be bad for you at all!" Wilson sat back in his chair and smiled. "I just thought about something ironic. Wouldn't it be fitting for you, the man who couldn't stand being penned up with the guys on the ship, to be stranded alone on this station? Just think, Ski, after we all kick off, you'll have the whole place to yourself! I even-"

"Knock it off," Millus said as he carried his tray to a table and sat down. Wilson scoffed and returned to his meal.

Ski thought about what Wilson had said. It was a possibility, and the thought of being stranded alone on the station made him shudder. *What if no rescue came? What if the Kestrel crew had been written off already? He had heard talk of new relay stations being activated. What if the ICA decided to just let this one go?*

A deep, rumbling cough broke into Ski's thoughts. He looked to see the captain standing in the doorway, leaning against the frame. He looked haggard, old, worn out.

"Captain, why are you here?" Millus asked, walking over to him. "You should be in bed."

Van Wert shook his head, waving him off. He coughed again and nodded to Ski. "What are you doing today?"

"I had nothing planned, Captain."

Van Wert nodded. "I thought so." He struggled to take another breath. "A mind like yours should not be kept idle, Ski." He took another deep breath, then coughed hard. Ski could hear rumbling in his chest. "I want you to start reporting to sick bay for duty, starting today."

"Sick bay, Captain?" Ski asked. "Do you mean as a medic?'

"In whatever capacity you can."

"Sir, I appreciate the need, but I have no medical training whatsoever."

"You're smart. You'll catch on soon enough."

Ski realized that the others were watching him. "Captain, honestly-"

"Listen, Doc is out, and soon I'll be out, too. I need someone to tend to these men as they get worse. I'll tell you all that I know, and we'll try to do some kind of turnover with Doc." He stopped to cough again. "Who knows? Maybe you'll find some clue that will help us."

Ski nodded and sighed.

"Bring your breakfast with you."

Ski heated a biscuit, and with an orange juice container, followed the captain to the station doctor's office next to the clinic.

"Here are the doctor's notes and journal. Foley's notes and journal are there, too," Van Wert said, pointing to an arrangement of thin, transparent computer notepads on the desk. "I've also opened some books on the doctor's pad about viral diseases." He coughed hard and spit into a handkerchief. "This room over here is the lab. All of the medical supplies are there."

"Is everything labeled?"

"Yes. I've decided to give the hemoglobin enhancer to everyone regardless of the severity of their symptoms. You'll find that on the lab table."

Ski nodded.

"After checking in on the men, I want you to have a look at the books and notes and things. Doc didn't believe it, but there's got to be something we can do to help ourselves."

"Maybe, but I don't know anything about this stuff."

"Well, I didn't either, but I learned a lot just by reading about it in these books." Van Wert said, pointing at the station doctor's pad. "And don't forget Doc's log and the records he kept. You can continue where he left off." The captain coughed and spit again. "Whatever you try will be okay. I just want an account of what happened."

"I don't want to do anything wrong."

Van Wert smiled. "You can't do anything wrong, at least nothing that would be held against you. Like you said, you've not been trained." He coughed again and seemed to lose his balance, bracing himself against the desk. "I've got to go lie down. Study this material. Around midday we'll make the rounds together."

Ski nodded and watched the captain leave the room, then he sat down at the desk and began to read.

****

At eleven a.m. Ski looked up from the doctor's computer pad to see Ensign Millus standing in the doorway.

"Hi, Ski. How's it coming?"

"Pretty well. It's a lot of material for a crash course. I started with Foley's log and records and then went on to Dr. Shahid's journal, but soon realized I needed more knowledge about the virus to make sense of the records, so I'm in the medical books now."

Millus stepped in and leaned against a cabinet. "Anything interesting?"

"Actually, yes. This is about how the human immune system fights off viruses with antibodies and killer T-cells and macrophages. The antibodies are produced to attach to the viral receptors on a specific virus, preventing the virus from attacking a human cell. Once they are produced, you will never get sick from that particular virus again. Then the T-cells and macrophages seek out and destroy the viruses."

"So why is it so hard to get over the flu?"

"Because the virus mutates. A drift mutation in the viral RNA may subtly change the receptor spikes, which makes the antibodies obsolete. The body has to play catch up several times before it can overcome the viral invasion."

"But people still get sick from flu year after year."

"True, but that's because there is another type of mutation which occurs. A shift mutation is when a totally new gene strand appears, which dramatically alters the surface proteins. It may go unnoticed by the immune system until a new wide-scale infection has begun."

"I remember reading about that. The mutations happen in the digestive tracts of some animals, right?"

"Exactly. A shift mutation takes place when the existing strain of flu virus combines with some other virus. Sometimes the new strain is more virulent than the original, other times it is less so. But the real interesting part is what happens when the virus attacks a human cell."

Ski turned the pad so the ensign could watch a video representation.

"Once the virus has evaded the immune system, it attaches itself to the human cell and begins to penetrate the cell wall. Once inside, the virus commandeers the cell's nucleus, inserting its own RNA into the cell's DNA, and forces it to manufacture new viruses using the cell's own reproductive system. The new viruses, produced en masse, leave the cell to infect other cells, and each one takes part of the host cell's protective membrane to form its own lipid envelope. After enough of the cell tissue is taken, the cell dies." The video ended.

Millus pointed to the medical lab. "What about antibiotics?"

"Well, that's the clincher. Antibiotics are designed to stop the life processes of bacteriological organisms, but a virus technically has no life processes to stop. It can't even reproduce on its own. It can be killed in a lab, but that's all. That's why the human body is totally dependent on its immune system to combat and overcome an invading virus."

Ski picked up another pad from the desk and said, "This is the station doctor's journal. He wrote, 'The Aldebaran virus mimics the influenza in every way, except that the drift mutation reoccurs four to five times as often. The patient's immune system can never catch up.'"

"So how did you recover?" Millus asked.

Ski set the pad back on the desk. "I don't know yet. The captain thinks if I can figure that out it might help the rest of us."

"Wow. Wouldn't that be nice?" Millus looked up at the ceiling and seemed about to say something else, but abruptly stood up. "Well, good luck. If I can help you, let me know."

"Thanks."

***

The lunch hour had passed without Ski's notice as he continued his study of the material. No one else had come by until nearly one thirty, when a congested coughing outside the office caught his attention. He looked up to see the captain enter and give a nod of approval.

"Make any headway?" Van Wert asked.

"Yes, as a matter of fact I did. It's very interesting reading, especially about the flu virus."

"Did you read about Pasteur?"

"No, not yet, but I planned to read that and all the other parts that you'd marked."

"Good." Van Wert coughed. "Let's do the rounds while I still have some energy."

"Where should we start?"

257

"Let's start with Doc. He's not doing well at all." Van Wert coughed and spit into a tissue. "Each day you'll begin by seeing the men who are the worst. Then you'll open sickbay to treat the others who come in."

Ski nodded. "Let me get Doc's bag." He walked into the lab and grabbed the medic's bag, then followed Van Wert to Foley's room.

As they entered the darkened room, Ski could hear the medic's shallow, labored breathing, and a chill went up his spine. They walked over and switched on the light over the bed.

"Get in the habit of checking breathing, pulse, heartbeat, and temperature," Van Wert said.

Ski took the medical recorder out of the bag and switched it on, then he placed the stethoscope over Foley's chest until he heard gurgling with each breath and let the machine record the sound. After a few tries, he found the pulse and heartbeat and did the same. He applied the thermometer to Doc's forehead and read the temperature and finally applied the automatic cuff and recorded the blood pressure.

Throughout the examination Ski felt very much out of place. He only did what he had seen Foley do, and he knew that he really couldn't interpret the symptoms. His only hope was to record the data and get a recommendation from the station doctor's computer.

Van Wert turned away to cough, and the medic stirred. Doc looked at Ski holding the medical recorder and grew incredulous, then he groaned and turned away.

"Not exactly a vote of confidence," Ski said, putting the equipment back into the bag.

"Don't worry about that," the captain said. "I think you should put him on oxygen after we check on Mac."

Ski nodded and switched off the light, then followed the captain into the next room.

They found the cook asleep on the bottom bunk, and Van Wert roused him. He sat up rubbing his eyes.

"Meanwhile, back in the jungle..." Ski said with a grin.

Mac gave a lopsided smile.

"How are you doing, Cookie?" Van Wert asked.

"Not worth a crap, sir."

"Where do you feel sick the most?"

"I feel sore all over. I feel like I gotta bad cold, and my chest feels heavy."

Ski recorded his vital signs and afterward Mac asked, "What's going on?"

"Doc is too sick to make his rounds. I'm trying to fill in for him." Ski answered.

Van Wert coughed hard.

"Are you okay, sir?" Mac asked.

Van Wert nodded. "Ski will give you something for the symptoms. Can we get you anything to eat?"

"No, thank you. I'm not very hungry."

"When did you eat last?"

"Late last night Dresden brought me some danish and orange juice. You know, sir, he really has changed. I mean, he was always an all right guy. He just got caught up with the wrong crowd. I think he's really trying to make good."

Van Wert nodded but didn't remark. "You should really try to eat something, to keep up your strength."

Mac shook his head. "I just don't have the stomach for it, sir."

"All right. Call Ski if you change your mind."

"Okay," Mac said. "I guess Doc must be pretty bad."

"He needs to rest," Van Wert said. "And so do you."

Mac nodded and frowned before turning on the bed to face the wall. Ski and Van Wert stepped out and returned to the doctor's office.

"I should take your vitals, too," Ski said.

"Yes, I suppose you should." Van Wert waited until Ski recorded the data before he spoke again. "As you read those books I recommended, you'll find that there's a common thread in how doctors have fought the different viruses over the years. Mostly they used an attenuated or killed virus to inoculate people against disease. That way the body can set up its defenses before the person is exposed to the real thing."

"Yes, but that doesn't help someone who is already infected, does it?"

"It sometimes can. Pasteur-" Van Wert coughed hard and spit into a tissue. "My chest is so sore." He took a few breaths before continuing. "Pasteur used an attenuated rabies virus to cure rabies in an infected boy. He cultured the virus in bottles that held animal spinal cords. He started with a weak dose then gave increasingly stronger doses until he was giving the boy full rabies. But by then the boy was cured.”

“How did it work in the immune system?”

“I don’t remember.”

“Well, how did he attenuate the virus?”

“I think he used formaldehyde. No, that was Sabin. Oh, I can’t remember right now. I get one confused with the other. But read about it. It makes a lot of sense.”

“I will.” Ski finished the exam and returned the machine to the bag. “Captain, I think you should spend the rest of the day in bed. You told us we needed to conserve our strength, and you’ve been running around the station as if there’s nothing wrong with you. I think you should obey your own order.”

Van Wert nodded in resignation. “There’s still so much to be done.”

“I think I can handle it from here. You’ve done enough for everyone else, now take care of yourself. Conserve your strength.”

Van Wert nodded and stood up, clasping his hand on Ski’s shoulder. “Thanks, Ski.”

Ski smiled. “Anytime.”

Chapter 48
"Desperation"

Ski brought a late lunch into the doctor's office and ate as he read the medical articles the captain had bookmarked. It soon became apparent that inoculations like Pasteur's rabies shot would be hard-pressed to work on a virus that mutated so rapidly like this one.

So what happened to me? He took up Foley's journal again and scanned through it until he found the entry when Doc had examined him.

It read, "Blood sample drawn 7 D.O.E. of J.A. Kowalski, Type A pos. Patient's blood evidenced an unknown strain of virus that is not the Aldebaran virus, but resembles it in many ways. Eleven months ago patient contracted a virus which caused fever, swelling of joints, and slight jaundice. Disease was found to be the Schadendorf virus of the Herpes virus group. Given the fact that the Schadendorf virus remains in the body in dormant state, it is possible that it played a role in the patient's recovery from the Aldebaran virus."

So that was it. That's how I recovered. He scrolled to the next entry and found another blood test the captain had ordered specifically.

It read, "Blood sample drawn from dead station crewmen T. S. Gregory. Type O positive. This crewman was found symptom free in a station lifeboat and had expired between ten days and two weeks ago of suffocation. Although blood tissue was in an advance state of decay, traces of a viral agent were found that are similar to the Aldebaran virus. Station medical records indicate that crewman also carried a dormant virus, possibly the Schadendorf virus."

Ski closed the notebook and stood up. *So the Old Man was right after all. The key to curing this virus is in me.*

Ski walked into the small lab and began pacing around. *I may not know very much about diseases and the human immune system, but it's only common sense that the Schadendorf virus had somehow combined with the unstable Aldebaran virus to create a less virulent strain. Had a shift mutation occurred? How can I know for sure?*

He paced around the room, his eyes glancing over the variety of lab equipment. *I can't know for sure. The only thing I know for sure is*

*that the dormant Schadendorf was present in the only two cases that
survived the Aldebaran virus so far. I also know for sure that time is
running out for the captain and the others.*

As he studied the laboratory equipment an idea began to
formulate in his head. *I must introduce the Schadendorf virus into the
others.*

The more he thought about it, the more determined he became.
He would draw a sample of his own blood, separate the virus, and give
it to the crew. He opened the drawers beneath the table top until he
found a kit containing a disposable syringe and a rubber tourniquet. He
took the protective cover off the needle, and a chill ran up his spine
causing him to shudder. It seemed an eighth-inch thick, its beveled end
menacing and sinister. He put the needle down and bent his arms
tightly against his chest.

"Oh, man," he said aloud.

He stared at the needle. *How has medical science come so far
and yet still relies on medieval tools?* He began to pace around the
room again and made a pass around the table. He looked down at the
needle again and shuddered.

Closing his eyes, he tilted his head back and took a deep breath.
"Dammit!" He shook his head and walked on. He feared needles and
syringes like some people feared snakes.

You can do this. You have to do this.

He stopped in front of the syringe again and quickly took up the
rubber tourniquet and passed it around his upper arm. Holding one end
in his teeth, he threaded a loop under it and drew it tight so that one tug
would release it. He opened an antiseptic swab and sterilized the inside
of his left elbow where a vein was already beginning to rise. He picked
up the syringe and held it by the plunger end so that he could draw it
one handed. He brought it toward his elbow, then dropped it again and
turned away.

"Dammit!" He began pacing around the table again.

*This is stupid. I can do this. People do this all the time. Some
diabetics used to have to stick themselves every day. It's just a phobia,
an irrational fear. Intelligent people don't have irrational fears. Get
over it. You can do this.*

Ski picked up the needle again. *Just insert it, draw the plunger to fill, and take it out. Then you'll be done with it. If there's a chance this idea will work, then it's worth a try. Come on.*

Ski stared at the needle and attached tube. His whole body felt as tense as a steel spring. By now his arm was beginning to tingle and the veins were enlarged. He would have to do it soon or take the tourniquet off. He picked up the needle and placed the point at the inside of the elbow, just above a large vein. He willed himself to just push it in. *Just push it in...*

Every fiber of his being strained to push the needle into his arm, but it wouldn't go. His mind seemed to scream out, and his hand began to shake. He threw the needle back on the table and removed the tourniquet then stood shaking.

"Dammit! Dammit! Dammit!"

Waves of opposing emotions buffeted him. Anxiety, determination, fear, and now self-loathing swirled through his heart, and he felt as though he might cry. He walked out of the lab and into the office.

Maybe there's someone who could help me. I wish Doc was well enough, but he'd shoot the idea down anyway. Millus or Flores? No, they wouldn't know what they were doing. One botched attempt, and I know I couldn't try it again. I've got to do this myself.

But what if I botch it? He drew a deep breath and began to pace around the office.

Look, you've seen this done. You've got good veins. Just one tube might be enough to help everyone. How would you feel if your idea would have worked, except that you were too much of a coward to draw your own blood? What if the captain died because of your cowardice? How do you come back from that? First you shoot Gradenko, and now more death through cowardice?

His questions needed no answers. Resolutely, he walked back into the lab.

The key is to get it over with as quickly as possible. Don't think about it. Don't give yourself time to think about it.

He walked directly to the table and picked up the tourniquet. He fastened it securely the first time and swabbed his arm at the inside of the elbow. Then, even before the vein had risen fully, Ski stuck the needle into it.

"Ow!" he barked, not so much from the pain, but from the shock of pushing through the threshold of his fear. He slowly drew out the plunger and watched intently as the tube filled with his blood. Nausea and dizziness began to rise in him. When the tube was nearly full he withdrew the needle and placed the syringe on the table. He tore open a gauze pad with his teeth, placed it over the hole, and bent his arm up. Then he pulled off the tourniquet.

"That's it," he said and began to pace around the table. A feeling of pride began to grow inside him, settling his nausea and anxiety. He had faced it down.

He looked around the lab until he found the centrifuge. Selecting a tube randomly, he removed the cap and injected the blood sample into it, then replaced the cap and placed the tube into the machine. Inserting another tube from the cooler across from his sample to balance the centrifuge, he switched it on at the lowest setting for fifteen minutes.

"I guess that should do it," he said. "Now I want something to drink. I wonder if they have beer in the lounge." He smiled broadly and, still holding his left arm bent, headed for the lounge.

***

After a late lunch and a celebratory refreshment, Ski spent the rest of the afternoon trying to separate the blood solids from the plasma and virus. The centrifuge had taken longer than he had expected, and he had to increase the machine speed and spin duration. After several tries, he'd finally done it and, with a new syringe, he carefully extracted the amber liquid out of the tube. He checked a sample under the microscope and saw traces of the attenuated Aldebaran virus and the Schadendorf virus. There was a lot less of the serum than he had expected, but maybe it would be enough. He didn't want to draw more. He capped the needle and headed up to Van Wert's room.

When he got there, the room was still dark.

"Captain?"

"Yes, Ski." Van Wert switched on the lamp by his bed.

"How are you doing?"

264

"About the same." Van Wert coughed hard. "What've you got?"

"I had an idea I want to run past you."

The captain raised his eyebrows. "Let's hear it."

"Foley ran a blood test on me and also on the crewman found in the lifeboat who had no symptoms. Both tests showed a mild form of the Aldebaran virus, and both the crewman and I had been previously exposed to another virus called the Schadendorf virus. It remains in the body in a dormant state and apparently caused a mutation."

Van Wert smiled weakly. "Good work."

"Thank you. My idea is to inject the Schadendorf virus into someone who is sick to see if it will cause the same reaction as it did in me."

The captain nodded. "Is the serum ready?"

"I think so, but I only have a small amount." Ski held up the syringe.

Van Wert studied the amber liquid in the tube. "Try it in me first."

"Captain, I don't even know the risks."

"If I don't get help soon, I'll be dead anyway. If it is lethal, then I'll take the responsibility personally. If it's a success, then we'll give it to the others." The captain coughed hard.

Ski took the cap off to expose the needle but hesitated.

"What's wrong?" Van Wert asked.

"Are you sure you want to do this?"

The captain nodded. "Yes."

Ski leaned over and injected the serum into Van Wert's arm.

"Now," the captain said, "be sure to write down everything that you are doing and why. And as far as this shot goes, you write that I urged you to give it to me. Do you understand?"

Ski nodded. He understood very well. If the old man died because of the shot, he didn't want Ski to be blamed.

"And now I'm going back to sleep." Van Wert settled back down in the bed and closed his eyes.

Ski shut off the light and left the room, placing the capped syringe back in his pocket. He felt mentally and emotionally tired, but also hungry, so he went to the dining area and selected something to eat and waited for it to heat up. A few of the others were already there or were just coming in.

"Well, Doctor Kowalski," Wilson said, "how're things going with your new practice?"

Not sure if Wilson was being sarcastic or not, Ski replied simply, "All right."

"Oh, come on, Ski. Haven't you made any new breakthroughs yet? You've been so busy."

"Actually, yes." He looked around and noticed that he had everyone's attention, so he explained to them about the dormant virus that he had found.

"So where do you go from here?" Millus asked.

"I thought we might try injecting the Schadendorf virus into someone to see if they get the same reaction I did."

"Who's going first?" Flores asked.

"The captain has already gone first."

"What?" Millus asked, raising his eyebrows in alarm.

"I gave it to him just a few minutes ago. Why?"

"Because just the other day, Foley told the captain that giving someone a new virus when they are already sick could kill them."

A tingle went over Ski's scalp. "Foley told the captain that?"

"Yes. I was there in sickbay when they were talking about it," Wilson said.

"Who authorized you to administer anything like that to anyone?" Millus said.

"The captain did." Ski said, a sense of dread welling up in him.

"What makes you think that you can just come up with an idea and then implement it as you please?"

Ski clenched his teeth. "With all due respect, sir, where the hell were you when the ideas were coming up? I seem to be the only one around here who's taking an active interest in fighting this thing, and I'm not even sick. All the rest of you seem to do is lose yourselves in your work or those MSES machines, or just sitting around bitching. If you don't like my ideas, then I'd appreciate some new ones."

The room grew quiet except for a ding on the food heater indicating Ski's food was ready.

Millus gave a sigh and tried to sound conciliatory. "Ski, I think we all appreciate the effort that you're putting in for us. But all I ask is that you don't run to the captain with every new idea you come up with. At this point he'd try anything, no matter now dangerous."

"Well, sir, as close as he is to the end, that sounds about right, doesn't it?" Ski gathered up his dinner and left the room.

Chapter 49
"He's Gotten the Word"

The next day, Ski entered the captain's room and turned on the light. The captain woke readily.

"Good morning, Captain. How're you doing?"

Van Wert spoke slowly, straining with every breath.

"The same, really. What time is it?"

"A little after seven a.m."

"You're up early." Van Wert coughed up some mucus, and Ski handed him a tissue.

"I was up most of the night. I kept coming in here to see if you were still breathing." He didn't mention that he kept having recurring dreams that the captain had died. "I brought the oxygen machine for you."

Van Wert nodded. "I guess it's about time." He drew a heavy breath. "How are Foley and Mac?"

"About the same as yesterday, but Mac is getting weaker. I need to set up a buzzer or something so he can call if he needs help."

Van Wert nodded his approval.

"Foley wet his bed. I never even thought about him being too weak to go to the head."

Van Wert smiled. "You're a better Operations Specialist... than you are a nurse." He coughed hard and spit into the tissue again.

Ski nodded. "I'll have to clean him up, but I'll need some help. I'll ask one of the guys."

"If you have any trouble, I'll assign people."

"All right." Ski placed the oxygen tube on the captain and turned the machine on. "Yesterday, Mr. Millus told me that Foley said giving someone a new virus when they are already sick could kill them. He said Doc told you that."

"Yes, that's true," Van Wert said.

"Well, why did you let me give you that serum?"

"I thought it was worth a try...Besides, it seems...to have been harmless...I thought that I would have had...some reaction by now, good or bad."

"Maybe it's still early. Or maybe you didn't get enough to do anything at all," Ski offered.

Van Wert shrugged.

The door opened and Millus came in, haggard and bleary. "Good morning."

"Good morning," Ski answered. "How are you feeling?"

Millus shook his head. "I woke up with a fever. Aches, too."

"I'll give you something for that as soon as I'm done here."

Van Wert gestured to the ensign and spoke to Ski. "Tell him about Foley."

Ski turned. "Doc wet his mattress. I'll need some help to clean him up and change the sheets."

Millus nodded. "I'll help you."

"Or you could just assign one of the guys."

Millus shook his head. "Flores is much worse this morning, and I'm about the best of the lot. I'll help you."

"Thanks. I was also thinking of asking someone to sit with Mac to talk or play cards or something. He seemed depressed earlier."

Millus nodded. "That's easy enough. Should I call quarters?"

Van Wert shook his head. "Just ask them." He coughed long and hard and spit into a tissue again, and Ski felt a surge of nausea in his stomach.

The captain looked up at Millus. "Have there been...any messages?"

Millus shook his head. "No. I check the receiver twice a day."

Van Wert's expression became a mixture of incredulity and despair. "Why?" His eyes implied an answer from the ensign. "Why haven't they answered?"

The captain began coughing hard, his whole body violently shuddering. When it subsided he was too weak to lift a tissue to his mouth. Ski took a clean tissue and held it to the captain's mouth. Van Wert spit into it and mouthed the words, "Thank you." Ski threw the tissues into the trash and placed another in the captain's hand.

"It's possible that they've sent messages on the military bands, thinking we were still on the *Kestrel*," Millus offered. "I've seen some military looking traffic come over the beam, but we can't decrypt it here."

"I'm sure that they're on their way, Captain," Ski said. "You've just got to hold on a little longer."

Van Wert didn't answer. He looked away from Ski to the wall.

"Can we bring you anything to eat?" Millus asked.

Van Wert shook his head and closed his eyes. Millus nodded to Ski that they should leave, so they quietly left the room and headed back to sick bay.

As they walked down the hall, Millus said quietly. "He's gotten the word."

"What do you mean?" Ski asked.

"That's an expression that military people use when someone realizes that his end is near. Like a pilot who gets all of his affairs settled before he goes out on his last mission. It's only a feeling, but somehow they know." Millus frowned. "The captain has gotten the word."

Neither man spoke again until they reached sick bay.

***

After dosing Millus with meds, the two went to Foley's room. Ski checked the oxygen machine, then turned to the officer.

"Let's clean him up first and then we'll change the linens." Ski leaned over Foley and gently shook him. "Doc? Doc, can you hear me?"

Foley moaned something unintelligible and then coughed violently.

Ski continued. "Doc, we're going to get you cleaned up and change your sheets. Okay?"

Foley didn't respond. His breathing was labored and made a rattling noise.

"He doesn't even know we're here," Millus said.

Ski frowned. "Let's get started."

The two worked like a team, and in half an hour they had the medic cleaned, dressed in fresh pajamas, and sleeping comfortably in clean sheets. They also placed an absorbent pad under him.

"That should do it," Ski said. "I think he'll rest easier now. Thanks."

"Anytime," Millus answered. "When someone's losing everything else, they should at least be able to keep their dignity."

Ski made an impression on Doc's arm and frowned. "He's dehydrating. I need to give him an IV or something."

"Do you know how to do that?"

"No. But yesterday I drew my own blood to separate the serum. Sticking someone else can't be as bad as that."

Millus grimaced and grunted.

"I'll study up on it first," Ski said.

"Make sure you do."

Chapter 50
"Doc"

After spending the morning studying about IV procedures, Ski went around to check in on the bedridden crewmembers. In Foley's room he found Dresden sitting next to the bed reading aloud from a computer pad. He stopped reading and looked up as Ski walked in.

"Hi," Dresden said.

"Are you reading to Doc?" Ski asked.

"Yeah. *Treasure Island*." Dresden held the screen so Ski could see. "I don't know if he hears me or not, but if he does, maybe it will keep him company."

"I'm sure he can hear you on some level." Ski checked the machine and looked to see what kind of veins the medic had. Doc's breath respirations were short and shallow. "You don't have to stay with him all the time, though."

"I know. Flores and I relieve each other every thirty minutes or so."

"That's really good." Ski nodded. "I may come in later to try to get an IV on him."

Dresden coughed and nodded.

"Don't wear yourself out," Ski said.

"I won't." Dresden lifted the pad and began reading again.

Ski left and entered Mac's room where Wilson and the cook were playing cards. Mac looked tired and didn't seem very interested.

The systems tech laid down a card and said, "So the chief turns to the warriors and says, 'He chooses death, but first, the Ururu!'"

Mac smiled and laid down a card.

Wilson picked up the card and said, "Aw, come on, man. That was a good one."

"How are you feeling, Mac?" Ski asked.

"About the same."

"Is that cough medicine helping you at all?"

Mac shrugged.

"I'm doing about the same, too," Wilson said, eyebrows raised accusingly.

"I was going to ask you next." Ski felt Mac's forehead, and it was very warm. He next placed his hand on Wilson's forehead, and it was warm as well. "Are you getting feverish? Body aches?"

Wilson nodded.

"I want you guys to keep drinking fluids as much as you can. Doc's already getting dehydrated, and I'm trying to figure out how to get an IV in him."

"I'd rather not get stuck by an amateur," Wilson said, laying down another card. "No offense."

"Then hydrate while you still can."

The cook gave a worried look to Ski.

"Can I get you guys anything, now? I'm going that way."

"Well, since you put it that way, I'd like a nice orange soda," Wilson said. "How about you, Mac?"

"Root beer."

"I'll be right back."

"How is Doc doing?" Wilson asked.

"And the captain?" Mac asked.

"Both are weak but resting. The captain is still taking nourishment," Ski lied, "but Doc is sleeping all the time. That's why I've got to fix an IV."

Wilson nodded silently, and Mac only stared at his cards.

Ski turned to leave.

"One more thing," Wilson said. "Is it okay to bring Mac to the lounge for dinner?"

"I don't see why not," Ski answered.

Wilson patted Mac on the knee. "Good. We'll get you out of here for a while, baby."

Mac nodded and smiled weakly, and Ski left the room.

He went to the dining area and filled the drink orders, then looked over the food items to see if there was anything he might bring them for a snack. He was about to make a selection when Flores came in hurriedly.

"Ski, I think you'd better come quickly."

"What's wrong?"

"Doc's struggling to breathe."

Ski put the drinks down and started for the door. "When did it start?"

"Just now. I came in to relieve Dresden, and he started making gasping sounds."

Ski followed him back to Doc's room where Dresden was leaning over the bed. He looked up as Ski entered. "He started convulsing like he couldn't get a breath, then he got still. His legs feel cold, too."

"He must've just stopped," Flores said. "He was still struggling when I left."

Ski nodded and checked for a pulse. He cut off the oxygen machine and leaned in close to listen for any sign of breathing but heard none. He stood up again and sighed, feeling utterly useless, and the despair he'd felt when Petey died began to grow in him again.

"Can't you do anything?" Flores asked.

"I don't know what I can do to help him. He's gone." Ski removed the oxygen tube and covered Doc's face with the sheet.

Dresden began to slowly shake his head. "I should have told you when I first thought something was wrong."

"No," Ski said, "it wouldn't have made any difference."

"What do we do now?" Flores asked.

"I better go report it to Mr. Millus."

"And the captain?" Dresden asked.

Ski thought about the depressed state Van Wert was in earlier. "Maybe." He picked up the oxygen machine and turned for the door. "Let's leave him for now. I'll tell Mr. Millus, and I'm sure we'll put him in the lifeboat soon."

The three left the room, and Ski put the machine in the sickbay before joining the others in the lounge. Wilson had come in and was helping Mac take a seat.

"I thought you were bringing the drinks to us," the systems tech said.

"I'd planned to," Ski started to say, "but-"

"Doc's dead," Flores blurted out.

"What?" Mac asked.

"Just now," Dresden said.

Ski nodded.

"So that's it, then?" Wilson asked. "It'll just keep taking us one by one until we're all dead."

"This is the way the frigging world shall end," Flores said, "not with a bang, but with a whimper."

The statement hung in the air like smog, and Ski felt the urge to walk out, desiring to be alone, but Ensign Millus came in and broke the silence.

"Ah, there you are, Ski. When can I get another dose of that cough medicine?" He looked around at the somber faces. "What's wrong?"

Ski drew a deep breath. "Doc's gone, sir."

"Aw, hell." He shook his head. "When?"

"A few minutes ago."

"Should we tell the captain?" Dresden asked.

Millus took a deep breath and blew it out between pursed lips. "Damn."

"I guess he's got a right to know," Flores said.

"Sure," Millus answered, "but in the state he's in I don't think it'll help his peace of mind."

"I'd want to know anyway," Wilson said.

"Is the captain that bad?" Mac asked.

Millus nodded. "He's right behind Doc, and I doubt if he'll be with us much longer." He let his words sink in. "If anyone feels he has something he needs to say to the old man, he'd better say it soon."

Hardly a word had been spoken during lunch. Ski sat at the table but had eaten nothing. He waited patiently until Millus, Flores and Dresden were finished, then the four of them went to Foley's room to move him. They wrapped him in a sheet and then carried him downstairs to the lifeboat that held Petey. When they were through, Flores went to Mac's room, Dresden went to check the power plant, and Ski returned to sickbay.

In the doctor's office, Ski tried to read over the articles again but couldn't stay focused on the material. His thoughts kept returning to Doc and Petey and Gradenko. Then he thought about all of the crewmen lost on the *Kestrel,* and his moroseness deepened. *So much death. How could this patrol come to so much death so soon?* Ski rubbed his face with his hands and then rested his face in his palms, shutting out the light. The numb emptiness in his heart seemed to swell into a cavernous void. *And more to come.*

The sound of the door opening invaded his preoccupation. He opened his eyes to see Ensign Millus standing before his desk, his expression grave.

"What are you working on now?"

"I don't know," Ski answered. "I don't know where I should go from here."

"Are you still working on placing an IV? The captain may need one before long."

"No. I can't concentrate." Ski sighed heavily. "I've feel I've got to do something, though."

"Maybe you should take a breather."

Ski nodded. "Did you tell the captain about Doc?"

"Yes."

"How was he about it?"

"I think you could say he took the news with resignation."

"Maybe you shouldn't have told him."

"He's still the captain. He wants to be kept abreast of what's going on."

"I guess so. How was his oxygen?"

"I didn't check it."

"The last time I looked, the filter was almost ready to be changed. I'll go change it now."

"Good idea." Millus put his hand to his forehead. "I need to go lie down."

The ensign left and Ski walked over to a cabinet. He took out a small filter element and unwrapped it, then headed for Van Wert's room.

He opened the door quietly and heard the captain's shallow, rumbling breathing. The lamp above the bed cast a soft glow over the room, and he thought the captain might be sleeping, but as he got closer to the bed Van Wert turned his head toward him, his face old and withered. He gave a weak smile.

"Hi, Captain," Ski said, trying to sound cheerful. "I brought a new filter for the oxygen machine."

Van Wert reached his hand out and patted Ski's arm weakly. "You're… a good man." Then he coughed hard, the phlegm rattling in his chest.

Ski knelt and replaced the filter, then he stood up and faced the captain. He thought about what Millus had said earlier and knew he had something to say, but he wasn't sure how to frame the words. He took a deep breath.

"Captain, I'm very sorry about how everything turned out. I think you deserve a lot better."

Van Wert patted Ski's arm again. "You've worked… very well. I…wrote…" He coughed very hard and it seemed to clear his lungs a little. "I wrote in my log… that you are to be… meritoriously advanced… to first class."

Ski blushed with embarrassment. "Captain, that's… Thank you, but that's really not necessary."

"You deserve it."

Van Wert coughed severely, and Ski wondered if he was damaging his lungs. He spit into a tissue and looked up at Ski. "You know, it wasn't my… first choice… to pass you over… for promotion… I was going… to bust you… to third class."

Ski frowned and nodded. *I probably deserved to be busted.*

"Do you know… why I didn't?"

Ski shook his head.

"Petey… talked me… out of it." Van Wert nodded his head and smiled. "I was mad… about that song… but Petey told me… how you had been… screwed over… by the former… CO. He said…" Van Wert coughed again but seemed to produce nothing. "He said… that was why… you had… an attitude. He told me… all of the good things… about you, so I only… held you back."

The captain stopped to rest, exhausted by talking. His breaths were shallow and didn't seem to go very far to strengthen him.

Ski bit his lower lip. *No wonder Petey always seemed to take the captain's side whenever I complained about being passed over. Petey knew that it could have been worse.* Ski opened his mouth to speak, but Van Wert continued.

"He was right. You are… a good man. You would make… a good officer."

The captain patted Ski's arm one more time before withdrawing it under the covers. He turned his face away from Ski and closed his eyes to sleep.

Ski stood dumbfounded, his heart like a stone in his chest. After a few moments he picked up the old filter and stepped out of the room. The hall was deserted, and an oppressive weight of loneliness pressed down on him. He realized the conversation he just had would probably be the last he would ever have with the captain. His throat seemed to close, and his face began to twist with grief. He wanted to be alone. The heavy emotional strain of the last several days was beginning to boil over, and he didn't want anyone to see him or speak to him or try to comfort him. He dropped the filter and headed for his room.

***

It was early in the evening when Dresden walked down the hall to the captain's room. All day he had been thinking about Ensign Millus' words, and they echoed through his mind now. *If anyone feels he has something he needs to say to the old man, he'd better say it soon.*

278

At first the words had chilled him, but now they haunted him. He wanted so badly to explain, to justify his actions, but no matter how much he wanted it, he just couldn't make himself face the captain. Three times he had come up to the room and three times he had retreated, chastising himself for his cowardice. Finally, imagining the captain dead and being loaded into the lifeboat goaded him back again. By then it would be too late for apologies. This time he would not turn back.

Like a condemned prisoner, he slowly reached out to the stateroom door and opened it. Inside, the dim lamp above the bed cast an eerie light on Van Wert, creating an appearance of a stone knight reposing on an ancient crypt. He walked over to the bed and saw the captain's eyes open, turning his head to face the young technician.

The old man's eyes were neither angry nor disappointed nor judgmental. They almost seemed to smile, as if the captain was glad to see him. His breathing was short and labored, and Dresden doubted that he would be able to talk. But that didn't matter. Dresden was here to do the talking.

He drew a breath to speak but couldn't. He had rehearsed a speech all afternoon, but now his mind drew a blank. Even the ideas that he had wanted to convey seemed stupid. He opened his mouth, and when he spoke, his heart took over, saying the words that needed to be said.

"Captain, I... I'm sorry," he stammered. "I'm really sorry."

He wanted to say more but couldn't. As he stared into the captain's eyes, he saw a tenderness that he had never seen there before. Van Wert slowly reached his arm out from under the covers and took Dresden's hand, squeezing it as tightly as he could and shaking it slightly.

Dresden placed his other hand on top of the captain's and held it. Without a word spoken, he knew that it was all right. He was forgiven.

At nine forty-five that night, Ski stood at the table in the lab studying an array of lab equipment and supplies spread out before him. He stared at the items, trying to compare them with the instructions from one of the medical articles, and felt bewildered. A cough at the door broke his concentration, and he looked up to see Millus enter.

"Damn, Ski, you're really burning the midnight oil, aren't you?"

Ski nodded. "How are you feeling?"

"Achy. I need something for this fever, too."

Ski went to a cabinet and produced a bottle of pills. "I should've come in to check on you."

"That's all right. When I woke up I couldn't get back to sleep, so I went in to check on the captain."

"How is he?" Ski asked.

"About the same. Sleeping." Millus gestured to the items on the table. "How is the work coming along?

Ski shook his head in disgust. "Dead slow. Sometimes backwards, I think."

"What are you doing now?"

"Looking up how to kill a virus."

"Didn't we see something on formaldehyde?"

"Yes, and that's a good substance to use, but then the only problem is how to remove it from the virus." Ski gestured toward the row of filters. "I thought about rinsing it with water and then filtering it, but that's a supreme pain in the ass. It took me two hours just to spin it and then separate the virus from the filter. Then I don't know if it was successful or not." Ski looked up at the ensign. "I really don't know what the hell I'm doing."

Millus nodded silently and looked at his watch. "Well, it's getting late. Why don't you knock off and hit it again tomorrow? Maybe you'll get some fresh ideas."

Ski nodded. "I just wish I could make some kind of progress. It's so damn tedious. Everything has to be done one step at a time." He looked around at the lab equipment. "I'm beginning to think that Foley

was right. I just don't know enough to make this work. I don't have
near enough information to have a snowball's chance in hell of finding
a cure."

"Foley wasn't a doctor."

"No, but he knew enough to know how fruitless this is."

"Ski, whether we live or die depends on a rescue party, not on
your medical abilities. I don't think anyone would blame you if you
gave it up."

"Yes, that's probably true." Ski looked at Millus. "But, I need to
know that I tried my best until the very end."

"I understand, but I still think you ought to get some rest."

Ski nodded. "You're right. I'll start again tomorrow."

Millus yawned and coughed hard. He held up the bottle.
"Thanks for these. Good night."

"Good night."

Ski studied the items for a few moments, separating them into
two groups. Then he studied the medical article again, but gave a
gesture of disgust and backed away from the table. He stepped out into
the hall, and the red lights seemed strange and lonely, adding to his
deepening depression. He went to the lounge and found it deserted. *I
must be the only one awake.* He glanced at the MSES machines but
decided against it. Instead he went to the elevator and pushed the button
to the transmitter module.

As tired as he was, he felt a strange restlessness, as if he needed
an answer to some inner question. As he ascended he thought about
Petey and his belief in God. The navigator had always seemed to know
that things would work out all right. Yet he died anyway.

Ski looked up toward where he thought heaven was and spoke
aloud. "Okay, God, if you're up there, why don't you tell me what to
do now?"

His voice held an edge of sarcasm. He had always believed that
if there was a God, He must be very impersonal, despite what Petey and
others like him said, but now, deep down, a small part of him hoped
that Petey was right, that he was somehow being heard.

"Surely, you can see that what I'm trying to do is a good thing.
Petey would have thought so." Ski frowned. "He never lost faith in you,

and to tell you the truth, I think you let him down. He was the first one to die of the virus!"

He remembered Petey once telling him that one should always be honest with the Almighty, no matter how one felt. God would not be insulted or put off.

"I didn't mean to tell you what you should do, but, if you're really up there, please help us. Please don't let anyone else die."

The elevator reached the transmitter module, and Ski stepped out. He looked down the hall in both directions, and his loneliness felt magnified here in the remote section of the station. He noticed the open hatch to the optical positioning room and went to the ladder below it. He climbed up into the cramped room and crawled to the optical positioning alignment telescope. He stood up next to it and peered into the eyepiece. AlCent B burned steadily with a yellow white light. *No one even knows what's happening to us here.*

He backed away from the eyepiece and looked out at the universe through the dome of glass where the vast, cold panorama of stars glowed indifferently, uncaring, unfeeling, unknowing. The usual peace that descended over him when viewing the stars would not come.

As he stared out at the universe, the corner of his right eye noticed a faint vapor moving past the station. He turned his head and watched it grow denser, like a river of mist traveling through space. Thicker and thicker it spread and soon began to glow as a stream of superheated gases. He drew in a sharp breath as recognition flashed in his mind, and at that moment he saw it. A long, narrow ship, its lower end surrounded by a cluster of large hydrogen slush tanks, came into view perhaps a half a mile away, flying engine nozzles first and decelerating at full power. It was going far too fast to be able to stop at the station, but then Ski noticed that the four large racks surrounding the upper portion of the slender hull were empty.

It's a BMAS! He must have already discharged the modules and is beginning his return trajectory back to AlCent A2! But where are the modules?

Instinctively he looked back in the direction from which the ship had come, but the receiver antenna blocked out the sky. *The radio!* With one last look at the Boosted Module Accelerator Ship now streaking away and getting smaller, he crawled back to the hatch and went below. Not waiting for the elevator, he ran to the stairs and descended two and three steps at a time.

At the lounge level he paused to shout, "Hey, everyone! It's a rescue ship!" Then he continued down.

Once at the Main Control level he ran to the communications panel and beyond the window saw four ships decelerating directly toward the station, the flames of their engines bathing the station with hot gas as they slowed. A young woman's voice calmly inquired from the radio speaker.

"Space Station CR3, Space Station CR3, this is Module One of the *USS Halsey.* Do you read me? Over."

Ski felt a rush of excitement. He grabbed the microphone and nearly shouted. "Uh, yes! This is station CR3. I read you loud and clear."

There was a pause, then the voice said, "Switch to AV mode."

Ski reached up and powered up the comms screen. A young officer's face appeared, but, before Ski could say anything, she backed away from her comm panel and an older man, a flag officer, stood in front of the screen, his voice abrupt but not unfriendly.

"This is Admiral Selig. Who am I speaking to?"

Ski stammered. "OT2 Kowalski of the USS *Kestrel,* sir."

"Where is your commanding officer?"

"He's in his rack, sir. He's extremely ill."

"Where is the *Kestrel?*"

Ski drew in a breath but hesitated, trying to figure out how to phrase his answer.

"Well, tech, where is your ship?"

"It was destroyed in a mutiny attempt, sir."

"Damn," Selig said. "Who is in command?'

"Ensign Millus, sir."

Selig opened his mouth to ask another question, but a new voice came in over the audio.

"Station CR3, this is Dick Maeda of the Interplanetary Communications Agency Module Two *SS RJ Branscome.* Please initiate the automated Out-mooring Positioning System in the Main Computer and depressurize the docking bay for landing craft."

"Uh..." Ski replied. "Aye, aye. One moment, please." Ski looked over at the main console but soon realized he would need Wilson to get the program running.

"Where is Ensign Millus?" the admiral asked.

"He's asleep, sir. I'll page him right away." Ski went to the intercom and spoke into it. "Ensign Millus and ST3 Wilson lay to Main Control, ASAP." Ski returned to the comms panel. "Mister... uh, ICA module, I need our systems tech to get the program up. He's on his way."

"Very well," Maeda replied over the audio. "Also, have him run the remote status board sequence so we can monitor the station from out here."

"Aye, aye."

Another voice broke in over the audio. "Station CR3, this is Dr. Arthur Shaw of the Disease Control Agency. I need a preliminary triage from you as quickly as you can get it for me. I need to know how many patients there are and their conditions."

"Aye, Aye!" Ski replied. As tired as he was, the flurry of activity refreshed him as it always did in the OPS shack of the *Kestrel*. He felt at home in chaos.

"Yes, son," Selig said, "how many crew members are left?"

Ski counted quickly in his head. "Seven, Admiral, including myself. We've already lost three men, and three others are in very bad shape. Doctor, are you going to be able to do anything for them?"

"We're going to try."

Millus dashed down the steps wearing only his khaki pants and a t-shirt. He gave Ski a puzzled expression.

Ski pointed to the comms panel. "Rescue ships are here. Admiral Selig wants to speak to you."

Millus' eyes opened wide, and he hurried to the AV panel and began speaking to the admiral. Coming down the steps behind him ran Wilson, Flores, and Dresden. Dresden collapsed into a chair as Ski waved Wilson over. The systems tech coughed hard as he stepped up.

"What's going on Ski?" he asked, looking out beyond the main window.

"Rescue ships are here. Four deceleration modules from the BMAS, the fleet module *Halsey*, an ICA module, a DCA module, and one other. The ICA man needs you to run the out-position program and the remote status board so they can monitor the station. Do you know how to do that?"

"Of course," Wilson said, taking a seat. "I'm not sure why the out-mooring one is off, but I'll get it."

"Good," Ski said. "Flores, would you run down and make sure the docking bay is depressurized?"

The engineering tech nodded and walked quickly to the stairs.

Ski looked over and saw Dresden completely exhausted in the other chair. Ski looked out of the main windows and saw that the four ships had now slowed to a stop and were taking up positions equidistant from the door.

Millus turned to face the main terminal. "Wilson, what've you got?"

"They're already communicating with out-position mooring system, and I'm hooking them up the remote status board…now."

"Very well."

The ensign stepped over next to Ski and watched as the ships maneuvered to the station's local down orientation.

Ski gestured to the comm screen. "Is the admiral still there?"

Millus shook his head. "He's getting ready to come over now."

Chapter 53
"Rescue Party"

Ten minutes later, Ski, Millus, and Wilson joined Flores at the docking bay window. They watched the *Halsey's* barge fly over the threshold of the docking bay door. Behind it flew a gig from the ICA module *Branscome* and two large shipping containers from the DCA module, one labeled *FS/H Ambulatory* and the other labeled *DCA Scrub Team*. The four vessels settled onto the floor and powered down.

Flores picked up the intercom microphone and nodded to Wilson. "All right, man, do it."

Wilson held an empty brass cable fitting up to the mic and double-tapped it three times with a screwdriver to produce something like a bell tone. Flores' voice followed.

"Commander, Fleet Operations, arriving."

The door of the docking bay closed, and Flores initiated the re-pressurization. Soon the doors of the boats opened, and people began filing out, all of them in vac-suits. The admiral was the first person out of the barge, and Ski's eyes followed the short stocky man as he walked quickly to the door and stood waiting for the green light that would signal an equalization of pressure.

Ensign Millus walked up and stood next to Ski. He wore his complete uniform, but his illness made him appear old and haggard. All of the crewmen present seemed to have gotten worse during the night, and there was a steady chorus of coughing and throats clearing.

The light turned green, and Flores pushed the button to open the door.

"Attention on deck!" Millus called. The men all snapped to attention.

The admiral stepped through the open door and spoke to them through the vac-suit helmet's microphone. "At ease." He turned to Millus and took his hand, shaking it vigorously. "Ensign Millus."

"Welcome aboard, Admiral."

"Thank you, son. We got your messages on the tachyon beam and on the radio, and we came as quick as we could. Where is Van Wert?"

"I'll take you to him, sir."

Selig looked around at the other crewmen. "Shouldn't these men be resting?"

"They were, Admiral, but they came out to lend a hand."

Selig nodded and made eye contact with each man as he spoke. "Bear up a little longer, men. We've got the best help on AlCent A2 setting up shop right now." He looked at Ski, and a puzzled look came over his face. "How come you're not sick?"

Ski almost felt offended by the question. "I was very sick, Admiral, but I got over it."

Selig nodded. "I'd like to hear more about that later," he said, then followed Millus toward the stairwell.

The group relaxed, and Ski turned to look past the door. The floor of the docking bay had become a whirlwind of activity. The group from the ICA ship, twenty or so, were unloading provisions and luggage. The admiral's barge crew came out and helped carry the boxes of supplies to the back wall. But of all the vessels in the bay, the DCA container vessels were by far the busiest. Some of the people were erecting a large cubical tent structure around the door of the ambulatory craft while others set up equipment on the floor within it. Outside of the other DCA vessel, scrub team workers were rolling out large pieces of equipment, some with attached sprayers and others with thick hoses. The teams of both DCA vessels moved with military-like precision and efficiency.

Having unloaded their provisions, the people from the ICA vessel gathered their personal gear quickly and approached the door in single file. Once through they split up, some of them headed downstairs to the power plant while the rest headed upstairs toward main control and beyond.

Flores nodded toward them. "I wonder who they are."

"I think they're the relief crew for the station," Ski answered, watching them until they were out of sight. Then he turned his attention back to the docking bay where one man from the ambulatory craft seemed to be running everything. The man said something to the scrub team leader, who nodded, then led some others from his own group toward the docking bay door. The group from the barge and the gig also started for the door.

As the DCA leader approached, Ski saw that he was a younger man, mid-thirties with hazel eyes and a closely trimmed beard. He spoke with a gentle smile.

"Hello, I'm Dr. Shaw. I take it you are the men of the *Kestrel*?"

"Yes, sir," Ski answered, "some of them. There are more upstairs."

"Very good. It is my understanding that we must work very quickly. I need you gentlemen to gather your things and go to the isolation/scrub tent over there." He pointed to the ambulatory vessel with the attached white cube-shaped tent. "We need to begin treatment right away."

"All right, but first we need to let our ensign know what's going on."

Dr Shaw nodded. "I understand."

"Are you going to be able to help us?" Dresden asked.

The doctor looked over at him, his eyes concerned but confident. "I think so. We're going to try."

"Ski," Flores said, "do we need to get our weapons and vac-suits from the gear locker?"

"The *Halsey's* people will probably take those."

The doctor held up his hand. "No. Nothing is taken off of this station until it has been scrubbed."

Ski nodded. "Good enough."

A party of four from the admiral's barge walked up, and Ski saw that the lead woman wore a captain's star. She looked at Ski as she spoke.

"I'm Lieutenant Commander Murray of the *USS Halsey*. Where is Admiral Selig?"

"He was taken upstairs to see Lieutenant Commander Van Wert."

"Will you take us to him?"

"Yes, ma'am. Of course." Ski turned to the other crewmen. "We don't have any personal effects aboard the station. Why don't you guys report to the isolation tent while I take everyone up? I'll tell Mr. Millus what's going on."

"Don't forget Mac," Flores said.

"I won't."

One of Dr. Shaw's medical assistants gestured for the *Kestrel's* crew to follow him. "Right this way, gentlemen."

"If you'll follow me, please," Ski said and led them to the elevator. At the lounge deck, they entered Van Wert's room, and Lieutenant Commander Murray pushed past the others and went right to the bed. She took Van Wert's hand and leaned over to speak to him.

"James? James? It's me, Jenny. Can you hear me?'

"He's not responding," Selig said.

She looked up at the admiral and then to Dr. Shaw. "How soon can you begin his treatment?"

"As soon as we can get him to the ship. I need the most able patients to report first, that way we will have more room to work with the others. I believe there is another who is also bedridden?"

"That's right," Millus said. "Mac is in the next room."

"Mr. Millus, I've already sent some of our crew to the tent," Ski said. "If it's all right with you, I'll go down with them."

"That would be best," the doctor said. "And the sooner you can join them, Ensign Millus, the better. My orderlies are waiting in the hall now with a stretcher for your captain."

"Very well." Millus turned to the admiral. "By your leave, sir."

"I'll go with you," Selig said.

Everyone but Dr. Shaw left the room, and his orderlies brought the stretcher in. As he stepped into the hall, Ski saw Mac being carried out of his room on a stretcher. He looked like he could barely breathe, but he looked up at Ski as he was carried past.

"What's going…on, Ski?"

Ski patted Mac on the shoulder. "They're taking us to a hospital ship to be treated. We're out of here!"

Mac smiled weakly. "Meanwhile…back in the jungle…"

Ski stepped out of the way, and a door opened behind him. It was the room where he and Petey had stayed. He looked over at the bunk where his friend had lain and taken his last labored breaths and grimaced at the thought that the navigator had missed out on this rescue. The star journal still lay on the stand next to the bunk. Van Wert's words came to him about Petey receiving full honors, but that just didn't seem good enough. *Full honors and then forgotten. That cannot be all.* He stepped over and picked up the star journal and stuck it in his belt.

***

Ski entered the double-flapped opening to the isolation tent and saw several nurses and medical technicians waiting for him, all wearing medical vac-suits.

"Where are the others?" he asked.

The tech nearest to him, an attractive young woman with blue eyes and black hair tied up behind her head, led him by his elbow to a camera set on a tripod. "They're already inside waiting for you."

She smiled at him, and he felt a tingle in his chest as he returned her smile. There was something vaguely familiar about her, as if he'd known her before, but couldn't remember when. She held up a small computer pad. "Please face the camera and state your name."

"Julius Kowalski. 'Ski' for short."

"Do you know your blood type?"

"A positive."

As two nurses took his vital signs, the technician spoke quietly and rapidly into the pad describing Ski's physical condition and lack of symptoms, feeling around his throat and armpits as she went. Once finished, the technician gestured toward a row of transparent plastic chambers against the wall that led to and covered the opening to the ambulatory vessel. The other techs began to power up the equipment controls.

"Okay, Ski, I need you to step into the first chamber there and disrobe."

Ski looked around. "In front of everybody?"

The young woman gave a wry smile. "I'm afraid so. No place for modesty in a hospital ship."

Ski rolled his eyes. Then he remembered Petey's journal and held it up. "What about this?"

The tech studied it for a moment. "We can sterilize it, and I can give it back to you later."

He placed the computer pad in her hands and held it for a moment. "It's very important to me."

290

The young woman smiled and nodded. "I'll get it back to you personally." She led him into the chamber and shut the door behind him. With his back to the others he removed his clothing and looked over his shoulder at the young woman.

"Place your clothes into the laundry bag, and then step into the next chamber to be scrubbed."

"Not with wire brushes, I hope."

The woman laughed. "No, no. Nothing like that. It's a non-invasive process. You won't feel a thing. Just hold your arms out by your side and place your feet shoulder width apart. Keep your eyes closed."

Ski followed her instructions and went through the scrub-down process, which included a chemical aerosol in one chamber and a blue light in the next. The last chamber held a stack of hospital gowns and disposable isolation suits on a table. Once dressed and suited up, he entered the ambulatory vessel.

Inside, Flores, Dresden, and Wilson sat in comfortable chairs against the inner hull of the vessel. Beyond them against the walls stood racks for stretchers where two medical techs prepared the equipment to receive Mac and the captain. Ski took a seat and looked at his three companions. Even though they were all very sick, Ski could feel the excitement that radiated from each man. They were on their way home.

After a few minutes, Ensign Millus joined them, and everyone began talking excitedly. Soon Mac came aboard carried on a stretcher, and finally, surrounded by medical people, the captain was brought on board, still unresponsive. As the medical team secured the stretchers in the aft part of the ship, some of the scrub tent personnel came aboard and took seats as the door was secured from the outside. Ski noticed that the black-haired girl was among them, seated opposite and too far down the row for conversation. He watched her as she connected her seat belt, fascinated by the grace of her movements. She looked around and noticed him and smiled, and Ski felt a tingle in his chest again. He returned the smile as she held up a sealed plastic bag that held Petey's star journal. His smile became a grin, and he gave a thumbs-up gesture.

Dr. Shaw came forward and took a seat at last, and the vessel began to power up. After a few minutes, the bay depressurized, and the vessel lifted off and headed for the hospital module.

Chapter 54
"War Plan"

Ski spent the rest of the morning alone in a room where the furnishings were Spartan, even by hospital standards. With nothing to do and nowhere to go, and once again in a ship's low-gravity environment, he spent most of his time napping.

Occasionally a lab technician or nurse would come in, always wearing a plastic isolation suit, and take a blood sample, or sputum sample, or some other bodily fluid sample. He would try to initiate conversation, but they would always politely exit in a hurry.

After a few hours, hunger began to gnaw at him, so he decided to petition the next visitor for food, but as it turned out his next visitor was Dr. Shaw himself without an isolation suit. Dressed in a lab coat he appeared younger to Ski than he had on the station, perhaps only ten years older than himself. *And he's in charge of the treatment and scrubbing operations,* Ski thought. He again wore a gentle smile and seemed very intelligent.

"Good morning, Petty Officer Kowalski. We met on the station already. I am Doctor Arthur Shaw." He held out his hand and Ski shook it.

"Yes, doctor, I remember. You're not wearing a suit!"

Dr. Shaw smiled. "Yes. It seems that outside of a topical exposure you had, you are completely free of the virus. I have no reason to hold you in here any longer."

"Great. I would really like to go get something to eat."

"Actually, I was hoping that we might go have lunch together while your shipmates are being prepped for treatment. I would like to talk to you."

"Excellent! Lead on," Ski said.

"I brought some better clothes, so as soon as you change out of that gown we'll head to the galley."

"Thanks."

***

Despite the shipboard low gravity environment, the galley was set up like a restaurant. Once they had ordered their food from a computer screen menu, Ski asked, "Doctor, how is the captain?"

"He's still holding on. We're going to be treating him first. He's being prepped now as we eat. I should think that he will require additional treatments because of the advanced condition of the infection."

"How long do the treatments take?"

"Working quickly, our portion should take about forty-five minutes to an hour. Then the patient's immune system must do the rest. That part takes from eight to twenty-four hours."

"What kind of treatment can you use against a virus like this?"

"We'll use various genetic therapy methods in four phases. Our treatments will accelerate the patient's own immune responses to combat and destroy the virus. This pathogen mutates very rapidly, and the human immune response is always playing catch up and inevitability falls behind. We can give the whole immune system a boost to destroy the virus before it reaches the next mutation."

"It sounds interesting."

"Yes, it is," Dr. Shaw said. "It's quite complicated, but it works very well."

"Will I be going through it?"

"No, no. You're clear. But I would still like to run some small tests on you when I'm through with the others. I'd like to confirm exactly why you recovered when the others did not."

"In the journal I wrote that I believed there is a connection to the Schadendorf virus."

"Yes, I read that. I believe that the Aldebaran virus antigens, or surface proteins, resembled the Schadendorf virus closely enough for your immune system to mount an immediate defense. That's what I'd like to confirm."

"I think that was what happened to the station crewman we found in the lifeboat."

"Indeed." Dr. Shaw took off his glasses and looked intently at Ski. "You know you are very lucky that the virus didn't shift. If you would have been exposed to a new shift mutation, your body might not have reacted in the same way. The disease might have advanced as rapidly in you as in the others."

"I never thought of that." Ski shook his head. "I'm glad it didn't."

Dr. Shaw smiled. "Me, too. That's why we must keep the patients isolated during the treatment." The doctor took a drink of water. "You know, as I read that journal you kept, I found your ideas very interesting."

"But not very helpful, it seems."

"Perhaps, but they were good tries, nonetheless. Your theories may have been incorrect, but your methods were sound. Have you ever had any medical training?"

Despite himself Ski smiled a little. "No, I haven't."

"You've never worked in the medical field?"

Ski shook his head.

"Perhaps you just have a knack for it."

"I tried to do what seemed logical."

"Indeed." Dr. Shaw looked at his watch. "I wish they would hurry. I really need to get back."

The waiter came shortly with their food. Despite the fancy surroundings, the meals served in plastic containers were similar to the shipboard fare of the *Kestrel,* and the two men ate quickly in silence. Once finished, Dr. Shaw stood up.

"Well, I must get to the Treatment Control Center. Perhaps we could share a more leisurely meal after the treatment of your shipmates is completed."

"I would love to," Ski said. "You know, Doctor, that gene therapy sounds fascinating. I really wish I could learn more about it."

Dr. Shaw considered Ski a moment, and then smiled. "Come with me."

Ski took one last bite and then followed the doctor out of the restaurant to an elevator. They both gripped the hand holds in the low gravity and rode it down four decks to one of the operating room levels.

Chapter 55
"Battling a Virus"

They exited the elevator and entered an airlock marked "Gene Decoding Lab." Dr. Shaw typed an access code onto a pad set in the wall and the outer door closed behind them. After a few moments, the inner door opened, and the doctor led him into a large dimly lit room that reminded Ski of the bridge on the *Kestrel*. But instead of fleet personnel manning consoles for weapons, scanning, and communications equipment, he saw medical technicians busily operating various numerical and biological computer displays and electron microscope images. Some of the consoles had the patient's names displayed across the top. The far wall was transparent, and beyond it were other rooms and other technicians busily working at laboratory consoles and work surfaces unrecognizable to him.

"This is our Genetic Decoding Lab. Here's where we bring tissue samples of the patients to analyze present surface antigens, pathogenic DNA, current antibody production, etc. We have also brought prokaryotic samples affected by the original virus from the alien remains the station crew found in the life pod. Here we identify the genetic sequences that will need to be deleted and spliced."

"Can you splice DNA strands here?"

"No. This lab determines where the splices are to be made, but that's all. The actual gene-splicing work is done in our Gene Splicing Lab." He pointed past the glass partition to the room beyond it to the left.

The doctor put his hand on the shoulder of the nearest technician and said, "How is it coming along, Rodney?"

"Very good," the tech answered, keeping his eyes on the screen. "I'm at an estimated eighty-six percent completion on this patient."

Ski noticed Dresden's name at the top of the console screen.

"Has the captain's entire treatment been prepared?"

Rodney looked up at them. "Yes, Doctor. Three of us worked on it together by mapping out different sections. We wanted to get his going first."

"Have the CRISPR/Cas9 sequences been sent to the GSL?"

"Yes, sir. All of the materials were sent to the GSL and VPR hours ago, and they've been producing the modified sequences and vectors. I believe they have everything ready for transduction as we speak."

"Excellent. Thank you. I'll be in the Treatment Control Center for the procedure. Have them bring the patient into the OR now."

"Yes, Doctor."

Dr. Shaw gestured to Ski. "Come this way."

They stepped over to another airlock and proceeded into another small room jammed with computer monitors and manned by four technicians. The screens appeared to monitor every aspect of the various stages of the treatment. To his left and beyond the glass partition was a room labeled "Gene Splicing Lab" and to his right was a room labeled "Vector Production Lab." Each room was divided internally by glass walls, and in the walls small airlocks allowed samples and other materials to be passed between the divisions. The personnel in both labs wore medical vac-suits. At the far end of the Treatment Control Center stood a narrow access passageway between the two labs, and beyond it was the Operating Room, also separated by glass partitions and small access windows to pass materials. As he watched, medical technicians in vac-suits carried the captain into the room on a gurney that floated easily in the low gravity environment. They secured the gurney on its stand and arranged the various tubes and lines attached to Van Wert so as to keep them out of the way during the procedure.

Ski looked up to see a raised ceiling surrounded by glass where many people were gathered to watch the treatment. Among the fleet personnel in the operating theater were Admiral Selig and Lieutenant Commander Murray. The others were medical personnel in white lab coats or scrubs.

Dr. Shaw donned a small headset and microphone and then took several minutes to look over the continuous feed of information coming onto the computer screens and to talk with the technicians, questioning and directing each in turn. Satisfied, he lowered the microphone and turned to Ski.

"This is the Treatment Control Center," he said. "Here we monitor every aspect of the gene therapy procedures. You might say this is where we do battle, Ski."

A woman technician in the Operating Room spoke into a headset microphone. "Dr. Shaw, the patient is ready to start the procedure."

Dr. Shaw raised the microphone to his mouth. "Very good. Go ahead with Phase One." He lowered it again and turned to Ski. "Instead of showing you around, I'm going to just get started. Keep close and I'll try to explain everything as we go along."

"Fantastic. Just don't let me get in the way."

Dr. Shaw smiled. "I won't."

They watched as a technician in the Gene Splicing Lab passed a small cylindrical container through an access port into the OR. A nurse took it and inserted a needle and syringe into the end and drew out the contents. Then she injected it into the IV port on Van Wert's arm.

Dr. Shaw turned to Ski. "They will now administer the nucleic acid to the patient. In this first phase, which we call the decoy phase, naked RNA is injected into the patient's bloodstream. What we were looking for in the alien life form were simple bacterial organisms that do not have a nucleus but were infected by the virus. In those we can find certain clustered regularly interspersed short palendromic repeating sequences from the invading pathogen. Those sequences are cleaved and duplicated and then processed to create crRNAs. The RNA strands carry the coded information that forms surface antigens. These antigens create the particular shape of the receptors of the cell walls and the viral spikes. In this phase, we flood the blood stream with vectors studded with proteins that resemble respiratory cell receptors. The Aldebaran virus spikes attach to these decoy vectors and thus slow the damage done to the patient's own respiratory cells."

"What are vectors?" asked Ski. "They seem to be important."

"They are important. Basically they are man-made viruses that carry genetic information into a host cell. As you already know, a natural virus carries pathogenic RNA strands into the bloodstream and uses its spikes to attach to a receptor of a host cell in the body. It then injects its cargo of RNA into the host cell and causes it to create viruses like itself, flooding the bloodstream with pathogenic viruses. Each new virus carries part of the cell wall with it, thus destroying the cell."

"So you inject a homemade virus into the patient?"

Dr. Shaw smiled. "No. We transduce a vector into the patient."

"Ahh," Ski said with a nod. "Are those the vectors produced in the VPL?"

"In subsequent phases, yes. But in this phase the vectors are created *in vivo*, which is to say in the patient's body. It is a much more efficient method of large scale production of vectors and has a reduced chance of rejection by the patient's immune system. The naked RNA goes into the patient's muscle cells and creates the vectors for us. For subsequent phases the vectors are created *in vitro*, which is to say in cell cultures using adeno and retro viruses. Empty viral shells are created and will carry the appropriate crRNAs into the body. Those vectors are produced in the VPL, and the ones for your captain are now ready to be used for the treatment."

Dr. Shaw watched the OR team for a moment. "The Aldebaran virus is the most remarkable of all the known corona viruses in how fast it mutates to stay ahead of the human body's adaptive and innate immune responses. The human immune system is highly effective, but in this case, by the time it mounts its defense, the pathogen has mutated, and the response is no longer effective. Our treatment speeds up the immune response before the next shift."

Ski nodded and looked past the partitions to the captain in the OR, trying to digest the flow of new terms and ideas. *I wish I had paid more attention to my biology classes in school.* "So in this phase, the RNA strands just travel the body randomly until they find a host cell to infect?"

"No. Under the operating table are electromagnets that generate an electromagnetic field in the muscles of the latissimus dorsi and the gluteus maximus. We target those muscle groups because they are large and are the least damaged by the virus. The muscles can stand more damage at this point than the respiratory system. These muscle cells now become packaging cells for the vectors.

"The naked crRNA strands we use in this phase and the vectors we use in subsequent phases contain iron oxide nanoparticles that respond to the magnetic field to target the cells of those muscles. The magnetic field also increases the permeability of the cell walls, which speeds the transduction of the nucleic acids to the cell nucleus. The iron oxide is not only magnetic but is also biodegradable. Those muscle cells will create the mass of single generational decoys."

Ski shook his head slowly. "Amazing."

Dr. Shaw smiled. "And this is only Phase One." He spoke into the microphone. "Amy, how is the transduction proceeding?"

A technician closely monitoring a computer screen help up a gloved thumb. "Seventy-seven, no, seventy-eight percent complete."

"Very good. I think we can begin Phase Two now."

The technician looked up as the nurse went to the VPL access window, and Ski saw that it was the same young woman he met at the ambulatory craft. All of the technicians watched as the nurse injected the liquid into the captain's IV port, then returned their attention to their computers.

Dr. Shaw turned to Ski. "Now this next phase is called the antibodies phase. Vectors from the VPL are transduced that will carry the genetic code of the antigen of the Aldebaran virus to the plasma B cells where the antibodies are made."

"What is the antigen, again?"

"That's the organism's outer surface that stimulates specific antibody production. The antibodies are Y-shaped proteins with receptors that fit exactly to the pathogenic virus spikes like a lock and key. The antibodies not only prevent the Aldebaran virus from invading new cells, but also tag the virus for destruction by the killer T cells. This is where we can significantly shorten the time it takes to fight off the virus. Because we can speed the information along, the antibodies specifically configured for this latest strain can attach before a new shift mutation occurs."

"So, you have decoys for the Aldebaran viruses to bind to, and you have antibodies to bind to their viral spikes," said Ski.

"That's right. It's redundant, but it helps to prevent further damage to the respiratory system."

Before Ski could answer, a low buzzing alarm sounded in the OR, and everyone in the labs stopped their work to watch. One of the technicians in the Treatment Control Center turned to Dr. Shaw and said, "The patient's lung is starting to collapse!"

The doctor nodded his acknowledgement but kept his eyes on the people in the emergency room.

The OR team worked rapidly to stabilize the captain. Ski could see the OR doctor place a mask and hose onto Van Wert's face, but his view was soon obstructed by the other OR personnel. The scene once again reminded Ski of how close his captain was to death. As he watched the team, he became agitated and turned to Dr. Shaw.

"Isn't there anything you can do for him?"

Dr. Shaw never took his eyes off of the OR team, but merely held up his hand. "No. Those people are professionals. They know what they're doing."

Ski couldn't hear what was being said, but the actions of the OR staff told him what was happening. Two of the doctors seemed to be having a dispute while a nurse gave an injection to the patient. Another nurse took out the cardiac arrest paddles and brought them to the bedside, but one of the OR doctors held up his hand. The nurse stopped and everyone watched the monitor for several moments.

Ski held his breath as he watched, then sighed as the paddles were put away and the activity resumed as before.

The technician with the earphones turned to Dr. Shaw and said, "The patient is stabilizing, but Dr. Gerald suggests that we delay the next two phases until he's stabilized further. He wants to-"

"No. Go ahead with the treatment. This patient doesn't have a lot of time."

The technician nodded and turned back to her terminal.

"Have they finished administering phase two?" Dr. Shaw asked.

The woman nodded. "Yes, Doctor."

"Then go to Phases Three and Four, one right after the other." The lab crews and OR staff nodded and went back to work.

Ski was concerned. "Is it all right to go ahead?"

"We have no choice." He looked at Ski. "It'll be all right."

They watched as a technician from the Vector Production Lab brought another vial to the OR access window. The nurse took it and administered the dose to the captain.

"Okay, Doctor," Ski said, "what are Phases Three and Four?"

Dr. Shaw took a deep breath as if to relax from the recent crisis. He turned to Ski and said, "Phase Three sends vectors into the body to stimulate production of various T cells and killer cells, which seek out specific "non-self" and pathogenic antigens associated with the

Aldebaran virus. When they find the virus, they secrete cytotoxic granules that contain powerful enzymes to perforate the virus membrane and destroy it. They also attack virally infected cells to stop the production of more viruses. By stimulating broad adaptive immune system responses, complete destruction of the virus is ensured. This is the most important phase since it actually targets the Aldebaran virus."

"Did you create the toxic granule idea?" Ski asked. "That's pretty cool."

Dr. Shaw smiled. "No. Mother Nature did that all by herself. All this is going on in our bodies every moment of the day, day after day, year after year. We only help it along so it can work a little faster to defeat these particularly virulent diseases. Isn't the human immune system fascinating?"

"Yes, it is," Ski said, nodding slowly. "It's very fascinating."

"Now, as to Phase Four-"

"But I thought that was Three and Four."

"Oh, no. The last phase is what we call the mop up phase, and it deals with the production of one generational macrophages. These are white blood cells that patrol the body and engulf and digest cellular debris, foreign substances, microbes, cancer cells, and anything that does not have proteins on its surface that indicate a healthy body cell. They also eat the remnants of the viruses, vectors, and decoys. They use enzymes to ingest and break down these materials, which are then either assimilated or expelled as waste. They also rid the body of worn out cells and are essential for wound healing, as they eat bacteria and damaged tissue. Macrophages are wonderful scavengers, and in these patients, their presence will also help provide increased resistance to disease while the patient recovers from the Aldebaran virus."

"That sounds good. But wouldn't having all of those white blood cells in the blood stream be like having leukemia?"

"No. First of all, there is plenty of debris in the blood stream for the macrophages to consume. Secondly, the effect is only temporary as they are only one generational."

"Wow," Ski said. "I'm feeling better about their chances of recovery already."

"Yes, but patients like your captain still have a long way to go. Each one will have to rest and let the treatment run its course."

"How long will it take before you know if this treatment is successful?"

"We'll be monitoring him constantly in another room to see the effects as they happen. But if all goes well, I hope to see him conscious in eight to ten hours."

"And then what?"

"He'll be in bed for at least a week. There is a lot of damage to be repaired in his system."

Ski nodded. "Well I'm completely impressed. I've heard of this kind of therapy, but I've never been this close to it before. It's really amazing."

Dr. Shaw smiled. "Yes, it is."

"How would one get into this field? I'm due to get out of the fleet soon, and I'm looking forward to getting back to school."

"Good! I have some information in my room about the schools I attended. I'll pass them to you. I'll be working on these treatments all evening, but perhaps we can get together tomorrow and talk more about it."

Ski smiled. "Thanks!"

"Don't mention it. I think that you would do very well in this field. I think you have the mind for it."

Ski nodded his thanks and then yawned.

Dr. Shaw patted him on the shoulder. "You must still be very tired from your ordeal. I have a cabin waiting for you on Level 2. Why don't you go lie down for awhile?"

Ski looked toward the OR and saw the staff lift the gurney and carry the captain out to a post operation recovery room. "Will they be treating Mac next?"

Dr. Shaw glanced toward a computer screen. "Yes, but all of the treatments are the same. Rest now, and perhaps you will be able to visit your friends later on tonight."

Ski yawned again. "Excuse me. Yes, I think I will. Level 2?"

"Yes. See the attendant there."

"Thank you again."

Ski exited the lab area and went to his cabin. He was still very tired from being up all night, and he knew that his friends were getting the best of care. He decided he would get some sleep and then check on them later.

His room was small but comfortably furnished. There was a single bed tube, a closet, and a small desk that was set into the wall. There was also an adjoining bathroom with a low gravity style shower. He kicked off his shoes, turned out the light, and climbed into the bed.

As he floated in the bed tube, he remembered the seemingly endless days of watch standing while underway, and he hoped that it would be a long time before he had to go out on patrol again. He would get thirty days of leave at least, as is the custom for survivor of a ship that is lost, but he had no idea where he would go after that.

Probably to another corvette, he thought. *Maybe I could work out some deal that would keep me at a desk job until I got out.*

As he lay there on the bed with his eyes closed, his thoughts drifted back to the *Kestrel*. He thought about his shipmates and the places they had visited and the things they had been through. The names and faces of Sansbury, Cauthen, Morrell, Lyons, Crosley, De Zurik, Doc, Gradenko, and Petey played across his mind, and as he thought about them, a heavy feeling of finality settled over him. They were all gone, irretrievably lost. He imagined the wives and children and parents being informed of the deaths of their loved ones, and his emotions plummeted. Realization of the magnitude of the loss was finally catching up to him, and as he lay there, alone in the dark cabin, Ski wept.

Chapter 56
"New Beginning"

When he awoke from his sleep, it was late in the evening and a
clock on the wall told him that he had slept almost seven hours. He got
up and took a shower, brushed his teeth, and changed into some clothes
that had been left in the small dresser. Then he left his cabin and made
his way to the attendant's station where a lone person was writing a
report.

"Excuse me, but where can I find Dr. Shaw?" he asked.

"Are you Ski?" the man asked.

"Yes."

The attendant pointed down a hall to a set of closed double
doors. "He's in room one oh seven with your captain. He told me to
send you in. And here, you'll need one of these."

He handed Ski a surgical type mask.

"Thanks." He walked through the doors and down the hall to
Room 107. He put on the mask and stepped inside.

The room was dimly lit, but Ski could see Dr. Shaw standing
over the captain's bed. There were several monitoring devices against
the wall, and a nurse was changing an IV bag. As Ski walked in, the
doctor looked and waved him over. The nurse carried the empty bag
out of the room.

Ski walked over to the bed and saw that the captain was awake.
His eyes were barely open, and he looked totally exhausted. To Ski, he
didn't look any better that he did when he was on the station, but at
least he was awake.

"Hi, Captain," Ski said. "How are you doing?"

Van Wert looked up at Ski and smiled weakly. His hand slowly
reached up and patted Ski's arm. His lips seemed to be trying to form
words.

Puzzled, Ski looked up at the doctor.

"He's still not able to speak, and his breathing is very weak." Dr.
Shaw said. "There was a lot of damage."

"Will you have to do another treatment?"

"I'm still not sure. We're watching him very closely." The doctor looked down at Van Wert. "But we've come a lot further than we had expected to with the first treatment."

Van Wert nodded slowly.

The doctor faced Ski. "I was just telling your captain that the treatments for the other crewmen have been completed and that the prognosis is very good."

"Even McElroy?"

"Yes. Now all they need is some rest."

Van Wert focused his eyes on the doctor and tried to speak. He was pointing at Ski, and he seemed to be asking a question.

"Yes." Dr. Shaw said in a reassuring tone. "Ski is all right, too. As a matter of fact, he was with me in the control center during your treatment. He seems to be taking a great interest in genetic therapy."

Van Wert looked over at Ski and seemed to be smiling weakly.

"That's right, Captain. I've decided to go back to school and study in that field when I get out of the fleet."

Van Wert raised his hand to his head and tapped his temple with his index finger. Then he pointed to Ski.

Ski smiled and patted Van Wert's arm. He was deeply relieved to see the captain doing so well. But more than that, he was filled with a sense of respect and admiration for his commanding officer. The struggle with the Aldebaran virus was another fight that they had come through together, and Ski realized that his feelings must be common to all who share death and share life together in battle. It was the brotherhood of fighting men.

Just then the door opened, and some people quietly walked in. Leading the way was Admiral Selig and Lieutenant Commander Murray with two staff officers. They surrounded the bed to speak to Van Wert, and Ski could feel himself being nudged out. While the Admiral asked Dr. Shaw questions about Van Wert's condition, Jennifer Murray spoke to Van Wert by his bed.

"James? How are you, love?" she asked. "They're telling us that you're going to be all right. The DCA people said that their scrub team is finished, and the hospital ship will be leaving for AlCent A2 soon. I wanted to say good bye and that I'll meet you in port when we pull in."

Ski backed away and headed for the door. He didn't feel like staying with all of the commotion. He also didn't feel like he belonged in their company. Besides, there were his other shipmates he needed to visit. He decided that he would eat dinner and then go see them. As he got to the door, he felt a hand on his shoulder. It was Admiral Selig.

"Son, Ensign Millus told me about all of the effort that you gave on the station for the men. I wanted you to know that I appreciate it."

"Thank you, Admiral. But I'm afraid I didn't really accomplish anything."

"Nonsense. Not only were your efforts valiant, but you also helped to keep the morale of the men up. I also understand that you took care of them when they couldn't take care of themselves. You stood by your shipmates, and I'm writing a letter of commendation for you because of that."

At first Ski didn't know how to reply. He had only done what was natural and decent. So he simply said, "Thank you, Admiral."

***

On his way to the restaurant level, Ski decided to stop on the recreation deck where large observation windows gave a full view of the station. He let his eyes follow every line and contour, and he couldn't help but to feel that he was leaving part of himself behind.

As he stood there, he noticed someone walking up to him. It was the technician from the OR, the raven haired girl he had spoken to in the isolation tent. As he watched her approach, he was again filled with a vague sense of familiarity. She was smiling and carrying something in her hand, and Ski's heart seemed to skip a beat in his chest. She was very beautiful, and her long black hair fell loosely about her shoulders. Even her blue eyes seemed to smile pleasantly.

"Ahh," she said. "I've finally caught up with you. Here is your star journal."

"Thank you very much." He took the computer pad and opened the cover absently. "Delivered to me personally, just like you promised."

"Of course," she said. "And you're welcome."

"By the way, what is your name?"

"Amy. And you're Ski right?"

"That's right."

Amy gestured toward the computer pad. "I hope you don't mind if I looked through the book a little. Those photos are very beautiful. Did you take them?"

"No, I didn't. This journal was put together by my friend Lawrence Peters. We called him Petey. He studied Astronomy, and these pictures are his."

"Is he one of the crewmen who came on board with you?"

"No, he died on the station. I wanted to have this book published for him. He was hoping to go to school to become an astronomer when he got back."

"I'm sorry," Amy said. "He must have been very talented."

"He was. And he was the kindest person that you would ever want to meet." Ski thought a moment and had an idea. "Have you had dinner?"

"No, I haven't. I missed it when I was in OR, and I just got out. Late supper is available, though."

"Well, would you care to join me? I was just heading up there myself. If you like, we could look at the entire star journal, and I could explain the pictures for you. Maybe I could tell you about Petey, too. He was a special person."

Amy smiled and nodded. "Yes, I'd like that very much."

Ski returned her smile, and the two turned around and headed for the ship's restaurant.

The End